LIFE'S GOLDEN TIME

by

BETTE VICKERS

Part Two of
Fed up to Top Attic

as serialised by
BBC Radio Humberside

HUTTON PRESS
1985

Hutton Press Ltd.
130 Canada Drive, Cherry Burton, Beverley
North Humberside, HU17 7SB

First Published 1985
Reprinted 1988

Printed by Clifford Ward & Co.
(Bridlington) Ltd.

ISBN 0 907033 21 0

For Pam —
whose loving support
is so precious

FOREWORD

In "Fed Up To Top Attic" we followed the tribulations and happiness of Thom and Esther's life in the Yorkshire coastal town of Bridlington in the late nineteenth century.

"Life's Golden Time" follows on from there. This time it is the story of Ada, one of the youngest of Thom and Esther's seventeen children, and Wilf.

Wilf and Ada's story starts when they both go to school for the first time. We follow them through their childhood and their friendship, which matures into love in their teens. And before their marriage, the First World War begins, disrupting their lives and the lives of all about them.

Bette Vickers writes with the same humour and pathos as in "Fed Up To Top Attic"; "Life's Golden Time" is the second part of the serial originally broadcast by BBC Radio Humberside based on memories of her family.

A third book on this family, "Ha'penny Top and Farthing Tail," will be published in the spring of 1986.

The publishers wish to thank Mr. Graham Henderson, producer of BBC Radio Humberside's "Chalk and Cheese" programme, for his assistance and the Bridlington Augustinian Society for providing the photograph of the Old Town of Bridlington taken in 1906 which appears on the front cover.

CHAPTER 1

They always said you could hear Ada coming a mile off. The sound of the distinctive clatter-clatter of her feet as she placed each one down with a ferocious precision was a familiar sound as she went up and down St. John's Street on some errand or other.

It was as if she knew exactly where each step was taking her. She never stumbled or faltered and walked with steps so quickly one after the other than you felt Ada could not wait another minute to get wherever she was going.

On first seeing her tiny figure trotting up and down, you might put the quickness down to size, thinking that her short legs needed to put in more paces. On being greeted with her old-fashioned, knowing look and a sharply delivered, "Na, then, weather looks bad over Tylan's Alley this morning," you would immediately know that Ada knew exactly what she was about. In short Ada had all her knobs on — and some to spare.

As the sixteenth child of Esther and Thom Skipton — and for eight years the baby of the family — you might assume her old-fashioned ways and sayings were due to being paid a lot of attention. Certainly she got more than any of the others had ever had. But Ada was a child that demanded attention and she would not settle until she got it.

Her Mam had a feeling — she sometimes called it a foreboding — from the moment of conception, that this child would be unlike any of the others. Ada was born after a lapse of four years and Esther hoped that her child-bearing years were over but she did not mind expecting again — a baby around the place was nice and with Daisy being at home to give a hand things wouldn't be too bad.

Thom was tickled pink with Ada, whom he called "short arse." He said that what she lacked in size she more than made up for in personality.

"She's got taking ways has that one," he would laugh.

Things were certainly much easier in the household now. He was a foreman over fifty men down at the Corporation yard, chairman of the Liberal Club, a committee member of several good causes and a well respected member of the community. But none of his children had seemed the least bit inclined to follow in his footsteps.

"They've had it too easy, Esther," he would say. But after all that was what he had striven for all his life — to give his wife and family a good life.

"It's a pity this one hadn't come a bit sooner then — she might have learnt a bit from our early struggles," Esther snorted as she spoke, for Ada was the only child they had ever disagreed about.

To Thom she was the brightest one of all — to Esther she was simply a "little bugger — a right Madam."

It came as no surprise that Ada never bothered with the tedious task of crawling, but at the age of ten months simply got herself up from the pegged hearth rug and walked, as straight as a die, across the black and red tiled floor. At just over eighteen months she could say several words and Thom would spend hours teaching her his favourite songs and hymns. It was quite a sight to see this little mite, so small that her clothes had to be taken up at least six inches, standing up and singing at the top of her voice. And this was another of her attributes — Ada had a voice — a voice that could be heard loud and clear.

She loved to perform for visitors and Thom encouraged it. Esther was not so impressed.

"A bairn of that age shouldn't be as far on — you'll turn her brain if you're not steady, Thom." But he paid no heed to the warning — Ada would be fine.

Until the age of four when she was finally allowed to run errands, her world was confined to the four walls of the house, the yard and the wall that surrounded it which gave a full view of the chapel next door, and its grounds. But Ada loved it all — there was always something to find out and being the seeker that she was — always something to do. It didn't take long for her to find that by getting a foothold in the cement of the yard wall she could heave herself up and sit on the top. She would take great note of all that went on — weddings, funerals and any other event — Ada knew all that happened and would relate the details to her amused brothers and sisters.

"Why do folk wear black for funerals, Mam?" she asked.

Esther tried to answer by saying it was to show respect — to show that people were sad to have lost a loved one.

"Miss Boldman says that to die and go to Jesus is what we are all aiming for so why be sad about it?"

Esther had no answer to that nor many of the other questions her daughter asked throughout the day.

Every nook and cranny of the house was explored and her favourite was the attic which held trunks and boxes to look through. The seven-piece suite was another source of delight and she would dig into its sides in search of treasure.

The only thing that baffled her was the hissing of the gas chandelier. She would sit and watch and listen to its plopping away as the gas fed through the pipes. It was an eerie sound that sometimes made her shiver although she could not have said why.

"She's never still a minute and she's getting a right nark on her." Esther usually said this after a scene when Ada could not get her own way — which was not often. Handling her was a right job for somehow she always managed to get what she wanted. She was never short on telling folk just what she thought, but Esther could never say she was cheeky — Ada just

6

stated the facts as she saw them and didn't seem to care whether you agreed with her or not. She'd said her piece and that was that. It was no use trying to talk or reason with her for once her mind was made up she would purse her lips, fold her arms across her little body and shut up — the matter was closed.

Esther had ten bairns still at home — two lasses at school, Daisy who helped in the house and the six lads at work. The others were either wed or in service and "Of course you know our little Isaac were drowned," Esther would recount.

It was the weekly visits to Isaac's grave that were amongst Ada's earliest memories. She did claim that she could recall being pushed in the wicker perambulator up the High Street, through the Baylegate and then on to the old cemetery. Once there she would investigate the other gravestones. As soon as she was old enough to realise what it all meant, she decided that these weekly visits were not for her. She would watch as Mam and Daisy cleaned up the grave and removed the old flowers to replace them with fresh ones.

One week she didn't go round the other graves but just stood near Daisy, silent and still.

"You're quiet, young lady. Are you sickening for something?" Daisy asked. Ada shook her head, but gave one of her rare smiles so that Daisy and Mam wouldn't go on about it.

The reason for the mood was made clear when they prepared for the next visit.

"I'm not coming." The statement was flat and firm.

"What do you mean, you're not coming?" Mam demanded.

"It's daft going up there and taking flowers and chucking them away when they are not even dead. There's nowt to see and nowt to do — I'm not coming."

"And where do you reckon you're going then?" Dad asked, having a damn good idea what was in her mind.

"I'm coming with you and our Bert and Jack to play football." And she did. Thom was pleased to take her along and Esther was just as glad to have a bit of a rest from her. But she got her own way too easy.

"Our Ada'll be a handful if we don't watch it, Daisy," she puffed as they pushed against the wind on the corner of Baylegate. Daisy laughed, reassuring her that Dad would never let that happen.

Ada did not encourage cuddles or kisses — she disliked any fuss except sometimes when she wanted Dad to agree with her about something. She used all her wiles, and, coupled with an almost photographic memory, could wheedle and charm if necessary. Her memory astounded them.

"Ask short arse — she'll know," would bring forth the answer to some query that might have otherwise baffled the rest of them.

7

Playing with other children did not interest her at all. But she loved to sit on the donkey-stoned step and watch them. Her enjoyment was in helping Mam and Daisy and running errands which meant she could chat to the folk in the street and the shopkeepers.

Soon after she was four she started to clammer about going to school and would bombard her two sisters with endless questions about what they had been doing. It wasn't long before she picked up, parrot-fashion, the times tables and these she would recite at the top of her voice without any idea of the value. Thom taught her to read and recognise her own name and to do numbers up to ten. She was so enthusiastic that she used up a whole exercise book in less than a week.

She didn't mind doing any useful jobs, but had favourites. One was the daily errand to Freddie Cligg's, the butcher. He loved to tease her and she loved his banter — Freddie Cligg was one of Ada's mates.

It was in Freddie's shop that she met and struck up a friendship with Wilf Tanner, a little lad around her own age. It was a surprising friendship for Wilf was a ragged-arsed little lad who came from one of the cottages on Ireland's Row. He didn't seem like Ada's type at all. The distance between the houses was a mere mile, but their worlds were poles apart.

Wilf was the middle child of Polly Tanner — a tall, gaunt woman who took in washing to eke out the parish relief she got as a widow. Harry, her eldest lad, was five-and-a-half and at school, Wilf was four and Gertie, two-and-a-half. Her husband, John William, had died when Gertie was only a few months old and none of the bairns really remembered him. It fell to the lot of young Wilf to do the errands, empty the endless tubs of water and to see to the copper fire. He worked hard but Mam never seemed to appreciate it — Harry got most of her attention.

"He's not strong you know — not strong at all," she would tell Wilf, but he thought Harry was strong enough when he wanted to be. Most times he was just bone idle.

Esther varied her meat dish every day, but kept to a weekly ritual. Ada soon taught herself to remember the day by the kind of meat she fetched. The money would be placed in a leather pouch and tucked into her pinny pocket and off she would go.

As she went down the street she would turn her head this way and that taking in the rare mixture of buildings and looking out for folk she knew to have a chat with.

Often, she thought that the people grew to look like the houses they lived in. Take little Miss Clegg — small and wizened like the worn grey stone of her cottage. Councillor Denby — a tall, thin, miserable looking man, who, when dressed in his frock coat and top hat, looked just like his tall, narrow, three-storeyed house. No light ever appeared in his windows and Ada likened them to his eyes — dull and lifeless. But old Mr. Forbes —

8

now that was a different thing. He was small and round just like his double-fronted low cottage which stood on the corner. He was a jolly bloke and his eyes danced with laughter just like the flames of his fire did when they reflected upon his window pane. Ada's world was so interesting.

She and Freddie had developed a routine. She would enter the shop, making sure that the brass door bell rattled well on its spring and then stand in front of the counter. She reached only half way up and Freddie would pretend not to see her until she came out with one of her pert sayings. This particular morning she had been waiting for a few minutes when the door opened quietly and in came this little lad. He was so quiet that Ada hardly noticed him.

Freddie came to the counter and, bending over, looked down at Ada and said, "Now then Miss Skipton — what day is it today?"

"You know damn well it's Tuesday — liver and hot cakes."

"Just watch your tongue now, Madam. We have other customers present, I don't want to have to tell your Dad on you."

"You just do that Freddie Cligg and I'll tell your customers how you weigh all fat and bone in with the meat and charge for it." Her answer was swift and sharply delivered.

Freddie leaned over and playfully cuffed her ear. "You're a bit early this morning so you'll have to wait until lad gets the offal cut up. I'll serve young Tanner here."

Ada turned and looked at the lad, eyeing him up and down with open curiosity. He was nowt much to look at and stood only half an inch taller than she did. He stood with his head hung down as if ashamed to be there, scuffing the sawdust with his worn hobnailed boot. He looked like thousands of other kids did, but he was cleaner than most. His boots were clean but not polished and patched here and there where the leather had worn through.

Ada's eyes travelled up his body and saw that patches seemed to cover most of it. His jersey, once again clean, had more darns than anything else and his trousers, once a dark grey serge, were now faded almost white and worn as smooth as soft cotton. With all the patches he looked like Joseph's coat of many colours. The only complete piece of clothing was his black new socks and they were miles too long for his legs and curled up round his ankles like a wriggling worm. Mam had had them given and he knew they looked a sight but they kept his legs warm, especially in bed when the covers had all been dragged off by Harry. Covers — that was going it a bit, for the only covers they had on the beds were a collection of coats they had grown out of.

"What are you looking so down for then?" Ada addressed him in her precise voice.

9

"I'm not down." He mumbled the words into his chest. Freddie moved forward and asked for his order.

"Two penn'orth bones please Mr. Cligg." He lifted his head as he spoke and Ada saw that his eyes were bright blue — almost as blue as Dad's. And they were topped by a mop of blonde hair too, like Dad's. But nowt so tidy. Somebody had plonked a basin on the lad's head and cut round it leaving a jagged hairline on a level with his eyebrows. Up to this line he was almost bald for his neck and lower head had been shorn to the skin.

"You got dicks at your house then?" Ada took a pace backwards.

"No, we ain't." Wilf's face and tone were sullen.

"What's your hair cut like that for then?"

"'Cos it saves Mam cutting it so often. She don't care much for cutting hair."

"You can tell that, lad." And then she turned away, her interest for the moment fading and Freddie was waiting with her order.

She dug deep into her pocket and took out the two bob piece — Mam always gave the right money. The packet was handed over to her neatly wrapped in white greaseproof paper. Wilf's bones were also ready and she noticed that they were roughly wrapped in newspaper.

"Why isn't his done up like mine?"

"Because, young lady, he won't pay until Saturday and I can't afford to give tick and wrapping paper as well."

"That's not right. It's class distinction and my Dad says that's all wrong. We should all be treated equally."

Freddie could not suppress his laughter — by hell she was Thom Skipton's lass alright.

"Get along with you." He smiled and watched as the two bairns left the shop. What a contrast — Ada so well dressed and neat, and the lad with hardly his breeches arse in. No matter how hard Thom worked for equality, they were still a long way from it.

Ada got to the door first and held it open for Wilf to walk through. He shuffled and hesitated not knowing quite what to do — folk didn't usually open doors for him — and then Ada heaved exasperatedly and shoved him through it. She'd no time to stand there messing about.

"Where do you live then?" she asked as she banged the door closed.

"Third one up on Ireland's Row — not that it's owt to do with you." It was an unexpected bit of spirit and it aroused her interest.

"Asking is the only way to get to know owt. My Dad says if you don't know then ask. What's your name?"

"Mind it, nosey parker." And with that, he shot off up the street.

It didn't bother Ada all that much. She had plenty of other things to think about and with a shrug of her shoulders she walked at a more leisurely pace towards home.

Her next call was at Mrs. White's shop for some tiger nuts. Mrs. White was another of her favourite people for she would chat to Ada about grown up things. Today's subject was the weather — and the pile of ironing still to be done.

"There's only one thing to do Mrs. White — roll your sleeves up and get on with it." This parting shot caused a laugh and she left the shop chewing vigorously on one of the nuts.

She stopped and sniffed the air — she'd know that smell anywhere — Blacky Johnson was shoeing. She ran and stood in the open doorway of the smithy and saw a large cart horse tethered to the back wall. Blacky was bent over the back foot busily cleaning out the hoof. She watched as his muscles rippled, saw the smoking hiss as he offered red hot metal to the hoof, and sniffed again.

Blacky heard her sharp intake of breath and looked up. "You going to be a blacksmith then young Ada?" he called out.

"Nay lad, I'm not big enough. But I've a mind to marry one when I'm old enough."

"Hurry yourself up then and I'll wait for you."

"Tha'll be shoving daisies up afore I'm ready to wed," she answered cheekily and ran off up the street.

She was approaching the chapel gates when she saw Wilf again. He was sitting on the kerb edge in careful examination of his boots.

"What you up to then?" Curiosity got the better of her and she bent over his shoulder.

"Nowt — I'm just having a minute." He paused and then blurted out, "It's Tanner — Wilf Tanner."

She knew what he meant but decided to play awkward and asked, "What is?"

"My name."

"Hmmm." She looked down with lips pursed. "Do you always run errands?"

"Mostly." He sighed wearily as he spoke.

"You the young 'un then?"

He had to think for a minute before he got the drift of her question. "Nope — our Harry's older'n me and Gert younger."

"Why do you always do errands then?"

"'Cos Mam says so." The statement was so definite that he thought it would put an end to her endless asking.

"You should tell her to let your brother take turns. You should stand up for yourself. My Dad says you'll never get anywhere if you don't stand up for your rights."

"Your Dad has a lot to say for himself. Anyroad Mam says Harry's not strong enough to do a lot of running about."

11

"What's up with him?"

Blimey — she didn't half ask some questions. "Nowt as I know on."

"He's her pet then."

She voiced a thought he had hidden for a long time. Harry always got the best bits because Polly said he needed to keep up his strength. Harry got the first pick of any clothes given to them. Harry got his hair ruffled when they climbed out of the tin bath on Friday night. Harry had the only bit of blanket on the bed. Bed — that was a laugh — bed was a straw palliasse — hard, itchy and uncomfortable.

The realisation hurt him and he decided not to answer her question, but instead to ask one of his own. "What's your name then?" She answered briefly.

"I've heard Mam talk about your Dad. He's summat on council isn't he?"

He dared not have told her what Polly actually said about Thom Skipton and his family. She thought them far too high and mighty for their own good. "I don't know how the hell they do it with all their lot. And who the hell do they reckon they are anyroad. I can remember when Thom Skipton hadn't ha'penny to rub together and now look at them. They've got big-headed since their lass wed gentry, but they forget we all know why that happened."

If ever Esther had heard all this she would have gone barmy. She was so proud of all her family and especially Isabella who had gone into service at Lord Burlingham's and wed the eldest son. Oh, the daft young things had got themselves into bother, but George had married her long before the bairn was born — long enough to make out it was a seven month child. And they seemed happy, too, in Sewerby Lodge. He was a good lad and never once shunned his wife's family. The reason for the marriage was never mentioned.

Wilf looked carefully at Ada and decided that his Mam must be wrong about Skiptons. This one seemed alright even if she was a bit nosey. He liked her bright personality and she was friendly enough.

"Everybody knows my Dad, but he's not on council. He were too good for that lot, Mam says. She says he's more trouble than he's worth and all sometimes." She laughed as she recalled Mam's words for she knew they meant nothing of the sort.

"You live up here then?"

She pointed to the big house next to the chapel.

"Come on, I'll show you."

He got up, brushed the dust from the back of his pants and followed her the few yards to the front door. She was far too small to reach the brass knocker and announced her presence by giving the door a hefty kick with her boot. For a little 'un she had some strength and the big solid door

12

shook with the impact. Wilf looked startled and he made to run off. "Hold hard a minute lad and come in. You can see Mam and our Daisy."

"No, I'd best be off." He didn't want to see the inside of this imposing house — it looked far too grand for the likes of him. Mam had been right — the Skiptons were too grand for his sort.

"Get your arse in." Ada was not to be put off and she reached out and grabbed him by the collar of his worn jersey. The impact ripped it without effort — right across the back and underneath the arm. A horror-struck look passed between them, she hanging on to the ripped collar and he looking white faced and scared out of his wits.

"Now look what you've done — Mam'll kill me," he cried out and the tears came to his eyes.

Esther came to the door and almost laughed outright at the scene on her doorstep.

"Now then buggerlugs, what are you fighting about?"

"I'm not fighting Mam, I just got hold of his jersey and it came away in my hands. It didn't look up to much anyway."

"Well, that's no call to go tearing it to bits. Come in, son, and let's see what we can do with it." She looked and recognised Polly Tanner's lad. Poor little mite, he looked frightened to death, and no wonder, with Polly for his Mam. Gently she led him through the passage and into the kitchen.

"Daisy, look what we've got here. Our ham-fisted Ada has torn young Tanner's jersey. Can you mend it for him?"

Daisy looked at the damage and shook her head. "Take it off son whilst I get mending basket. Come on Ada give him a hand," she instructed, and Ada helped to pull what was left of the jersey over his head.

"Can we go in yard Mam?" Esther nodded. "Can we have some milk and a piece of pound cake?" Esther nodded again, wondering where the hell she put all the grub she ate.

"I'm not hungry thanks," Wilf almost whispered.

Ada ignored him and fetched out two mugs of milk and two huge pieces of cake.

Wilf took the offered share and followed her out into the yard where they sat on the wooden bench Dad had made. They munched and sipped in silence. He'd never tasted anything like it before. The cake fair melted in his mouth and the feel of the cold milk on his tongue was sheer delight.

"You starting school soon then?"

He nodded and told her after the Whit holiday.

"That's when I start — I can't wait can you?"

He looked dumbfounded — nobody wanted to go to school. "Our Harry says school's a waste of time and Mam says I'll know I'm born when I get there."

"That's daft. You have to go to school to learn so's you'll get a decent job and get on."

She got down from the seat and stood in front of him. Wilf stopped his munching and took his first good look at Ada Skipton. Her hair was raven black and hung down to her waist, tied back with a white ribbon. Her black dress reached to the top of her shining boots and he could see the deep hem that had been turned up to make it short enough. Her pinny was pure white and edged with lace — by hek — they must be posh. She brought to mind a tiny sparrow and when he looked at her eyes he saw that they were speckled grey — just like a sparrow — sharp and missing nothing.

"Why do you have to learn to get a decent job?"

Now it was her turn to look him up and down. His vest was shabby but clean — not like Mam's washing — but clean enough. His whole appearance was the same — shabby but clean.

"Well — just look at you and me for a start. We've got a big family and if my Dad hadn't learnt himself to read and write he'd still have been a labourer and we'd be as poor as church mice. Learning got him a better job and gave us more. What has your Dad done for you?"

"He's dead." It was a fact stated without any emotion. The only memories Wilf had of his Dad were vague and from the way Polly spoke of him it was no great loss when he died.

"Oh." Faced with this statement Ada was, for once, non-plussed. "Well, happen he's better off where he is." She did not understand what she said, but she had often heard the words in the house when news of a death was received.

Daisy's voice called out to them and they went back into the house.

"I can't do owt with this, lad, but I've found one of our lad's that'll fit you. Come on, put it on and tell your Mam she's welcome to it." She held out a brown jumper with not a darn or hole to be seen. Quickly he pulled it over his head and arranged it around his small body.

"That looks fine, son." Esther smiled and thought what a bonny little lad he could have been with a bit of love and care. Oh, she wasn't blaming Polly, for she knew what it was like to try and provide on parish money. In fact she quite admired the woman for the way she worked. It was a pity she was so unpleasant about things though. She was that awkward she might just send the jersey back. Still, it would make him decent to go home in. Polly could please herself then.

Wilf preened as he looked down at himself. The jersey felt thick and warm — by hek Mam would be pleased with this. "Thanks missus — I'd best be off now or Mam'll be bothered."

He picked up his old jersey and the packet of bones and went out in to the passage.

"Shall I walk a bit of the way with you?" Ada asked as she opened the door.

"Nay thanks. I'd best hurry on." He didn't want her to see where he lived. He wasn't ashamed of it for it was clean and tidy, but nowt like this place.

She accepted his refusal and smiled at him — a smile that lit up the whole of her face. He grinned back shyly.

"I'll look out for you when I do errands then," she said and closed the door behind him.

Daisy asked how she had met him and Ada told her the story.

"Do you know they only have bones to eat?" Her voice held contempt.

"You just think yourself lucky, my lass, that you weren't born a bit sooner. When your Dad was out of work I've made many a meal from bones," Esther chided, but Ada took little notice being more interested in helping Daisy to set the table.

"Get a move on then. Straight after dinner you and me are off up to our Isabella's to see the baby."

Ada grunted. "I'll bet they won't have bones for dinner either."

Esther made to clip her ear, but had to laugh. Little bugger — one of these days she'd get a right shock. Thom said she took after Granny Raines, Esther's mother. He well remembered the sting of her tongue. But she didn't have Ada's wit and humour — that came from him.

And with all her cheek she was Granny's favourite. The others were a bit scared of the old lady, but not our Ada. She would march up to the house, kick the door and be let in with a smile and warm greeting.

"I just thought I'd call and see what you're up to. Can I do owt?" she would ask, and Granny would always think of something and then reward her with some goodie.

It was a warm, safe world. She knew where the next meal was coming from and that it would be better than bones — she was well dressed and had a good bed to sleep on and the love and friendship of her family. How different from Wilf Tanner who lived in the shadows.

She set the table and sang 'Sunshine Corner' at the top of her voice. The smell of liver and hot cakes made her mouth water with anticipation. Thank God they weren't having bones.

Bones were for dogs.

15

CHAPTER 2

Wilf hurried home as fast as his legs could carry him. He wanted to show his jersey off to Mam and Gertie.

The greeting was not what he expected, for as soon as he got through the door Polly yelled at him, "Where the devil have you been all this time?" She looked down at him from where she stood ironing at one end of the table and spotted the jersey.

"And where did that come from?" Her voice was sharp — not in the same way as Ada's, but biting and bitter. It was a voice she seemed to save for Wilf.

"Ada Skipton ripped mine and her Mam gave us this one." Maybe that would please Mam.

"Oh, she did, did she. Well you can bloody well take it back after dinner and tell her to stick it. We don't need Skipton's charity."

Well, he should have known, but his heart sank in disappointment. Still, it was no use going on about it for if Mam said it had to go back then that was that. Not even this jersey was worth one of her clouts.

"Get a move on then and get some bread cut for Harry's dinner, he'll be in from school in a minute."

Wilf busied himself with the hard mound of home-made bread and thought of Mrs. Skipton's pound cake. He decided not to tell Mam about that. Harry came in and without a word grabbed the bread and pushed it into his mouth.

"Where's our Wilf got that jersey from Mam?" he asked through a mouthful of crumbs.

"Skipton's. Their lass ripped his and they gave him that one. He's not keeping it though don't you fret. I'll mend his own and he can take that one back where it belongs."

Harry decided to take a closer look — this one didn't have any holes or darns.

"What you doing that for?" he asked.

"We don't need Skipton's charity here," Polly answered.

"Don't be daft Mam — it would fit me. I could do with a good jersey for school."

Wilf saw an immediate change in Polly's attitude. She stopped the endless to and fro of the iron and looked at the offending garment.

"Happen you're right, lad. Here, take it off, Wilf, and let Harry try it on. He needs it more than you with being at school. You have his old one and then you'll both be set up."

Without any protest Wilf obediently did as he was told. And, of course, the jersey fitted Harry perfectly — better than it did him if anything. Harry patted his belly and spun round looking at Polly for approval. Wilf

16

took the cast-off and putting it on ran outside. It was always the same, always Harry who got the best bits. Tears prickled his eyes and he sat on the kerbstone pushing the dust around with his fingers and then rubbing his eyes, pretending that some of it had gone into them. He wasn't going to let anybody see him cry — not about a bloody jersey.

He was still sitting there when Ada and her Mam walked by the lane end on the way to Sewerby. She spotted him sitting there and saw that the jersey was not the one Mam had given him.

"Where's our jersey then?" She spoke without any preliminary greeting.

"I let our Harry have it. He needed it for school." But his voice and expression belied his true feelings.

"They took it off you more like. You want to stand up for yourself, Tanner. Go and tell them we gave it to you — get some gumption in you, lad."

He didn't answer and Esther came and pulled her away having got the gist of the conversation. Ada was more than capable of going and telling Polly what she thought.

It wasn't right to take the jersey off the lad, but at least Polly had kept it. It didn't really matter who wore it so long as it was put to good use.

Wilf watched as they walked away and thought hard for a minute about what Ada had said. It was given to him — it should be his. By gum, he'd have a go like she said.

"Where've you been and what are you looking at me like that for?" Harry asked as Wilf marched into the kitchen and purposefully went towards him.

"I want that jersey back — it's mine." Wilf's voice shook, but his manner was determined. Harry's mouth fell open and he gaped stupidly at his brother. Wilf didn't usually make any fuss.

"Mrs. Skipton gave it to me — give it here."

He could hear the words but couldn't believe they came from his mouth. Never before had he dared to voice so much as an opinion let alone defy his Mam. He ran towards Harry and began to pull the jersey over his head. Harry struggled and the lads fell to the floor in a tangled heap of flying legs and arms. Polly slammed down the iron and went to separate them. She was dumbstruck — Wilf had never rebelled before — he was the quiet one like his Dad. She bent down and clouted him across the head making him yell out with pain. Gert saw her pick up a wet towel and decided that under the table was the safest place — she'd never seen owt like this before.

The crack of the wet towel across his legs made Wilf yelp and jump up with fists flying, but this time they warded off another blow from his Mam.

"Stop that lark my lad. You're getting just like your Dad — mean as

17

muck and as awkward as hell when you can't have your own way." But Wilf was past caring and as she rained blows upon his head he kicked and screamed like a wild animal. Harry had bolted from his brother's grasp and got behind his Mam's skirts.

He was scared and surprised at his brother's outburst. Wilf might only be little but he was making enough row to waken the dead. Polly had to do something to stop the racket before the lad had a fit or something.

"Oh, give him his bloody jersey Mam and let him keep it." Harry tore it off his back and threw it down on the floor, half expecting Wilf to give in. But he grabbed it and clutched it to his chest whimpering and muttering to himself.

Polly put her arms around Harry. "Don't bother son, I'll see you get it back," she tried to appease.

"No he won't, it's mine and I'm keeping it."

The three onlookers were so astounded that they just stood there and stared as Wilf took off Harry's cast-off jumper and put on the newer one. Never, ever in his life before had Wilf acted like this. It was such a show of defiance that Polly thought she'd have to watch this one or he'd be trying to rule the roost before long. They always said the quiet ones were the worst.

So Wilf got the jersey — he had won his first battle for his rights. But the fruits of victory were bitter for he was treated with a sullen silence from his Mam and brother that lasted several days. He was sorely tempted to take the thing off and give it to Harry, but he kept recalling Ada's advice — "Stand up for yourself, lad." He hoped he could.

At bedtime he would curl under the coat and softly cry himself to sleep. Polly would go in and tuck up Harry, but never so much as said goodnight to Wilf.

After a day or two he got up one morning especially early, and cleaned out the grate in the hope of earning some approval or word of kindness from his Mam. His only reward was a grunt.

"Shall I go down to Cligg's for you, Mam?" he asked.

Polly grunted again and he took this as an assent. He always went down to Cligg's — they had to eat even if it were only bones. Slowly he trundled down the street to find Ada waiting for him outside the house.

"I thought you might come down today. You got it back then?" She nodded at the jersey.

"Aye."

"You don't sound all that pleased — what did they say?"

"Nowt much — didn't mind really."

"I'll bet they didn't." Ada knew it all.

"They didn't — but Mam's been a bit quiet since I took it back. It'll be alright at dinner time though."

"Why don't you take something special to eat then. When I'm in bother I always try to do something special to say I'm sorry — well maybe not sorry — but want to be friends like."

"What can I get?" He emphasised the "I."

"Some offal for dinner maybe — it'll be a sight better than bones."

What a grand idea. They only had offal at Christmas and he knew both Mam and Harry loved it. By hek, that would put them in a good mood alright.

Freddie questioned him about the order but, with his heart pounding, Wilf assured him that Mam knew all about it. He couldn't wait to get home with his packet and refused Ada's offer of milk and cake.

Polly was bent over the washtub when he went into the house and took no notice of his entry.

"Look Mam, look what I've got for dinner." He put the parcel on the table and unwrapped it to reveal a bloody mass of offal.

Polly yelled out and, wiping her hands on her pinny, stood and stared at the meat. Liver, heart and kidney — a full offal. She put her hands to her face.

"What the hell made you bring this lot? I can't afford this. Skipton's didn't give it to you did they?" Her voice rose in anger and frustration.

"No — no — it's alright Mam. We don't have to pay for it till Saturday."

"And where the hell do you think the money's going to come from? I can't pay for stuff like this today, Saturday or any other day. You daft little sod."

She didn't clout him as he half expected, but the anguish in her voice hurt far more. He'd not given a thought about the money — oh bugger Ada Skipton and her big ideas.

"Am I to take it back then?" His voice was a mere whisper.

"Freddie Cligg won't have it back, but I'll teach you, you little bugger. This lot can last all week and you'll not have any of it. You can make do with bread and gravy."

She sank down into a chair and stared at him. "Whatever made you do it, Wilf?"

But he couldn't tell her that or she'd go barmy. His answer was to burst into tears and run outside.

True to her word, Polly dished out his plate with bread and gravy whilst the others had part of the offal. Wilf kept his eyes fixed down on his plate as she told Harry, in bitter tones, what he had done. And he didn't want them to see that his mouth was watering. It smelled so good — like Christmas. Harry's smirk made him feel ten times worse. Oh, hang it all — no matter what Ada Skipton said, nowt was worth all this lot. He got up from the table and began to take off his jersey.

19

"Here — you can have this," he mumbled into its folds as it came over his head.

"I don't want it now — you keep it," Harry laughed unkindly.

It seemed he could do nowt right. Polly nodded her approval to Harry — he was more like her — independent and proud. Wilf shrivelled further into himself. This sticking up for your rights was not as easy as Ada made out. It hadn't got him anywhere — he was more of an outcast than ever.

He made up his mind not to meet her anymore — Ada Skipton was no friend of his.

About a week after the pavement meeting Ada realised that Wilf was avoiding her. It dawned on her when Daisy asked if "that little lad" was still wearing his jersey. She decided to keep a special lookout for him. But it was several more days before she finally spotted him as she was on her way to visit Granny Raines.

Granny lived up on Gordon Road at the top of the Old Town which meant that she had to pass through Ireland's Row if she took the long way round. And she quite liked roaming around if she got the chance — she saw some of the cottages and their lack of privacy and amenities — these must be the hovels Dad was always on about.

If Wilf was around somewhere she'd be sure to see him. And see him she did, but walking through Applegarth Lane and carrying his usual newspaper packet of bones.

It was a bit out of his usual way but he'd done that on purpose so as to avoid her. She shouted out to him and on seeing who it was Wilf took to his heels and ran, head down, through the Baylegate. She knew he had heard her and was running away from her. Oh well, she didn't care, she'd only wanted to see if he was still wearing the jersey — and he was.

That dratted jersey was one of the reasons Wilf did not want to meet Ada for, since that awful day, his Mam had made him wear the damn thing day in and day out, without washing or wiping it.

"You can keep the thing on till it drops off," Polly had snapped at him.

He was now aware of just what that meant, for the jersey was almost stiff with muck. He'd tried dabbing at it with the bit of cloth that served as dishcloth and flannel, but the stains were now so ingrained they showed up in stiff rings all down the front. But Polly remained adamant — the jersey was his and he could keep it — muck and all. He had made it clear it was nothing to do with her and things could stop that way.

Wilf wondered if she would make him start school in it. There was only a couple of weeks to go now and he was dreading it — what a sight he'd look with his patched pants and a mucky jersey — they'd all laugh at him.

And what would Ada Skipton have to say about it all?

CHAPTER 3

With only a short time to go, Wilf was beginning to dread the thought of school. Harry delighted in telling him how the bigger lads bullied the starters. He listened in fear about the Headmaster — Mr. Appleyard — who gave the cane for the smallest reason.

"Old Applepie can't half twang that cane — makes your hand bleed sometimes if he's really mad," Harry said.

To Wilf, school looked like being a terrifying experience — that and the thought of seeing Ada every day.

For her the preparation for school life was an entirely different matter and filled her whole life now that time was drawing near. Mam and Daisy busied themselves making her black dresses and pinnies — a clean one every day — and she was taken to Machin's for new shoes and a dark grey coat.

All through these days she would ask Aggie and Cissie endless questions until they got so fed up they told her "to wait and see for yourself."

"I only hope she settles down as well as she's reckoning on. If she doesn't take to it, life will be hell on earth," Esther remarked to Thom one night after Ada was finally in bed and, for once, completely silent.

Thom assured his wife that Ada would be fine, he had no fears at all.

"You mark my words, she'll be a star pupil," he said. He was quite sure that if any problems arose, Ada would deal with them — she'd sort things out one way or another.

At long last the great day dawned and Ada was up at the crack of dawn, washed and dressed and ready for off.

"It'll be a long day for you my lass, getting up at crow shits like this." Esther looked down at her and saw that Ada's face had been scrubbed until it shone and her hair was brushed until it gleamed like silk.

She looked such a little mite that Esther had to swallow hard to stop the tears — after all this was her baby starting school.

"Eh lass, it doesn't seem five minutes since you were born," she whispered and patted her on the head.

"Shall I come up with you?" she asked as Ada made for the door.

Ada shook her head to that one. She was big enough to go up with her sisters — she wasn't a baby any longer.

Esther watched as the trio walked up the street. Ada skipped along in the front leaving the other two dawdling behind. As she turned back into the silent house she realised just how much she and Daisy were going to miss Ada — she was a handy lass to have around the place.

When the girls reached the imposing iron gates in front of the school, Ada stopped dead in her tracks as if her spirit had for the moment deserted her. She peered through the railings at the playground which was teeming with children. Some of them were playing, some crying and others clinging to their Mam's skirts and refusing to go inside.

"Come on our Ada, you go round there in the infants playground." Cissie took her hand and led her round the corner and then through the double oak doors above which was written in stone lettering *First National School*. She took another look round before going inside — this was a big step she was taking.

Inside there were lines and lines of kids waiting to start school. They stood with their mothers, bigger sisters and brothers or alone and forlorn. She swallowed hard and clung to her sister's hand.

"Shall I wait with you until you get enrolled?" Cissie asked.

Brusquely Ada shrugged her off — she intended to start right and would manage on her own thank you.

But Cissie did notice that as she walked towards the lines, she took out her hankie and blew her nose hard.

"Independent little madam, she won't ever give in," she muttered to herself as she went to her own part in the senior school.

Soon Ada was lost in the interest of watching the long line dwindle as the children gave their particulars to the teacher and then were sent to their respective rooms. She listened in wonderment as she heard them struggling to give their name, age and address. Half of them didn't seem to know who they were or where they lived. No wonder their Mams had to come with them. She took note of the way they were dressed, some neat and tidy and others ragged and mucky.

"Shouldn't wonder if they haven't got dicks," she mused to herself.

Now it was her turn and, squaring her shoulders, she marched up to the big polished desk and vainly tried to peep over the top.

"My goodness, you're a little one," the lady teacher said. "Are you sure you're old enough to start school?"

It was always as well to make sure, for it was not unknown for mothers to try and get children into school early just to get them out of the way. A year was often added to the age with the plan of them leaving a year early to start work. Many parents still considered school a waste of time and who could blame them with big families to provide for?

"Yes I am," Ada's firm answer startled Alice Naggs.

"Miss," she prompted and Ada looked at her with raised eyebrows.

"You say *Miss* when you speak to me."

"Yes Miss, I am," Ada repeated firmly.

"Come along then — what's your name?"

"Ada Skipton, Miss." Well, at least she had picked that up.

"And how old are you?"

"I'm five next birthday — June 27th — er — Miss."

"Are you sure you're five?"

22

"Well, I were born five years ago so I must be." The answer came as quick as a shot.

"Miss — Miss Naggs," the teacher again prompted.

"Yes Miss." Ada was now looking at her at bit old-fashioned. This teacher was a bit fussy.

"And do you know where you live?"

"Of course I do. 64 St. John Street — Miss."

And then Alice Naggs realised — of course, this was one of Thom Skipton's daughters. This one must be alright or she would never have been allowed to enter school. In spite of the big family, the Skiptons were all well thought of in the school. They never gave any trouble over attendances, never got lice or impetigo and were always polite and well-behaved.

"Thank you Ada. Now go over there and start another line until we have assembly." Ada did as she was bid and was soon joined by another girl who, thankfully, looked as clean and tidy as she did.

"What's your name then?" she lost no time in asking.

"Hannah Wilson — what's yours?"

Ada told her and they began to chat in whispers, wondering whose class they would be in and what the lessons would be like. Ada informed her new friend that she could count and read and write her own name. Hannah was suitably impressed and admitted that she had no such knowledge.

"Well, don't fret yourself, I'll help you."

They were deep in conversation when a raised voice made Ada turn sharply. She saw a little lad snuffling into his sleeve and Miss Naggs getting impatient with him. By hek, it was Wilf Tanner. Now Miss had got up from behind the desk and was shaking him by the shoulders.

"If you can't tell me your name boy, you can't expect to start school. How shall I be able to put you on the register?" she shouted.

Quick as lightning Ada ran across the hall and pushed Miss Naggs aside. "You can put Wilf Tanner because that's his name. Leave him be, he's only a little 'un. He lives at third cottage on Ireland's Row and he'll be five just after me."

Miss Naggs stared at the scene, not knowing whether to chastise Ada or just be thankful that she had come to the boy's rescue. But what a little madam — she'd have to watch Ada Skipton.

"Well, we must be sure. Get your mother to write a note when you go home for dinner and put down all the details."

Protectively Ada put her arm around him and led him across to the line. She noticed he was still wearing the jersey, and it was mucky — covered in stains and bits. If she expected any gratitude she was disappointed, for huffily Wilf shrugged away from her.

23

"I can manage," he grunted.

"It looks like it and all," she snapped and went and stood near Hannah and noticed that Wilf kept close behind her.

Once all the formalities had been dealt with the children were joined by the rest of the school children and teachers. They were hushed into silence and then from a small glass room which stood at the end of the hall there emerged a tall, thin man who mounted the platform which stood in the middle of them all. He raised his hand and silently, like shadows, each child moved forward and stood on one of the brass spots which were set in the parquet floor.

Ada had been told of this routine and she followed suit, hastily joined by Hannah and Wilf and finally the rest of the new starters. Alice Naggs noticed the leadership and mentally planned to see that it was channelled correctly.

"Good morning children." The man spoke softly, but his voice was heard clearly throughout the hall.

"Good morning Mr. Appleyard." The answer came as one voice.

"Hands together, eyes closed," he instructed and all heads were bowed and he led them in the Lord's Prayer. Then the piano struck up and they sang the morning hymn.

"God bless you and have a good day." This was the dismissal and the children answered "Thank you, sir," before leaving, class by class, marching to their rooms to a rousing tune from the piano. Now only the new ones were left.

"This way children," Miss Naggs called out and obediently they followed her into a bright room that had rows and rows of bench desks set out. Each one was shown to their place and told to sit down. Hannah managed to sit next to Ada and on the other side a grubby-looking lad with grey skin and black greasy hair matted to his head.

"Have you got dicks?" Ada demanded. He stuck out his tongue. She retaliated by digging him in the ribs with her elbow and he yelped with pain.

"Now stop that nonsense and listen," Miss Naggs called out and proceeded to tell them all about behaving well in school. They were not babies any longer and must learn to obey orders. Next she handed each child a slate and pencil and boxes of bright red counters.

The first lesson was numbers and going to the blackboard she wrote down one to five.

Pointing to each number each child was told to count out as many counters and then to write them down.

"Now let's see who can remember them." She pointed to number four and asked those who knew the number to put up their hand.

Ada's went up immediately.

"Four Miss," she called out in her clear precise voice.

Miss Naggs said well done and then pointed out another one. Again Ada gave the answer.

"Are you able to count and read numbers, Ada?"

Proudly Ada nodded and told teacher that she could do them all up to ten. "I can add up as well, Miss," she added.

The morning passed quickly, and before it seemed possible, playtime arrived. Hannah and Ada stood in the corner of the yard a little apart from the rest and watched as they fought or played together. Without being too obvious she kept her eye on Wilf, but all he did was to hang on to the iron railings, swinging his feet in the air and then dropping to the ground. But she noticed he kept looking across at her and Hannah.

"Do you want to come over here with us?" she called out.

Wilf shook his head and put all his concentration into dropping safely on to the ground.

"We don't want him do we Ada — he doesn't look all that clean to me," Hannah said.

"Wilf's alright. He can come across if he wants to." Her tone defied any argument.

The infants were allowed to leave five minutes before the older ones and at dinner time Ada decided not to wait for her sisters. She was dying to get home and tell Dad all about it, and skipping lightly, she made her way down the Old Town hill and towards home. With a hitch and derry, with one foot on the pavement and the other in the gutter, she counted each limping step.

And then a feeling of being watched made her turn round. A few paces behind was Wilf, copying her limping and counting.

"What do you want?" she asked.

"Our Mam can't write," he said.

For a minute she could not think what he was on about. Of course, she then realised he needed a note to take back to school.

"Oh, can't she?" She wasn't going to make any offers, not after the way he had rebuffed her at school.

"And I'm not five until October."

She pointed a finger accusingly in his face. "Oooh — you shouldn't be at school then."

"Don't say owt will you. I'm not all that keen to go to school, but it's better than being at home with our Mam always on at me."

"What are you going to do then?"

He looked at her, with an unspoken question written all over his face.

"Shall I ask our Dad to write it for you? But we'll have to tell fibs about your birthday. I'll tell him it's two weeks after mine or you'll be sent home again."

25

His face lit up and they made an agreement to meet outside the school gates.

Mam was waiting and watching at the door for her with dinner ready to be served. All through the meal Ada recounted to them the happenings of the morning so explicitly that Esther felt she had been there at her side.

When the meal was over Ada asked her Dad to write the note for Wilf.

"His Mam can't write and I said you'd do it. They want his name, address and birthday. If he doesn't take it back with him he'll be sent home."

Both Esther and Thom wondered why Polly had asked for their help, but knowing Ada, no doubt she had volunteered to help out. Carefully Thom wrote the note and they had to think hard to work out his birthday. After counting out the dates they came to the conclusion that Wilf was born on July 10th — or thereabouts.

"It won't matter to a day or two, but I still can't think why Polly asked for you to write it," Esther said and quickly Ada suggested that it might be out of gratitude for the jersey.

She got the note and went gaily back to school to find Wilf waiting for her as arranged. He clutched the piece of paper gratefully and smiled his thanks.

"Your mother can write then?" Miss Naggs asked in surprise, and Wilf had the grace to blush. Pretending was one thing, but a downright lie was another matter altogether. He hadn't bargained for that.

"Please Miss, my Dad did it for Mrs. Tanner." Ada saw Wilf's plight and quickly came to the rescue.

Miss Naggs accepted this, for illiterate people often got others to do such things for them. This was no exception.

Wilf was dumbfounded. Fancy Ada telling a great fib like that. He hoped his Mam never found out, but Polly had never given a thought about the note. She had taken Harry the first day and given all the information and assumed they would know who Wilf was once he gave his name.

She had not asked one word about school during dinner time and though he had made vain attempts to tell her about it her short grunts had stopped him. Harry was given all the attention.

Ada enjoyed the afternoon and to a certain extent so did Wilf — a lot more than he had expected anyway.

He was nothing like as sharp as Ada, but he paid attention and especially liked the peace and quiet as he listened to the poetry Miss Naggs read out. She noted him as a plodder — slow — but he would get there in his own good time.

At a quarter-to-four the big bell rang out and the children stood for the final prayer.

26

"See you in the morning," Ada called out to Hannah and then set off with her usual gait down the street.

"Thanks Ada," she heard Wilf's voice call out from behind. He always seemed to be hanging behind her.

"Come up here instead of hanging back there." She stopped to wait for him.

"Thanks for not saying owt about the note, but we shan't half get into bother if anybody finds out." His voice trembled.

"Then we'd best see that nobody does find out." Clearly Ada was not in the least bit bothered.

"What made you do it?" Wilf had not known anybody put themselves out on his behalf before.

"'Cos — 'cos — I like you, that's why." She hung her head down with an unknown shyness.

"Me — why?" The open admission had startled him.

"'Cos you're little, like me, and need seeing to. Do you like me?"

What a funny thing to ask, he thought, and decided not to answer.

"Well, do you?" She wasn't going to let him off.

But he was embarrassed and didn't rightly know what to say. He didn't really know what it was to like or dislike anybody. He knew he liked goodies, which he rarely got, but people — he wasn't sure what Ada meant. He gave it some thought and then said, "Well, I must do or I wouldn't be walking down here with you, would I?"

"That's it then — we're friends." Ada liked everything cut and dried and his answer pleased her.

"Friends — what — you and me?"

"Yes, you and me, you great barm pot. My Dad says it's always policy to know who your friends are and now we know. You're my friend and I'm yours — right?" She looked him straight in the face.

"Ay, alright — if you say so Ada," came the somewhat bewildered reply.

They looked at one another and then her face lit up with one of her bright smiles. It was so smitting that slowly his face too creased into a wide grin.

"Come on then lad — follow me and I'll see you right." She laughed and he turned dutifully and fell into her footsteps to follow her down the street.

27

CHAPTER 4

Right from the start Ada's schooldays were good. She enjoyed the lessons and, although her character did not allow her to be a teacher's pet, she was appreciated for her quick brain and the way she could keep things in her head.

Very soon she was working with children a year older and by the age of ten was high on the list of possibles for the higher grade school examination. If she passed then she could go to the Girls High School. It would be a feather in her cap and look well for the school too.

On the other hand Wilf stayed with his own age group and though he did not show much academic talent, he always listened attentively, and slowly but surely absorbed the aknowledge. He did have one shining talent which took the form of great aptitude with his hands. This showed clearly in the elementary woodwork lessons.

The firm friendship that developed between the two — apart from a few childish squabbles — soon became an established part of their lives. Wilf would wait for Ada at the corner of Baylegate and Scarborough Road as they went to school and then outside the gates at home time.

They always shared their goodies and though Ada had more than he did, he managed to buy a few from the coppers he earned by scrubbing out Freddie Cligg's shop on a Saturday night. He gave some of the money to Mam and also the bits of leftover meat that Freddie gave him. The first time this happened he couldn't wait to get home and give it to Polly and for the first time Wilf thought he saw a glimmer of gratitude on her face.

He enjoyed the job in spite of the buckets of stony-cold water that chapped his hands. He also liked chatting to Freddie when they finished off with a mug of hot sweet tea.

But the highlight of his life was Ada's friendship and the best times of all were the days when they would go off up to Sewerby to see Isabella and George. The Right Honourable George Burlingham — son and heir to the title and estate.

On the way up they would look at the houses on Scarborough Road — big houses with big yards.

"I'm going to have a house like that one day," Ada announced and Wilf never doubted that she would.

She loved to spend time at Isabella's, to take tea out of china cups and to be the grand lady. Very often she would mimic her sister's ways and sometimes Esther would worry that she was getting big ideas.

As always Thom told her not to fret. "Ada will be fine. She'll have just as much as Isabella and she'll get it herself, you wait and see," he added. Thom had great faith in his daughter.

She loved to brag about her sister's home and future title. "Our George will be a Lord one day — that'll be a do for our Isabella. She'll be a proper lady — a proper one."

Ada liked things proper, and it was her intention to have everything proper, just like Isabella, when she grew up. It was not a dream but a plan for life. She would have the best no matter how hard she had to work for it.

Wilf would smile at her as she talked of such things and be suitably impressed to be the friend of a future lady of the land.

Polly was not impressed and was always sarcastic about the friendship. Once or twice she tried to put a stop to it, but Wilf was adamant — Ada Skipton was his friend and nothing would change that.

"You're a right sissy playing with a lass. Why don't you lark about with lads like Harry does?" she would say, and Harry also tried to get him with his gang, but it was no use.

Esther also shared some of Polly's feelings about what, to her, seemed a strange friendship, but sensibly she decided to let things be.

The visits to Sewerby fascinated Wilf. He had long outgrown the jersey that started the friendship, but he was no better dressed than before. In fact, he looked a right urchin at the side of Ada and it surprised him to be treated just the same as she was. After a time he accepted their kind ways and grew to feel comfortable in their presence.

Isabella's husband, George, took the trouble to show him round the farm and estate and Wilf was always glad when they came to the animals. The pheasant-rearing puzzled him a bit for he thought it wrong for such lovely creatures to be reared only to be shot.

"Why do you rear them just to kill them?" he asked George, who patiently explained that they were like the other animals being fattened for food. The killing was just done differently.

He mentioned it to Ada who told him not to be so soft. "George always sends us some down and they aren't half good when Mam's cooked them. I shall have pheasants one day when I'm grown up."

Isabella always gave them something to eat and drink and on one memorable Sunday they had lunch — or rather dinner — there.

They sat down at a table so big that to Wilf it looked as big as their kitchen. And the stuff they had to eat — roast beef, tatties, Yorkshire pudding and greens, two sorts. The broth they started with was the best he'd ever tasted and he saw George smile as some ran down his chin. The memory of that meal stayed with him for years and would come to mind in vivid colours when hunger rumbled in his belly.

Most of the toffs he knew ignored or shunned him, but not George and Isabella. There he was accepted as Ada's friend.

Isabella often resisted the temptation to send down some clothes for the lad. If he'd been dressed right he would have been right bonny. But she knew Polly would never accept anything.

She would only take spite out on the lad and perhaps try to put a stop to the visits, and Isabella knew what that meant to the lad.

It was a marvel the way the two got on together and although Wilf might be the one to do most of the giving in, it was very much a partnership.

With all the talk of the higher grade examination, Wilf worried a bit that Ada would not want to be his friend if she passed. There were only two others thought anywhere near good enough to take the exam and one was Hannah. The other was Claud Jones, the son of a prominent businessman.

"I'll put my money on Ada Skipton," Mr. Appleyard said with assurance. His only worry was Thom and Esther — would they allow her to go to High School?

"I don't think there will be any problem there. Thom Skipton is self-taught and always a good supporter of education. I think he'll be proud of Ada," said one teacher, but Mr. Appleyard was not so sure.

And he was proved to be right for when the results came through to show that Ada had passed with flying colours her Mam was not impressed. Thom was delighted and said she must go to High School. Esther said no.

"She's not going, Thom."

The statement fell like a thunderbolt into the room, so heavily that Ada could feel her Mam's voice bouncing around the walls. She couldn't believe what she had heard.

"Not going — now what does that mean, lass?" He looked bewildered at his wife.

"It means what it says — she's not going to High School. For one thing it's not fair to the other bairns to let her have any better education than them." Her tone was firm.

"But you can't do that to the lass, Esther. That's not right. The bairn is bright and she's worked hard to pass. You can't deny her the right to get on. Nay — you can't do that, Esther."

"I'm not going to talk about it, Thom. She's not going and that's that."

They couldn't believe their ears. Ada's face began to pucker.

"You can stop piking your eye, my lass," Esther snapped.

"Why can't I go Mam — can't we afford it?" Ada cried.

"It doesn't matter whether we can afford it or not, you're not going. If you've got the brains they say you have, you'll make out alright. It's a daft idea putting all that learning into lasses. You'd be kept at school until you're fourteen or fifteen and I'm not having that."

For the first time in Ada's life she went to bed in a flood of tears. All the pleading and Thom's reasoning fell on deaf ears. Through her sobbing

Ada could hear her Dad and Mam having an argument about it all. The next morning it was obvious that Thom and Esther were not on speaking terms, but Esther appeared to have won the day.

Wilf saw her downcast look as soon as they met and asked what was wrong. Ada briefly told him.

"Well, that's not right. It's real mean. I don't know as I want you to leave our school, but I reckon you've a right to what you've won," he said.

"It's all Mam's fault — now Hannah Wilson will go in my place."

"I'm sorry Ada." His shoulders hung down to match hers and they walked slowly up the street sharing the disappointment.

"I'll bet your Isabella wouldn't side with them. She'd not see it that way," Wilf said as they reached the school gates, and in this statement Wilf had given Ada what she thought to be a brilliant idea.

"You're right lad — you're right. Here, come on, let's go up to Sewerby now and tell them," she shouted.

"What about school?"

"We'll play hookie — come on lad." And she set off running with Wilf close on her heels.

"By hell we'll be for it if we're found out," he panted, trying hard to keep up with her.

"Well, make sure they don't. Mine will know anyway when our Isabella sorts it all out." Her faith was blind.

They ran down the lane and found Isabella taking young George for a trot around the garden. Breathlessly Ada poured out her story. Isabella listened patiently without a word. She couldn't make any promises. Mam was a threat to be reckoned with. If she'd made up her mind it would take an earthquake to move it.

Her sister's attitude disappointed Ada. "I thought you would stick up for me," she sulked.

"I didn't say I wouldn't, but you should not have skipped school like this. It won't make things any better."

The young truants were quickly despatched on their way, but decided to take the morning off anyway.

"I shall have to own up, but what about you?" she asked Wilf.

He decided he wasn't going to say anything unless Polly found out for herself. He'd face it then.

They spent the rest of the morning wandering around the old gravestones in the Priory churchyard. Ada knew by doing this they could keep well hidden and she could also keep an eye on the time from the tower clock. She enjoyed reading the funny old names and took note that rich folk seemed to afford large headstones and plots. "When owt happens to me, I shall have a big stone like that. I shall have written on it 'a noted member of the town'."

31

She pointed to a large stone surrounded by wrought iron fencing.

"I shan't care where they put me — it's too late to bother then," Wilf laughed.

"That's 'cos you've nowt about you. Me — I'm going to work hard and have everything I want. My funeral will be a grand event."

"Well, knowing you, that wouldn't surprise me. Me — I reckon they'll shove me in the corner of a field somewhere." He giggled at the thought.

"If you take notice of me Wilf, you could end up a hero. You might even have a gold watch."

In childish innocence they laughed gleefully — a hero — a gold watch — what dreams!

During lunch Isabella told George what had happened, saying that she felt she ought to go down and have a word with her Mam.

"It does seem a bit unfair not to allow her the chance. I don't suppose it will do a bit of good but at least I feel I ought to try," she said.

George looked across at his wife and smiled. She was so thoughtful and kind. He was well aware that they were not of the same class, but he blessed the day they wed, whatever the circumstances. At off times her little ways irritated him, but they were too minor to worry about.

"Shall I come with you? I might be able to help, and anyway, your mother may have made some of that pound cake."

Isabella laughed. Mam's cooking was becoming famous. She felt so lucky at the way her life had turned out — it could have been so very different. George need not have wed here — they could have shunned her, but neither he nor his family did that. At first they were a bit funny, but now they had grown to enjoy a mututal respect and were quite proud of their daughter-in-law. She hoped her position would be able to help Ada. Knowing Mam, she very much doubted it.

Ada made no secret of her morning's visit deciding to risk her Mam's wrath for playing hookie rather than for telling fibs. Hookie might get a sharp clout round the earhole — a downright fib got a real good tanning.

Esther pursed her lips at the story and looked knowingly across at Thom as if to say, "I told you this one would be trouble." He took the easy way out and concentrated on his dinner.

Ada was just thinking that Isabella had let her down when a knock on the door heralded not only her sister but also George. Oh hek, now Mam would be real mad for putting them to this bother. Still it would be worth it if they did any good. She ran down the passage to greet them and Isabella asked, in a whisper, if Mam knew anything about it.

"You can stop whispering there together, I know what's going on," Esther shouted from the kitchen.

"Well, now Mother — are you keeping well?" George spoke so respect-

32

fully to her, just as if she were gentry too. Tonight it had little effect.

"She's not going." Esther dispensed with any preliminaries and spoke out.

"But you must consider it very seriously. If it's a question of finance, I would be delighted to help out. The girl has got a good brain and could do well — you can't deny that," he said.

"It's not a matter of brass, lad — not just now anyway — but whether we could keep her there is another matter. But I don't think it's right she should be made any different to the others. She's got enough big ideas as it is. Ada will stay where she is until she's old enough to take Daisy's place at home. After that she can go out to work same as rest of them."

Her tone was such that all of them knew any arguments would fall on stony ground. Ada would take her chance with the rest of them.

Even Mr. Appleyard called at the house to try and persuade Esther to change her mind, but it was of no use. He felt saddened that all his and Ada's work had gone in vain. He prayed that the girl would not lose heart and would continue to work hard. She could have another go at the examination when she was twelve — if they could get Esther to change her mind.

But Ada was not of the stuff to let a disappointment, no matter how big, worry her for long. Once the first bitterness had passed, she seemed to become inspired to work harder than ever at her lessons and became so good that she was sometimes allowed to help the little ones who found their work too difficult.

"There's a teacher in the making if ever I saw one," Miss Naggs said.

As Ada's first teacher she took a pride in the girl's achievements. Ada was patient with the youngsters and would take ages to explain the basics of reading and writing.

But in addition to Ada passing the exam, that year was to be marked by another momentous happening — Esther gave birth at the age of fifty to her seventeenth child.

Ada had no idea that the event was expected although she did say once or twice that Mam was getting rare and fat. Esther made no mention of her condition and Thom thought she seemed a bit ashamed to tell the bairns, especially Isabella.

"They'll reckon we should have stopped all that lark," she said shyly.

"Well, we haven't and I'm not sorry. You never know lass, it might run in the family," came the laughing answer.

Isabella took it in very good part and even teased her parents about it, saying she hoped all this child-bearing didn't run in the family.

"As long as you're both alright Mam, that's all that matters," Isabella said and Esther could have kissed her for it.

33

The morning that the baby was born Esther stayed in bed with a supposed bilious attack — she often had these and Ada gave it very little attention.

"Best leave Mam, love, and get off to school. You can go up and see her if she's a bit better at dinner time," Daisy told her.

At dinner time she was surprised to be greeted by a delighted Dad who told her to go upstairs and see what Mam had got to show her.

"Is it a gold watch then?" She laughed and scampered up to the big front bedroom. Esther was sitting up in bed looking pretty in a white cotton nightie and silk bed shawl over her shoulders. At one side of the bed there was the old bassinet which had obviously been repainted and frilled.

"What's all this then?" Ada asked in her cheeky way.

"Have a look for yourself," Mam told her.

She crept on tip-toe, instinctively, and peeped inside the cot. A bundle of cream blankets lay inside and nestled in the folds slept a fair-haired baby.

"What is it?" Ada asked and Mam introduced her to her baby sister, Lillian.

"By hek, she came a bit quick, didn't she? What did you get her with — Brooke Bond stamps?" Ada smiled and stroked the baby's head whilst Esther smothered a laugh at her daughter's perky turn of phrase.

During the past few months she had often wondered if she had done the right thing in not letting Ada go to High School, but she still held the firm belief that Ada would make out fine whatever she decided to do. And with another mouth to feed, keeping her on would have been impossible. Soon Daisy would have to go out to work and Ada would have to take her place. She had already applied for a labour certificate so that Ada could stay at home in the afternoons to help around the house. With putting in such good attendances, there was no problem with the authorities. The application had disturbed the teachers, but they were powerless to do anything about it.

"What does Ada say about it then?" Thom asked and was told it was better that she knew nowt about it until all the forms were passed.

"Don't you think you should mention it to her?" Daisy asked, and Esther snapped, feeling a little guilty, that she'd find out soon enough. She didn't relish breaking the news and decided to be out when Ada was told. By God — she would create.

At this point Thom took a stand and said he was having nowt to do with the matter.

"You seem to think you know what's best so you can get on with it," he told her.

Many others tried to get their children exempted from school to bring a bit more money into the home. Polly relished the thought of her lads

34

leaving to start work — things would be mighty easier then. She tried to get Wilf off, but she had kept him at home too many days to help with the extra loads of washing. But she planned to ask for him to leave on hardship grounds as soon as she could. Harry would then be old enough to leave and she was going to make sure that the burden of wage earner was not going to fall on his shoulders alone. Wilf would have to take his share.

On the morning of Ada's eleventh birthday Mr. Appleyard mounted the platform and stood looking down at the full view of children gathered before him and sighed. After the usual greeting he called out, "Ada Skipton — will you come to my study straight after prayers please?"

Ada shuffled her feet and tried to keep them on the brass spot. She felt all eyes were looking at her and bent her head to try and hide the colour that had risen to her cheeks.

"What you done then? — looks like you're for it now, Ada," a voice said behind her.

She missed Hannah, who had gone on to High School and it had hurt to see her friend all dressed up so smartly in the dark green uniform. For a time they had remained friends, but Hannah made new ones and now virtually ignored Ada.

She brightened up thinking that maybe she was to be given another chance at the exam and after prayers went and stood outside the study door. She was still very small for her age, but bore herself with a confidence that showed she was quite capable of looking after herself. The large gloomy hall swamped her tiny form and as she looked across the floor the brass spots danced before her eyes.

"Oh God, please don't let me be sick," she prayed.

Lately she had often felt giddy and sick and couldn't understand when Mam called it "her age." Ada wondered what being eleven had to do with feeling sick. Did everybody feel sick when they were eleven?

"Come along in child, I'm not going to eat you." Mr. Appleyard spoke kindly, having seen the look on her face.

He opened the study door and sat behind the big desk. Ada's face still only showed just above the carved edge. He leaned forward to see her more clearly.

"Well, today is the day, Ada."

"What, sir?" She looked puzzled.

"Your labour certificate has come through. Your mother applied for it some weeks ago and it came through this morning."

"Labour certificate — what does that mean, sir?" Mr. Appleyard tried to cover his impatience. The child was obviously ignorant of it all.

"It means that now you only attend school in the mornings. With your good attendance you have been given partial exemption."

"When does it start, sir?"

35

He told her immediately and had to stop himself from adding, "I'm afraid."

Ada stood silent and her eyes clouded over.

"What's the matter, Ada?" he asked.

"I like school, sir. I don't want to stop coming. I thought that with the others working I might get another chance at the exam. I've worked hard, sir, and I've tried to help Mam too. I thought she might give in and let me go." Her tone was sullen with disappointment.

"I'm sorry Ada, but I have to abide by your parents' decision. There is nothing I can do about it now." He got up and went and stood by her side placing his arm on her shoulder.

"Couldn't you ask again, sir?" she pleaded.

"We've been through all this before, Ada. You must accept it as a lesson in life — part of growing up. This is your first big step and you must face up to it, no matter how unfair it may seem." He spoke more harshly than he intended and saw tears well up into her eyes.

"Now come along, that's enough of that. Go along to your classroom and give this paper to Miss Baldwin to keep until dinner time."

Ada shrugged her shoulders and muttered, "Yes sir, thank you sir," and slowly went towards the door.

"Ada — I'll try and help all I can during lessons you attend and if you're really keen, I'll give you some work to do at home."

Her face brightened. "Thank you, sir," she called out and skipped into the hall.

As she entered the classroom she heard poetry being recited. This was one of her favourite lessons. Miss Baldwin knew the reason for the study interview and was prepared for a difficult morning. Ada was a bit of a handful if upset. Ada gave her the paper and she was surprised to see the girl smiling. Well, perhaps things were not as bad as expected after all.

"Come and sit down, Ada. Wilf is going to recite for us."

"Can I say it, Miss — I shan't have many more chances?"

Miss Baldwin nodded assent, deciding to allow a little favouritism for once. She told Wilf to sit down. The class giggled for they were always teasing these two for spending all their time together.

Wilf and Ada took no notice of them. Wilf treasured the friendship for Ada was his inspiration. She was the only one who ever encouraged him to do anything.

"Go on lad, have a go. You never know what you're made of if you don't try. Get on with it — you might win a gold watch." This was her usual saying when he dithered over anything.

"Wilf Tanner's sweet on Ada," someone whispered, but Ada gave them a withering look and silence reigned.

She stood, straight as a ram-rod, tossed her hair behind her shoulder, clasped her hands in front of her white pinny and started in a clear voice, to recite.

" 'King Bruce of Scotland threw himself down in a lonely mood . . .' " The words poured forth and Ada was lost in the story of this great king whose strength had lain in his perserverance. Ada admired perseverance.

The class listened in rapt attention for Ada was good at reciting. Miss Baldwin listened too, and sadly wondered how many other girls had been wasted as Ada was now being. Bright girls who would have made excellent teachers if given the chance. Most of them went into service or the local laundry before marrying, far too young, and bearing large families. She felt her work was in vain and helpless to do anything about it.

The bell stopped further reciting and they sang " 'Thank you for the world so sweet.' " Ada had to swallow hard to stop tears falling. Why hadn't she played hookie more often? She could have stayed on then. Leaving school was the privilege for behaving, working and attending — some privilege!

Wilf waited for her to come out of the girls' entrance and immediately asked her about Mr. Appleyard.

"Did you get into bother about summ'at?" he asked.

Briefly, and without any emotion, she told him what had happened.

"You lucky begger — I wish I could leave," he said.

"Aye — you would. I like school and I don't want to be a duffer like you. I'd change places with you and stop on."

He could see that she was really upset and tried desperately to cheer her up.

"Well, there's one thing — I shan't have to share my goodies with you this afternoon," he teased, trying to get a smile but, truthfully, he too was sad at the thought of not sharing their adventures as they went to and from school together.

When they got to the end of Ireland's Row he paused and looked at her.

"Ada. . ." He spoke hesitantly.

"What?"

"Oh, nowt," he muttered and ran along the cobbled roadway, turning as he reached his door to shout, "I'll miss you."

Slowly she walked home and went into the house to find Mam and Dad alone for once — except for the baby lying in the cradle beside the fire. She plonked down the paper in front of Mam, who unfolded it and passed it to Thom, asking him to read it out to her.

"That's nice then — she'll be a real help to me and Daisy in the afternoons, won't she?" Esther breathed in deeply as if satisfied that, at long last, a tiresome item had been dealt with.

"Ada will be a great help, never fear. She's a good little worker," Thom agreed, having long ago given up the fight for his daughter's education.

Esther placed a plate of broth and dumplings in front of her, but Ada just looked at it.

"Mam, Mr. Appleyard said he thought I ought to stop on, but if I can't he'll give me some work to do at home to keep up."

Esther's face clouded. "Well, you're not. You can put a stop to them fancy ideas once and for all. You'll be the same as others and ruddy well work for your living." Education to Esther was not work.

"I would get a damn sight better job if I stayed on and learnt a bit more," Ada's temper flashed.

Thom was fed up with the whole thing and wanted nothing more than peace to reign in the house.

"Don't you talk to your Mam like that my girl. It's quite finished and done with now. Let it drop."

"What's good of education anyroad. Before you know it you'll be wanting to get wed," Esther snorted.

"Don't bother about that Mam. I'm not saddling myself with a houseful of bairns and a ruddy bloke to wait on hand and foot. I want better than that."

"They all say that. You'll change your mind quick enough."

Esther looked across at Thom and smiled, but he was deep in thought. Ada's sharp words had gone deep and hurt him. Was that what she had learnt from her home life — a houseful of bairns and nought but hard graft?

Her brothers and sisters came in and seeing her quiet mood asked what it was all about. Esther told them.

"You'll enjoy that better than school, and it won't be long afore you're old enough to come and work with us at laundry. You are growing up now." Lizzie spoke encouragingly, but Ada scowled and stuck out her tongue.

"We'll soon knock that out of you when we get you with your arms stuck in a bowl of hot suds. There's nowt like a pile of mucky washing to set you straight," Lizzie grinned.

Ada bit her lip to stop any sharp retort. It couldn't do any good and maybe cause a row. It wasn't worth the bother.

When they had gone back to work, Esther wrapped a big black pinny around her waist and pointed towards the mountain of pots and pans waiting to be washed.

"Get some water out of the boiler and start on that lot. Rub your cloth with Sunlight soap and get a good lather."

Grudgingly, Ada did as she was told.

"You can count 'em if you fancy schooling all that much. I'll teach you a thing or two, my lass, without school."

Ada looked at the black fire-scorched pans, the piles of greasy pots and the cups with tea leaves stuck with sugar to the bottom. Her belly curled in revulsion at the sight.

"I don't need to count. There's ten of us sat down and that's forty pots, forty cutlery, four pans and a bloody steamer." She felt the blow of a wet cloth around her ears for her cheek, but ignored it and, rolling up her sleeves, tackled the job by starting to recite at the top of her voice.

" 'King Bruce of Scotland threw himself down. . .' "

Her voice reached out into the backyard where Esther was shaking out the cloth. At first she felt angry and then remembered her own youthful resentments and laughed softly. "Little bugger," she thought.

Ada worked steadily through the afternoon, washing the pots and pans and drying them until they shone, turning the beds, sweeping the lino surrounds and shaking the mats.

"I'll give the little bugger her due, she can shift the work," Esther later told Thom.

At half-past three she kept a close eye on the clock and as it struck four she ran to the door shouting out that she was going to meet Wilf. She went a little way up the road and spotted him walking pegged-legged in the gutter.

"What's been going on then?" she greeted him and fell into step with him.

"Nowt. Bobby Grice got a swipe for making a mess on his reading book with aniseed ball, but that's all."

"Nobody ask about me then?"

He shook his head. "I missed you at playtime," he spoke softly.

"Don't talk so daft. You missed my treacle toffee, that's all." She gave him a hefty shove with her elbow and sent him sprawling into the gutter. He lay there looking up at her — Ada — his idol.

"I did Ada — honest — and I've kept you a gob stopper." He got to his feet and reached into the depths of his trouser pocket, finally bringing out a crumpled ball of newspaper which held the goodie.

"Thanks Wilf. Come on I'll suck it until it turns colour and then you can have it."

She took the goodie, stuffed it into her mouth, lodging it carefully to one side so as not to swallow it. Noisily she sucked and he laughed as they fell once more into step — Wilf behind Ada — and walked home.

39

CHAPTER 5

The half day schooling did not work out at all. At first Ada resented the time spent at home and then as she realised that soon she could be earning money she resented the half days at school.

She began to enjoy working at home and had become very aware of the value of money. It started when Thom began to give her threepence a week for helping Esther, and as she became quicker at her set jobs and had more time to spare, she took to doing odd jobs for other people.

Mrs. Bibby's front steps was her first task — all five of them — and then she saw Mrs. White struggling to take some groceries to Fensby's and offered to help. This too became a regular thing and also brought in more brass.

With Dad's threepence, and sixpence a week from the steps and the deliveries, she soon had one and sixpence a week coming in — wealth indeed! She kept her money in an old toffee tin under the bed and only spent when necessary and then very carefully. Thrift was a natural gift and soon she had three pounds tucked away. Her family teased her about being stingy but Ada never had to ask Mam for money for Sunday school or anything — she was always solvent.

At thirteen she was allowed to leave school completely and was glad that at last her twilight life was over. She would have to wait until she was fourteen to begin work proper, but that would soon pass and now she could take on extra outside work.

The first full week she worked at home she made a careful note of the extra work Mam gave her. On Friday night Dad pushed the threepence across the table as usual, but Ada pushed it back to him and shook her head.

"I want more than that Dad — double in fact. I'm home all day now and I do a hell of a lot more work. That should mean more brass."

Thom laughed at her. "Well, I'll be buggered. What do you reckon, Mam?" He looked at Esther for confirmation and she had to admit that Ada had turned out to be the best help she'd ever had in the house.

"Can't we negotiate?" Thom asked in mock seriousness.

"What are you offering?" Ada's voice was brisk and businesslike.

"Four pence." He banged the table to strike the bargain.

"Five pence ha'penny, and that's my final word." She banged the table too, and Thom thought what a good union man she would have made.

Laughing, he agreed, and so each week Ada received the odd sum of five pence ha'penny. She had only expected four pence and the extra bit tickled her pink and spurred her on to ask Mrs. Bibby and Mrs. White for more and she got another penny a week. Ada was learning fast.

It was not so with Wilf. Polly managed to get him off school when he was thirteen and immediately began harping on about getting a job.

"You'll not be able to do much — you're far too little — but there must be somebody as wants a hand somewhere," she nattered on.

Since Harry had been left, he had got — and lost — three jobs. He was shifty and idle, never pulling his weight if he could get away with it. Polly excused him with the usual "he's not strong."

"If you ask me, he's just bloody idle," Wilf confided to Ada.

"Just see to it that you're not like that, then. Anyroad, what do you want to do with yourself?" she asked.

"I don't rightly know. I've a chance to sweep up and deliver for Kidd's and there doesn't seem to be owt else to do. I reckon I'll take that."

"Why?"

"What do you mean why — what else can I do?"

"Look for a better job — you never know what you can do unless you put your mind to it. Put your stall out lad. Just look at me. I've got money coming in every week and I'll soon be up at laundry earning more."

Wilf thought it was easier for a lass and said so, but who would take a lad like him on for any job worth owt?

"Why not think about learning a trade?"

He snorted at this and could just imagine what Polly would have to say.

"Forget other folk, Wilf. Get on and do something for yourself. Why not try Uncle Joe's up at carpenter's shop or our George?" she suggested.

"I don't know as I fancy working on a farm, but up at carpenter's — that's different. Do you reckon your Uncle would take me on?" His interest was aroused, for he had always liked woodwork.

Ada knew Uncle Joe would help if he could, and if she asked him, but Wilf ought to start looking out for himself. Still it was worth keeping in the back of her mind.

Wilf started at Kidd's the furniture shop on Quay Road as no more than an odd-job lad. His money was half a crown a week, of which Polly took all but three pence.

To keep a bit extra in his pocket he kept on Cligg's scrubbing out job and kept that money for himself.

"How much does Harry fork out then?" Ada asked when he grumbled about his finances.

Wilf had no idea, but guessed it to be very little, if anything.

Being at work left little time for meetings and these were cut to three times a week, apart from chance encounters.

On Wednesdays they would go to the Young People's Meeting and on Saturdays and Sundays go for walks or up to Sewerby. Wilf was not yet in the habit of calling openly for Ada and would wait outside the house whistling loudly until she came out. His face would light up when he saw her and off they would go as happy as larks.

They loved the summer months when they went along the sea front and up the cliffs. This was Wilf's favourite spot. They would scramble up and down the chalky sides shouting to one another and needing nothing else but each other's company.

Their closeness bothered Esther when she thought about it. After all, she could still recall how she and Thom had had strong feelings for each other. These could run high if young people spent a lot of time together and though Ada and Wilf were still very young, you could never tell. She made up her mind to have a little chat with Ada — no use waiting until it was too late.

But the friendship was perfectly innocent in spite of their closeness and fondness for each other. Wilf had never so much as kissed Ada — or even tried to. Holding hands as they walked was an unusual event and lasted only a few moments before one of them would go haring off, usually Ada leading the way.

The thought of any other contact never occurred to either of them but once — only once — did Ada feel a need to see what Wilf was made of.

It happened one Sunday afternoon in the late summer when they were walking at the back side of the cliffs. They had been out about two hours and Ada's bladder being what it was she was cut short.

"I'll have to squat down behind them bushes," she informed Wilf and without any more to-do hid herself from view, bent down, parted her open drawers and proceeded to pee with a gush that would have done credit to a stallion horse.

It took Wilf aback a bit, but he stood guard in case anybody came along. The sound of her water made him want to go too and so he popped behind the bushes just a second before Ada had finished.

"I'm sorry Ada, but I can't wait any longer, you've made me want to go." He blushed but Ada didn't bother — she was used to lads in her family and told him to get on with it.

"You've only got a john willy same as our lads," she said in a matter of fact voice.

"You seen them then?" he asked in surprise.

She shook her head and busied herself with her clothes.

"You seen a lass's mary-ann?"

Wilf stared back and shook his head.

"You can have a look at mine if you want." And without any more to-do, she lifted the skirts of her dress at the back, parted her drawers again and bent down to give Wilf a full view.

He went forward to take a closer look and she stood still for a second and then asked cheekily, "Seen it all then?"

It was too bad if he hadn't for Ada had had enough of her private parts

42

being inspected — the wind blowing off the sea was a bit cold and she downed her skirts.

"Let's have a look at yours then."

"What if somebody comes?" he asked, never thinking that he would have to take a turn of inspection.

She just laughed and shyly he undid his buttons and brought out his john willy. It measured about one and a half inches long and looked to Ada like a large fat worm. She bent over it and tentatively gave it a prod with her finger. Wilf winced and jumped back.

"It's not much to shout about is it?"

She pulled a face and Wilf put the offending object away. The incident was over and neither of them ever referred to it again.

Ada was far too occupied with other more important things than Wilf's "privates." Things like growing up — earning money — and getting on. She was also thinking it was time she went up to see Uncle Joe about setting Wilf on, for that job at Kidd's was no use at all for somebody who wanted to get on.

By this time, Thom was a well-established agent for the Sunday papers. He collected them at five in the morning and delivered them to newsagents before setting up his own stall near the pier. He also ran a delivery round and Ada took her papers up round Priory Close. Dad paid her and she often got tips from the customers who rather pitied such a little lass pushing the barrow laden with papers. Ada took it gladly for she knew her size could be used to good advantage.

She asked Wilf if he would like a round — perhaps they could share in a bigger round. He thought about it, but when Polly found out she would have none of it, not even for the extra money. Earning money from the Skiptons was not allowed.

Ada never visited the house. "It wouldn't be good enough for the likes of her, would it?" Polly sneered.

The reason was that Ada felt it best to keep out of what looked like an explosive situation. If she went up there and saw any injustice to Wilf she would more than likely say something and that would only make things worse. If she wanted Wilf she knew that she could catch him on his way to and from work.

On one of her Sunday morning paper treks, she decided that it was time to tackle Uncle Joe about Wilf.

"Is Uncle Joe up yet?" she asked her aunt as she delivered their paper.

Aunt Cissy smiled and nodded towards the front parlour where Uncle Joe was trying to light the fire. Ada went straight through and found him poking away at a smoking mass of coal and sticks.

"Now then Ada — what do you want?" he asked fondly.

Ada was also one of Joe's favourites. He liked the streak in her character

43

that was so like her Granny and with the added bit of spice she was a right good lass. Her youthful dreams and opinions gave him many a laugh.

Joe was the spitting image of his Dad — Grandad Raines — he was rather small, but with a commanding presence. When he had taken on the flourishing business he had not been put under any pressure for he loved the work. Now he ran the whole lot, but old Joe still had a bit of a say in how things were done and he put in a damn good day's work too.

"Can you do with another hand in the yard?" Ada asked outright.

"You're not thinking of coming are you?" He wouldn't have put that past her.

"No, I'm not, you great fathead. I were thinking of Wilf Tanner. He can do with a better job and he might be a good prospect for an apprenticeship later on."

"You standing reference for him then?" It was like talking to an old woman.

"I can do that right enough. He'll make a good worker and a job with you would have more future than the one he's got down at Kidd's."

"You making plans for the lad then — you thinking on weddin' him?" Joe teased.

"Don't talk so daft. Th'onny man I'll wed will have to have his arse hung in diamonds and every diamond worth a thousand."

"Aye, I bet he will and all." Joe and his little niece laughed heartily together.

They were not particularly looking for another lad, but he could not deny that an extra pair of hands would be useful. Business was good and there was always room for a good lad.

"Tell him to come up and have a word then," he told her.

"Right then, I'll bring him up this afternoon as we go to Sewerby." She wasn't going to lose any more time. This needed settling as soon as possible. Her aunt offered a cup of tea but Ada refused.

"You know what my water-works are like. I shall have to be nipping behind hedges if I drink owt." She bid them cheerio and left them laughing as she usually did.

When she and Wilf met she looked him up and down to see that he was presentable enough to go up to Uncle Joe's. He was always clean, but some of the clothes he wore — well — the less said about them the better. And the haircut had not improved much. Still, that would all come when he got a decent job.

Wilf was not as pleased as she had expected when she told him where they were going.

"You should have mentioned it first, Ada. What's Mam going to say?" He paused, then said, "She'll reckon I'm going behind her back." "She can't say a lot if you get more brass, can she? She'll not turn that away."

Wilf mused to himself for Ada had a point.

Joe already knew Wilf well enough for he often visited with Ada. He liked the lad whom he nicknamed "Ada's shadow" and thought him a nice, polite youngster.

Ada shoved open the door and shouted, "Can we come in?" and without waiting for an answer walked through the door. Wilf hesitated and she pulled him behind her.

Joe welcomed them, said, "Sit yourselves down" and then started to ask Wilf some questions.

"Can we talk in private, Mr. Raines?" Wilf asked after the first one or two.

"Why — what have you got to say in private?" Ada demanded.

"This is men's talk Ada — private."

By hek, Joe thought to himself, the lad has got a bit of spirit hidden in him. He got up and led the way into the kitchen leaving an open-mouthed Ada with her aunt.

"Now then lad — you fancy a job in woodwork I understand?"

Wilf nodded and answered all Joe's questions quietly and honestly. Yes, he had always liked woodwork and yes he would like to be considered for an apprenticeship if he showed promise.

"If the money is right that is."

Joe looked at the lad carefully — clean but shabby but with an open countenance that showed an honest wish to better himself.

"How much is Kidd paying you?"

Wilf told him and after a bit of thought offered three and six. He knew a little about Polly and the extra would be a godsend.

Three and six — a fortune — surely Mam couldn't say owt against that? Happily he accepted and on a handshake made arrangements to serve a week's notice and start the following Monday at seven sharp.

"You keep good time and no shirking mind you. We are only a small business and everybody has to pull their weight," Joe warned.

They went through to join Ada and Aunt Cissy and told them that Wilf had a job with Raines & Son, Carpenters and Cabinet Makers. Ada smiled and heaved a sigh of pleasure and satisfaction.

"Come on then, let's get on up to Sewerby and tell our Isabella."

Joe listened to her firm instructions and pitied the man she wed. She'd be a handful and no mistake.

As they walked along, Wilf was more than usually silent. His courage was waning a bit at the thought of facing Polly. She might not like it that Joe was related to the Skiptons.

Ada sensed what was on his mind. "You getting a bit windy now, Wilf?"

He shook his head but didn't fool her for one minute.

If you'd asked, she couldn't have told you why she bothered with him.

45

He didn't look much and hadn't a great deal about him, but there was something about the way his face lit up when he smiled at her, the way his eyes would sparkle when he was roused with pleasure or anger and his dog-like devotion. She knew there were hidden depths in Wilf and she intended to bring them out. He would turn into a good lad if handled right. There were little unexpected twists to his character that kept surprising her and livened her interest and besides, she could never, ever, hurt Wilf.

When they got to Sewerby, Isabella and George were delighted with the news and their enthusiasm gave Wilf a bit of courage to face his Mam. They were asked to stay for tea, but Wilf firmly refused. He wanted to get home and get, what he felt sure would be a row, over with. He was resolute in his determination to go to Raines's no matter what she said, but it would be no easy matter to talk her round.

"You stop if you want Ada," he said, but she decided to walk home with him and perhaps tell him what to say — how to handle the situation.

"Don't be so scared Wilf. Tell her straight and if she doesn't like it tell her to lump it like cats do dumplings," she told him.

"I know what I'm going to say without you telling me. I know Mam better than you do," he snapped and the rest of the way was walked in silence.

"Sure you don't want me to come in with you?" she asked and then stopped herself short for he gave her one of his looks which said "no" plainer than any words could have done.

"See you later?" Wilf just shrugged his shoulders and turned into the cobbled street.

He got in and saw the tea laid, wishing for a minute he had stopped up at Sewerby. Bread and dripping — that was it. Still, he couldn't blame Polly for she did her best. But he noticed that Harry had jam spread on his bit of bread and felt angry. Why the hell should he have the best bits? He never brought much, if owt, into the house.

"I expect you've had tea with your posh friends," Polly greeted. Wilf shook his head.

"Well, we've nowt that they've got here."

"I've never said owt have I Mam? I've never grumbled about how you manage?" he asked her.

"No, you've not enough about you for that. You're too like your Dad."

"And who's he like then — ruddy king?" He nodded towards Harry and then bit his lips for he'd never said anything like that before.

Polly's colour rose and she bit her lip. "Enough of that. Here, get yourself sat down."

He could see that he had ruffled her feathers. Well, might as well get it all over with.

46

"Mam, how would you like an extra tanner a week coming in?" He watched her face closely and saw surprise in her eyes.

"How do you mean?"

Patiently he explained and left out the part Ada had played, for that would make her mad.

"I'm to get three bob a week." He lied, praying she wouldn't check up on him. Wilf was learning fast — that other sixpence could be saved for himself like Ada said.

"I can't deny it won't help." She spoke grudgingly, and he knew he had won. Whatever spot he had touched upon had shut her up without a fight. It might be worth remembering. And to think he had nearly messed himself in fear of her.

"You'll be getting a right big head our Wilf — a job and then a trade. You'll soon be too big for the likes of us. Next think you'll be off down to live at Skiptons." Harry was jealous and had to say his piece.

"Shut your gob — it's about time you got off your arse and brought in some steady money," he rounded on his brother.

"Leave him be Wilf, Harry's not strong, you know that."

She would have to defend him, but he thought it best to leave matters alone for the moment. He had got off without a row and that was enough.

The first thing Monday morning he told Mr. Kidd he would be leaving at the end of the week. He was sorry to lose the lad, but wished him well and readily agreed to give him a reference.

The days passed slowly, for Wilf was keen to get started in his new life. As Ada had said, there was no telling where it could lead — he might even go into business for himself one day.

Bright and early the following Monday he presented himself at the yard gates. It was ten minutes to seven — he was early as Mr. Raines had said to be. He felt good, for this was the new beginning and Mam had grudgingly wished him all the best as he left the house. Well, almost.

"I hope you know what you're about, our Wilf. You be a good lad and do as you're told." These were her exact words, but Wilf knew, in her way, she was wishing him well.

At first the work was menial, just sweeping up and bagging the sawdust and seeing that the workbenches were tidy and the tools cleaned and oiled for the craftsmen. But one day somebody would be doing this for him, and that was worth striving for.

After a week or two he saw that a great deal of wood was wasted and burnt in the old tin out in the yard. He pondered upon it and then came up with what he felt was a brilliant idea.

"Mr. Raines, you know that wood we burn? Well, if I chop it up in my own time, could I take some home for Mam and maybe sell the rest to make a bit of extra money like?"

47

"I don't see why not lad," Joe told him.

And so every day after the others had left, Wilf would stay behind and chop up all the odd bits and pieces and bundle them up to take home. Mam was pleased with it and soon found that she had far more than she needed.

"I'm going to go up and down street and sell rest," he told her and proceeded to knock on each door. He found that he had a good trade at a penny a bag. It was good value and soon he had a regular round which he did every Saturday afternoon after finishing work.

Polly accepted the extra money with bad grace, but an odd kind of gratitude. He began to get bits of meat on his plate and jam on his bread when she packed his snap for mid-morning.

The extra tanner she knew nothing about and as the money from the sticks mounted up he began to save. Every week he would religiously put a bit aside in the broken leg of the old dressing table when nobody was around to see. He had a plan — first to get his hair cut decently and then, when he had enough, to get a proper suit from Machin's.

One Saturday afternoon he was a bit late for his dinner and when he entered the house both Polly and Harry gawped at him with mouths open.

"Whatever have you had done to yourself?" she asked.

It was plain to see that Wilf had had his hair cut properly and the difference it made was unbelievable. Jim Lawty had done a good neat job with what he had to start with and the result was a neat back and sides and a front quiff that showed off the hint of a wave.

Wilf ate his dinner quickly and then got out the enamel bowl and gave his hair a good wash with Sunlight soap. After brushing the sweep of the quiff it showed a golden gleam. Now — what would Ada have to say to that?

"Well, I'm blowed — you do look different Wilf. I'm right proud of you," she praised and he glowed. Just wait until he got his suit.

Carefully he kept watch on Machin's window and noted the price of suits, realising with delight that he only needed another fifteen bob. He could get one for August Bank Holiday.

The stick round was increasing and he had to spend most of Saturday afternoon delivering.

"Why don't you ask your Harry to help out — offer him a bit of money. He might jump at the chance," Ada told him.

Wilf was not too keen on the idea, but thought he might give it a try.

"No I'm bloody well not — I'm not skivvying for you — you take your own sticks out," Harry bawled at him.

Wilf looked across at Polly — surely she would say something in his favour?

"If the weather got bad, he wouldn't be able to do it Wilf, you know how he gets cold easy."

He might have known, but he had at least tried.

"But you're not above having what sticks bring in, are you, you idle sod?" he grumbled and marched out.

"It's that Ada Skipton that's doing all this to him Mam — she'll ruin our Wilf if he's not careful."

Polly grunted in agreement.

When Ada learnt of Harry's reaction, she suggested young Stanley — her elder brother's little lad — he'd be glad of a copper or two in his pocket. Stanley would often go with them on walks and hero-worshipped Wilf. He would be glad to be thought big enough to help out.

"Only give him threepence though — he's not big enough to earn more than that," she said.

Stanley was tickled pink to earn goodie money and happily dragged the bags of sticks up and down the street. He did St. John's Street and Back Lane taking in his Granny Skipton's house.

Thom laughed like hell when Esther told him she had paid a penny for sticks which Joe would have gladly given her for nowt, but she liked to encourage the lads, especially young Stanley who was the apple of her eye.

On the first day Wilf finished his deliveries and went to find Stanley only half way down the street.

"Come on, I'll give you a hand to finish." He took hold of the bags and went to alternate houses until all were delivered.

"You'll not knock my money down will you, Wilf? I'll get better as I go on."

Stanley looked up and Wilf had to smile for he was a right chip off the old block. Stanley wanted his full whack.

The suit he had set his heart on was dark grey serge, one that wouldn't show the muck. When the last needed penny had been earned he couldn't wait to get home and count his money. No-one knew a thing about it — wouldn't they just be surprised when they saw him all dressed up?

He rushed his dinner down and ran upstairs to get out his hoard. Carefully he lifted the broken leg, sat on the bed, undid the knot of the piece of rag and began to count. One shilling, two, three — on and on he went until the money ran out. He counted again and again, but could not make it reach the amount he needed — he was ten bob short. He couldn't have gone wrong — he counted the weeks — yes he was ten bob short.

A wave of disappointment — greater than he had ever known — swept over him. And then anger began to burn in his gut, a slow creeping anger that finally flared. With a yell that was almost a scream, he leapt from the bed, jumped the ladder stairs two at a time and flew straight to Harry who was sat at the table.

"You bugger — you rotten bugger — you've pinched my money haven't you?"

Harry was not prepared for the onslaught. He'd never thought Wilf would miss the money from the pile. He hadn't known Wilf was saving for something special. He tried to brazen it out, but it was no use. Wilf knew where the missing money had gone. He flew at Harry, grabbing him by the hair and punching his back.

Polly tried to get between them shouting "Stop it — stop it, you wild bugger — you'll kill him. I took the money — I took it."

Wilf stopped and stood still, clinging on to Harry's hair. Gertie stood back in fear for she had never seen Wilf so angry.

"Look, you're frightening Gert. Leave Harry be, it's me you want to go at."

Wilf looked her straight in the eyes. "Where did you get it from Mam — where did you take the money from?"

Quickly he stopped Harry from answering by clamming his hand over his mouth. His voice was deathly quiet, but his manner more frightening than the wild temper.

Polly felt the back of her neck prickling — this would take some dealing with. With a tired sigh she gave in, seeing that it was no use pretending — Wilf knew she was lying, for whatever Mam might be she would not take anything that was not hers. She raised her hands above her head in a desperate appeal and Wilf removed his hand from Harry's mouth.

"Tell Mam where it was Harry." Still the same quiet voice.

"Under broken leg of dressing table." The voice was sullen.

Wilf again set about his brother with a ferocious anger.

"Leave him be — leave him be, Wilf," Polly pleaded and again tried to part the lads.

"I only took it for you Mam, 'cos I knew you were always short. It wasn't fair him having all that lot and you scrimping," Harry whimpered.

"Listen to him Wilf — he only did it for me."

"I never let you go without Mam, not if I know it. Ask him what he did with the money, Mam — how much did he give you?"

But his anger was spent. He looked down at Harry's red face and then saw the bare patch on his head where the hair had come out by the roots. He walked away to swill his hands and face and saw teeth marks where Harry had bitten. An emptiness filled him — not just for the money, but because even though he was guilty, Mam had still sided with Harry.

Without another word he left the house not knowing where he was going, but finding that his footsteps led to Ada's doorstep. He whistled and she came out.

"Whatever's up with you?" she asked, seeing that he was upset about something.

Quietly he told her what had happened. Now and again she breathed in heavily, sighed and murmured "by hell," but otherwise she let him finish without a word.

"What are you going to do now then?"

He shrugged.

"Where's rest of money?"

He pulled out the rag and showed it to her.

"You could get a cheaper suit — Machin's have them cheaper."

"I wanted that one. Never mind, I'll think on something." He turned to leave now that he had unburdened his heart.

"You coming down later?" she called after him.

"I expect so." What else was there to do?

She stood and watched as he ran up the street. Poor Wilf, fancy having a family like that. She could leave all her money out and not one of her family would touch it.

As he went up the town he peered into Machin's window and looked at the suit. It would take a few more weeks yet to get enough money and not in time for August Bank Holiday.

When he got back his tea was ready and waiting, but not a word was said. He didn't care if they did clam up on him.

He took the remaining money out of his pocket and laid it open on the side table.

"I'm leaving it there, Mam. Every week I shall save a bit more and if you need any, then take it, but if our Harry so much as touches a farthing, I'll slaughter him."

She stared sullenly, knowing as sure as Wilf that not another penny would be touched.

When he stood outside whistling for Ada, she came out carrying something over her arm.

"Mam says to come in and try this on. It belonged to our Jack, but he's grown out of it. Mam says you can have it if you want."

She did not expect the reaction she got.

Wilf took the suit and threw it to the ground, stamping his feet upon it as it lay there.

"I don't want your bloody suit — I want a suit of my own, not a bloody Skipton's cast off." He was shouting at the top of his voice and tears were rolling down his cheeks.

"We were only trying to help — what more do you want?" She tried to calm him down, but Wilf was having none of it, not this time anyway.

"That's your trouble — you're always trying to help, to manage other people."

51

"If you don't like it lad, you know what you can do."

Now Ada's temper was rising and Wilf stopped his tirade and looked at her.

"I'm sorry Ada, but can't you understand — I wanted to do this myself, with my own money."

"As you please," she snapped.

"I'll not come out tonight — I've a bit of a cold coming on."

He was trying to hide the choking tears. She turned and shut the door in his face.

Now he didn't quite know what to do. He didn't want to go home and he didn't want to spend the evening alone either. Feeling bitter and empty, he trudged up the street. What if Ada fell out with him now — what if she didn't want to be friends any more? That would be a fine thing. No more Sewerby, no more lovely teas, no more walks and talks. Then what would he do?

Behind him he heard the quick, quick patter of feet. That was Ada, there was no mistaking her walk. Turning, he smiled through his tears.

"What you want?" he asked, but she knew he didn't mean it.

"Well, I don't know what you were thinking of doing, but I'm going up cliffs. Coming?"

Of course he was!

He re-told his story and she listened carefully.

"You did right, you know, to put money out in open. You should have done that at first and he daren't have touched it. Face up to them Wilf and you'll get on better. Forget it now — come on, let's go around Flamborough Cliffs."

"Do you reckon we should? Them cliffs are dangerous."

"Come on lad — have a go — you'll never get anywhere if you don't try. You never know, we might find a gold watch."

He laughed and they scampered up the street and along the road to the cliffs.

She was a right lass was Ada — but he'd be lost without her.

CHAPTER 6

As her fourteenth birthday drew near, Ada couldn't wait to get started up at the laundry. She felt the past year had been a waste of time. Admittedly she had earned a good bit of brass, but working full time in a real job would bring in wages — then she could start to get somewhere.

Her sisters arranged for her to go up and meet the manageress, Mrs. Price, and see about getting set on.

"We'll take you up if you like," they said, but Ada refused. She wanted to do this herself. If she knew the lasses, she would finish up like them — just filling in time until they got wed. That wasn't for her. She wanted to find out what the prospects were and not just start at any old job.

She walked up to the laundry through the Priory Fields and stood looking at the red brick building. Three great chimneys were puffing out clouds of white smoke — well if the smoke were that white, clothes must be clean, she thought to herself. The windows were small — about three foot square. They were glazed with tiny panes of thick glass and didn't look as if they opened at all. But the great doors were open — all of them — and she could see the steam-filled caverns within. Everybody seemed to be happy, for she could also hear singing — 'Goodbye Dolly Grey' came through — and not bad at all.

She went round to the front which faced Breakneck Lane and knocked on the door marked "office." A young lass, not much older than herself, answered.

"Good morning. Can I help you?" she asked politely.

Ada asked to see Mrs. Price, the manageress. "I have a meeting with her so she'll be expecting me."

The door was opened and she was taken through the front office and then into a back room where she got her first sighting of Mrs. Price, the woman who, to Ada's thinking, held a great power over her future.

"Good morning young lady — you'll be Ada Skipton. Your sisters have told me about you." Muriel Price looked down at her and for a minute the two eyed each other up and down.

Ada saw a tall woman of about forty — old really — her features were thin and she had the smallest-set eyes — almost like two pin pricks in her face. She did not look unkind — firm maybe and a bit strict — but that didn't bother Ada. She was dressed fashionably in a brown skirt edged with a deep frill that fell around her ankles showing just a hint of crocodile skin boots. They had pointed toes and a small heel. Ada took note — by hek, one day she'd have some of them. Her blouse, as one would expect, was beautifully laundered and was made of cream lawn, soft and silky. It had the new leg o' mutton sleeves and frill down the centre of the front, where it fastened with the tiniest pearl buttons she had ever seen. Well, if the manageress were that well-heeled then the business must be good. Muriel Price thought how like her sisters Ada looked. Clean, well scrubbed and shining. But there was something else about her. For one, she was a tiny girl — she looked as if she had stopped growing at twelve — her apron was of spotlessly white handmade linen and her mane of black hair was tied back with a white ribbon.

It was her face that caught her attetntion and her eyes darting everywhere that compelled her to think that this one was different. In spite of the uniform clothes that most of the girls wore, this one had a presence, a sharpness that was almost compelling.

"You've come about a job?" Mrs. Price asked. Now that was a daft question for a start.

"I shouldn't be here if I weren't." Ada was abrupt and Mrs. Price was somewhat taken aback.

"Yes, well, now let's see. Do you want to work with your sister Lizzie in the sorting room or Aggie in the pressing room?"

"I don't want to work with either of them. I want to learn job proper — I want to start at the beginning and go through, like you must have done."

It wasn't often, if ever, she had come across this request. Most of them wanted to start where the money was best.

"Why — why do you want to do that?"

"As I see it missus, there's no future in just standing sorting out mucky clothes or just stood pressing them. After a bit you can do that with your eyes shut. I want more than that."

"Oh, do you now? And what about bottom drawer and looking for a chap to wed as soon as you're old enough. Most girls only think about that."

"Not me. I've a hell of a lot more to do with my time afore I think of getting wed."

This was a new approach, and it reminded Muriel Price of how she had once been.

"Well, before you make up your mind, let's take a look around shall we?"

This again was without precedence for usually she told the girls where they were to work, the wages and that was it. They reported for work the next Monday and started on the treadmill until they either got into trouble or wed.

She opened the door and ushered Ada through into the main washroom. The steam and noise knocked her back for a minute and she couldn't see a thing until, slowly, forms began to emerge and she saw lasses at great tubs pummelling their arms backwards and forwards as they worked.

"Here, we do the heavy stuff like sheets and things," Mrs. Price said.

She looked at Ada's tiny figure and thought, "We'll have to get a box for this one to stand on."

They went through to the starching room, then the linen room and ironing room, where the noise of gas irons seemed to fill the air like the hiss of snakes. Finally they reached the boilers — where the heat from the large iron coppers was overpowering. No wonder they had the doors open.

They walked on, Ada taking it all in. "This is really where it all starts — in the sorting office." They were now in a room behind the front office and Ada saw groups of lasses sorting the baskets of clothes, marking them and putting them into other baskets which stood behind them.

From there they went into an adjoining room where all the ironed clothes were being placed in neat piles according to the numbers marked in special ink.

"Do you ever lose any?" she asked.

"No, not often — this is a very good system." The lass certainly wanted to know about the job.

It was her usual procedure to give the lasses a mild lecture on promptness, good attendance and cleanliness, but she didn't feel this was necessary with Ada and instead did something she had never even contemplated before — she asked her to have a cup of tea and to sit down for a chat.

"Now, how do you feel about the job?" she asked.

"Oh, it'll be right enough. Where shall I start?"

"How about the sorting office and from there to the starching tubs and if you're still keen to learn the job properly we'll have another chat and see how things are."

For the first time, Ada smiled, and Mrs. Price was surprised at the way it lit up her whole face and eyes. This lass was really genuine. Well, that was something new.

"Yes please missus — how much shall I get?" she asked.

"The going rate is four or five shillings a week, but if I'm to take time teaching you the trade properly then I think we must make allowances and treat you differently."

"How do you mean?"

They were talking money now and this was of paramount importance to Ada.

"You will be like an apprentice — I think we should settle for four-and-sixpence."

Ada grunted and thought for a minute. It wasn't as much as she had expected and it would mean keeping on two or three of her little jobs, but if she was to learn the job properly, then it might be worth it.

"But it won't be a proper apprenticeship will it — lasses can't do that. How do I know you'll stick to the bargain?"

"If you do, then I will, Ada, but I don't want to waste my time and then find you going off and getted married or anything. I want you to promise to stay until you become really useful and then work on for a year or two."

"Aye, I'll do that if you keep to your side. How long do you reckon it'll take then?"

"Well, if you're as keen as you say, about a couple of years at least."

"Oh, that's fine. I thought you were going to keep me say five or six years. I'll only be sixteen then and nowt like thinking of getting wed. Will my wages rise then?"

"I'll give you a rise as you become good at a particular job. How's that?"

"That's fine by me, missus." The bargain was struck — Ada's future was planned.

"What will your parents have to say about it all — do they know what you want to do?"

"Oh, they'll be fine, don't you worry. I can give Mam some money and do extra for my pocket — they'll be alright."

It was arranged for her to start the following Monday at seven sharp.

"You'll go through every department — it won't be easy," Mrs. Price warned, but Ada answered with another smile and just bid her good day.

She walked home slowly and half way down decided to call in at her Uncle Joe's yard.

He was carving out the stand for a towel rail and she stood watching as his hands worked so deftly.

"That's a nice bit of work," she said and he laughed at her.

"Do you want one for when you get wed?" he teased.

"Not yet, Uncle Joe — not for a while yet." She told him about her job at the laundry and he listened to her enthusiasm.

It was a change to hear a lass talk like that, and a bit strange and all.

"Is Wilf getting an apprenticeship then — he'll be fourteen soon," she asked.

He might have known there would be something behind the visit. "Well, he's shaping up nicely is the lad, but that's between me and him, Ada." Joe remembered how Wilf had asked to talk in private when he first came for a job.

Ada asked no more for she could see Uncle Joe wasn't going to discuss Wilf's business. She wasn't bothered anyway. She had got her job and seeing Wilf got on proper would come later.

Esther was a bit uneasy when she heard about the conditions of Ada's starting. It wasn't the money, but the way Ada seemed to be so forward — it wasn't natural in a lass.

"Why do you want it like that, lass — why not just take a job like others and look for a nice lad?"

"'Cos I don't want to Mam. It must be a miserable lot to work your insides out and then there be nowt at the end of it. I want summat different to that."

"Well, I can't see that there is owt else myself — but still you have a go if you want to."

Thom, on the other hand, was pleased one of his lasses was trying to get on and Esther couldn't say much about her not being natural for she could knit, sew and crochet as good as, if not better than, the others. And she could cook and all and tackle any job around the house. No — Ada was the bright one and she had something about her.

When she told Wilf, he was glad for her for she seemed to be getting what she wanted.

"You want to think on about getting your apprenticeship next. You'll soon be old enough. Don't let it pass by, Wilf," she warned him.

But he hadn't forgotten, and was already planning to have a word with Mr. Raines about it.

"Does you Mam know yet — have you said owt?" she asked him.

"Aye, I told her long ago. But she didn't say much only that I would get too big for my boots."

"Is that all?" She couldn't believe Polly would stop at that.

"Oh, aye, and that you would be the death of me one day." He laughed as he spoke and she cuffed his lug hole.

Monday morning saw her up bright and early with her snap wrapped up in a linen cloth and on her way to start her first day's work. She walked quickly and her sisters shouted her to go steady.

"You'll not be so keen next week," they called, secretly a bit peeved that she was going to be a special case at work.

But she wasn't made out all that special for, if anything, Mrs. Price made her work harder than any of the others.

The sorting room was a bit dark and they had to have the gas lights on all the time. She liked the system of numbering and lettering the clothes and sorting them out.

After the first few tentative weeks she became popular with the other girls. Her devilry made them laugh especially when, if she got a bit bored, she would regale them with long recitations. They loved it and Ada would play up to her audience with exaggerated voices and actions.

"By hell, you've brightened place up a bit," Lily Hartley told her after one hilarious performance of 'Me Father's duck eggs.'

She and Lily had got rather friendly and would walk to and from work together and sit on the baskets to eat their snap. Ada often gave her some of her Mam's pound cake and Lily would eat it, relishing every last crumb.

"Your Mam must be a good 'un to do like this," she said.

"Well, you've got to try your best Lily. It's no good giving up you know. You never know what's round the next corner. There might be a gold watch."

"Oh you are a daft bugger, Ada," Lily laughed and then looked up as Billy Acton, one of the delivery men, came through the door.

He kept casting his eye in Ada's direction, but she never seemed to notice — she never gave a thought to any lad except Wilf and with him it was still only a deep friendship.

"Why are you always talking to yourself, Ada. It's one of the first signs of madness they say," Billy teased her one day after he had heard her muttering to herself.

"'Cos it's best way, lad — you get right answers then," came the cheeky answer.

He grabbed her by the waist and tried to pull her towards him.

"Just you mind it, Billy Acton. I'm not one of them lases that'll lay down for you in blanket room. Get off me, you're mucking my pinny up." She gave him one of her sharp kicks that sent him sprawling.

"Leave her alone, Billy — she's only a bairn, and anyroad she's already spoken for. She's courting Tanner," Lily shouted across to them.

But she could see the approach did not bother Ada — although she might be little, she could handle his sort. Coming from such a big family had taught her to stick up for herself.

What did startle Ada was Lily's reference to her "being spoken for." She wasn't spoken for — not by Wilf — not by anybody. Ada belonged to herself.

At break Lily took her usual place beside Ada. "Watch out for that one Ada, he can be trouble and he does seem a bit keen on you." She referred to the Billy incident.

"Don't bother yourself about that Lil. I'll soon settle his skylarking, even if I have to chuck a bucket of cold water over him."

"It's all very well Ada, talking like that, but if he keeps hanging around you could have trouble with Molly Drayton 'cos she's mad keen on him and she's a devil if you cross her."

"I'm not bothered about that either. I'm more bothered about you saying I was spoken for — I'm not you know."

"Well, why do you keep company with Wilf Tanner so much then?" Lily asked.

"We started school together — we've been mates for years."

"Mates — what do you mean mates? Aren't you courting then?"

"Don't talk so daft — course we're not courting."

Lily looked puzzled. "Don't you ever gum suck then?"

"What?"

Ada's startled look showed that she had no idea what Lily was on about. "Kiss and cuddle a bit like."

"No, we bloody well don't. We're mates me and Wilf — good mates."

Really, they did go on. Just because she and Wilf had been mates for such a long time — courting indeed — she'd more to do than go courting.

Her work at the laundry progressed and, as promised, she was put through every department. She liked the way Mrs. Price worked and ran the place. The girls were all made to wear large white pinnies and frilled caps to cover their hair. Every week their heads were inspected for lice or nits, which they could have brought from home or caught from some of the washing. Some of the boarding house stuff was alive and it was for their own sakes that she made the girls go through such inspections.

She was also very wary of consumption which could be caught from infected laundry from the isolation hospital. If a girl was heard coughing a lot or losing weight quickly she made sure no time was lost before sending her to the doctor. Mrs. Price kept a tight ship, but it paid off.

The worst thing the lasses had to deal with was their red raw hands and arms which they got from washing, elbow deep, in hot suds of soda and rough washing powder. They always said you could tell a laundry lass anywhere by the redness of her hands and arms. Ada learnt from Mrs. Price to rub glycerine on hers and it gave a lot of relief and took away the harsh redness.

The first day she was put on the tub she went home with her feet sodden wet through. In spite of huge rubber aprons wrapped around them there was no way they could stop the water splashing over the sides, down the apron and onto their feet.

She often thought it was the biggest wonder there wasn't more sickness amongst the girls, for most of them coughed and barked like broken-winded horses through the fumes of ammonia that was used for badly soiled clothes.

Consumption was her greatest fear, ever since she had seen young Jenny Constable die at an early age of fifteen. In spite of being told not to, Ada had gone to see her as she lay in the throes of death.

They had not been all that friendly, but Ada had liked Jenny for her spirit and sparkle. She had always tried to keep herself neat and tidy, but coming from a big family who were poor, she didn't have much chance. Ada gave thanks to her parents — they could have easily been like Jenny's.

Jenny's home was awful, mucky, smelly and without hardly a stick of furniture. She lived near Wilf and when Ada had been asked in she almost passed out with the sickly sweet stench that seemed to hover all around.

She followed Mrs. Constable up the ladder that served as a staircase and saw Jenny laid in what looked like a bundle of rags. The window was so small and mucky that hardly any light filtered in. But she swallowed hard and went to the bedside.

"Now then Jen, how are you?" she whispered.

"No so dusty when I'm well brushed." Her voice was weak, but there was still the hint of the old spirit. They smiled at one another.

"I've pinched some of old Beacon's apples on way down. I thought you might like one."

"You little bugger — but it does look grand. Just pop it on bed and I'll have it after." She lifted herself up on one elbow, but the effort was too much and she slumped down again.

Ada had to choke back the tears. "I'll not stop long love. I can see you're tired, but I'll come again love — promise."

Jenny saw the hushed tears. "Come on Ada — it hasn't been all bad you know. I've had a lot of laughs — you've made me laugh at lot. You can't take that away you know."

"You just get yourself better, my lass, and then we can have some more." It was daft to talk like that for they both knew there would be no more times.

"Get along with you. You'll be getting wed to young Wilf afore long."

"Tell you what Jen — you can be bridesmaid. How about that then?" And they laughed together for the last time, for within the week, Jenny was dead.

Ada took her death hard — something that neither her Mam and Dad nor Wilf could understand.

"You weren't all that friendly were you?" Wilf asked and Ada shook her head.

"Not really — but I did promise she could be my bridesmaid. That didn't half make her laugh."

"Oh aye — you're thinking of getting wed then are you?" He looked puzzled.

"Well. . . ." She couldn't think what to say now.

"Who to?" he asked frowning. She might be getting sweet on somebody and that wouldn't do — he would miss Ada.

"Any bugger that'll ask me." She laughed now, thankful that Wilf had not made more of it and flustered her.

Thom saw that she was really upset about Jenny.

"What's bothering you then?" he asked her.

"I don't see the point of it Dad. What did Jenny ever have — nowt — so why was she born?"

"Eh, that's something I can't answer. The only thing is that it's a lesson to the likes of us to be thankful and to try and see that things are better for Jenny's sort."

"They should be better Dad, but they haven't all got folk like you and

60

our Mam. I reckon you're miracles — both of you." She hugged him and then he had to choke back the tears. That was his Ada, full of cheek and sharpness, but with a heart of gold. Oh, if only she had been a lad, she could have gone on the council and, who knows, maybe parliament?

"She's a good lass is our Ada," Thom told Esther of the little incident.

"Oh aye — she's got a heart right enough if you dig deep enough to find it — but she's as hard as nails if she's a mind to be."

Esther bothered about Ada and her ambitions. She was now nearly seventeen and doing well at work and bringing in more than the other lasses put together. Wilf went into his apprenticeship and they still spent all their spare time together, but nowt was ever said about courting or anything.

The lasses at work teased Ada a lot about Wilf.

"Is he a bit slow on the uptake then your Wilf?" Lily would ask.

"How do you mean?" God — they were always on about her and Wilf.

"Well, slow in coming forward like."

"Lily I don't know what the hell you're on about. Me and Wilf are good mates."

"Don't you get up to nowt then when you go on those walks and things?"

"No, we bloody well don't. Anyway, what is there to get up to?"

Lily couldn't believe it — it was just not possible that Ada was so green.

"Well, don't you ever listen to the other lasses talking about what they get up to with their lads?"

"You know damn well that they don't talk like that to me, not in the position I am." She was so good at her job that Mrs. Price considered her to be second in command.

"You're my right hand now, Ada. You've done well and before long you could take over if ever I'm away or anything."

Ada preened at the praise, but felt it was well-deserved for she had worked hard.

Wilf, too, was in pretty much the same position, for although the lads at work talked amongst themselves they didn't say much to Wilf — him going out with the boss's niece like.

But, in spite of these drawbacks, they were both liked and popular with their work mates. It never bothered Ada that Wilf didn't "get up to owt" so why should it bother other folk?

Wilf took a great deal of teasing from Harry, who would jibe and sneer as he got ready to call for Ada. She still had never visited their home and he had no intention of asking her to do so. Polly would watch as he washed and put on his best clothes.

"You getting dandied up for her, then? Before much longer you'll be going off and marrying her — just when you are out of your time and you could be some good to me." It was more of a question that a statement.

He didn't rise to it for although he thought the world of Ada and could not imagine how he would manage without her he wasn't going to rush off and do owt daft.

Even George and Isabella started to ask questions.

"Will you be getting engaged soon or are you going to wait until Wilf's twenty-one and out of his time?" Isabella asked her when George and Wilf were out of the way.

"Not as I know on. Why do you keep on about it?" Ada snapped a bit and began to feel niggled. Was there something missing between her and Wilf after all?

She looked down at her clothes, a navy tailored suit and white blouse, grey crocodile skin shoes — like those she had promised herself when she had first seen Mrs. Price's. The outfit was complemented with a navy straw boater hat. Why, she was as well-dressed as any lady, and Wilf was almost as smart. They went off on day trips to Hull and Scarborough and were planning a visit to London to see the Crystal Palace. They were alright as they were.

Lord Burlingham had now retired and although George could not take the title until his father died, he did run the estate and all its business. He had been bought a commission in the county's regiment and served in the Boer War — not gone overseas mind you, but in an administration post in London holding the rank of Major, a rank he was referred to when he returned home.

In 1907 he was called to a very important meeting in London and asked by the authorities to form a battalion of the Territorial Association. This idea was born by Lord Haldane, who wanted an efficient army reserve to call upon should they be needed. These men would come from all walks of life, they would train as soldiers at night and weekends and for a bounty of one pound attest their willingness to serve overseas in case of war. They would replace the old Militia Reserve, the Yeomanry and the Volunteers.

It was not well received at first, but George could see the sense in having a backing of a trained stand-by army instead of three differing ones who did not use the same arms or have the same training.

The Territorial Association would be as one if called upon to serve their country. He returned home full of enthusiasm and began the task of forming the Bridlington battalion, which would be known as the Fifth Battalion.

At first the call was not answered by many and he tried to think of a way to get more recruits.

"How about you joining, Wilf?" he asked, but Wilf shook his head. A soldier — no, that wasn't for him.

"I'm not cut out for that life, George," he said.

Over tea, George mentioned that he had been trying to get Wilf to recruit and that he had refused.

"You mean be one of them Saturday night soldiers?" Ada laughed.

"You might well laugh young lady, but you may be glad of them one day," George reproved.

"What do they do there?" she asked and listened patiently as George told her of their duties.

"You mean they only have to serve if there's a war, like?"

"Yes, but they have to go away to training camps and learn to keep up with all the modern techniques."

"How much do they get?"

"Five pounds a year and of course all expenses and pay when they are at camp — as a regular soldier does."

She looked at Wilf. Five pounds a year. Well, that would help and if he would be associating with George and his like it might help him to get on a bit more — give him better ideas.

She talked to him on the way home and, for once, slipped her arm through his.

"It might do you good Wilf. It would get you out and about and a bit more brass. You might enjoy it."

"What about having to serve if needed?" he asked.

"Oh nobody will tackle us lad — you'll not have to do that."

"It would mean not always being around at weekends though. What about that?"

"What about it?"

"Wouldn't you miss me?" He stopped walking and turned to look at her. She wasn't half a nice looking lass — not pretty but nice. Her hair was done up in plaited wheels and her hat was perched prettily on top. She dressed well and he was always proud to be seen with here.

Still he wasn't so bad himself if the lasses who shouted after him were owt to go by. His hair was golden and he wore it with a swept quiff at the front. He had a good suit and his shirt was always white, for Ada took it up to the laundry to be washed every week.

They were both a bit short — him five foot four and her five foot two — but they were a nice looking pair for all that. And by hell they had come a long way since their school days. Nearly out of his time now, well dressed and earning a bob or two. They went out a lot and enjoyed each other's company and he knew he owed most of it to Ada. Without her he might be like Harry, going from one job to another and without a penny to his name.

Ada blushed as he looked at her — something she very rarely did, being much too self-assured. It took a lot to ruffle Ada.

63

"Well, yes, I suppose I would." she admitted uncertainly.

He enjoyed the moment of seeing that he had disturbed her, for usually it was the other way round. He laughed and decided to try a bit of devilment.

"Tell you what, I'll strike a bargain."

"What's that then?" she asked, now even more uncertain than ever, for Wilf had a gleam in his eyes that she had not seen before.

"Give me a kiss and I'll join."

And before she knew what was happening he had put his arms around her and was holding her close. She found herself trembling and didn't know what to do or say. She liked the feel of him close to her — his soft face next to hers. So this is what being forward meant.

He moved and looked down at her.

"You aren't half a short arse," he whispered and bending his head kissed her softly on the lips.

"But just the right size for you, eh?" she smiled and whispered back.

"Just right." He kissed her again and this time she leaned against his body and responded.

It lasted only a short time and they giggled and laughed like a pair of school bairns as they drew apart.

Wilf pretended to jump in the air.

"I'll join owt for that," he laughed, and she took his arm and held it close as they walked home.

Instead of his leaving her at the corner of his row he continued walking.

"You don't reckon to come down this far," she said.

"I know, but I don't want anybody else getting a chance, and, besides, I want another kiss." She tingled at the words.

They stopped in the doorway of Limon's shop and Wilf drew her close again and kissed her. Ada drew away — she wanted to get something sorted out — a loose end like.

"Wilf," she asked nervously.

"Yes, love." He had never called her that before.

"Are we courting?"

He thought about it. "Yes, I reckon so. If that's what this is all about then I suppose we are."

She knew now what she wanted to know and, laughing, she looked up at him.

"And not before time either," she said and pulled the quiff of his hair.

CHAPTER 7

Very little enthusiasm was shown for the forming of a Territorial Association and the Honourable George Burlingham met with a lot of unexpected opposition. As an officer who had seen service with the colours — and the son of noted local gentry — he had been the obvious choice for the task.

The War Minister, Lord Haldane, had warned him that it would be difficult to convince civic dignitaries and authorities that it was a much-needed commodity.

"None of the army top brass are supporting me and I am getting some opposition from the government. I feel so strongly that the regular army need the back-up of trained units instead of the uncoordinated ones we have now of Militia, Volunteers and Yeomanry, but I fear your task will meet with a lot of ridicule and obstacles," he told George.

And one of his biggest obstacles was old Thom Skipton.

"What the hell do we want an army association for? It will only breed war." Thom spoke fiercely for he was a peace-loving man who felt that if any wars needed to be fought it should be the working class against the bloody-minded bureaucrats. But he was not a member of the council and would have no say in the matter.

His power in the Liberal party would have been useful and George needed their support as much as any. Most of the young voted Liberal and he was looking for the main body of his recruits from that sector.

"Wilf Tanner has agreed to join and I've enlisted most of the men from the estate — it will be good experience for them. Training will develop their characters — make men of them — now you can't say that isn't a good thing can you, Father?" George asked.

"Did he join of his own free will or did our Ada shove him into it 'cos of the extra brass and the opportunity to, so call, better hiss'en?" Thom knew how his daughter's mind worked.

"But think of the good it will do — it will take a lot of young lads off the street and out of the pubs, smarten them up and make them begin to think for themselves."

Thom was not convinced.

"We shall only call upon them to serve if we are attacked by a foreign force — they will act as a back-up in an emergency," George went on, trying to impress Thom and, as he spoke, looked across at Ada for moral support.

"I should have thought you would have been for it Dad. You're always on about giving working classes a chance. Well now they've got one — a chance to improve their thinking. And, you never know, you might find a

65

few budding politicians or councillors if you rattle their brains a bit." She smiled across at Thom, who raised his eyebrows.

"That what you want for Wilf then?" he asked.

"I want owt that will help him to get on. The extra brass will be a help, but not as much as the chance to mix with folk from other walks of life."

No matter what they said, no matter how they argued, Thom would not give his support and there was an angry scene when his two elder lads, Thom and Jack, decided to join. They, too, were more concerned with extra brass than any thought of patriotism.

"I shall join as soon as I'm old enough, Grandad," young Stanley informed Thom, who replied, "Not if I have owt to do with it."

Support and money from organisations and civic amenities was, to Thom, like pouring water down a drain. Any spare money should be spent on bettering living conditions.

"It'll never come to owt — you mark my words," he warned.

But he was wrong, for in spite of the jibes and taunts the Territorial Association was finally formed.

"Saturday Night Soldiers" became ridiculed by all and sundry. Politicians, religious bodies and the ordinary bloke down the street who did not join, laughed and said it would soon fade out.

"Haldane's Horse, Feather Bed Heroes" — they were called everything and Ada got into heated arguments both at work and at home about the rights and wrongs of it all.

"If you hadn't made Wilf join then our lads wouldn't have gone either. Who the hell's going to come over here and tackle us? They can't get over watter for one thing and I can't see bloody Zulus or any others fighting on pier. It's all daft and they'd be a sight better pushing in bill to get pensions for the old folk," Thom shouted and appeared to blame Ada for the whole of the Bridlington force of territorials being formed.

At first, the jibes and mockery bothered Wilf, in particular when groups of people gathered outside the Drill Hall to watch them being put through elementary paces.

George had hoped to pick and choose his men, but when he felt the general opinion he was glad to take what came. But, gradually they came — labourers, office workers, tradesman and those out of work. Perhaps not for the right reasons, but they came.

He grew to learn the weight of wisdom behind the saying 'Soldiers are born not made.' His task was to refute that saying — to make his men into soldiers. He had hoped that the volunteers from the former Militia and Volunteers would take on the job of teaching the raw recruits drill and the basics of army life. He was wrong for they argued about the way they were trained and the commands were so varied that they only succeeded in bewildering the men.

And then he hit upon an idea. He applied for a regular soldier to be posted to his battalion, which had become the Fifth Yorks. The Association would raise his pay and he would set out a training programme and take command as in the regular army. Some humming and hesitation took place, but finally the idea was accepted and later taken up by other battalions.

Sergeant Major Bradley of the Army Service Corps was detailed for Bridlington — an old sweat with over nine years service.

He was billeted on Pansy and Ada Hebblewhite, who had no one eligible for the force. George had taken care to make sure of this so as to avoid any involvement and trouble.

Tutt Bradley — or, to give him his full name, Harold Joseph Bradley — had seen active service with the colours and had discharged his duties well. He had an excellent record.

He was used to handling raw recruits, but these men were different for after an hour or two's training they went back home and forgot all about the army and most of what they had been taught.

The age range was wide and varied from eighteen to thirty-five. Some were set in their ways and most looked upon the training sessions as a hobby. Very few were ardent patriots.

It became his prime task, amongst others, to drill into them a sense of duty, obedience and swift reaction to orders. It was hard going, but he made it his business to mix with the men during time off and would go into the pubs, meet them on street corners and chat, even call at their homes on some pretext. Anything to get to know them.

His nickname came about because of his habit of saying, when things went wrong, "Tutt, tutt, my lad, that's not the way now is it? Let's try again shall we and this time do it the way I say — right?"

If this didn't work he would use barrack square language and blast the eardrums of the men until he got the results he wanted.

He stood over six feet tall and his uniform gave him a majestic presence. The swing of his hips, as he strutted up and down the lines, became a joke with the men, who likened him to a rowing boat in a gale. They soon stopped laughing when he brought up his stick and twanged it across a backside — more than one had felt its sting.

But underneath his military bearing, Tutt Bradley was a decent bloke and because of this had been specially selected for the training of what he secretly termed 'toy soldiers'.

"You've got two left feet, Tanner — put them down one in front of the other, lad," Tutt would bawl out at the top of his voice, much to the amusement of a watching crowd.

This ever-present audience caused bother and he could see that unless he got rid of them things were not going to work out. Things really came to

67

a head when Frank Jordan's missus came down one night and hauled him out of the lines.

"I want you at home, my lad, to give me a hand. Get yoursen up here or I'll give you a clout," she cried out and Frank had sheepishly left the lines and followed her.

The following drill night he cordoned off the road and the audience soon tired of watching from a distance and dispersed. At last he had got them in his hands and no interruptions.

The issued rifles and equipment were those discarded after the South African war. They needed a lot of bulling and sweat before they came up to the gleaming standard Tutt looked for, but with perseverance and brute force they did and the men too shaped up.

George regularly visited to see how things were going and he noted that progress was being made. Slowly, but surely. And once they got the bit between their teeth, the men began to want to do more — to train more extensively and show off what they had learnt. Weekend camps were introduced and, looking at his men, Tutt hoped that whoever was organising them would get on with it before his battalion lost interest.

One of the first breaks came when the town council invited the battalion to parade with the fishermen and other organisations for the annual February parade to commemorate the Great Gale.

Uniforms were pressed and tucked and made to fit — rifles were cleaned until they shone like the sun — boots were rigidly laced and polished until you could see your face in them and the men marched and counter-marched until they reacted like clockwork.

The invitation was a back-handed compliment and a bit of an after-thought, but to Tutt and George it was a chance to gain credibility.

The final drill rehearsal was held in full uniform and George attended to march at the head of his men. Having served with the colours he was very experienced and when the men saw him at the head of the column in full dress uniform the first feeling of pride swept through them. As he lifted his sword and held it in a straight line with his nose, the men squared their shoulders and marched smartly to command.

"Well done, Sergeant Major, and congratulations to you all. This turn-out will make them eat their words. You've done a good job," he praised Tutt, but in true army fashion, would not allow the praise to go to the men's heads.

"They're not perfect yet sir, not by a long chalk, but I reckon we'll give them something to look at on Sunday." The praise was enough to encourage the men.

Promptly at one o'clock on Sunday afternoon the men assembled for inspection and Tutt was gratified to see how smart they looked. It was an almost professional turn-out.

He lined them up and then marched down to the parade assembly point near the harbour. As they turned the bend in Quay Road the watching crowd stared, the thought of laughter frozen upon their lips. Each man marched in perfect step, rifle held straight as a ram-rod sloped on his left shoulder. Eyes were kept strictly to the front as they left-wheeled and finally came to a halt at the rear of the parade. The town band was to lead and the Territorials were given the rear position behind the Salvation Army band.

"We'll be marching to 'Abide With Me'," Sid Wilson laughed.

"Quiet in the ranks — you'll march to whatever tune they play — and in time my lad," Tutt shouted.

He saw the leading band raise their instruments, and gave the order in his best barrack square tones: "Aaaaaatention! Riiiiiiiight turn! Quiiiiiick march."

And to his delight the good old Sally Army struck up with 'My Gel's a Yorkshire Gel', in strict marching time.

The men felt their feet tingle and their bodies react to the swing of the tune. They marched, straight and true, heads held high, rifles steady and in complete precision.

George headed the men, together with three more county officers bearing drawn swords and in full military dress. The whole scene presented an imposing spectacle.

Being rather on the short side, Wilf was placed in the middle of the third rank and though he was sure nobody would see him he nevertheless marched proudly. It felt good to be swinging along in time to the beat of the music and the jibes turned to cheers as the column came into view.

As they reached the corner of Ireland's Row, he saw his Mam standing on the kerb with Gert at her side. For a moment great shyness overcame him and he felt himself shrink, but Tutt's training came through and he marched along proudly. Gert shouted and waved, but Polly showed nothing except — except that Wilf could have sworn he saw the hint of a smile across her face.

Although he had been born and bred in the town, Wilf had never been inside the Priory Church let alone attend a service and apart from the rousing singing he thought it boring. The men had trouble placing their rifles as they entered and they found the seats uncomfortable and the sermon long and uninteresting. The national anthem roused them a bit and they sang loud and strong, standing stiffly to attention.

It was only a short march to the Old Town Market Place where the parade was dismissed, but Tutt kept his men standing at ease until the crowds had gone.

"Well, we showed 'em, didn't we lads? They laughed on the other sides of their faces this afternoon. Just you wait until we've had a spell at camp

— then you'll be real soldiers." He smilingly dismissed them.

Wilf walked down the street, followed closely by Stanley.

"I'm going to join and all Wilf, when I'm eighteen — that's only three years off."

Wilf laughed and ruffled his hair. He heard Ada's voice calling out to him and stopped and waited until she caught up.

"By hek, you were grand. What did I tell you, aye? You keep on Wilf and you'll soon get somewhere, you mark my words." She hugged his arm close to her side and walked proudly up the street.

"You seem taller somehow." He braced his shoulders at her words.

They decided to go on up to Isabella's and perhaps have tea. Ada wanted to show Wilf off — weekend soldier indeed — there'd be none of that now.

Isabella greeted them warmly, but George, still in his full uniform, was somewhat distant and embarrassed.

"Wilf, you should not have come up here in uniform and certainly not carrying your rifle, not with my being your superior officer," he said.

Wilf blushed and Ada frowned.

"What are you on about?" she asked, paying no heed to his rank. He was their Isabella's husband, uniform or no uniform.

"It's just not done Ada. It doesn't matter one jot when we are out of uniform, but with Wilf only being in the ranks we cannot possibly mix socially whilst dressed like this."

"Well, I'll be buggered."

Ada stood and stared at him and Isabella looked flustered and uneasy. Wilf felt just very foolish — there was a lot more to this lark than he'd thought.

"Come on then Ada — we'd best get home." He made to take her arm.

"And that's another thing — you are not supposed to walk through the streets with Ada on your arm and never carrying a rifle — you should have taken that home first," George went on.

"You're coming a bit aren't you George? Who sets all these daft rules anyroad?" She was getting in a paddy now.

"It's all in regulations, as Wilf will find out. When in uniform there is a dividing line between us and there is nothing I can do about it or even want to. These are the rules," George spoke firmly.

"Come on love — let's be off. I don't want any bother." Wilf tried to usher her out for he knew that George was right.

"All right then — we'll not stay where we're not wanted, lad." They made to leave.

"Haven't you forgotten something, Private Tanner?" George asked curtly.

Wilf had, but he quickly remembered and brought his right hand up in a smart salute almost knocking Ada's hat off her head.

"Sir," he said and turning smartly left with Ada trailing behind him.

"Whatever made you do that?" she asked, referring to the salute.

"Because it's the right thing to do. He's right you know in what he said."

She started to argue but he told her it was no use going on for they couldn't change the system.

"Well, I don't reckon it's right anyroad." She pursed her lips. "I shall tell our Isabella when I get her on her own. It's not right you being who you are with Geroge."

"And who am I, like?" he asked.

"Well . . . you're my young man and he's my brother-in-law and I thought we were all friends," she finally blurted out.

"Exactly — but we are friends off duty only. Otherwise to him I'm just another soldier."

"You don't reckon it'll make any difference to us going up there do you?" Now she was thinking perhaps this Territorial business hadn't been such a good idea after all. If things changed she would miss the visits and the one-up of being on such terms with gentry.

"Oh, you know old George, any other time he'll be the same friendly bloke as always. It's not easy for him either you know."

Maybe Wilf was right, she thought. Still, they'd have to see.

"Could you be an officer?" she asked after a long silence.

"Not much chance of that. The likes of me don't get to be officers and gentlemen." He laughed at the thought.

"Why not — you might if you tried."

"I'll get a gold watch first — I'll bet you on that."

She sighed heavily. "I just hope all this lot won't make any more difference to us, that's all."

But a difference, a very great difference, was slowly creeping into their lives. One thing was the drill attendances which took up two nights a week and sometimes Sunday mornings. With Wilf working overtime to see that Joe didn't suffer from this new interest, little time was left to meet Ada.

Preparations were also underway for the first camp, which was to be at Dane's Dyke at Whit weekend. They had all been issued with field kit — mess tins, mugs and cutlery — and it had to be cleaned along with the other kit. It took time for the Fifth wanted to show that they could match up to the other battalions at the camp.

"What will you do with yourself all weekend?" he asked Ada.

"I reckon I shall work. It's always busy at Whit and the extra cash will come in handy. I shan't have owt else to do."

"You must have a tidy bit put together now Ada. What are you reckoning on doing with it all?''

It was the first time he had mentioned such a thing. Ada's money was a very private matter and never discussed with anyone — not even Wilf. She set great store by money and he often wondered what her final ambitions were.

"I've got my ideas lad, don't you bother yourself. I've got it all planned out in my mind."

"Who for Ada — you — me — or both of us?" It was a blunt question and stumped her for a minute. She thought hard before answering.

"I don't like talking about plans — I reckon if you set too much store on things they never happen, something goes wrong. But if you really want to know I rather fancy going into business — something that brings in profits for us."

"Us?" The question hung between them.

"Yes, Wilf — us — if things go right — why not?"

"Aye, lass — why not?" He laughed now, feeling glad that he had a place in Ada's future which he had no doubt would be a good one, planned to the last detail and safe and secure. He warmed to the idea.

"How do you fancy a laundry and cabinet makers business then? They don't go together, but it would be something different?" He was teasing now.

"I don't know — you could make dolly pegs and tubs and I could do laundry. It might be a good team."

"And shall we both have gold watches to tell when workers clock on and off?"

"Might — but we'll have a ruddy great clock set up in the wall then everybody'll see it." She was giggling like a schoolgirl and as they parted Wilf took hold of her arm.

"Ada — don't make owt of that business with George — he was doing right and I don't want to look a fool."

She promised to keep her peace.

That Friday the battalion was due to leave for camp and Joe Raines was none too pleased at having to give Wilf the Saturday morning off.

"I hope this lark isn't going to happen too often Wilf — I can't spare you that much."

It was a compliment to Wilf for they had come to rely on him his good workmanship. He obviously loved making wood into beautiful pieces of furniture and enjoyed his work. Joe never regretted taking him on and called him one of his finest assets.

Ada and Wilf's relationship puzzled him a bit and he would try to draw the lad out by asking him if he would soon be starting make stuff for their bottom drawer.

"You can have what wood you want lad — you know that," he would say, but Wilf would only smile and keep his silence. But they seemed happy enough together and so Joe let it rest.

Leaving home for the first time, be it only for three days, was a new experience for most of the Fifth. Some had never been on a train and it was a boisterous, almost holiday-spirited crowd that gathered at the station. Tutt sensed the tense excitement and laughed — they'd soon find out what a real bit of soldiering was like.

The journey took almost an hour and the wooden carriages became hot and stuffy as they travelled. One stop was made for the men to relieve themselves, which they did thankfully.

The train arrived and they formed up and marched to the camp. As they approached, Wilf saw the imposing row upon row of white tents set against the green grass of the cliff top. The contrast was stark and the wigwam shape of the tents made him think of blobs of ice-cream.

"There's home sweet home for the next three days, lads," Tutt told them and Wilf thanked God that at least the weather was bright and dry. He'd never been in a tent before — never seen one for that matter and he didn't fancy freezing under their flimsy covering.

The tents were rigged up around a large square which was to serve as the parade ground. They marched towards this and mustered in line with other battalions who looked just as hot and sweaty as they did.

"We'll have a wet and a bite first. Take out your dixies and get in line at the mess tent over there." They looked towards where Tutt pointed and sighed.

"Bloody hell, there's thousands before us, it'll be night afore we get owt," Sid groaned.

But, surprisingly, they did not have to wait too long and gratefully accepted the mug of strong black tea and a dixie full of stew with a hunk of bread dolloped in the middle. The service was quick, but not very efficient, and slops of tea and splodges of gravy spilt on uniforms and boots.

"Look out — I cleaned them this morning," Wilf grumbled.

"And you'll clean the buggers again tonight — move on up the line." He moved sharply as he was threatened with a ladle of stew.

Dumping their kits on the ground they sank down and ate and drank. The meal tasted wonderful and Wilf mopped up the last morsel with his bread. Tutt came up to show them their tents.

"Take it alphabetically — A company in the first, B in the second and so on. I'll be round to you all in a few minutes when I've got the orders."

They went to the tents and looked at the straw palliasses which were to serve as beds. Dumping down their kit they lay down and closed their eyes.

"I'm going to have a sleep — I feel whacked." Sid took the bed next to Wilf and was just about to rest when Tutt's voice rang through the air.

"Rise up there — I've got our orders. Get over to the stores and pick up

73

shovels and picks — we're in the field." The reverie was over.

"What's these for, Sergeant Major?" Sid always asked the questions. Tutt told them they were at war and they were going to learn the art of digging trenches — at the double.

"Where are your kits then?" he asked sarcastically as they faced him with a various assortment of picks and shovels.

"Back in the tent."

"You'll need them with you — we are to live in trenches for the next two days — get a move on and fetch them."

Again they ran and picked up the packs. As if on parade Tutt marched them towards a large field which was staked out in oblong patches.

"Get down to it and dig your trenches — six foot deep at least so as guns can't get you sighted."

They dropped the kits and set to work. After a few minutes of trying to force the tools into the hard ground they found to their dismay it was part of the cliff clay and chalk. Off came the hats, jackets and shirts. They dug and grumbled, sweat rolling down their bodies, making very little impression upon the ground.

"Come on lads — get a move on — dig, dig, dig," Tutt bawled.

They dug and the ground gave way to their efforts. As night fell they finished and Wilf looked down into the wide chasm of earth that was his bed for the night.

"Rations will be round in a minute — get your groundsheets out and make ready for the night."

"Sergeant Major, we haven't any groundsheets. Shall I fetch some?" Wilf asked in all innocence.

"No you won't — if you are daft enough not to have drawn full kit then you can sleep as you are."

Wilf and Sid looked at one another and sighed, thinking of the hard earth — the stones and lumps of heavy clay. And when the rations arrived they sighed even harder — another dixie of stew and mug of strong back tea.

Just as he was about to close his eyes, Wilf heard an eerie sound piercing the air. It was a trumpet blowing a melancholy tuneless sound over the field. Heaving himself up he looked over the side of the trench to see, standing underneath a lowering Union Jack, a young soldier blowing a bugle. As the flag lowered Tutt stood to attention and saluted.

"What was that all about, Sergeant Major?" he asked.

Tutt explained the procedure of lights out. Wilf curled up and slept without waking until, once more, the sound of the bugle rent the air. He remembered Tutt's words and raised himself up and stood to attention as, this time, the flag was slowly raised. Sid stood beside him and as he gradually opened his eyes he saw that dawn was creeping over the cliff top.

74

"Show a leg there — get on with it — the day is half over." Tutt came strutting along the trenches.

Slowly and stiffly they stretched and yawned, taking in great gulps of the new morning air.

"Over to the ablutions with you and get swilled down. Sharp about it now." Tutt's voice woke them into brutal reality.

"What time is it Sarge?" Sid asked.

"Five o'clock," said Tutt.

God — what an unearthly hour. Wearily they strolled over to the ablutions.

"On the double there." He was everywhere.

Ablutions — they had expected something primitive, but nothing quite like this. Rows of barrels filled with water around which stood groups of men swilling themselves down. The urinals were merely holes dug into the ground and hidden behind canvas riggings. Wilf stood and looked at the barrel of water and then removed his hat, undid the buttons of his jacket and dunked his hands into its depths — it was freezing cold.

"Strip off lad — down to your waist and let the air in."

Wilf cursed, but stripped off and stood shivering and shaking like a small buck rabbit about to be skinned.

"For God's sake get on with it." Tutt came up behind him and, grabbing him by the shoulders, downed him, head first, into the freezing cold butt. The shock on impact made him squirm and wrestle. He coughed and spluttered, but he was held firmly until he was gasping for breath. Finally he was heaved out.

"You rotten sod. What did you do that for? You nearly drowned me." Wilf grabbed a towel and held it to his face and then began to rub his body in an effort to bring some warmth and feeling to his goose-pimpled skin which had turned into patches of red and blue.

"Less of that. If I didn't know you better I'd put you on a charge. Get a move on and get that bum fluff off your face."

Without hesitation, the others followed suit, stripping to the waist and giving themselves a good swill down.

"We'll all get pneumonia at this rate," Sid moaned, but Wilf didn't answer.

At that moment he had neither the inclination nor the breath and he was swiftly getting into his clothes to try and cover his withering body.

If this was the Territorial Association they could keep it — he'd resign as soon as they got back no matter what Ada or anybody else said.

Bugger this for a lark.

CHAPTER 8

In spite of the outdoor life and the rough-and-ready treatment, all in all, Wilf enjoyed the camp weekend.

If Ada had asked him about it he would have hesitated before telling her — if indeed he would tell her at all — that only one thing marred it. The rather odd way George acted. Not just towards him mind you, for after that first rebuff, Wilf did not expect any favours. It was the funny way he acted and reacted when confronted with any situation. It was as if he thought himself above being out in the field and whereas some of the other officers mucked in and roughed it with the men, George would hang back, find other important jobs to do — like staying in the headquarters whilst they were on recce, or on one occasion disappearing completely.

"Well, we know where the bugger will be if we ever have to face an enemy," Tutt scoffed.

"How do you mean, Sarge?" someone asked.

Tutt looked sideways at Wilf before answering. "I've seen his sort before — all uniform and glory but no backbone."

It made Wilf feel uncomfortable, being sort of related to George. He felt anything George did reflected upon himself. They all knew that he was courting George's sister-in-law. Not that it made any difference — he seemed to pick on Wilf more than any of the others. But the men treated him rather warily because of the relationship.

The officers never told them who had won the war they were supposed to be fighting and Tutt said if the truth were known he doubted if the silly buggers knew. "Especially if they were all like that Burlingham," he scoffed.

Wilf got the idea that, as a soldier, Tutt didn't rate George very highly, and with only one weekend behind him, he didn't feel justified to make a judgement and so he tried to ignore all the remarks that came flying past his ears when it appeared another bungle had been made.

Wilf had never been away from home before and he found in that short weekend that he did a lot of growing up. He had mixed with other men in close relationship and contact and you soon lost all modesty when you wanted the closet and there was nowhere to go but an open field in which you were dug-in for a mock battle.

He listened to the men talking vulgar sometimes, but in the main good-humouredly. They talked about their womenfolk in a way that Wilf felt was disrespectful. He would never ever mention Ada like that.

Although in themselves the days and nights seemed long, the whole weekend passed quickly and he lost all track of time. It seemed only a short time before they were all back on the train heading for home. Wilf looked round the carriage — how brown they had all got. Somehow they seemed to have changed too, become more independent. Maybe the army did make men out of boys after all.

"Remember what I said, Tanner, and don't do anything I wouldn't do."

Wilf knew he was referring to him and Ada and he smiled and shook his head, blushing as he did so.

Tutt seemed to have taken to him and he talked more to him than to the others. He told Wilf of his life and of how he had made the army his whole world.

"You never miss having a family then Sarge?"

"If I'm really honest, no. Maybe sometimes when I have leave, but I always find a good billet somewhere and pass the time away."

"How?" Wilf asked.

"Well, I have a few drinks, find a woman to set me up with what I've missed on duty, and I'm alright."

"You never married then." Tutt frowned and Wilf saw that he had touched a raw spot.

"Once lad — once — but she didn't care for army life. She wouldn't live in quarters and that meant she was on her own a lot. I decided it best to make a clean break after the South African lot, and never went back."

"What happened to her then?"

Tutt told him that he had once slipped back to the town where she lived and on learning that she had found someone else decided to leave it at that.

"I made sure he was a good bloke — met him as a matter of fact without him knowing who I was — and then caught the next train back to London."

"No bairns then?"

"Not our luck lad — it might have been different if there had been. Still it were for the best as it turns out."

"And you've no regrets about leaving? I don't reckon I could just walk away like that."

"Then you must love your Ada, lad — really love her. Mind you, don't spoil it all by being a silly bugger like I was."

Wilf detected a note of regret in his voice and contemplated the word 'love.' He couldn't imagine a life without Ada, but love — he'd never thought on that.

"How do you know when you love someone, Sarge?"

Tutt looked at him for a long time before he answered. "What would you do if Ada died, or went off with another bloke?"

"Ada would never do that and she's as strong as a horse — little, but strong," Wilf laughed.

"But what if it did happen? What if she got consumption or met a bloke at work she fancied more than you?"

"She wouldn't, not Ada. . ." Wilf spluttered, but the thought disturbed him deeply. Ada was his whole world.

It surprised him to find her waiting at the station with the other women — but it pleased him.

"I'm right glad you came down," he said in greeting as he got off the train and, without thinking, bent down to kiss her as most of the others were doing.

"Mind what you're doing. You'll knock me hat off," she laughed in embarrassment.

"Bugger your hat," he said firmly and gave her another kiss.

It was surprisingly difficult to return to work after the excitement of the camp, for it all seemed so tame and uneventful. He missed the comrade-ship of the other men, of being his own man and not just what Tutt referred to as a 'pappy boy.'

Several times he was on the verge of telling Ada of his doubts about George, but when they went up for Sunday tea the next week he was his usual affable self and made them both very welcome. No reference was made to the weekend or indeed to the Territorials at all. It was as if it had never happened. Wilf assumed that George kept one side for the army and another for home. Well, if that's what he wanted, it was fine by him. He decided to keep his tongue between his teeth. No good making trouble out of nowt.

As they took their leave after one of Isabella's substantial teas, George even put his arm on Wilf's shoulder and told him to bring Ada up for supper next Sunday.

"The children will be in bed and we can have a good chat and a couple of glasses as well, old chap."

'Old chap' indeed! Well, they always said there were nowt funnier than folk. Wilf was learning a lot lately.

On the next Territorial night he was somewhat surprised and a bit disturbed to be called into Tutt's office.

"Now what have I done, Sarge?" he said gloomily.

"I don't rightly know, Tanner, but whatever it is, it's got you a Lance Corporal's stripe."

"A what?" Wilf sounded, and looked, gob-smacked.

"Lance Corporal. Mr. Burlingham contacted me last Monday and asked for names to be put forward for promotions and asked if I thought you would be any good."

"And do you, Sarge?"

"You wouldn't have got the bugger unless I thought so lad."

78

He held out the stripes and told Wilf to get them sewn on before the next week.

Wilf was puzzled — he'd never thought of himself as being the right sort for promotion. Maybe Ada was right. He might be on the way to being an officer — well, a non-commissioned one anyway.

He called at her house on the way home and, smiling all over his face, held out the stripes.

"Will you stitch these on for me?"

"What is it?" She could see his delight.

"It's Lance Corporal's stripes. I've been promoted."

"That's grand, love. Come in now and I'll do it straight away. By hek I'm proud of you."

She took his arm and pulled him through the door and without more ado fetched out the sewing basket and sewed on the stripes that showed the world Wilf Tanner was promoted from the ranks.

"It gives me a bit more brass you know, lass, another two quid a year," he told her.

"Well, that'll please our Ada — she's a bugger for her brass." Thom's voice rang out from the doorway as he came into the room. He stood watching as his daughter sewed neatly and quickly.

He still did not approve of this part-time army — he felt it would only brew wars and he'd no time for killing. They'd not got life right yet, as far as he was concerned.

Wilf watched Ada working away deftly with her needle and he thought again of the way blokes had talked about women. He could never talk about his Ada like that — she was different.

She bit the cotton to break it and held out his jacket. "Put it on then, lad, and let's see what it looks like."

He stood proudly before her, preening and turning round.

"Wilf, I reckon we're on our way. You've got promotion and you're in a good job, and I've got a bit of news for you and all. I've been asked to become supervisor. That means I'll be next to the missus. It'll be a good raise in money as well as position."

"Have you taken it then?" he asked and felt a little disgruntled.

"Of course I have. I'd be a bloody fool not to. It'll mean more responsibility, but it'll be worth it."

He felt she might have talked it over with him first. He very rarely did owt without first talking to her. She saw his disapproval.

"Now what's up?" she asked.

"Nowt. What are you planning to do with the extra brass then?"

"Well, now that you've got a bit more and all, it might be a good idea to save — save for that business we intend to have and that gold watch. We might get one each."

79

He had to laugh at this — him and Ada in business. He might have known she'd have some plan to better things.

"Do you reckon we ever will then? We'd make a rare team," he laughed.

"You ought to know now Wilf that our Ada will do whatever she makes her mind to. Her Mam always says that Ada will do what she's set on if the devil stood at her head," Thom intervened again.

"She's alright, Mr. Skipton. She's fine as far as I'm concerned."

Wilf spoke proudly and Thom wondered if they were at last planning something.

"Come on lad, let's go for a short walk. I want to show you off."

She got her coat and went into the passage and he walked proudly at her side.

"We're making quite a bit of brass now between us Ada?" It was a question.

"Aye. If we go right away about it lad, we'll be fine."

"What way's that then?"

He stopped as they turned the bend of Squire's Lane. They were hidden from sight and, anyway, there wouldn't be many out walking at this time of night. It was dusk, a summery dusk with a stillness that made him feel that he and Ada were the only two people in the world.

"Ada," he whispered, as if not to disturb the stillness.

She looked at him. Underneath the sternness of the army hat, his face was soft and oh so young. She felt protective towards him — her little Wilf.

"Ada," he spoke her name again and held out his arms. She took a step and reached him and laid her head on his shoulder. He held her tightly, pressing his cheek into her neck and then lifted her head and kissed her softly and gently.

"We'll always be together, me and you, won't we, love? You'd never go off with anybody else would you — or go and get owt like consumption and die would you?"

She looked startled and then began to giggle. "Whatever made you say that, Wilf Tanner? Who the hell would fancy me — and if I got consumption then I'd give it to you and we'd die together."

He knew it would all sound daft to her, but Tutt's words troubled him. "Aye — that's right — we'll die together and if you ever think of going with somebody else I'll . . ." He couldn't finish the sentence for the thought of Ada doing that was more than he could bear. Instead he kissed her again, this time with more intensity of feeling to which she responded. Feelings stirred inside him — feelings he'd never imagined, and he held her closer.

She stirred. "Your uniform's scratching me," she said, but Wilf felt that she too was disturbed at what was happening to them.

Ada, in fact, was remembering her Mam's warning — 'when a bloke begins to feel like that then it's time he were wed.'

She had no intention of getting wed just yet. There was no way she was going to burden herself down with a home and family — not afore she'd got that business.

"Come on, it's time you were getting along, or you'll be late for work in the morning." She spoke lightly, trying to break the fusion of feeling between them.

It wasn't that she didn't want Wilf to kiss her and hold her close — she enjoyed that — but you had to keep your sense about you if you didn't want to land up in trouble. She'd seen enough of that with lasses at work. Bairns most of them were — barely out of nappies before they found themselves expecting and either having to get wed with nowt behind them or left to fend for themselves. She wasn't having any of that. Ada had plans to better herself.

She was not ashamed of her background, or of Wilf's either, but she had seen enough of the other side by mixing with Isabella and George, and although she knew she could never be like them she could — and would — see to it that when she wed she would have a good standard of living. It was her intention to own her own house, but she'd be careful not to mention that for they'd only laugh at her. She could just imagine what her Mam and Dad would say. But Ada had got it all worked out.

Wilf sighed and released her, sharply returning to reality. He was surprised at the depth of his feelings, the way he tingled at the feel of her body. But Ada was right as always. They'd best be sensible.

"Come on then, short arse, I'll race you to the end of Lane."

And they set off, sprinting down the narrow lane, swerving to avoid the high-grown thorn hedge and stopping, breathless and panting, as they reached the main street.

"You can still plant them feet of yours when you need to," he laughed. And they kissed briefly and parted.

During the next few days he broached the subject of saving together being as how she had plans for a partnership, but Ada brushed the suggestion aside. She was far too independent to want to let anyone in on her private business, and her money was private. When the time came she would share all she had with him — but the time wasn't right — yet.

She took to her new position as if she had been born to authority. The lasses knew she had the job at her fingertips and they respected her for it. She could turn her hand to anything that needed doing just as well, if not better than they could. This, in turn, brought them and herself higher bonuses. The work was got out on time and she personally inspected everything before letting it go.

Wilf's job went on as usual, but he got such enjoyment out of it that it did'nt bother him. He knew there were no prospects of promotion at Joe Raines' yard — he was a time-served apprentice and that was as far as he'd go with them. But Joe paid fair wages and there was a chance of quite a bit of overtime which made his pay up to more than the average. Life looked pretty good for them both.

"I don't care what anybody says, our Ada's made a right good lad out of Wilf. If he'd been left to himself he'd not have done half so good," Esther told Thom with pride in her voice.

'Old Polly,' as Ada always called her, began to see where her bread was buttered. Wilf paid her a good lodge whereas Harry paid in bits and bobs — when he was in work. With young Gert working up at the laundry now, she was better off than she'd ever been in her life. And although Ada never called at the house, she had been a great sway in getting Gert set on and she kept her eye on her too.

But Polly still thought Ada, and the whole lot of Skiptons, far too big for their boots. Fancied themselves that lot did, and Wilf was getting just as bad. But she kept her mouth shut. She knew that without his money she'd be hard pushed to manage. She often wondered if they were any nearer to getting wed, but Wilf never said much in the house about Ada at all, and it wasn't likely he'd mention marriage. He'd become too canny for that. Still, she did wonder — maybe more about the money that would be taken out of the house than the loss of her lad — but she would miss him, there was no doubt about that. No matter what she liked to think about Ada, she'd made a man out of Wilf. He wouldn't stand any bother from Harry — not since he'd stood up to him about the suit money. Harry never said or did much when Wilf was around. If he wed Ada and left, Harry might start chucking his weight around. It was better with Wilf at home.

The thought of marriage had not really entered either Wilf or Ada's minds. They talked about setting up together and at the back of their minds the thought was there that it would mean getting wed. But that was a long way away. They'd got to get stuck into some work and save a bit before then.

As each birthday came along, Esther waited expectantly for them to at least get engaged. She tried to broach the subject about a bottom drawer, but Ada brushed the talk of linen and such with, "What do I need all them for? I get enough of fine linen up at laundry."

"Well, you might have a home of your own one day," Esther said.

"Might, aye, might — and pigs might fly," Ada just laughed.

And then something happened which they thought at first would change their whole planned destiny. Uncle Joe Raines died suddenly and just as suddenly the yard closed down. Wilf looked like being out of work.

CHAPTER 9

To Thom and Esther, and indeed the whole of the Old Town, the closing of Raines' business seemed the end of an era.

The funeral service was attended by hundreds of townfolk who all wanted to pay their last respects to not only 'young Joe' as he had always been called, but to a family that had played a very great part in their lives. Not many of them were without some piece of furniture made by the Raines'.

Wilf and the other two men were asked to act as coffin bearers and they were proud and pleased to do so. Joe had been a good boss and this was one way they could pay their respects to him.

"You'll need a black tie and cap, you know. I'll call and get one from Machin's on my way home from work," Ada told him.

He'd never thought about black. He didn't really much hold with all this dark colour for death, not if you could believe all the religious teaching which said death was the prize of life. He couldn't see how they worked that out either. Death to him was the end of everything and as for heaven — well — what was heaven? He'd rather have a gold watch any day. But Ada got him the necessary things and on the day he wore them just to appease her.

As he walked up the path towards the open grave bearing Joe on his left shoulder, Wilf felt the prickle of a tear behind his eyes. What would happen now? Would he be thrown out of work? By hell, Ada wouldn't think much to that. They lowered the coffin into the open grave and he stood with head bowed looking down at the inscription on the brass plate. Was this all that was to show for Joe Raines' life? Oh, he had bairns, but they were not interested in the business, just in the money it might make. But there should be something more than a wooden box and a gravestone to show for a life. He'd want more than that. He'd like to got out in a blaze of glory and leave something behind worth remembering.

The parson's voice droned on. "We come into this world with nothing and we take nothing out. The Lord giveth and the Lord taketh away."

Maybe you couldn't take owt with you, but it would be nice to be remembered for something great, like an important invention or having saved somebody's life.

The thought went through his head and was only disturbed when Ada came to his side and took his arm. He saw that amongst all the family she was the only one who had not shed tears. It was not because she didn't feel anything, just that, for her, life was life and death was death.

"No good blithering about something you can't do owt about," she would say.

Wilf wondered how she would react if anything happened to him. She'd miss him for a bit, no doubt, but he doubted very much if she'd mourn all that long, not even to appease convention.

"Well, that's that then." She looked at him as he straightened his black cap, trying to tuck the golden quiff underneath the peak. "I shall cut that off one of these days," she laughed, as it sprang out again.

They walked down to the yard and into the house where an enormous and elaborate spread had been laid out. This was another thing that puzzled him. How the hell folk could eat at a do like this. But when he was offered a plate of cold ham and beef, he found himself eating heartily. Maybe funerals did give you an appetite after all.

It came as no surprise when the house, yard and business were put up for sale. It broke Esther's heart to see her old home going, but she had to agree that Joe's wife couldn't keep it on and had done the right thing to get one of the new houses up on Oxford Street.

It was a business with a good name and soon sold to the highest bidder, a large firm of joiners and cabinet makers — Prestons from Sheffield — who were wanting to expand. They seemed decent enough and were willing to keep the men on. They brought a yard foreman in who lived in the house and they offered Wilf the job as his assistant.

"You want to take it lad. The extra brass will be fine. We'll be million-aires soon," Ada told him.

Her aim of a business partnership was so important to her. Sometimes he thought it was more important to her than he was.

But no matter how he tried, he could not settle down to his work. They were all for getting work done and out quick, and not too much bothered about the finish. Wilf had always been taught by Joe that the finish was important. Orders from the townsfolk dropped off, but this didn't bother the Prestons. They were after bigger fish and soon introduced machines to cope with mass orders from furniture stores that were now getting popular. Wilf had to admit that they were good. These stores offered furniture at far cheaper prices that Joe could ever have turned out. But the work — well he reckoned most of the stuff would drop to pieces in a few years. It wouldn't last a lifetime like good furniture was meant to.

Ada sensed his dissatisfaction, but ignored it in the hope that it would pass once he got settled into the new ways.

"They're not bad to work for are they Wilf?" she asked when he told her that he was now earning an extra twenty-five shillings a week.

"Aye, they're alright, I suppose," he spoke grudgingly.

"Well, you're getting brass aren't you? What more do you want?" Her tone was sharp and snappy.

Wilf looked searchingly into her face. Was she that much of a money-grabber?

"Don't you ever think of owt else, Ada?" he asked.

"Like what?"

They were standing on the cliff top, a favourite spot where they always seemed to finish up when out walking.

"Like all this." He waved his hand dramatically and looked over the white cliff top and down towards the green that seemed to go on forever inland. They could just see the spire of the Priory in the distance and, if they peered, a nestle of fishermen's cottages at Flamborough.

He loved this part of the town, in fact he loved it all — the cobbled streets, the quay, the sea and the boats sheltering in the harbour. Money could never buy this.

But he was not happy at work. He could not complain about the way they treated him; they treated him fine in the knowledge that he was a good craftsman, but at the end of the day there was no fulfillment, no feeling of having done a good job.

He found his enjoyment these days from the Territorials and when another weekend was arranged for weapon training, he looked forward to it with a joy that bewildered Ada.

"Anybody would think you were glad to be off again. And it's another holiday time and all."

"Well, it's not far this time. It's only on the cliff tops on some of George's land at Sewerby."

He couldn't very well say that he was looking forward to being with the other blokes again, could he? She'd take right umbridge at that.

The part George had allotted for the headquarters was almost in the grounds of the house. For George and Isabella it would be very much a social weekend with many county big-wigs to entertain.

Ada listened with envy to her sister's plans for a dinner party which would round off the weekend. She vowed her turn would come. Oh, she would be as good as Isabella one of these days. Just wait till she and Wilf got that business.

"I might have asked you, our Ada, but I can't really with you going out with Wilf. You see that, don't you?" Isabella spoke softly and almost without any accent at all. George had evidently been teaching her in readiness to meet his fellow officers.

"Oh, don't fret yourself, lass. I'm happy enough as I am. I wouldn't want your lot for a fortune," she answered, using a broad dialect. But she was fooling nobody and Isabella knew she would love to be in her shoes.

Tutt Bradley had got the situation sized up. "It's just as I thought it would be, Tanner. All this hob-nobbing. You mark my words, he'll be promoted after this lot, and not for his shooting ability either." The words were muttered scornfully.

"I'd love to see Burlingham's face if you and Ada turned up for Sunday tea or dinner." He laughed as he spoke, but it was clear to Wilf that Tutt Bradley had no time for the Major.

He made no comments, for he felt it would have been unfair to Ada and her family to do so, but he, too, was having his doubts.

When the visiting associations began to arrive, Wilf felt a pride surge through him as they gasped and stood gazing at the green-topped white cliffs with the rolling sea at their feet. A large number of them had never seen the water before, let alone a cliff top. He watched as they breathed in the air and then went scrabbling down the cliff sides. There was nowt like this in the whole world. He'd like to be buried on the cliff tops when owt happened to him.

The training in weapons was interesting, but exhausting, and at least the issue was a hell of a sight better than the first lot. At least the weapons worked.

As a Lance Corporal — an NCO as Tutt called him — he was given charge of his tent. Tutt watched him closely and saw that this rather shy little bloke had a presence and quiet authority about him that men obeyed. He'd be a good lad to have around if you were ever in trouble. Wilf gave his orders quietly, but with authority, and carried out those given to him in the same efficient manner.

"Wilf Tanner's a dark horse, isn't he? I reckon that his Ada has drilled some of this into him — that, and him being sort of related to the CO, like," Sid Wilson remarked, but it was said without any malice.

Wilf liked the feel of a gun between his hands. It gave him some sort of power, and he enjoyed being in charge in a minor way. His men got praise for being on time, smart and quick to learn. He felt good, and promised himself that on the usual last night booze-up, he would treat them all to a drink.

They were shooting the final rounds on the rifle range when he was summoned to headquarters.

"Lance Corporal Tanner — you are to be relieved of your present duties to form a guard up at the lodge tonight for the CO's dinner for the visiting officers. Get yourself smartened up in this dress uniform and then report back here."

Tutt looked at him wide-eyed and innocent as he gave the instructions and handed over a red and navy gold braided uniform, complete with a wide stripe on each arm.

"What's all this, Sarge? I've never mounted guard. Who says I'm to do it?"

"Yours is not to reason why, lad. The CO personally asked for you. The

86

guard is to be made up of a man from each of the visiting associations and he asked for you to represent us."

"A bit of a feather in my cap like?" Wilf smiled.

Tutt smiled too, but with a sardonic wonder at Wilf's innocence. He was personally of the opinion that the Major asked for Wilf to show off his superior class, to emphasise the difference in their standing. He had seen that being married to the sister of his lance corporal's young lady was beginning to rankle the CO a bit.

Major Burlingham was a funny bloke with more than two sides to his nature, none of which impressed the old sweat at all. He could turn on the charm when he wanted anything, and calmly blame somebody else when things went wrong, and nine times out of ten if they went wrong you couldn't find him.

Wilf got ready in the uniform, which fitted perfectly. He preened in front of the mirror that had been set up in the guard room. By hek, if Ada could see him now. The other men were from Barnsley, Scarborough, Whitby and Hull. They seemed a decent bunch and as tickled as Wilf to be all dressed up.

Two were posted — one at each side of the big front door of the lodge, another two to receive and direct the carriages when the guests arrived and two to relieve every hour.

As the guests arrived, Wilf watched closely. The women were in gowns all flowing and silky. He'd never seen anything like it before. The officers were in so much gold braid, he wondered how they could carry it, and the visiting dignitaries from the town were in full evening dress. By hek — it was a colourful sight. He made mental notes to tell Ada all about it.

Isabella and George waited at the door and greeted their guests. He was in full military dress and she looked grand in a flowing dress of silvery blue silk which hung in points around her silver slippered feet. She looked a lot like Ada, a bit taller, but with the same facial expression.

She made to go and speak to Wilf, but George, with a gentle push on her elbow, turned her away. Wilf saw the gesture, but took no offence. They were way above his class and he knew procedure meant that on this occasion they could not mix.

The other sentry posted with him was a lad from Barnsley and when they were relieved they sat having a drink and got talking. His name was Alf Aylward and he was a miner. Wilf listened as he spoke, matter-of-factly, about the conditions down the pits.

"By hell, I wouldn't like that job," Wilf frowned.

"Oh it's not so bad. And I've known nowt else. I've been down pit since I were thirteen. What do you do for a living then?"

Wilf told him about Joe and how it used to be and then found himself talking about his discontentment under the new bosses.

"By hek, lad, you could earn a tidy bob or two at pits making props."

Wilf looked up from his drink and raised his eyebrows in a puzzled way. He'd never heard of pit props. Mining to him meant going underground and digging coal and he didn't fancy that, not when he saw how the grime still showed on Alf's skin, and how it was ingrained in his cracked hands and fingernails.

"Pit props — making wooden props to shore up." The lad spoke eagerly and almost in envy as if he wished he had the skill to stay on the pit top instead of underground.

He was only twenty but looked years older — nearly thirty if not more. His complexion was grey and pitted with tiny pieces of coal — his nails were broken down to the quick. He was a nice friendly lad — and decent too — Wilf could sense that. All his family worked in the mines — him, his Dad and three brothers.

"There's nowt else round our way," Alf explained, with a shrug of the shoulders.

"I've always thought that mining were a rough sort of job, and I've always thought miners rough blokes — present company excepted, of course."

He saw Alf's eyes flash.

"And you would be and all if you had to work in some of the conditions that they have to work in. Where do you have your snap?"

Wilf told him they brewed a can of tea and sat at the bench or on fine days went out into the yard.

"Well, we have it down pit, just where we are working in all muck and grime. And where do you shit?"

"Shit?" Wilf was agog. "There's a lavvy down the yard." He couldn't think of what he was on about.

"Well, we shit and do whatever else nature calls for right where we are — down pit. It's no joke eating your snap when a bloke next to you is relieving himself just behind the next bit of coal."

"Never!" Wilf shook his head in disbelief.

"I'm telling you, mate. And that's trouble — most folk don't think what conditions are like. They buy coal and shove it on fire and never think about the blokes that dig it out."

"And you're trying to tell me that pit propping would be better than my job." Wilf laughed outright.

"It's nowt like that on top. You want to think about it, mate. Money's good there and I know they want more blokes. You could earn a tidy sum, what with overtime and that."

Wilf mused to himself over the words. He'd never thought of leaving Brid and Ada, but the idea was sown and it began smittering at the back of his mind.

"Get yourself down there. You can stop with us. We're not grand, but Mam's clean and there's always a good table. Think about it and get yourself down to have a look."

It was time again for senty duty and as the guests left he stood smartly to attention. He watched as Lord Burlingham and her ladyship stood with George and Isabella to bid them farewell. Aye, it was a right funny old do this. Here was his lass's relations lords and ladies, and him a short-arsed nobody, standing to attention for them. It was at that precise moment that he realised that if he and Ada wed, then he too would be related. How would George take to that?

"You've given us a splendid weekend. I shan't forget this, old man."

He heard the senior officer's voice clearly, and saw him pat George on the back.

Another faint voice spoke in a whispered tone behind him, "I'll bet he won't. He'll be promoted next bloody week." It was Tutt who had come to inspect the guard.

The whole incident had given Wilf food for thought — the way George had stopped Isabella from making public recognition of him, Alf's talk about the pit prop job, and Tutt's scathing opinion of his CO. It might not be a bad idea to move away, earn more money. That way he might make something of himself and get his own business started quicker.

When everyone had left, Tutt bought them all a pint. Wilf sat for a long time looking down into the froth that covered the top of the mug.

"Alf, did you mean it about my coming down to Barnsley?"

Alf nodded. "Come next weekend if you like, lad."

At least it would give him an insight into another world, and if he didn't like it, then no harm was done. They exchanged addresses and made arrangements for Wilf to travel down after work on the Saturday afternoon.

It did not occur to him until later that week that he had not said a word to Ada about this arrangement. As he worked, he thought deeply about his life. Ada seemed to be his world. Like Alf with the mines, he knew nothing else. But how would Ada take his going away for another weekend?

"What's on your mind then? You've been as quiet as a mouse since last weekend."

He might have known she'd spot something was on. Maybe that was the trouble — they knew one another too well.

With a courage that surprised him, he told her about Alf Aylward and the pit prop job.

"What's all this leading to then?"

"I thought of going down this weekend and seeing what it was about. It can't do any harm," he said in a clear determined voice that took her aback for a minute.

"You mean you're thinking of leaving Brid?"

The idea stunned her. Wilf never made any decisions without her. He hadn't that much gumption.

"If it came to owt it might mean that. I'd come home at weekends like, if I weren't working."

Ada fell silent, trying to imagine what it would be like without Alf at her beck and call. She swallowed hard before answering, pride overtaking the hurt she was feeling.

"Well, you can but see, lad."

"You'll not mind then?"

Now he had taken the plunge he was half-hoping that she would raise some objection.

"Not if that's what you want, and it might mean more brass for when we go into business. You'll not forget about that, will you Wilf?"

Her voice told him that she was bothered and he squeezed her hand reassuringly.

"I shan't do that, love, never you fear. That's the main reason why I'm thinking of going."

His promise gave comfort, but she was very quiet for the rest of the evening.

"You wouldn't like me to come with you, would you?" she asked as they parted.

He shook his head. "No thanks love. I'd rather go on my own."

He bent his head to kiss her, but she turned away with a "Ta-ra then," that was too bright, and marched into the house.

A strange feeling came over him. This was something he had to do on his own. Never before in his whole life had he done anything without her but being in the Territorials, and seeing how the other blokes went on, taught him something. He wanted some of their independence. Life without Ada was unimaginable, but the thought of the coming weekend excited him and, as he walked home, a sense of freedom bordering on gay abandon swept through his body.

CHAPTER 10

He half-expected Ada to be at the station to see him off and he kept looking expectantly over his shoulder as he bought his ticket and climbed into the carriage, but there was no sign of her and he had to admit that he felt relieved.

As the train made its way through the countryside, the carriage became airless with the heat and the rough serge of his trousers started to itch at his legs. He stood up, flexed his knees and opened the window, taking in great gulps of the rushing air. This was the last stage of the journey to Barnsley and so far he had travelled alone in empty carriages. Barnsley was not a place that many people visited for the weekend.

At their last meeting Ada had simply and politely enquired if he was all ready and what did his Mam think to it all. Wisely he had not told Polly anything until Friday night. This meant she had less time to nag and ask endless questions. She'd made the most of it, blaming Ada for this new-fangled idea of leaving home.

"I shall see you alright, Mam, so you needn't go on. I might not be going yet and anyway, if I do, I shall be home most weekends."

Polly was not to be mollified by these promises. That Ada Skipton was putting all these notions into her son's head — her and her big ideas.

As the train approached Barnsley he looked at the huge piles of coal slack, like black mountains reaching up to the sky. He went to the window again and looked out, feeling the grit and grim beat at his face and eyes in the rush of wind. Slamming it down, he wiped his face with the white hanky Mam had put into his pocket — it was covered in soot! The air at Brid was fresh and clean, and he had a second's thought about this being such a good idea. Wilf put great store by being able to breathe in clean air.

The train drew slowly into the station and he jumped down, tripping over the bottom step of the doorway.

"Now then lad, had one over the eight then?" He looked and saw Alf standing by the station sign, accompanied by a brown haired, mousey-looking lass, of about eighteen.

"This is Beatty, my young sister I told you about." They shook hands and Wilf took in the rough cloth of her black skirt, the dull grey woollen shawl that covered her shoulders over what looked like a man's checked shirt. He couldn't imagine Ada dressed like that.

Beatty smiled at him and her face lit up. She looked a little sprite, with her twinkling eyes set in a thin face that was surrounded by a mass of corkscrew ringlets held back untidily by a black bootlace.

"So you're the great Wilf Tanner then?" she said with a laugh.

"Not 'great' as I know on, but Wilf Tanner, yes." Her laugh was infectious and he grinned back at her.

"Come on then, Mam's got dinner ready for us."

Alf went to his side and they began to walk up the grey cobbled street. It seemed to Wilf that everything was grey — the houses, the curtains, even the sky. But there was laughter in the air as the folk greeted Alf and Beatty, everybody smiled as they spoke. Wilf couldn't see all that much to smile about if first impressions were owt to go by.

The Aylward house was set in the middle of a row that seemed to stretch on and on. There must have been thirty or forty of them, all built of cobble grey stone.

Alf's Mam greeted him warmly. "Come on in lad, set yourself down. Dad'll be done in a minute."

He saw, in front of the blazing fire, a big tin bath in which sat a man, covered in lather. He stared as the man stood up — he was completely naked and young Beatty didn't bat an eyelid.

Wilf blushed to his hair roots and Beatty laughed again. "We're not proud chaps here Wilf. If you'd been a minute sooner you'd have seen Alf and the other two in there and all." She was taking delight in his embarrassment.

Len Aylward held out a damp hand and, still in his birthday suit, took Wilf's and shook it firmly.

"You're welcome lad. I expect you'll find things a bit different, but you're welcome to what we've got."

They were so genuine, so pleased to see him that he forgot his shyness and smiled brightly saying thank you for their hospitality. Beatty smirked at the big word and he saw Alf nudge her into silence.

They sat down, still with the bath by the fireside, around the table. Mrs. Aylward motioned him to sit between Beatty and Alf. The other two lads, Jack and Kez, were placed at the other side and Mam and Dad at each end of the table. Kez, short for Ezikiah, took delight in teasing his young brother about being a part-time soldier, but Alf took it good heartedly.

The meal was a plateful of broth with dumplings — even they looked grey — but the family ate heartily, almost hungrily. Wilf noticed how they all slurped and champed and how they all watched him eating with his knife and fork while they had spoons. God, he was made to feel like visiting gentry.

Alf wiped his face clean on his shirt sleeve. "I've spoken to pit deputy about you coming Wilf and I'm to take you up there about three this afternoon," he said and then they began to tell him wild stories about working in the pit. He took it all in good part knowing that, in their way, they were making him feel at home.

As they stood up to leave the table he could not help comparing his clothes with theirs, and the freshness of his skin.

In spite of bathing they didn't look half as clean as he did and their eyes were still encircled with black grime. Well, it might be a good sign. They always said 'where there's muck there's brass.' But the Aylwards didn't seem all that well off.

As they walked to keep the appointment they chatted easily. He was a nice lad was Alf. Wilf felt they had been friends for a long time instead of only a few weeks.

"After tea I'm taking you down to miners' club for a drink. You can meet some of my mates then."

Wilf felt he was being shown off.

They gave their names in at the front office and then Alf left him to get on with things. A young lad showed Wilf into an inner office with a large window that overlooked the main pit. He saw, in the yard, stock piles of short wooden poles — these must be pit props. There didn't seem to be much to them and he wondered why they wanted skilled men for the job.

A tall, thin, gaunt man came into the room.

"You Wilf Tanner then lad?" He held out his hand. "I'm Amos Crosby — pit deputy." He looked about sixty — too old to be working in a pit.

They talked about the job and it was more skilled than Wilf had realised, needing him to go down the pits to shore up the roof and sides and to see that the old ones were still safe.

"The men's safety depends a lot on your work. I don't want you unless you are a conscientious and reliable man."

Wilf told him about his apprenticeship with Joe Raines which appeared to have little to do with this job but Amos Crosby thought he had been well trained.

"We'll give you the training for what we want — money is £3 a week, and overtime which will make it up to £4 or £5 if you want."

For a minute Wilf hesitated — it was a big step to take.

"Are you interested then?"

He nodded. "But I'd like to talk it over with somebody first."

He thought of Ada. The money was good, there was no doubt about that, but what would she think to the work — and the area?

"Your wife — tied to apron strings are you?" Amos smiled.

"No, I'm not wed, but I've got a lass and I'd like to see what she thinks."

"Take a bit of advice lad, never let a woman get the upper hand of you, and not afore you're wed or you'll never be able to call your soul your own."

The words jolted Wilf. Mr. Crosby was right.

"I'll take it then — when shall I start?" As the words came out they stunned him. Was this Wilf Tanner making a decision on his own? He shrugged his shoulders as if shaking off a haunting shadow.

Amos noticed the reaction — he was a shrewd man. He hoped his remark had not made Wilf do something he would regret.

93

"When you're ready lad. Best not be too hasty. You go back to that seaside town of yours and write to me next week when you've had time to mull things over."

They shook hands on it and Wilf went outside to find Alf and Beatty waiting for him.

"How did you get on then?" Alf asked and Wilf told them about the interview and Amos's parting bit of advice.

"You courting then?" Beatty asked.

Wilf just smiled, giving no firm answer. He knew he should have said yes but — well, Ada was in Brid and he was in Barnsley until tomorrow night. He might as well enjoy a bit of freedom.

They spent what was left of the afternoon looking around the town. It was a busy bustling place, not as big as Brid but not as sleepy. The folk seemed more alive, happier and relaxed.

They had a nice tea of ham and bread and cake and then Len Aylward beckoned him to sit by the fireside whilst they talked. He was an interesting man — a man of deep thought and insight. To Wilf he was the kind of man he would have chosen for a father — a caring but firm man who was master in his own house. He clearly thought a lot of his wife, Annie, and she of him, but he was the boss. Was that what women wanted — somebody to take the lead? He wondered what Ada would think to it.

"Come on then Dad — get your boots on and let's get up to miners for a sup."

Alf fetched his Dad's boots — all shiny and bright — and laid them at his feet. Len didn't kiss his wife as they left; he walked over to her and touched her shoulder.

"Don't you be too late — and don't get a drop too much," she warned him, but smiled as she spoke.

The club was just a large room in a building that had been put up by the pit owners for the men's recreation. It had a bar, a dart board and tables set out for games of dominoes.

Wilf was not a drinking man and soon the smoke-filled atmosphere and the beer took hold of him. He felt dizzy and sick, the room began to spin and his head thumped in rhythm with the tune being played on the piano in the far corner of the room.

"I'm just off round back a minute, mate," he said to Alf and pushed his way towards the door. He got out but didn't make it to the lavatory before being sick down one of the drains.

"Get it off your chest lad. I thought you weren't used to supping."

He was bent double, retching and heaving, and could not look up, but he recognised the voice — it was young Beatty. What the hell was she doing here?

He shook his head, stood up and leaned against the wall for support.

94

Beatty walked over to his side and plunged her hands into his pockets, taking out a grimy black handkerchief. Carefully she wiped his mouth and eyes. He stared bleary-eyed at her. He wasn't drunk, not by a long shot, but by hell he was feeling a bit queer. This beer was a bit rough.

"What are you doing here?" he asked, gasping for breath as he struggled to straighten up.

"I were on my way from Aunt Peg's — Mam's still up there. I saw you coming outside and guessed you were a bit bad. Come on, lean on me and I'll take you back home for a lay down."

"What about Alf and the others?"

"Oh they'll be far too gone to bother about you. Come on afore you fall all over the place."

He was glad of her support, glad she had turned up when she did, for he didn't fancy going back inside and drinking any more. His stomach wouldn't take it.

They walked and stumbled down the uneven street. He puffed and blew but Beatty kept tight hold of him and when they reached the house she propped him up at the side of the door whilst she opened it. With a rough shove she sent him sprawling through, making him almost lose his balance.

"I reckon you ought to have a lay on bed. Come on, I'll get you upstairs."

He couldn't protest, he was too buggered. But he was sensible enough to realise that Beatty had done this before. She was an old hand. With strength that belied her size, she dragged him up the stairs and flung him down on a bed in a small room that he noticed had a low sloping roof.

"You're in here with Alf. Come on, let's get them clothes off or you'll look like a rag bag in morning."

She took off his jacket and then made to slip his braces over his shoulders to down his trousers. Quickly he grabbed her hand.

"I'll manage now, thanks."

She just laughed, and going to the end of the bed undid his boots and with a sharp tug pulled his trousers over his feet.

"Oh, don't fret yourself, lad. I've seen it all before. It's nowt new with our lot."

But it was new to Wilf. Nobody, not even his Mam, had undressed him since he were a little lad.

A heavy feeling engulfed him, his eyes felt like lead, his mouth clogged and clarty, his lids drooped in sleep and he felt Beatty pull a cover over him and tuck it beneath his chin.

"That's right, you sleep it off," she whispered and crept out of the room.

He awoke lying on his belly. He stretched, moving each limb in turn. He felt better now. Without turning over he sensed that someone else was in the room. Perhaps Alf had come home. A hand reached under the covers and he jumped as it touched his bare backside.

"By hek, you're a bit scared, aren't you?" It was Beatty again. She had brought him up a cup of tea and set it down on the chair beside the bed and sat down beside him. He hutched up, clasping the covers around his neck.

"Come on, it's only a cup of tea." She handed it to him and he drank thirstily. It was good, she had put plenty of sugar in and as it coursed through his body, he felt refreshed.

"You got a lass back home then?" she asked.

He didn't answer. He just stared at her above the rim of the cup. The feeling of a lass in his bedroom disturbed him.

"You scared of lasses, then?" she asked.

Again he didn't answer, just stared with piercing blue eyes. By hell — she'd taken off her top clothes and was sat there, bold as brass, in her shimmy and drawers.

She shivered in a false, affected way. "It's a bit thin out here." She laughed again and then slowly crept underneath the covers until she was lying at the bottom of the bed with her feet underneath his thighs.

He lay there like stone. His heart was pounding, but he couldn't move — he couldn't move a muscle. He knew he should have told her to move — to have got out of bed and left her there but, under this fear, he was enjoying the feel of her feet rubbing against his thighs.

"Your feet are like ice." The words came from his throat in a whispered croak.

"I'll warm them then." Her eyes twinkled and she pushed her feet between his legs and wriggled her toes. Their eyes met and transmitted a feeling that Wilf could not have denied if the devil had been stood at his head.

With one united movement they reached out and met in the centre of the bed. She was kissing him, wildly and passionateiy — he was responding in a way that he had never dreamed of. A momentary picture of Ada crossed his mind, but now Beatty was fondling him with her hands and gently stroking him. He kissed her eyes and throat and roughly explored her body.

"Take it steady, lad. You're like a buck rabbit. Haven't you done this afore?"

He didn't bother to answer and she took his hand and placed it between her legs. He felt the soft furry hair and flesh between them. He'd often wondered how you went on in bed — how he and Ada would go on when they finally wed. Now passion was taking over and he felt an urge to press his body into hers. She slid under him and with an ecstatic groan he thrust himself inside her. He pushed once, twice, three times and then as the sensational climax swept through his being he groaned and pressed his feet on the bed head as he pushed his full weight into her body. It was over, leaving him with a calm exhausted feeling of peace.

They lay quite still for a while, neither wishing to disturb the stillness between them. Finally he lifted his head and looked down at her. She tickled his ear with her fingers.

"For somebody who's not done it before, you're not half bad, Wilf Tanner." Her voice was teasing.

He looked at her dishevelled state, her hair tumbling around her shoulders, the crumpled bed and the pile of clothes at the side. The thrill began to wane and cold reality awoke his mind to what he had done.

"I'm sorry, Beatty — I never . . ." She hushed the words on his lips with a soft kiss.

"Stop bothering. I wanted it as much as you. I fancied you from the minute you stepped off the train. You're not like the lads round here. You're clean and shiny and bright."

He supposed she was referring to his fresh complexion — unlike the lds round here who were coal-grimed and grey.

In his ignorance he wondered if it was the first time for her too. She saw the look of inquiry cross his face and stopped the unasked question before it was uttered.

"Don't ask, Wilf — that would be telling, wouldn't it?"

Was Beatty as innocent as she looked. He doubted it, remembering her skilled caresses. No, Beatty knew what it was about all right.

What would Alf say if he found out his mate had been buggering about with his young sister? What would Ada say if she found out. God, she'd never forgive him. His heart and mind were in a turmoil. The sensation he had experienced was something he'd never forget. Was this what they all called love, then? It was something he'd never felt for Ada and not in his wildest dreams could he ever imagine her doing the things Beatty had done. He felt lost, like a small boy again, and had to gulp to stop the sobbing that rose in this throat.

"Don't take on so, Wilf, if often gets you like that. It were good though, weren't it?"

He could only nod in answer and before he made a complete fool of himself he swung his legs over the side of the bed and started to dress, turning his back to her with a shyness that was so naive and innocent.

"What time is it?" He tried to sound normal.

"About ten — come on, it's a grand night — let's go and meet the others from miners."

They dressed quickly and she straightened the bed. She stood in front of the mirror and tied her wild unruly hair back, tossing the ringlets of curls over her back. He wanted to run his finger through her hair again — to feel her body close to his — to make sure it hadn't all been a drunken dream. She was pretty in a wild sort of way — a way that disturbed him and made him think deeply on his true feelings for Ada. Again the thought of her passed swiftly — she was in Brid — Beatty was here at his side.

They walked slowly through the streets up to the club, not saying a word. He kept turning to look at her, unable to believe or take in what had happened only minutes before. She tucked her arm underneath his elbow and the feel of her nearness made him tingle.

Alf the club Alf tried to get him to have a nightcap, but Wilf was still feeling the effect of the last one. He didn't want to make a fool of himself again, not in front of Beatty now.

"Young Beatty been showing you round then — the sights of Barnsley?"

Wilf blushed and then nodded and smiled to hide his guilt.

"You'll have to take him up pit side in morning while Mam gets dinner," he addressed his sister.

"You'll come and all?" Wilf asked quickly. He wanted to be with Beatty and yet he was afraid — afraid of the emotion she sent through him.

"Oh, I'm working, lad — she'll look after you and then I'll be back in time to see you off home."

The gas lamps were lit and sent eerie shadows across their faces. Beatty's hair had tumbled out of the lace and cascaded around her shoulders. He put out his hand and only just in time curbed the urge to grab the curls — to pull back her hair and kiss her face. She felt his shaking and, pressing her hand into his side, squeezed his arm. Surely Alf could see that something was going on between them? If he did he made nothing of it and continued to talk about the town and the work at the pits.

"You'll be alright here, Wilf. We'll see as you get good lodgings. Mam won't be able to put you up, but she'll know somebody who'll be glad to oblige. Aye, you'll be fine here and I'm right glad you're coming."

It made him feel guilty to see the friendship on Alf's face and wondered if he would have the cheek to come back at all after what had happened.

Beatty didn't seem to bother and try as he may the thought that she had done it before rankled at the back of his mind, leaving a nasty taste in his mouth. Surely to God he wasn't jealous of this bit of a lass he'd known only a few hours? But he couldn't bear the thought of her caressing anyone else or anyone else caressing her.

With thoughts so troubled and muddled he thought that sleep would escape him but as soon as Alf blew out the candle Wilf was in a deep slumber, only awakening to the sound of his bedmate using the chamber pot.

"You go back to sleep, mate, I'm up for work."

Wilf stretched and murmured sleepily and woke again to find Beatty standing by his side with a cup of tea in her hand.

"You awake yet, Wilf?" He roused himself and she told him to get a move on and they could walk with Alf up to the pit top.

"At this time of day?" He reached over and ruffled her hair — it felt so good to touch her again.

"We might see sun rise over main pit. It might come up to standard of that place of yours."

He knew she was teasing him as she slipped through the door, leaving him to get dressed, swill himself down and shave in the bowl of water that stood on the table by the bed.

He made the bed and could almost hear Ada's cutting comments at the colour of the sheets and blankets. They were clean enough — but white — well not exactly — more of a pale black.

When he went downstairs and pushed open the door leading into the kitchen, Mrs. Aylward was standing at the table. She looked tired, as if the effort of plastering the bread with butter was taking all her strength. But when she greeted him her voice was warm and welcoming.

"Slept alright, lad? Come on, sit yourself down. We've not much for starters, but you're welcome to what there is."

Wilf wondered if he should offer to pay something for the extra food he was eating. As if she knew his thoughts, she told him to keep his hand in his pocket. What bit he was eating wouldn't make all that much difference.

"We might not be up to your ways, but we manage fine."

He realised then that they thought him a cut above the mining community.

"You're taking job then?" It was a statement and he nodded as he plunged his teeth into the bread.

"I reckon Jessie Waybotham will take you in. She's a good cook — clean and in need of a bit of brass being widowed like. Her Arnold were killed down pit last year."

He realised then that these people worked with the threat of death and disaster. No wonder they were so happy with their lot — they might not live to see tomorrow.

"It's good of you to take all this trouble, Mrs. Aylward. I do appreciate it." Wilf smiled at her and leaning forward she ruffled his hair.

He could never understand why women did that to him — they all wanted to ruffle his hair — even Ada. Ada — he felt a shiver run through him at the thought of her.

Beatty and Alf got up from the table and motioned to the door.

"Come on them mate — that's buzzer sounding."

Wilf listened to the wailing sound — a mourning wailing screech. Beatty put on her shawl and again Wilf thought of Ada. She'd never go out dressed like that, not even to work. But for all her shabbiness Beatty had a sparkle and fun-loving way about her that Ada lacked. He wished Ada had a bit of it and not be so keen on the money lark and trying to live up to George and Isabella. Her promise of a gold watch did not seem so good in the light of what Beatty had given him.

As they walked with Alf they were joined by other groups of men on their way to the pit. They greeted him warmly and when Alf mentioned his new job they chatted away teasingly.

"Do you reckon he's up to it then, Alf? We don't want bloody pit roof caving in on us."

"He's alright is Wilf. He mixes with gentry you know."

So, he had been boasting about him. Wilf wondered if George would measure up to these men's standards if necessary. It was the first time he had questioned George, but it was the first time he had mixed with any other sort of people — and Barnsley was certainly different to the world he knew.

They left Alf at the gates and he turned to follow Beatty as she started to walk up a steep green slope explaining as she did that it was an old, grown-over slack heap.

He wanted to take her hand in his, but dared not, for she didn't seem to want any contact with him. Finally they reached the top, both gasping with the effort of the climb. Beatty sat down and patted the ground.

"Sit down — I shan't bite you."

The nearness of her set his heart pounding. He thought of last night — how they had loved. He put his hand on her shoulder and turning her face towards him kissed her gently, and then with increasing passion. She pushed him away.

"Not now Wilf. You'll soon be back and then we'll have plenty of time to pick up where we left off. I don't know about you love, but last night was special for me. I don't want to spoil it."

He saw tears in her eyes, but the rebuff made him uncertain of what to do. They sat silently — a silence that made him uncomfortable and wonder if he had done the right thing in taking the job.

"That lass of yours in Brid — are you courting strong?"

So that was it. Alf must have made some mention of Ada.

"I reckon we are. We've been mates since we were at school and I don't know what I'd have done without Ada. I know this much, I wouldn't have had a trade in my hands nor been dressed with suits and that."

He remembered how Alf had gone out last night, how all the others had worn odd trousers and jackets, and not a tie but just a neckerchief around the tops of collarless shirts. Wilf had stood out in his suit, shirt and tie and matching cap.

"Ada." Beatty mulled over the name. "Is that what you want then — fancy trimmings?"

He could not answer, for at that moment he didn't rightly know what he

100

wanted. He wished Ada had a bit of Beatty's warmth and Beatty had some of Ada's side. He thought of Ada's tentative kisses and how she pushed him away when his feelings got warmer. Granted they'd never been alone long enough like he and Beatty had been, but he doubted if Ada would have done owt like that — not even for a gold watch. Ada had priorities — enough brass for a business and a fine house. She had George and Isabella to live up to.

Beatty saw his wondering look and she kissed him full on the lips letting her tongue reach into his mouth.

"There's better things than brass you know. But don't bother yourself — we'll see what happens when you get settled here."

Wilf wanted to go on kissing her — to hold her close enough to feel her breasts, her whole body pressing into his. But now was not the time nor place.

Oh bugger women, he thought, why did they have to be so bothersome.

Holding hands, they stood up and looked down the great mound on to the town below. He saw rows and rows of chimney-stacks, smoke rising up into the clouds. He saw the great pit wheels churning and wondered what it was like underground. Well, he'd soon find out.

They returned to the house and Beatty busied herself helping her Mam to get the dinner ready, far too busy to take notice of him and hardly saying a word in his direction. Maybe she was having second thoughts about making a bit too much of things. Wilf was more puzzled that ever.

When Alf came home they sat round the table and ate hungrily. Wilf compared their manners with Ada's. The Aylward lads gobbled the food and slurped the gravy into their mouths by holding up the plates and scooping it down. They all did it — even Beatty. No one took any notice of the way he wiped his up with a piece of bread. His stomach recoiled as he watched — they were like ignorant beasts. Not even his Mam would stand for manners like that. He saw Beatty lift up her pinny and wipe the gravy that had trickled down her chin and on to her shirt. He didn't fancy kissing her now, nor letting his tongue explore the depths of her mouth.

As soon as the meal was finished, it was time for him to leave for the station. He was glad when Beatty made no effort to accompany him and Alf. He looked at her stained pinny and shirt — he'd have been ashamed to be seen with her like that. But they'd made him welcome and he thanked them gratefully as he said goodbye.

"Be seeing you lad," Len called out to him.

The train stood waiting in the station and he hurried his steps to reach one of the open carriage doors.

"Thanks Alf. I've enjoyed these two days. I'll write and let you know when I'm coming. There's one or two things I want to settle up first." He took his friend's hand and shook it warmly. None of the happenings had weakened his feeling of friendship for Alf — he was a good-hearted lad. But he was beginning to hesitate about leaving Brid. He was just wondering if this kind of life would suit him. Ada had done a good job with him and he felt his life with her was far better than this. Wilf was getting cold feet about going out into the world alone.

He leaned out of the window and they shook hands again. It was as if Alf was reluctant to see him go. Slowly the train puffed its way out of the station and he leaned out of the window for a final wave.

He sat down, took a deep breath, and tried to sort out the events as they had happened. Sat here on his way home to Ada he couldn't be sure any of it happened. Trying to recapture the setting he could hardly bring Beatty's face to mind. But he knew it had happened — it was no dream — the sensation of being with a woman was something he'd never forget and he'd always be grateful to Beatty for that.

Staring through the window he began to nod off to sleep as the fields and hedges raced by. In his dreamy state he relived the moments of passion — but this time it was Ada. Ada was kissing him, caressing him and loving him.

He jumped as he heard the whistle of the guard and putting his head out of the window found the train just about to leave Brid station — he'd almost overslept and missed his stop. He leapt out of the carriage, clearing the two steps and slammed the door behind him as if closing the end of a chapter.

Pausing, he took in deep breaths of air — it was so fresh — you could smell the sea — almost hear it rippling against the cliff sides.

"Wilf — Wilf — I thought you'd missed this train."

He saw Ada running towards him, arms open wide in welcome. Oh, he was so glad to see her. They hugged, but as he bent to kiss her she turned her cheek to his mouth.

"People are watching," she said.

"Oh bugger them." Wilf kissed her soundly, praying to God she would never find out about Beatty.

Seeing her there, waiting for him, dressed so smartly in a suit and hat, had made him realise that he could never hurt his Ada. It didn't matter if they never had a business — never came up to any of George's or Isabella's standards — Ada was worth more than anything — even a gold watch.

102

CHAPTER 11

As they walked home, Ada hugged his arm close to her and he thought it was because she was glad to see him.

"I've got something to tell you — a surprise," she beamed.

Ada with a surprise! Whatever could this mean? She wasn't one for surprises.

He felt tired now — tired and dirty. The grime of Barnsley lay heavy on his body and his mind. How could he have been such a damn fool?

"Don't you want to know what it is then?"

Well, it must be something unusual or she wouldn't be making such a song and dance about it.

Her eyes twinkled and she looked just like a little sparrow bobbing about by his side.

"Well, I know you'll tell me sooner or later love, and to tell the truth I'm just a bit tired. You've not asked me how I've got on yet."

"Oh I'm not bothered about Barnsley, you'll not have to go there to work." She spoke with smug conviction.

"How do you make that out?" Now he was curious.

"Come on, let's go and sit in Town Hall Gardens."

She pulled him and led him towards the bench near the gate. God, he was glad to sit down, to look at the gardens and breathe the clean air.

"Now then, what's all this about?"

Her smile and joy were so infectious that he found, in spite of his troubled thoughts, he was smiling too.

"It's Uncle Joe — he's left you some brass — a tidy bit and all."

"What?" He turned and faced her with a look of disbelief and astonishment. "Left me money — how come you know that?"

"Well, it seems that all the business has been settled now — the selling up and that — and our Mam got a letter on Saturday to say she'd been left a bit, through her Dad's will like, and a copy of both wills, Uncle Joe's and Grandad Raines'. It mentions all beneficiaries — them's that's been left owt — and you're in it."

It took some taking in. Him with money? Well just fancy that now.

"Does it say how much?"

She shook her head, squeezed his hands in hers and crinkled up her eyes in glee.

"It might be just what we need to set us up though I've a tidy bit saved and with that and what you've got aside and now this it could set us up."

Her excitement infected him and his thoughts went riot.

What a relief it would be. He'd be able to stop in Brid and forget about Barnsley and Beatty. Being back at home had made him realise more than ever he could never live in the mining town. He liked the fresh clean air around him and he didn't fancy taking up with Beatty again either. Oh please God it would be enough.

"What do I do then? Like finding out about it all?"

"I should think there's a letter for you at home. You left before second post. Come on, let's go up and see."

They hurried, almost ran up the street, until they reached his house. By hell it might be poor, but it looked like a palace compared to where he'd just spent the weekend.

He banged on the door and then pushed it open, calling out to his Mam, "It's only me, Mam."

He got right inside before he realised that Ada was still standing at the door.

"Oh get yourself inside."

Impatiently he opened the door wider and pulled her in. She stood at the table corner looking uncomfortable and uneasy. It was the first time she'd set foot over the doorstep of Polly's house. Polly had been upstairs and when she came down and saw Ada standing there she nearly passed out. The two women stood eyeing one another uncertainly, until Ada broke the silence.

"Evening Mrs. Tanner."

"Oh — er — yes — sit yourself down — if you're not a proud chap."

Polly beckoned her to a chair and setting the skirt of her costume straight Ada sat down. Oh they were poor alright — but by hell nobody could say old Polly wasn't clean. Nothing was polished, but it was scrubbed as clean as a new pin. Too clean maybe, for in her zest Polly had fetched up splinters on the wood. Ada felt one catch her skirt.

"Is there a letter for me, Mam?" Wilf looked towards the clock on the mantlepiece where she usually stuck any cards or letters that came, not that they had that many.

"Oh aye. I've put it up there. It came just after you left and Gertie said it was for you." Wilf remembered that his Mam could hardly read or write.

"Would you like a cup of tea then?" She addressed them both and Wilf was just about to shake his head when Ada interrupted and said, "Yes, thank you, that would be nice."

If he'd not been so busy with the letter he'd have realised that this was the most words the two women had ever spoken to each other, but Ada was putting herself out on this occasion. She wanted to see that letter.

Polly busied herself and Wilf took the letter and opened it. He read through it slowly, making Ada sigh impatiently.

"What's it say then?"

He passed the letter over to her, grinning all over his face. "Three hundred quid — three bloody hundred — it's a fortune."

He was laughing now and Polly turned sharply at his words. What was all this talk of money, she thought to herself, and her ears sharpened.

Ada read the letter carefully taking note that it had an added rider that said to inherit one hundred and fifty pounds Wilf had to still be in the Raines' employment at the time of Joe's death and to inherit a further one hundred and fifty he had to be still 'keeping company' with his niece Ada Skipton. It appeared from the tone that the other two workers had also been left a one hundred and fifty pounds legacy. The added money was because of Ada, and left by Uncle Joe.

She smiled as she thought of him and the way he always teased her, about being sharp. But he was a sharp old lad too. He couldn't have left her anything and not the other members of the family, that would have been favouritism, but he'd found a way round it right enough.

She knew she'd always been his favourite niece and that he had loved her old-fashioned mannerisms as they chatted together.

He had watched her grow up and how thrifty she was and knew that, given the chance, she would go far. He had liked Wilf too and had hoped to live long enough to see them wed. But that wasn't to be. The legacy was, in a way, his wedding present to them both.

Polly made the tea and set it down in front of Ada before sitting herself down at the table. "Summat up then?" she asked.

Ada smiled at Wilf, nudging him to tell his Mam. She was so excited she couldn't have been awkward with anybody.

"Mr. Raines, Ada's uncle, has left us some brass, Mam."

"Oh aye." Her voice held the unasked question.

"Go on, tell her how much Wilf." Ada was openly gleeful.

"Three hundred quid."

Polly's mouth fell open. "Only three hundred if we're still going out together." Ada was quick to add the rider. Even at this moment she wasn't going to let Polly get any ideas.

"What about the other then?"

She might have known Polly would pick that up.

"There's a hundred and fifty for me, straight like, and another hundred and fifty for me and Ada."

"Got any plans then?" She put the question to Ada, who was sipping her tea.

"We'll have to see about that, Mrs. Tanner. But it does mean that Wilf won't have to go away to work now."

Wilf looked thoughtful.

"Doesn't it?" Ada spoke louder.

"Yes — yes it does. I'll have to let them know at Barnsley though. I'll do that first and then we can sit back and think things out."

"I expect you'll have got it worked out, haven't you?"

105

She spoke to Ada again, but her voice held no expression.

"Well, yes. If it's alright with Wilf like." Ada's answer was careful.

"It's usually women who sort things out."

Polly raised her eyes and stared straight at Ada. Their gaze held and then they smiled in happiness for Wilf's good furtune.

"I know what Wilf — why not give your Mam a bit? And why don't we take her out for a day — her and Gert?"

He thought Ada might be overdoing it a bit in her excitement, but he agreed.

"Why not? Would you like that, Mam? Tell you what, we'll take you up to Machin's and get you something nice to wear. You've never had owt decent as I can remember. How about that?"

Now they were all excited. Wilf thought his Mam might refuse the offer, but she seemed pleased with it all. The two women started planning and chattering about clothes. Ada suggested a nice costume, they were always useful. And a blouse and a hat maybe?

Who'd have thought that last week at this time they'd hardly ever exchanged a word together? They were like old friends now. Wilf began to see the power of money. But he was glad — glad that he could stay in Brid and start definite plans for the future.

With a Mother's intuition Polly felt his thoughts. "You'll be planning on getting wed now then?" she asked them both.

The question silenced the conversation.

"We'll see, Mam — we'll see," was all Wilf said in answer.

To tell the truth, he couldn't get over the change of heart both his Mam and Ada had shown. If he'd mentioned getting wed before, Polly would have bitten his head off. By hell, money talked alright.

It was dark when they finally left Ireland's Row. Polly saw them to the door and told Ada to call any time she'd a mind to.

"I know I've not been all I should to you two, but I can see now you've got best interest at heart for my lad. That's good enough for me. See as you don't waste too much time afore setting the date. Don't leave it too late."

"Shall we then?" Wilf asked as soon as they had turned the corner into St. John Street.

"Shall we what then?" Ada knew what he meant, but for some unknown reason she felt shy of him now that a wedding was definitely in the offing.

"You know damn well what — shall we set a date?"

He put his arm around her shoulders and hugged her close. This time she didn't move away. Oh how wrong he'd been about Beatty — how he regretted that weekend. How he could have thought of loving anyone else but Ada, of making love to anyone else but her? He wished he had kept himself for her. The thought of Beatty made him feel unclean and impure.

What on earth had possessed him to do such an shameful thing?   "I think we ought to start looking for premises for a business first. Somewhere with a house like Uncle Joe's place. Once that's settled then we'll set a date."

They talked about whether to buy or rent. If they bought, it might take the biggest part of their money and that wouldn't leave much for the business.

"I think we should plan for you first, love. Get a yard where you can set up as a joiner and cabinetmaker. Get that going first and then I'll set up. I can carry on working until time's right."

Good old Ada — she'd work things out right.

"I shall have·to let them know at Barnsley though, shan't I? They made me that welcome I owe it to them to let them know straight away." Yes, he'd like to get that over as soon as he could and rid himself of a burden.

"You could write straight away, but better still, why not go over next weekend and tell them yourself, that would be better." Her words stunned him. He didn't want to go back, he didn't want to face Beatty again.

"I don't know about that, love. Shan't we be too busy with things like?"

"You've said they made you welcome and that, why don't we both go? It'll be a nice day out, and I've never met this Alf of yours. If he's as nice a lad as you reckon, we might ask him to be best man. Get letter off and tell them we'll go down for day next Sunday."

His stomach felt like lead. If he tried to avoid it, she'd soon see there was more to it than just not wanting to go.

"I don't think you'll reckon much to place, Ada. It's not like Brid," he tried vainly to put her off.

"That doesn't bother me. I've never been far out of Brid. It'll be a change if nowt else. Tell them not to get a lot ready. I'll take a basket with cold meat and that."

Reluctantly he agreed to write to Alf.

"They might not want us."

Ada peered at him in the light of the street lamp.

"Well, they can tell us if not, and then you'll write again and explain things." Now she was determined to go, and Wilf knew there'd be no putting her off.

Thom was looking down the street for them and called out as they neared the house.

"Come inside both of you and tell us about it." Of course he would know from Mam's letter that Wilf had come into money.

Esther had another cup of tea waiting and the table was laid with bread and butter, jam and cake. Wilf never could resist her baking and readily sat down to eat and drink. They told Ada's parents what the letter said and Thom leaned forward and patted him on the shoulder.

"I'm right glad for both of you, lad. This'll put you on your feet and no mistake."

107

Thom looked at Wilf and waited expectantly. Wilf munched through his bread and butter, his thoughts in too much of a turmoil to realise what they were waiting for. Ada kicked him under the table, and the penny dropped.

"Yes, Mr. Skipton it will. We are going to start looking for a place and then we'll make plans for the future."

If Thom expected more he was to be disappointed. He listened to them talking about setting up in business, of looking out for a place with a house, out-buildings and yard, and it puzzled him, for he heard nothing of the plans for marriage. Oh, he knew looking out for a place meant they had plans for getting married, but the business and money seemed to come first. That was no way for a young couple to behave. They should be over the moon and not be able to wait to get wed. It didn't seem right somehow. Still, Ada was a bit funny about these things. She seemed to set great store on Isabella's way of life and wanted to pattern herself on that.

Isabella had been one of the lucky ones. But had she? Thom wondered. George was right enough, but he wasn't one of them. He was gentry, and that put him out of touch and he was making Isabella the same way.

Esther told him to shut up when he went on about it. "She's his wife Thom, she's got to keep up to his standards. Remember he could have done a lot better if he'd not done the right thing by her." She would snap Thom into silence and he supposed she was right.

But all Thom wanted for his bairns was that they should be as happy as he and Esther were, and that they should share a love that he had known. No money on earth could buy that.

Wilf rose to leave and Ada followed him into the passage.

"By gum lad, we'll show them, we'll be as good as our Isabella afore we've finished," she whispered and again threw her arms around him spontaneously.

"Is that all you want, Ada — money and security?" Wilf asked.

"Course it isn't. I want you. But money makes life a damn sight easier."

He would like to have kissed her, to have talked deeper and further about her feelings for him, but her parents were only through the door and at the end of the passage, and he knew Ada wouldn't allow any more goings on in case they heard.

He wished for once she would let herself go and say what was in her heart. And then he thought of Beatty and was glad that Ada was so pure and straightlaced. At least he knew that no-one else had touched her.

"Get yourself down to solicitor's in morning and get things settled. Tell them I'll go down in my dinner hour," she instructed him and he left the house and walked out into the darkened street.

All sorts of things were going through his mind. You go on for years in the same old rut with not much happening and then all of a sudden something started off a run of events that moved with the speed of lightning.

Two nights ago he'd been a virgin — now he had tasted the forbidden fruits. Two nights ago he'd just a few quid put away — now he was almost a millionaire. He wondered if the money had made his feelings for Ada any stronger — if they had made her more so for him. No. He loved Ada, not in spite of her faults, nor because of them. He loved his Ada with all her faults. A tear trickled at the back of his throat. How he wished he'd never let her down like he had. She would never let him down. But one thing money couldn't do — it couldn't turn the clock back, nor right the wrongs. His episode with Beatty was a cross he had to bear. But he did wonder why, when he thought about the lass with the tousled ringlets, he felt a tingling in his loins.

As he was bid, he went down to Tinker's to see about the will. They greeted him with respect and told him that once they had proof in writing from Miss Skipton they would make the settlement.

"She'll — er — Miss Skipton — will be down in her dinner hour," Wilf informed them.

"Then we shall settle up at the end of the current month." The man held out his hand and Wilf, after hesitating, took hold of it and shook it.

"If you want any advice about the money, please don't hesitate to consult us."

Wilf said that Miss Skipton would see to all that. "She's the brains of the partnership," he laughed.

When Ada went down she was dressed in her best navy suit. Wilf had gone in his working clothes. She sat primly in front of the desk, gloves folded on her lap.

"Well, this will be a nice start in life for you, my dear," Mr. Tinker smiled indulgently.

"I suppose so, but we'd have managed if needs be." She spoke sharply. She wasn't going to be patronised by him, solicitor or no solicitor.

Ralph Tinker had been practicing in the town for nigh on ten years, and his father before him. He'd met all sorts in his career — farmers, fishermen, business people, tradesman and, on rare occasions, some of the working class.

No matter who or what they were, he divided them into two classes — those that knew and those that didn't. This one knew — she was from that unusual breed of women who had a brain and used it.

"Mr. Tanner said you had certain plans. If I can be of any help, please do not hesitate to consult me," he repeated the offer made to Wilf. "Yes, well, we'll see about that Mr. Tinker. I believe in having the best you can afford. If we need a solicitor then we'll have to see."

She stood up and pulled her gloves over her hands. He noticed how small she was compared to himself — barely five foot nothing. And yet she stood as straight as a die, head held high underneath a wide-brimmed navy hat that almost drowned her tiny face. He noticed, too, the large black plaited wheels of hair, wound around her ears. It must reach past her waist when brushed out. Her costume was of good quality material and fitted her perfectly and she had set its dark colour off with a cream lace blouse — that was clever. White would have made her complexion look sallow — cream gave it a dusky hue. Even her shoes, with a curved cuban heel, were in navy and fastened with two-tone buttons at the side, the colour of the buttons matching her blouse exactly. This young lady had some taste as well as brains, and she had had a good teacher somewhere.

"Are you in business at the moment Miss Skipton, if I may be so bold to ask?"

"You can ask right enough lad. No, I'm not. I work up at steam laundry — but I'm assistant manageress. I started at bottom and worked my way up. I know what I'm about." She spoke with a broad dialect, but with a preciseness that intrigued him.

"Well, my offer still stands." He held out his hand and she shook it firmly, answering quickly, "Ay, and so does mine. We'll see when time comes."

A right little madam to boot. Her face seemed to have a familiarity about it and he wondered where he had seen her before, but decided not to ask.

Ada left the office walking sedately, but once she had got clear of the corner she set off at a run to get changed and into her working clothes.

Tinker's eyeing her up and down had made her feel uncomfortable. She didn't like smarmy fellows like that.

Ralph Tinker, on the other hand, was wondering what on earth Ada Skipton saw in young Wilf Tanner. He seemed such a pale character at the side of her.

He was drawing up the necessary papers when it dawned on him that, of course, she was one of old Thom Skipton's daughters, and it was one of his daughters who married George Burlingham. He had dined at the lodge and now compared Isabella with her sister. That was why he thought they had met before — the family likeness was quite striking. Not the colouring, but the eyes, the bone structure and the upright stance. Well, he was meeting George for lunch at the club next week, perhaps he'd have a word with him.

Ada began immediate enquiries about properties in the town and found that there were three possibilities — two were for lease-rental and one to buy.

110

"We'll go round them on Saturday afternoon shall we love?" she asked Wilf.

He was in too much of a daze to think seriously. Best leave it to Ada.

Sunday was worrying him. He was bothered about Beatty and how she would behave. Would she give the game away? Had she said owt to her Mam or Alf about what had happened? And if she got too lippy what would Ada say, or do, for that matter? It could spoil things altogether for him, and just when he seemed set right.

He didn't say anything to Prestons about the plans. Best leave it until things were definite.

The manager had heard about the money and invited Wilf into the office for a chat. "You could do worse than buy shares in this business. It's thriving and you'd get a good return on your money as well as be assured of a job. We couldn't sack a shareholder!"

Wilf knew bloody well they wouldn't sack him anyway. He was too good a craftsman for that.

"I'll think about it all when I get brass in my hands," he said and left it at that.

"They'll have got wind of you setting up on your own, that's why they said that. They know damn well you'd be strong opposition," Ada said when he told her about it.

"But it were nice all the same." The idea of being a shareholder quite tickled him.

"Well, if we need to think owt about that, then we'll take advice."

Wilf knew she'd got that from Tinker.

"Don't forget, it's my money Ada. I'll have final say." His voice was peevish.

"But you'd never have got a smell of it if it hadn't been for me, my lad. I got you job in first place and if we'd not been going out together you'd be a hundred and fifty quid worse off. We're partners Wilf — you remember that."

"Shall we be partners Ada — really partners — in everything?"

If she knew what he meant, she wasn't letting on and brushed him aside with a nudge and, "Oh shut up Wilf, and don't be so daft."

They looked round the properties and there was not much to choose between them. It would be best to take the rental. One was in North Back Lane and the other on the bend of Scarborough Road. Both the houses were large, too large Wilf thought, but Ada thought they were grand. The Scarborough yard was the biggest, and the outhouses could be turned into a workshop.

"I reckon we ought to take this one. I know it wants a bit doing to it, but this will suit us down to the ground."

111

Ada had made her decision and he saw no reason to disagree. He watched her prancing about the house. She had already got it decorated and furnished in her mind. Would he take second place to it all?

"Ada, come here for a minute." He was standing by the window of the front bedroom that looked down into the yard and over the top of the old town.

"What now?" she sighed and sounded exasperated. Trust him to interrupt her house planning. But she went and stood by his side.

"What do you see down there?"

What on earth was he on about now?

"I see a mucky yard and a lot of hard work that needs doing to it."

"Can't you see owt else?" He spoke softly and placed an arm around her.

Ada shook her head.

"I see a busy yard, I see a garden with a seat on it and you and me sitting on it. In that corner I see a swing with two bairns fighting to get on it. That's me and you Ada — and our bairns — the living proof of our love."

"Wilf," she gasped, but got no further for this was one of those rare moments when Wilf Tanner showed his true mettle. He kissed her hard on the lips, stroking and rubbing her back and her neck. She struggled to free herself but Wilf was having none of it — he wanted to know if Ada really loved him.

"Ada — Ada — did you know in all the years we've been going out I've never held you like this, I've never felt you like this."

He closed his eyes and began to kiss her throat. Again she struggled to free herself, but although he ceased his kisses he would not release his hold.

"Wilf — what do you want — what are you asking me?"

"I want to know if you love me Ada — really love me — more than all this?" He waved his arm around the room.

"Wilf, just settle down a minute, love. Here, come on, let's sit on the windowsill."

He let her go and they sat closely side by side on the deep sill and she took his hands in hers and gently stroked them.

"I've always loved you Wilf. If you don't know that then all these years have been a waste of time. But I want things for us love — for us both. You've not had as much as me and I want you to have all those things — and more, much more. I've always known that underneath your shyness there was a strength and goodness, far beyond any bloke twice your size. Just now, when you took me by surprise — that's one of the things I love so — your sudden power and strength, Can't you see that?"

His distrust of her feelings had upset her and she was crying. Oh what a fool he'd been to ever doubt his Ada — what a blind silly fool. She put her head on his lap and he gently patted her hair.

"I'm sorry love. Only sometimes you do seem set on things — money and like — more than me. I'm sorry love."

"But I'm not having a houseful of bairns. I'm not having any until we're on our feet." Practicality was again taking over.

"But how?" he asked, with a naive frown on his face.

"Oh, there's ways and means. You'll not miss out my lad."

She laughed and blushed. "Come on or we'll not be ready for tomorrow. Don't forget we're off to Barnsley."

How could he forget?

CHAPTER 12

Wilf tossed and turned all through the night, dreading the coming day and yet thankful when it came. He wanted to get it over and done with as soon as possible. The thought of Beatty repulsed him, but there was a tiny part of his heart that wanted to see her again.

Talking things over with Ada had made him see that she did love him — loved him in her way with all her heart. He closed his eyes tightly and mentally pictured the two women — Ada whom he had known all his life and to whom he owed so much — Beatty the tousle-haired little mining lass who had given him her body and made him into a man. Each in their own way had done so much for him. He was no longer torn between them — he knew now that his destiny lay with Ada. Why was he bothering so?

"I'm shit scared, that's what it is, in case Beatty opens her mouth or gives me away by some sign. Ada would soon catch on." He sighed to himself and got up to face the day.

Polly had become very genial to him since Ada had called and kept her promise to do so again. Plans were made to visit Hull on Easter Sunday and Polly was as excited as Wilf had ever seen her.

"By hell you've changed your tune, our Mam," Harry grumbled, but Polly told him to keep his tongue between his teeth — Wilf could do a lot worse than Ada Skipton.

Wilf wondered, with a wry smile, what Mam would have thought to Beatty.

Feeling a bit like a condemned man he ate the porridge Polly put before him. "Eat it up lad, it will set you up for the journey," she told him.

Anybody would think he was going on an expedition. But she meant well and he smiled at her show of indulgence. It was good to see her brighter and in better moods. Not that she still didn't go off at times, but Ada calling had made a world of difference. Maybe she enjoyed the company of another woman.

Ada was all dressed and waiting when he called for her, as he knew she would be. She didn't like folk being late and never kept them waiting either.

"Time's time and it's bad manners to be late." That had come from Isabella.

"You look nice and smart, love," he greeted her, with a kiss on the cheek.

"Well, it's nowt special, only my second best. I thought it better from what you said not to get too fined up."

But she would put Beatty and Mrs. Aylward in the shade with her grey skirt and short black coat. She had on a pink lace knitted blouse and Wilf knew she had made it herself and another of her wide-brimmed hats — Ada loved those hats. He felt proud as he walked beside her to the station.

He was quieter than usual on the journey, only acknowledging Ada's remarks about the passing scenery with a nod and occasional, "Hmm — aye love, it's grand."

"What's up with you then? Cat got your tongue?" she finally asked after several attempts to get him to talk.

"No. I were just thinking about things. The house and that."

"There's not much we can do on train, lad. Forget that until Monday and we'll go up and see old Wigglesworth and see what he has to say."

Wigglesworth was the landlord and though they both knew he would be glad to let the property, he was a close old bird. They wanted several repairs doing or a reduction in the lease before they took it. Wilf knew he would drive a hard bargain, but Ada would be a good match for him.

"I don't think you wanted me to come with you. Have you got some hidden secret at Barnsley?"

Her voice was teasing, but the chance remark made him blush. She must have seen his colour rise as it always did when he was put out, but she said nothing and was silent for the rest of the ride, looking intently out of the window.

"We're here, love." He smiled down at her as the train slowed down and puffed and pushed its way into the station.

She stood up, eased out the creases of her skirt, looked into the mirror and straightened her hat before alighting daintily by taking his outstretched hand.

"Wilf — Wilf, over here, lad," he heard Alf's voice calling from the gateway and looking up saw thankfully that he was alone.

They greeted each other warmly and then introduced Ada. Alf looked at her and then doffed his cap as if before gentry.

"Pleased to meet you, miss," he said, with great respect.

"I'm not 'miss' — I'm Ada, you daft ha'pporth." She laughed and eased the tension.

"Well, she's a fine lass and no mistake, your Ada," Alf beamed. "A right lady, just like you said."

Ada looked pleased when she heard this and taking Wilf's arm gave it a squeeze.

"Come on you two, Mam'll have dinner ready and waiting."

As they walked along, Ada looked around her. Wilf was right — it was a mucky hole. Not mucky muck — black muck like coal slack. And then she realised that's just what it was — dust and slack from the pits.

The family were waiting to greet them and Wilf was thankful that nobody was having a bath. Ada would have fainted at that. Beatty made no special recognition and simply said 'hello' and then shook Ada's hand.

It was plain to see they were all a bit uncomfortable in her presence. She seemed such a lady beside them. And when she opened the basket with a piece of ham in it, and a fruit cake Esther had made, they stood open-mouthed. It was all wrapped up in linen white cloths, as white as snow and it looked so out of place on the plain wooden top of the kitchen table.

"You needn't have gone to all that trouble lass." Mrs. Aylward was clearly ill at ease.

"That's alright love. We didn't give you that much time to get owt extra in, did we?" Ada smiled and, taking off her hat and coat, spent some minutes wondering what to do with them.

"Put them on that chair back," Alf's Dad told her.

"Why can't she hang 'em on back of door same as we do?"

Beatty's voice was peevish and showed her envy of the way Ada was dressed.

Wilf took a deep breath, wondering what Ada would say. He prayed to God she wouldn't give one of her sharp answers and start trouble — trouble that could mean the truth would come out.

"Indeed — why not?" Ada marched to the door and hung her clothes on top of the black-grimed coats. Wilf sighed with relief.

She and Mrs. Aylward carved the meat, cut the bread and made ready the meal whilst Wilf told them the purpose of his visit.

"You were that good to me when I came down for the job I felt it only right to come and explain things like."

"You're a man of means now then lad, I'm glad for you." Alf sounded genuine. "I can understand why you'll not be coming here."

"So can I — we won't be good enough now." Again Beatty sounded crabby and peevish. Wilf noticed she looked white and drawn around the eyes and, if possible, more shabby than ever.

"It's nowt like that Beatty. I'm sure Wilf and Alf will remain friends. I know he'll be welcome to our house anytime." Ada spoke sharply as if to a small child and Beatty went silent and sullen.

"You're planning on getting wed now then, Wilf?" Alf asked, pushing another peice of ham into his mouth.

Wilf watched as Ada stopped eating and sat looking mesmerised at their table manners. He hesitated before answering.

"That's right mate. We've seen a place and once we've got that settled then we'll make plans." He felt Ada kick him and he pretended not to notice.

"Go on, Wilf, ask him." She liked the look of Alf Aylward — he was a nice genuine lad and in the hands of the right lass would turn out a real good bloke.

Again Wilf appeared to hesitate.

"Oh hek Wilf, you are bashful. The thing is Alf, we'd like you to come up to Brid when we get wed and stand for Wilf — be best man like."

Alf beamed all over his face — by gum that was an honour.

"I'd be proud to do that mate — real proud. I'd best start saving for a new suit then."

The whole family were beaming, except Beatty. "You're not bashful are you, Wilf? Not with a bit of egging on." She looked straight at him as she spoke.

"Nobody is, if they get the right encouragement, but Wilf does know his place." Ada had seen the look. She wasn't going to have this bit of a lass speak to her Wilf like that.

"And just where is your place then, Wilf?" Beatty spoke quietly, with a ring of sarcasm, addressing her remark directly at Wilf.

She looked straight at him, making him choke and splutter on his mouthful of bread. A silence fell around the table. It was as if she was asking a question in Parliament — upon which hung a great decision. God, why couldn't they both shut their gobs and leave it alone?

But Ada and Beatty were waiting for an answer. He surprised himself when he finally spoke, for the words came slowly and deliberately.

"My place is with those I love." He looked at Ada, who with a smug smile upon her face, now busied herself with her meal. It seemed to put an end to any more such questions and the talk turned to the business and Alf's role as best man.

He had told the truth — his place was with those he loved. He knew he should have said Ada, but at that particular moment he couldn't bring himself to say her name. Oh, they would never know the passion he had shared with Beatty, but he loved Ada. Life with her was what he wanted. She had done a good job on him with her ways and fancies.

"You know Wilf, if we do alright, we might be able to set Alf on with something better."

"We'll have to walk afore we start running lass," Wilf told her.

Her thoughts were running away with her, but by hek she'd taken a right shine to Alf. That pleased him if nothing else.

She helped to wash up and clear the table and when she had finished, the pots shone and the table top, if not white, was a damn sight cleaner.

"I can see you're used to a bit of work," Len Aylward spoke admiringly.

"I've worked all my life. Mam and Dad saw to that. There's seventeen of us you know." The pride shone on her face and in her voice.

Mrs. Aylward gasped. "Seventeen! By hek, and I think I'm hard done by with four. Your Mam must be a living miracle."

"She's a good 'un is my Mam. She brought us all up well and Dad never earned a decent wage until this last few years. They were on Parish at one time, but Mam managed."

"You weren't born to money then?" Beatty asked.

117

"No, I've worked for what I've got, and so has Wilf. But I've got a sister that married gentry. She'll be a titled lady one day."

"Oh, aye — Major Burlingham." Alf and Wilf exchanged knowing looks and wry smiles behind her back.

Alf decided to walk up to the pit with Wilf, offering to show Ada the town whilst Wilf dealt with the business in hand.

"Are you coming, Beatty?" Ada turned at the door and politely asked.

"No thanks, I'm a bit tired. I'll stop here and wait for you."

"I don't know what's up with the lass — she's been right off it these last few days." Mrs. Aylward sounded worried and peered at her daughter.

They walked through the town looking in shop windows that surrounded the town square.

"I don't think you've got the variety we have at Brid," Ada remarked, thinking about her own wardrobe. The fashions were so different — so plain and old-fashioned.

"It's a different world, Ada," Wilf told her.

She could see that and gave silent thanks that Wilf wouldn't be working here. Good old Uncle Joe had come up trumps just in time.

The pit deputy was disappointed but not surprised that Wilf was refusing the job. "I didn't think you'd come lad. You're not our sort, if you don't mind my saying so. You haven't had the rough edges knocked off you enough for this job." Wilf wondered just what he meant.

Whilst they waited Alf took Ada up the pit side and she had to agree that the view of the smoke-covered town had a certain gaunt beauty.

"Would you like to get out of it, Alf?" she asked.

Alf had never thought about it until Ada had put the idea in his head and told her so.

"I don't mean to encourage you to leave home, I was just trying to be helpful, seeing you and Wilf have become such mates."

"It's alright Ada. The more I think about it the more I like it. It would be grand to work with Wilf. He's a good man is that. I've never known anybody afore, like him, nor you for that matter."

She was clearly impressed. "Well, you're welcome any time lad — any time."

And she meant it, for she could see in Alf a hard-working lad with a lot of character and backbone. She mused on the thought of introducing him to Lily Hartley — they'd make a good pair.

"Your Beatty — does she work at all?" she asked him, curious about his apparently sullen and rather unpleasant sister who was not as welcoming as the rest of the family.

"Aye, she does rough work — scrubbing floors and like — for Mrs. Sellars, the pit owner's wife. It's not much of a job, but there's nowt much else around here. It only pays two bob a week."

118

Ada felt a sympathy for the lass. No wonder she was unpleasant when she saw how Ada was turned out. What the hell could you do with two bob a week, and no future either?

"Is she courting then?"

Alf shook his head. "Beatty likes a change in her fellows, says she's looking for a prince charming who'll take her away from all this."

He laughed, but Ada knew how the lass must feel. All she could look forward to was a drab life — marrying a pit lad and living in grime for the rest of her life.

They went back and found Wilf waiting for them impatiently. "We ought to be thinking about getting back Ada."

He was wondering if Alf had said owt about him going to the club. He had asked him not to, but Ada had a way of getting things out of folk. But all seemed well and she was particularly amiable as they walked back to the house.

Mrs. Aylward offered them a cup of tea before they left, but they refused under the pretence of being short of time. Neither Ada nor Wilf wanted to sit through another slurping session and Ada made a mental note to correct this awful habit in Alf as soon as she could. If he was going to eat at her table, he would have to shape up better.

"What do you do in your spare time, Beatty?" Ada asked, not really interested, but thinking she might help with some advice.

"Not a lot," came the curt reply.

"You don't knit or sew?"

Beatty shook her head. "We don't have brass to spare for things like that. The only time women round here do that is if a bairn is due or for mending."

Beatty jumped up out of her chair and rushed out of the house, saying she wanted to get something before the shops closed. A thought crossed Ada's mind, but she bit her lips.

Alf saw them off with a firm promise to visit them as soon as possible. Ada might be a bit fine, but he had taken a liking to her and could see why Wilf was walking out with her. She would make a damn good wife and he hoped he would find one as good. But there was a fat chance of that happening.

They settled themselves in the carriage, one sitting each side near the windows, facing one another.

"I'll bet you're glad you're not going there, Wilf, aren't you?" Ada spoke matter of factly, as if the answer were a foregone conclusion.

"Well, yes, I suppose so in one way. But they are nice folk and I'm sure I'd have been made comfortable and welcome."

"Oh, they'd have done that alright, especially that Beatty of theirs. I don't reckon much to that one."

119

She frowned and looked thoughtful before adding, "I reckon you're well out of that lot."

"How do you mean? She's not a bad lass, and Missus did say as she weren't too well. She might be sickening for consumption or something."

Ada snorted impatiently. "If you ask me she's consumed a damn sight far too much for her own good." Men were so blind sometimes.

"Whatever do you mean by that?" Wilf was all innocence — genuine innocence.

"Well, unless I'm mistaken, and I aren't as a rule, that one's in the family way — she's expecting."

The words fell like a rolling boulder between them. He jerked involuntarily and sat bolt upright. Lights flashed before his eyes, his stomach turned a violent somersault until he thought he was going to be sick. His heart and pulse thudded so loud he was sure Ada would hear them. He felt the veins sticking out in his neck as he fought to control his fear. The red plush of the carriage seats, the mirror on the wall, and the leather arm rests mingled in light with the flashing countryside. For one terrifying instant he thought he was going to black out completely.

CHAPTER 13

Arranging the lease of the house and yard on Scarborough Road took pride of place all the following week. Wilf was so thankful that Ada had her mind on other things and didn't mention Beatty's condition again.

No matter what he did, it was always at the back of his mind. Every post that came, he waited, with bated breath, in case there was a letter for him from Barnsley. Every time he turned the street corner he half expected to find either Alf or Beatty standing there waiting for him. He felt sure the tension would show somewhere, but apparently he was a good actor for no-one seemed to take any more notice of him that usual.

But what would he do if Beatty were as Ada said, and he had no reason to doubt her, for she could spot this kind of thing a mile off. Would the Aylwards demand marriage and how could he face Ada and her family — or his for that matter? Now that his Mam and Ada were on friendly terms he would not half be in for it. A few months ago Polly would have laughed and welcomed trouble between them, but not any more.

Aye, women were funny creatures. After almost a lifetime of ignoring one another, Ada and Polly were now as thick as thieves. Polly was even offering to go and scrub out the house for them.

"We'll do it together love. You're not going to be my servant. You're Wilf's mother."

Wilf watched Polly preen at this remark.

The excursion to Hull was something else that took their attention. It was arranged for the following Saturday. Ada asked for the morning off work for Gertie and herself. It was better to go at this time before the busy season got into full swing.

Polly and Gertie were almost beside themselves with excitement. Harry would listen to their chatter and interrupt with snide remarks.

"You shut your gob, our Harry. You've never done owt for me as I can remember so you've no reason to talk," Polly quickly shut him up.

She washed their best clothes and Wilf had to admit that she and Gert looked as nice as he'd ever seen them as they set off on the great day. They looked brighter around the face too, glad for once in their lives to be alive and have something to look forward to.

In spite of his deep set fears about Beatty he'd had to laugh to himself as he heard Polly boasting to all and sundry down the row that "Wilf's young lady — Ada Skipton you know — was taking them out for the day." She cleaned the house as if they were leaving for a month or more.

"I don't know what's come over her, I really don't," he told Ada.

"Well I do. It's because for once in poor lass's life somebody is taking an interest in her. It's given her a new lease of life."

It was no use him going on about thinking that she had never liked his Mam. Best to leave it. Any further delving would only complicate things and he had enough on his plate at the minute.

Esther asked them in to wait until Ada put on her hat and coat and Polly stiffly accepted. She had got used to Ada, but Esther was another kettle of fish.

"Would you like a cup of tea Polly? You've plenty of time to get down to the station."

Oh, they had that, thought Wilf. Polly had been ready since six o'clock that morning. The train left at ten and they were sat here waiting for Ada at a quarter to nine. They could have set off and walked to Hull and reached there before the train at this rate.

Polly accepted the tea and sat looking around the gleaming kitchen. "It's a big place is this, Esther. I never thought it were like this inside."

"Well, with our lot Polly we need a big place. Sometimes it's not big enough. I used to find it hard work, but now with lasses able to help it's not so bad. There's many a time I'd have liked a smaller place, but breeding like we did it wouldn't have been much good." She laughed kindly showing that she didn't really mind one bit.

"I'll say this for you though, you're a good woman. There's not many could have done as you have." For once, Polly spoke with sincerity, and Wilf detected a note of admiration in her voice. By hell his Mam wasn't half changing. Did money talk all that much or could it be that now he and Ada were taking some interest in her she felt differently towards them? Was it love or money — he wished he knew the answer.

"I had a good bloke, Polly. I couldn't have managed without him by my side."

Ada always marvelled at the way her Mam and Dad spoke about each other after all these years. There was so much love in their voices. She looked at Esther, now greying and a little tubby. She thought of Thom, still tall, still with a full head of hair, now going whiter but still thick and plentiful. It was a love match alright. Please God it would be the same for her and Wilf.

Polly looked down at her feet as Esther spoke about Thom, going on to tell her some of the little happenings in their life — how she'd shut him in the closet up the yard when he first started playing the trumpet. How he'd insisted upon sleeping with her instead of the midwife when the bairns were born. By hek, that had caused a right to-do.

"Sometimes, you know, Esther, you don't realise the worth you've got until it's too late." Polly swallowed hard and then, raising her face, looked straight at her son. Her eyes were moist, but she didn't cry — crying was not Polly's way.

At last Ada was ready and together the foursome marched down Quay

122

Road and over the hill that led to the station. As they came out of the house Polly made to walk behind Ada and Wilf with Gertie at her side, but Ada had pushed her to the front to walk with Wilf.

"Me and Gert will follow behind you two. We can have a gossip about work, can't we love?" She smiled at the lass, thinking that if she were done up proper she wouldn't half be bad looking. She might let her be a bridesmaid when the great day arrived.

But first things first — the house and business needed the ends tying up before all could be finalised. She had not realised just quite how much it took to get these things organised. Oh, they had enough brass, but it were things like what to call the business — whether to employ an odd job man straight away — tools, benches, and oh so many little things they'd never thought of.

They had kept on with Tinkers as solicitors, as Mr. Ralph Tinker was so helpful — a bit too much at times Ada thought — but he seemed to know what he was about and had given them some very good advice.

He'd come up with a name, something neither Ada nor Wilf had given a thought to.

"Why not keep on your grandparents' name, Miss Skipton? They were very well respected throughout the area. Mr. Tanner learned his trade with them, it would be nice to keep an old tradition alive."

The family had no objection, and Esther thought it was a grand idea. And so 'Raines, Cabinetmakers, Joiners and General Duties' came into being. Underneath, written in smaller letters and in brackets, would be 'Proprietor: J. W. Tanner.'

Wilf felt it paid a debt he owed, not only to Uncle Joe, but to Ada and her family. Without them none of this could ever have happened.

Mr. Tinker also suggested taking on an odd job man as soon as they got started. He had been surprised at the amount of money they had saved between them. He could see it was mainly due to Ada's thrifty ways and business foresight and it would give them a damn good start.

As Ada chatted to Gertie she thought about Alf and mused on the thought of these two young folk matching up. That would be nice, and it would please Wilf no end. You never know, it might happen if they got him to come and work for them. Gertie was still a bit young, barely seventeen, but she was a nice looking lass, and could be better if she was looked after and smartened up a bit.

When the train arrived on the platform Polly was so excited she was like a bairn. Ada and Wilf had to get behind her and shove her into the carriage or she'd have missed the train with her dithering.

They pointed out to her all the villages and places as they passed them, and Polly kept saying over and over again, "Well, I never — who'd have thought it," until they all burst out laughing.

They arrived in Hull around eleven and when they stepped into the busy street the noise was almost deafening.

"Just look at them trams rushing about. A body could soon get killed in this place." They laughed again at Polly's face, aghast in wonderment.

"Come on, we'll go to Hammonds and get a cup of tea first."

They made their way to the big store and nearly lost Polly in the swing door. She went round and round, three or four times, before they could catch her.

"I've never seen owt like that afore. They're like roundabouts. I feel a bit giddy now." But not too giddy to stop at every counter and display on the way to the café. It took them at least an hour to get up to the third floor.

"We might as well have dinner now, it's gone twelve," Ada laughed.

She was really enjoying seeing Wilf's Mam having such a good time. The old girl wasn't half so bad when you got to know her. They ordered a meal and Ada noticed that they ate in a good-mannered way — Wilf must have said something to them. But there was no stopping Polly licking her lips as she ate the last morsel of her pudding.

"That's the best meal I've ever had — the best," she said and sat back contentedly.

"Well, don't get too comfortable. We've got to get this shopping done." Ada stood up and brushed down her skirt.

"You always look nice, Ada. I've always said you dress lovely." Gertie looked at her admiringly.

"Thank you love, that's nice of you. You'll look smart and all when we get you turned out."

And what a time they had. Wilf thought he was going to be fed up, but to see his Mam's and Gertie's faces light up at the array of clothes was like a tonic. By hek, Ada knew what she was doing. Finally they got what they wanted. A nice suit each, Polly in black and Gertie in flannel grey. A blouse each, shoes, hat and gloves.

"Whatever will folk think to me Wilf? But I shall keep it for special occasions — your wedding and things like."

He saw tears in her eyes and realised that his Mam had been as she was because of circumstances. Perhaps he'd never really known her. In the new rigout she looked a different woman — younger and almost pretty. And as for Gertie — well it was just amazing to see what decent clothes could do for a lass. "Do you want owt to take back for our Harry, Mam?" Wilf asked.

Polly's face clouded over. "No — he's had enough." The answer was abrupt and ended further discussion.

She wouldn't let Wilf carry the parcels, but hugged them to her body all the way home, even nursing them as she sat in the train.

"Are you coming to our place for a cup of tea?" Ada asked just as the train drew into Bridlington. It had been a good day — tiring, but she'd enjoyed every minute.

"Why don't you come to our house? I'd like a word or two with you both."

Ada didn't mind. Maybe Polly would be a bit embarrassed at having been bought all the things. She might not want Esther to see them all just now.

They trudged up the street, tired but laughing and teasing about the day.

"I reckon she'll sleep with that lot under her pillow tonight," Wilf teased.

"Maybe I'd be the same in her position," Ada mused.

The house was empty and Polly told Wilf to get the fire going and the kettle on. She had gone deep in thought and wandered about getting the pots out as if in a dream.

"Gertie, get yourself off to bed now, you'll not be fit for work in the morning." She pointed to the stairs.

"But it's Sunday, Mam. I can have a lie in."

Polly was having none of it, and Gertie was despatched up the stairs like a child.

"You'll have to stop treating her like that Mam. She's a young lady now. Afore long she's going to start going out with lads."

Polly frowned. "She'll mind what she's about and all. But, I suppose you're right. Anyway, there's something I want to tell you two. Something I want to get off my chest."

Wilf wasn't sure he wanted to hear. He'd enough on his mind without his Mam adding to it.

"Now what's up?" He sighed and looked at Ada.

"Nowt — at least nowt fresh. I want to make amends, that's all."

He made to stop her, thinking that perhaps the day's outing had made her a bit maudling. It was no good her going on about being sorry — that was all in the past and not worth raking up.

Polly raised her hand, half pointing towards the bedroom above them.

"When I were a young lass, not as old as our Gertie, I were right bonny. All the lads chased me." She smiled in thought before going on.

"But I were a silly young fool. I thought none of the local lads were good enough for me and I fell for a right dandy the minute he started sniffing around. Your Dad were hanging around me at the same time, but he were that slow and gentle, I'd no time for him. I kept telling him I wanted a proper bloke. When Harry took notice of me — and I made sure he did — I gave John the elbow." She put her head in her hands as if to rest from the memories.

"Harry — is that why you called our Harry by that name?" Wilf asked.

Ada didn't know quite what to say, or what Polly was going to say next. She would much rather have left and gone home, but Polly wanted her to stay.

"I called him that because that was his father's name — Harry. I got myself into trouble — and serve me right and all. I asked for it, thinking he would wed me, but when he found out he didn't want to know me. Called me names like 'guttersnipe.' I'll never forget that. And then I tricked your Dad into marrying me. He were that soft he'd have done owt for me. I'd maybe have thought a lot more about him if he'd stood up for himself more. I used to think you were the same. Now I know what you're really like and what your Dad might have been if I'd given him the chance — but it's too late now. I couldn't rest until things were right between us though. I've been so wrong, lad."

They sat silently — Polly lost in memory — Ada and Wilf digesting what she had just told them.

"No bother now Mam, it's all past now." Wilf smiled at her and thought what a worry it must have been to her, what a burden to bear. Beatty might turn out . . . he stopped his thoughts and shivered.

"Who was his Dad then?" Ada couldn't see any sense in beating about the bush and so far they'd only heard half the tale.

Polly's shoulders fell and she had to compose herself before she could go on. "He were gentry, like your Isabella's husband. She were lucky and I weren't. Maybe that's why I've always despised your lot. Jealousy is a bad thing."

"But who . . ?"

Wilf raised his arm for Ada to wait a minute. He could see it was taking Polly all her time to make the confession.

"Nobody knows this — only him, God and myself. The name on the birth certificate is Tanner. Your daft Dad thought he were his lad after I led him on, but he's not, anybody can see that. Harry's like his Dad — a waster. I used to kid myself he were a gentleman that's why I treated him different. But a gentleman is what you are Wilf — kind and good and gentle."

"But who was the bloke, Mam?" Now Wilf was getting impatient.

"Harry's father was Harry Burlingham — your George's uncle — the one who went off to foreign parts. That's one reason why I hated you going up there. I used to think it were our Harry's rightful place, not yours."

"I've never heard owt about an uncle." Ada's voice was puzzled.

"You wouldn't have lass. It were a long time ago and he were what they call a philanderer. They were glad when he upped and went to foreign parts. He went and got himself killed, and bloody good riddance and all — he were a bugger. I've no time for them," Polly scoffed and the years of hatred rose in her voice.

126

"But you can't blame George and his family for that. He's not like that." Ada had to defend the family, but she was shocked by what she had just heard.

"And you say nobody knows about it then?" Wilf asked.

"Not as I know on. Once Harry found out I was expecting and ready to tell the world, he was off like a shot and all I heard after that was that he got himself killed by some foreign natives. But they had a memorial service up in Priory for him as if he were a hero, and there's a monument in the churchyard. Some hero."

The trio sat silently by the dying fire embers. Ada wasn't all that bothered once the shock had subsided, but Wilf was uneasy. He was sad for his Mam's years of bitterness — sad for his Dad who never knew and who had been treated so badly. God, some blokes were beasts. They were like animals where women were concerned — but who was he to talk?

They promised not to say a word to anybody — especially Harry.

"He'd be sure to try and make something out of it if he found out and it's best buried."

Polly seemed to brighten up, as if a great weight had been lifted from her body. She leaned forward and patted Ada on the shoulder. "Look after him love. He's a good lad, though I say it myself."

"I know that, Polly. Come on love, I'd best be off."

"You'll not say owt at home, lass?" Polly asked earnestly. "I don't want to make bother, not with your lot being related."

Ada promised.

They stood at the door for a few minutes gulping in the fresh air as if cleansing their bodies and minds.

"That wasn't your Harry running up there was it?" Ada peered into the lamplight.

"God — I hope not. I hope the bugger hasn't been listening at the window."

They looked up the street, but it was empty. Wilf shrugged and taking Ada's arm walked her home.

"Shall we write and ask Alf to come down and have a look at things then?" she asked and told him of her thoughts about him and Gertie.

"You little monkey. Matchmaking now are we? Alright then, I'll drop him a line and ask him to come down next weekend. I'll send him train fare and all, if that's alright by you?"

"Of course it is. He can stop with us if you like. There's not all that much room at your place."

They spoke very little as they walked arm in arm, finally kissing goodnight lightly on Ada's doorstep.

Wilf plunged his hands deep into his pockets as he left. It had been quite a day. Never in a million years would be have guessed it to turn out like

127

this. He was glad it was Harry and not him that was born that way, it made him feel cleaner somehow — more of a real person in his own right.

A worry nagged at the back of his mind. He knew Ada wouldn't say owt, and for the life of him, he didn't know what made him so uneasy. Maybe it was his ever returning thought of Beatty. If she was expecting, he'd hate to think of her being like his Mam — or that it was his fault. But it was done now and nothing could alter it.

He wrote to Alf the next day and made arrangements to meet him at the station. Esther said it was fine for him to stay with them and Wilf was glad. If Ada was matchmaking, he didn't want Alf and Gertie thrown together too much without a chance to make their own minds up.

He received a reply within three days, written in Alf's awkward hand, and the paper smudged with sooty marks.

'Dear Wilf,' it read, 'I shall be glad to come down next week but I don't know whether I can come and work for you. We have a bit of bother on just now with our Beatty. I will tell you all about it when I see you. It will do me good to get away. Alf.'

CHAPTER 14

For the first time in his life Wilf knew the terror of real fear. Apart from silly little things when he was a lad, he'd never done anything bad enough to carry dire consequences and certainly nothing to measure with his episode of love with Beatty.

"Nowt's worth all this bother," he thought to himself over and over again. It was on his mind all the time and throughout the days before Alf's visit he could hardly speak a civil word to anyone. Admittedly Alf had not said what was wrong, but Wilf didn't need telling — as Ada's eyes had perceived, Beatty was expecting.

Ada gave him a funny look as she tried to talk about plans for the business and found him too many miles away in his thoughts to answer.

"You're not having second thoughts are you, lad?" she asked pointedly. "If you are, best say so now afore things go too far."

That was a laugh — too far — they'd gone too far already. More than once he'd been on the verge of spitting it all out to her and getting it over with, but something held him back. How would he begin to tell Ada a thing like that? She'd never believe it of him and what would his Mam say, especially now that she and Ada were getting on so well. What a bloody awful mess. Fancy a bloke of his age going and doing a thing like that and just when things were going right for him and all. A business — a house — a good wife — it looked as though he'd thrown them all away for a moment of passion.

The thought of having to marry Beatty was a sickening thought for now, as he looked back, he could not think what had appealed to him. He couldn't stay in Brid that was for sure. He'd have to take that job in Barnsley and set up home there. His stomach felt like an empty bucket as he thought of leaving all this behind. He couldn't bear to think of there being no Ada to turn to. He did wonder about buying Beatty off, giving her some of the money to keep her mouth shut and provide for the bairn. But if the bairn was his then he'd have to stand by it and take his medicine like a man.

Ada couldn't help but notice that something was bothering him, but when he assured her that he wasn't having second thoughts she put it down to nerves.

"Maybe he can't grasp all that's happening," she thought to herself. After all, Wilf had never had much in his life, and all this happening so sudden took a bit of sinking in. But she'd had no bother at all. To Ada it was as if she had always known that something like this would happen. She'd planned all her life to be a somebody — like Isabella — and this bit of money from Uncle Joe had just brought things forward a bit.

She spent hours talking to Isabella about her house.

"If all goes well, our Ada, you might be able to afford a woman to do the rough cleaning," Isabella said, peering at her sister over the gold rim of the flowered china tea cup.

Ada preened herself but made no reply. That was just another thing to think about. But just imagine it — a woman to do the rough work.

George asked her a rather funny question one day — something that she did not quite understand.

"Are you sure you're not wasting yourself Ada by marrying Wilf? He's a grand chap, one of the best, but if you'll forgive me saying so, not up to your standards. I don't necessarily mean in breeding, but in brain. You seem like a woman who could go far — the brains of the partnership. Ralph Tinker was impressed with you."

What a funny thing to say. Of course she wasn't wasting herself on Wilf. The questions and remarks put her out a bit and she answered huffily that it was none of his business.

"George was only trying to help, Ada. He doesn't want you to make a mistake by throwing yourself away." Isobella could see that her husband had said the wrong thing. Ever since Ralph Tinker had met Ada and told George how much she had impressed him, he had been trying to put a spanner in the works.

"Wouldn't have minded a formal introduction, old man, if she hadn't been spokend for," had been Ralph's way of putting it.

And how George would have loved to have given him that introduction. Having Wilf in the battalion as an NCO was already embarrassing enough, but if they wed and he became his brother-in-law, it could become even worse. What would his superior officers think, and how would it affect any further promotion? Admittedly Wilf never stepped over the mark by being too familiar, in fact he kept things very cool when they were on duty, but once he became related things could be very different.

Oh the lad was right enough and George knew he had encouraged him to visit with Ada,but the trouble was he'd never thought of things getting this far and with the Territorial Association and everything it somehow didn't seem quite the thing.

"Why not give an informal dinner party, my love — ask Ada and Tinker and one or two other people?" he put the idea to Isabella.

"What about Wilf?" She knew the way her husband's thoughts were leading, but in all honesty she couldn't be mean enough to try and put a rift between her sister and Wilf. And anyway, unless it was handled very carefully, Ada would soon turn round and tell them what to do with their ideas.

"Yes, well ask him too. It might show Ada how different he is compared to other men."

George was cunning at times, Isabella thought to herself, but she agreed to organise the event.

"Make it soon, say this coming Saturday, if you can arrange it." George thought it better to strike now, set the seeds and try to help them grow.

When the invitation was offered, Ada, having forgotten all about her brother-in-law's remarks, agreed excitedly. With Wilf also being included she never thought of an ulterior motive.

But as if the Gods were against Wilf, fate played right into George's hands, when Ada told him of the invite, adding, "It's a bit of an honour you know Wilf — being asked formally to dinner. I reckon it's because of us planning the business and that. A bit of encouragement like."

Wilf, knowing nothing of the motives, did know that any invite from George wasn't an honour. He more than likely was up to something.

"I can't go love — not with Alf coming. I do have to talk to him and it might be an idea to see him on my own — go for a drink like and have a man-to-man talk. You go. I'm sure they won't mind."

Ada was disappointed, but it was a relief to Wilf. This meant he could have a long natter with Alf with no-one else around. They could really talk without interference. It seemed a godsent opportunity.

Ada thought Isabella would say they were to wait until they both could go, but she didn't.

"I know Wilf would come if he could, but he's right love, you come and let him and his mate have a night out together," she told her.

George was delighted with the turn of events.

"I hope you know what you're doing. If our Dad found out he'd play hell up."

George reassured her that he was really doing it all for Ada's sake. "Give her a chance to see if she really knows what she's doing. She's never been out with anyone else, this might be just what she needs," he said and smiled at his wife.

But Isabella had been right about her Dad, who didn't say much until he saw Ada trying on her long navy moire-silk dress which, to him, revealed far too much of her shoulders to be decent.

"I only hope you know what you're about Ada. And why ain't Wilf going I'd like to know?" he snapped.

"Dad, I've told you — he's got Alf Aylward coming down and anyway he doesn't mind me going. It's better than me hanging around on my own. He's having a night out as well you know."

Thom grunted to himself and frowned at Esther, who told him to shut up and leave the young 'uns alone.

"Our Ada's not daft Thom. She won't come to any harm at our Isabella's," she told him.

As she looked at her daughter, Esther thought of the tiny sparrows —

Ada looked just like one — with her tiny shining eyes, and her small frame topped by jet black hair, which they decided to put up in a chignon instead of her usual plaited wheels. And, like the sparrows, Ada was sharp and quick-witted enough not to come to any harm. And anyway, what harm could she come to with George and Isabella?

Wilf feigned interest in the dress and all the goings on.

"They are sending the coach down for me you know. You don't think this dress is too daring do you."

Wilf looked at it and said, "No, it's fine, love."

She had hoped he would express a little jealousy, but he was too wrapped up with Alf coming. Well, she wanted him to be interested in the business and after all that's what Alf was coming for. But it would have been nice if he had been going, or at least shown some interest.

Somehow she felt that Wilf's opinion of George had gone down since they joined the Territorials. Maybe he didn't like his future brother-in-law being a senior officer, but somehow that didn't sound like Wilf. Oh well, it would sort itself out. Things might change for the better when the business got going. After all, she and Wilf weren't really in their class — not at the moment — but they would be once things got going.

This dinner party would be good experience, give her an idea how to go on like. Ada always took great notice of things around her. She'd see how to act proper. It might be an idea to buy one of those etiquette books to read. That way she would be sure of not letting Isabella and George down. On the way to work she stopped at Hoppers the newsagent and bought a little booklet — 'Etiquette for ladies and gentlemen' — and read it at break time.

Wilf was only too glad that she was so occupied with other things. It left him alone with his thoughts.

His Mam asked once or twice if things were alright. "You and Ada not rowed or owt, have you?"

He shook his head and told her he was fine.

"I've a lot on my mind just now Mam with the business and that."

Polly seemed mollified with this answer.

During this time Harry was so sickly nice that it bothered Polly — he was up to something.

"Do you think our Wilf will find a job for me, Mam? After all, I am his brother."

The words were emphasised with an underlying tone that made the hairs on her neck creep. He'd got something in his mind that was for sure. Surely it couldn't be that business she told Wilf and Ada about? No — he'd no idea about that and she'd see he never did have. Oh, she'd been so wrong about that one — but maybe it was her fault. In the early years she'd made such a baby of him, as if to make up for things like, to give him

132

some of what she felt it was his rightful duty to have. But she'd been wrong, she could see that now.

Ada went with Wilf to meet Alf, who greeted them both warmly.

"By hek you're right about this place Wilf — it smells lovely and fresh," he told them.

Wilf searched his face for a sign of anger or blame, but Alf seemed as friendly as ever.

They went up to Ada's house for Saturday dinner and Alf was surprised to see the kind of home she came from. Nothing posh or fine, but the house was, according to his standards, beautifully furnished and spotlessly clean. The meal was up to Esther's usual standards — meat and potato pie, apple pie and custard and a good strong cup of tea. He noticed the absence of mugs — cups and saucers they had — why, they were almost gentry.

"By gum Missus, that was grand. I reckon you're a marvel," he told Esther, and wished that his Mam could have seen it all. Poor old Mam — all she got was coal grime and soot. She couldn't keep her house shining like this if she'd tried and now with this Beatty business . . .

"You two are having a night out on your own tonight. I'm off up to my sister's for dinner," Ada couldn't resist telling him.

"Oh aye?" He looked across at Wilf.

"We can talk things over like without her chattering on." Wilf tried to make light of things. He was dying to get Alf on his own, but it was seven o'clock that night, when they were settled in front of a pint at the Ship Inn, before they were alone.

Alf noticed the difference between Wilf's home and Ada's. Polly's house was clean, but nowhere near as good as Ada's Mam's. He wished he could have worked for Wilf and Ada, lived in the fresh clean air, but he couldn't, not now. He had to stay at home and help out.

Polly noticed his shabby clothes and coal-grained skin. Poor litle bugger looked like an old man at the side of Wilf, who was dressed so nice in a suit and shining boots. He'd a hell of a lot to thank Ada for had Wilf.

"What's to do then mate?" Wilf asked straight out, unable to put off the awful moment any longer. He had to know about Beatty.

"Well, you know our young Beatty . . ." He paused for a minute and Wilf had to prompt him.

"Well, she's a bit of a one. You maybe hadn't time to see that. But she's a right one for the lads. Now she's gone and gotten hersen in family way and Mam will need all our money to help out like with another mouth to feed."

Wilf listened to his words, "You hadn't time to notice maybe." Beatty hadn't said owt then — oh thank God — but he wasn't out of the wood yet. She would have to tell before long.

"Has she said whose it is then?" he asked. Alf shook his head.

"To tell you the truth Wilf, I don't think she rightly knows. She's a bugger for the lads is Beatty, but we never thought things had gone this far."

Wilf sat looking at his drink. Should he say owt or leave things as they were? "You've no idea then?"

Alf shook his head and sighed. Before he knew what was happening Wilf found himself saying, "It could be mine Alf, did you know that?"

To his surprise Alf looked him straight in the eye and nodded.

"You knew?" Wilf was astounded.

Again Alf nodded. "I thought summat had happened that Saturday night when you went off. I thought she'd get round to you with you not knowing what she was like, I thought she'd lead you on a bit. It's alright mate — there's been plenty of others — I'm not going to blame you."

Again a long silence fell between them. By hell, Alf were a mate and no mistake. Fancy him taking it like this.

"It were first time for me Alf — God's honour — I've never touched a lass before — and not since. Ada's not like that."

"I believe you mate, I know you're not that sort. And I'll tell you summat now — I've never been with a lass either. Never fancied anybody to tell truth. But I must say I like your Gertie." He beamed at Wilf and Wilf smiled with relief.

"We'll all go for a walk tomorrow — me and Ada and you and Gertie, if she wants to. We're having dinner at Ada's but we'll have plenty of time in the morning."

Alf warmed to the idea and plodded along at Wilf's side.

"Well, I wouldn't object mate, you're a grand lad and no mistake. Any man would be glad if you went out with his sister. But what about your Beatty, Alf? I feel a bit guilty — I feel as how I ought to do something — after all bairn might be mine."

Alf shook his head firmly. "Nay, she got herself into this mess, it could be anybody's bairn. We'll manage, Wilf."   But Wilf protested so strongly it was agreed that Alf should take twenty pounds back with him to help out. "And I'm not taking no for an answer about you coming to work here. You're coming and we'll sort money out for you to send home each week."

Tears sprang to Alf's eyes. "I never dreamt of owt like that. What will Ada say and won't she wonder about you giving me this twenty pounds like?"

Wilf answered that he would tell her the truth — well half of it — that he'd given twenty pounds to help out so that Alf could be free to come and work in the business.

"You cunning bugger — she'd kill you if she ever found out." Alf smiled as he spoke. But Wilf had no fears — Ada would not find out from Alf. He'd lay his life on that.

They enjoyed two or three more pints and then decided to have a sit down fish and chip supper at Murgantroyd's. They ate and laughed and made plans.

"By hek, time's getting on, it's nearly eleven. Come on, I'll tell you what we'll do — we'll have a walk up to Sewerby and meet Ada." Wilf was a little in his cups and so relieved he gave no thought to his welcome.

They set off, deep in conversation about wages and hours. Ada would have the final say of course, but they were making plans. It was a fine night — semi-dark but with a shadowy visibility so that Wilf was able to show his friend all the landmarks that he loved so well.

They had only gone a few yards when a voice called out to them. "Straighten up there lads. You look like a pair of double holed closets slouching along."

They knew the voice well and turned to greet Tutt Bradley.

"What are you doing here then, Aylward?" he asked and Wilf explained the mission.

"You'll be able to join with our lot if you do take Wilf's offer lad. We could do with a lad like you in our batallion."

They stood and chatted for a while and though Tutt never asked, it was clear he was wondering where Ada was — it was unusual to see Wilf without her.

"Ada's gone up to Sewerby to dinner with her sister. I was asked but I couldn't go because Alf was coming like," Wilf explained.

Tutt raised his eyebrows but said nothing. He didn't care for the Major, but it would be wrong to say so to the men, especially as Wilf looked like being related. He'd had years of experience and if he was right he knew bloody well Burlingham wouldn't take kindly to one of the ranks, not to mention a lad like Wilf, being part of his family no matter how distant. He was up to something.

The arrival of the carriage from Sewerby at Thom's door had caused quite a stir. He wouldn't go out to see her off, but Esther did and smiled as she saw Ada wait for the driver to open the door before lifting her skirt daintily, climbing the two steps into the carriage. She almost forgot herself and closed the door, but then remembered and waited for the man to do so. Little bugger wasn't half playing the lady.

She settled back into the velvet seat and savoured the moment. She'd have one of these one day — for her and Wilf. She brushed a crease from her skirt and giggled at the thought.

The dress was perfect — not showy but subtle enough to reveal the outline of her dainty figure. She loved navy which, in spite of her rather sallow complexion, suited her, and the shine of the taffeta complemented the glowing raven hair. Aye, she'd do right enough — she'd do good enough for Sewerby and anybody who was going to be there. It never occurred to her to wish that Wilf was going with her — he was on business and that was that. The thought did wrinkle at the back of her mind that had he been going he would have had to buy a new suit and just now they couldn't run to it, not with all this investing going on. They would need every penny. At these thoughts a guilty feeling ran through her because of the dress. Still, it might be worth it in the long run. Another investment so to speak.

The carriage rolled smoothly to a standstill and as the carriage door was opened she saw George and Isabella standing on the stone steps waiting to greet their guests. By God, George was in evening dress — and so was that other bloke. She peered and saw that it was Ralph Tinker. Thank God Wilf hadn't come, she'd never have got him to wear one of those monkey suits and he would have looked out of place in an ordinary one.

George went forward to meet her. "How lovely you look Ada, you are a credit to us all. May I introduce you formally to Ralph Tinker? I believe you have already met through business. He is to be your escort tonight and will take you into dinner."

Ada's eyes met Isabella's and she frowned at her sister. Ralph Tinker eh? Isabella smiled openly and Ada brushed all thoughts of any conniving to one side. She might learn a thing or two from Ralph Tinker — after all he was working for her and Wilf.

CHAPTER 15

As George made the formal introductions, Ralph Tinker inclined his head slightly towards Ada and smiled down at her.

My, she looked a delicious little thing. He offered his arm but Ada ignored it and walked by his side up the three stone steps that led into the house.

She couldn't deny he was a handsome bloke and towered above her. She was so used to Wilf's smaller stature that Ralph's height made her feel protected, more womanly, and he was the perfect gent too, quickly putting her at ease until they were chatting away like old friends.

"Your cloak, Madam." The butler stood by her side and spoke quietly. She hadn't got a cloak — she'd never given that a thought and anyway would not have bought one if she had. She needed all the brass and the dress had cost quite enough.

"I haven't got one," she answered brusquely.

Ralph smiled at her forthright manner. "The evening is warm; a cloak is not really needed," he said.

"Well, if it was cold I would have worn a coat. I haven't got a cloak. I don't go in for that kind of thing — not yet."

He noted the 'not yet.' He found her openness refreshing. She didn't mince words. Most of the women he knew twittered and simpered and agreed with everything the men said, mainly because they felt it would win them a husband. She was definitely not in that category.

They went into the sitting room to wait until dinner was announced. Ada looked around her. She had been in the room many times before, never on an occasion like this. Isabella looked lovely — a proper lady in a pale yellow silk dress that fell in soft folds around her waist. It set off her blonde hair and pale complexion. By hek — she'd done alright for herself had Isabella — and she played the part right and all — the proper lady. George stood behind his wife and placed his hand upon her shoulder as she sat down. No matter what anybody said, it was obvious he loved his wife — and who wouldn't — she was a credit to any man.

At odd times Ada found it hard to think of Isabella as one of her family, but when she really thought about it, Mam had a certain something about her. A ladylike manner that put her a cut above other working class wives. She thought it might be something to do with her grandparents being in business that had instilled in Esther the good standards she always kept. And Dad was alright too — a proper gent — well, until something upset him and then he could sound off. Esther might be given credit for making him what he was, but the old lad had plenty about him, there was no mistaking that.

Ada thought highly of her family. They were honest, outspoken, and never smarmy to those supposedly above them. They were good folk and well respected. Mam and Dad had been to Sewerby on several occasions, but not at a formal do like this. Thom wouldn't have any of that, no matter what Esther said.

"We'll go like we do to the rest of the bairns, as part of the family. I'll not be a guest in my own daughter's house no matter who she's wed to," he said firmly and Esther let it be.

Ada was sat in a large wing-backed red velvet chair that would have hidden her from view if she had not perched herself on the edge. Ralph stood behind her with his hand placed on the back on the chair. "My God," she thought, "We look like a scene in a melodrama."

"Who else is coming then?" She directed her question to Isabella.

"The vicar and his wife, that's all. Six is a nice number for an intimate dinner party."

"Not too intimate I hope," Ada spoke and turning looked up at Ralph, ignoring her sister's tutt-tutting.

They sat chatting about the weather, and politics, about which Ada knew very little. Not to be left out, she tried to turn the conversation to her and Wilf and the business, and got a little annoyed when George and Isabella quickly stepped in and steered it to other things. Oh well, maybe you didn't talk about yourself at formal dinner parties.

Finally the vicar and his wife turned up in a bit of a fluster. "Confirmation classes I'm afraid," was the excuse. George introduced them.

"Ada, this is the Reverend Hilary Willmot and his wife Cecily — this is my wife's sister Ada."

Ada thought she had heard wrong, Hilary for a bloke's name? Perhaps George had got it wrong. But they were a nice middle-aged couple and they smiled pleasantly at her.

"Miss Skipton — may I call you Ada? I was just thinking that in spite of your contrasting colouring, you and your sister are remarkably alike. Do you have any more brothers and sisters?"

"Seventeen in all."

George gulped at her answer and tried to avoid any further discussion, but the vicar's wife was fascinated.

"Seventeen?" she gasped.

"That's right — ten girls and seven lads. One lad got drowned in Gypsy Beck when he was eleven, but there's sixteen of us around, live and kicking."

Ralph thought the last statement very apt.

"However did your mother manage that?" Cecily asked, and as their eyes met, Ada could have sworn Isabella nearly cracked out laughing.

138

"In the usual way I expect — they haven't invented anything new as far as I know."

Isabella blushed and George coughed and spluttered, but Ralph broke into pure delighted laughter.

"I can see you believe in calling a spade a spade, Miss Skipton. May I also call you Ada?" he laughed.

"I don't know about a spade — more of a shovel, but I don't see any sense in mincing words. We were brought up to say what we think, weren't we, our Isabella?"

And Isabella, laughing, agreed.

"Please call me Ralph." He was going to enjoy this evening. The more he watched Ada, her quick movements and reactions, the more he liked what he saw and heard. She had a mind of her own and she used it. What a change from the usual run of women.

"I don't know about that — maybe I will for tonight." She turned to the Willmots and added, "Mr. Tinker — Ralph — is employed by me as my solicitor, you know. I am organising some business and he is dealing with it for me."

George thought she was going to go through the whole business and sighed with relief when dinner was finally announced.

Ralph offered his arm and Ada was going to refuse again, but she saw Isabella taking the vicar's arm and decided to do likewise. After all, she must not let the side down.

The large mahogany dining table looked magnificent, set with silver and crystal. Little bowls of roses gave the finishing touch.

"What a beautiful setting," Mrs. Willmot complimented Isabella.

"It is nothing special Cecily. Being just a group of intimate friends we did not make it too formal."

"Well, it's a damn sight more than you were ever used to." The words were out before Ada could stop them. This time she clearly saw the embarrassment she had caused her sister and brother-in-law. "But Mother always kept a good table," she tried to make amends.

Ralph saw the situation and turning to Hilary Willmot said, "What do you think of the Austrian situation, vicar? Will our cousin the Kaiser bring us to war?"

Hilary Willmot murmured that he was afraid so.

"It might do us good — we are far too complacent — the working classes need a good shaking up."

Ada looked up sharply as George spoke. "What do you mean war — who said anything about a war?"

"Don't you listen and read the papers? There have been rumblings going on for months." Isabella was glad the subject had changed.

"I've enough on with my own business without thinking of war." It was

139

daft talking about war. Who would dare to tackle England? Ada was being patriotic, and blinded by her own affairs.

"Well, you had better start thinking about it for Wilf will be one of the first to go. Has he not said anything to you?" George asked.

Ada shook her head. Wilf had seemed a bit preoccupied of late. Maybe it was all this war business.

"He won't have to go. You can't force anybody to go. Can you?" She turned to Ralph.

"I don't really know, but if Mr. Tanner is in the Territorial Association then I'm afraid he will have no choice."

Ada frowned. Well, he could leave the Territorials. She wasn't having her future buggered about by some ruddy German.

"That will mean you as well won't it, George? As an officer surely you'll have to lead the men?"

George puffed himself up and beamed. "I shall answer the call if necessary," he said.

They ate in silence. Ada had read her etiquette book well and never made a wrong move. She had practised with the pictures shown in the book and felt confident that she was not going to make a fool of herself.

"Are you in the Territorials?" she asked Ralph.

"No, not at the moment. But if there is going to be a war then I shall certainly join," he replied.

"Come down tomorrow night Ralph, and see what we are up to. I might even enlist you. You would get an immediate commission, you know."

Ada wondered why he would. Why was it that the upper classes got the promotion? Wilf was a good lad, calm and capable. Why couldn't he have a commission? Still, if they were right about the war, she'd have him out before the weekend. Nobody was going to mess her life up.

It was the first time Ada had drunk wine and although she didn't care for the taste, she drank two glasses. It had the effect of loosening her tongue and soon she was telling Cecily and Hilary about her plans.

"Are you engaged then Ada?" Hilary asked.

This silenced her for a moment. Engaged? — she didn't really know about that. "Well, some time in the not too distant future I am planning to get wed to Wilf Tanner. We've been courting for a long time — in fact we went to school together. But we've a bit to do before that day comes."

"You're not officially committed then?" This time Ralph asked the question.

"If that means have I got a ring on my finger then the answer is no. But Wilf and me are as committed as anybody can be. We are tying our money up together and you can't get more committed than that in my opinion."

But Ralph was thinking that he might after all stand a chance. When he had first asked for a formal introduction he had not thought of anything more than a light flirtation. But that was not Ada's style. Being in her company on a social level had shown him that she was quite a woman — a woman he would have been proud to have by his side. He could see why George had married Isabella — these Skipton girls had great characters.

The wine made her sleepy and it was an effort to keep track of the conversation, but she murmured and nodded, and hoped they hit the appropriate spots.

Ralph never left her side and it was credit to him that she managed to keep awake. He was a nice bloke, she thought to herself. He would make a good friend.

"We must be going Hilary, my dear. The excellent food and all this talk of war has quite exhausted me." Cecily rose from her chair.

"You should try a day's work at the steam laundry, then you'd know what it's like to be really tired out," Ada roused herself.

"Yes, I suppose so. One never thinks of the poor girls that have to slave in places like that. I never cease to be thankful for my lot, don't you?"

"I work up there, Missus — I'm assistant manageress." And she was not ashamed of it either, but it seemed to embarrass poor Cecily and the Willmots hurriedly took their leave.

"A night cap old man?" George motioned to Ralph.

"I think if you'll excuse me I'll be on my way. May I take you also, Ada?"

George smiled and winked at his wife. Old Ralph seemed really smitten. He couldn't be sure about Ada, but who would miss a chance of having Ralph Tinker against that of Wilf Tanner. He was sure Ada wouldn't, she was no fool.

"That is kind of you Ralph. I must say I am ready for home, but I have enjoyed myself our Isabella, it was grand. And I'm right proud of you. You're a real lady."

The two girls embraced, and for a moment Isabella felt guilty at the reasons for asking Ada to dinner. After all, they were sisters, and having her here had recalled a lot of the old days at home. Sometimes she missed the laughter and fun of her family and although she would never have given up George for any of it, it was nice to hear some of the old humorous sayings and doings.

"And I'm proud of you too love. You shall come again," she told Ada.

"And you too, old man." George shook Ralph by the hand.

He helped Ada into the carriage and gave Ralph a nudge as he climbed the two steps. "Make the most of it."

Surprisingly Ralph frowned at him. No man in his right mind would try to make the most of Ada Skipton.

She settled herself down on the leather upholstered seat, leaned back, and looked across at Ralph. "You're not a bit like I thought you were you know," she said.

"And neither are you. You're quite a surprising lady, Ada."

She smiled. Lady, eh? Well, she would be one day.

"Well, you know what they say — good things come in little packets." She giggled and he joined in her laughter.

God, what an amazing evening. He'd gone just to have a laugh and a bit of fun and he ended up by being deeply attracted to Ada. He felt he wanted to encircle her small waist in his hands, to stroke her raven hair and to kiss her tiny ears. But she would never allow that. Ada was not the type. He felt nervous and unsure of himself — him, Ralph Tinker — Bridlington's most eligible bachelor feeling like a raw schoolboy, and all because of a snippet of a laundry girl.

"Do you mind if I smoke?" He had to do something to stop himself from going over to her and taking her in his arms.

"You go ahead lad, I don't mind."

Her dialect touched him — she was so honest.

"Have you enjoyed this evening — really enjoyed it?" he asked and she nodded her head so fiercely that some of the pins fell from her hair and it cascaded in a mass down her shoulders. The beauty of its colour and the heavy waves shook him. Oh how he would love to run his hands through those shining locks.

"Oh hek — now look what's happened — I've lost all my pins."

She bent down and as he leaned forward to help her look for them, he felt the sweep of her hair touch his face. He stayed, transfixed from the effect, and as she raised her head their eyes met and locked. He wanted so much to kiss her and felt that she wanted that too.

Ada had never felt a sensation like it in her life before — not even with Wilf. She was a little in awe, and frightened now of this man whom only minutes before she had begun to think of as a friend. It wasn't friendship shining in his eyes. She pulled back, wondering how to break the spell, and with an overwhelming thankfulness saw Wilf and Alf walking past the carriage.

"Stop the carriage — stop it," she shouted and Ralph thought that she had become frightened of him.

"It's alright Ada — it's alright."

"That's Wilf — Wilf and Alf." She wound down the window and leaning out shouted at the top of her voice, "Wilf — Wilf, it's me. Come over here and have a ride in a carriage."

Wilf and Alf had been deep in conversation and they turned and looked for the voice.

"Come on lad — it's Ada — come on and we'll ride home in style." They ran and Ada opened the carriage door. Wilf stopped still when he saw Ralph sitting rather uncomfortably in the far corner of the carriage.

"I'm sorry sir — excuse me — is it alright like?"

"Yes — yes — it's alright Mr. Tanner. Come along inside."

Wilf sat beside Ada and Alf beside Ralph. She was trying to pin up her hair and twisted it into a plait, letting it lie down her back. It almost reached her waist and both men looked on in admiration as it coiled down.

"Had a good time then, lass?" Wilf asked and she nodded.

Ralph saw the look that passed between them as they smiled at one another. There was no way he could come between these two and he would never do anything to hurt Ada. But he would not give up hope completely.

Alf leaned back and closed his eyes. "By gum, our lot will never believe this — me riding in a carriage." He laughed at the very thought.

"Then we'll take a little run." Ralph tapped to the coachman and told him to drive along the sea front.

"I always think the sea looks lovely at this time of night," he spoke to Wilf.

"Aye it does that, sir. I can see you're a true Brid man, like me. It's a sight you'll not forget, Alf, I'll tell you that for nowt."

They rode in silence. If Wilf noticed that Ada was a little flustered he said nothing, but he did feel a tension and wondered if that Tinker bloke had tried to get fresh with her. He laughed silently. Ada would give him short change if he had.

Ada looked across at the three men — what a contrast! Ralph was such a gentleman from the upper classes, Wilf a working lad, but a cut above Alf who showed the grime of his mining background. It wasn't half a funny old world.

"Do you know about this war they are all talking about?" she asked Wilf.

He nodded. "Aye, I've heard them on about it, but I've not taken all that much notice. I reckon we've enough on our plate without bothering about some bloody foreigners." He took her hand and squeezed it.

Oh, it was good to be near Wilf again — to feel his skin. She caught Ralph's gaze and for a moment allowed her imagination to wander. Did he really fancy her? That would be a right turn up. But she had Wilf — Wilf and the promise of a business that would start them off on a new life.

She didn't want any more than that. Not for the moment anyway.

CHAPTER 16

It turned out to be a good weekend after all and left Wilf with a feeling of relief. Now he could get down to setting up the business with Ada.

Although the time had been short, he and Alf had talked long and deep, cementing a friendship that seemed as if they had known one another all their lives.

Reluctantly Alf took Wilf's offer of twenty pounds to see that Beatty was alright. He even told Ada about it, with a fairly light heart. She agreed because of Alf. She could see he and Wilf would get on fine together and that would make for a successful business. And she felt a little bit of sympathy for the lass as well.

"But she shouldn't mess around like that — if you play with a bull you always get horn up your arse. She should have more respect for herself."

Wilf could say nothing, for at the time his affair with Beatty had not seemed to cheapen either of them. Only in the cold light of the day could it be dirty or wrong.

Both of them were delighted to see that Alf and Gertie were getting along fine together. The four of them went for a walk on the Sunday morning and after setting off with the two girls in front, it soon separated into Ada and Wilf at the front and Alf and Gert at the back.

"She seems to have blossomed, doesn't she?" Wilf turned and looked at his little sister as he spoke.

She was dressed nicely, thanks to Ada, in a smart skirt, blouse and jacket, and now that Ada had shown her how to put her hair up, she looked a pretty little thing — shy, mind you, but with a twinkle in her eyes that Wilf had not noticed before.

Come to think of it, his Mam was a sight better these days and all. It was as if a great burden had been lifted from her shoulders when she had told them about Harry's birth. Wilf didn't hold it against her at all. Poor old Mam — she must have felt so bitter and guilty all these years.

His feelings for Harry had not changed. No matter how he tried to find some brotherly love he couldn't. He was such a sly devil, peeping and creeping about the way he did, with never so much as a thought about earning a living.

"I'd have thought we'd not be good enough for you now, our Wilf, with all these big ideas of yours," he mocked.

"Just shut your gob while you can. If you shaped up a bit it might make things better."

"It might help if you offered him something Wilf. He might not deserve it, but it might set him an example." Polly was not proud of Harry, but she couldn't blame him altogether for the way he had turned out.

"Oh don't fret yoursen. I wouldn't work for him if he were last bloke on earth. I've other plans." His voice chilled Polly. What the hell did he mean by that she wondered. Still, best not to make too much of it. Harry couldn't know anything and if he did it was best not to dwell on it.

He was barely civil to Alf, who felt embarrassed, as if he was pushing a member of the family out. But Wilf and Ada seemed determined to set Alf on and he had to admit he was looking forward to settling down in Brid — for Gertie, if nothing else.

After Sunday dinner, which they all had down at Esther's, Wilf and Ada made to go down to the station with Alf.

"You'll come and all, Gertie?" Alf turned shyly to her, and she nodded shyly in reply.

"I reckon we've got a match there," Wilf whispered, and Ada looked contented at the situation.

That would be nice — round things off like, nice and tidy. But she'd never press them into anything. They must make up their own minds.

At the back of her mind there lingered the memory of the dinner party and Ralph Tinker. She went through the carriage ride home and could not get out of her mind the look in his eyes. It made her feel a woman, a real woman, a feeling she had not experienced before. Oh, Wilf was fine, but she felt they were equals. With Ralph there was no doubt that he was superior. He would be the man in any partnership.

She had an appointment with him the next day and thought of it with some caution. He would make a grand friend but no more. And how the hell could they be friends? They were worlds apart.

They left Alf and Gertie alone for a few minutes before the train drew out of the station, walking away as they waved farewell. Somehow, Ada felt a bit down, almost as if she were saying goodbye to Alf for the last time.

"What's up love? No regretting asking him to come are you?" Wilf asked.

She shook her head. "No, it's not that. He's a grand lad and we'd not get any better anywhere. It's just a funny feeling I've got. Maybe it's all this talk of war or something."

Wilf laughed at this. "Don't believe all that rubbish. Come on, brighten up. War'll not happen in a hundred years."

She tried to laugh with him, but the feeling lingered at the pit of her stomach. As she turned for a final wave, she saw Alf lean forward and shyly kiss Gertie on the cheek. Well, Wilf seemed right about that. Maybe he would be right about the war as well. She hoped so.

They slowed down to wait for Gertie, who ran to catch them up.

"Alright love?" Ada asked.

"Yes, I'm fine. He's a nice lad, isn't he Ada?"

Ada put her arm around Gertie's shoulder and squeezed her

145

affectionately. "He is that love. And you both seem smitten with each other." "We'll be having wedding bells soon. We'd best get a move on Ada or they'll beat us," Wilf teased and Ada told him to shut up. He was making Gertie feel daft and shy.

But his words touched her. Maybe they should get on with it — get wed now and not wait for business to get going. They could do the house up a bit, decorate a room or two, and it would be fit to live in. Maybe that would make her feel better. She'd mention it to Wilf as they walked home and get a date settled on. That might stop all this daft romancing about Ralph Tinker.

When she broached the subject, Wilf was in full agreement. He, too, would feel better with a date in mind, something to work for and look forward to.

"That just rounds off this weekend grand, love. When shall we do it then?"

She thought for a moment and then said, "How about the middle of October? That would give us a good two months to get things ready."

"That suits me grand, love. Oh it will be great. Just think on it — me and you wed and in our own home after all these years. I can hardly wait."

He held her close, but she eased herself away from him. "Nothing wrong is there, love? You aren't having second thoughts?"

She tried to smile. "No, of course I'm not. I just don't want things to get out of hand — you're a bit of a spark if I let you loose." She leaned her head on his shoulder feeling sad that she had rebuffed him. Surprisingly tears came and she could not control the sniff to hold them back.

"Come on love, what is it? Tell me, we can't have secrets now you know." He felt disturbed. This wasn't like Ada.

"Oh I expect it's wedding nerves now we've set the date. Lasses do get them you know. I'm maybe a bit scared of all the planning and that."

Wilf thought it best not to reply. The 'and that' gave him an idea of what she meant. Ada was a little scared of the bed part of married life.

They went into her parents and told them of their plans. Thom let out a yell of delight. "About bloody time and all. I thought you two were going to be past it before you got wed."

Esther shushed him, but they had to laugh at his bluntness.

Polly was just as pleased, but a little sad at the thought of Wilf leaving hime.

"I'll want you to give us a hand with the house and that, Polly. Mam hasn't time to help much and I shall need you."

Good old Ada, thought Wilf. She knew just how to make things right.

"Who are you having for best man, Wilf?" Gertie asked and he grinned at her.

146

"Now I wonder — Harry — one of Ada's brothers. I don't know, do you Ada?"

"You daft ha'porth, you're having Alf and you're to be my bridesmaid, Gertie. I can't ask any of our lot or I'd cause trouble. I'll have just you and that's settled."

Gertie was so excited she did a little dance on the hearthrug. A bridesmaid — and Alf best man — that was something to really look forward to.

"But I expect you'll be seeing him before that, won't you lass?" Wilf asked.

"He says he's going to write and he wants me to go up there and meet his family in about two weeks."

"You were right lad — they'll be wed afore us if we don't watch it," Ada laughed.

But Wilf was frowning. "You're not going up there. They're too rough and ready for you. You're too young to be going up there on your own."

The three women stared at the vehemence of his words.

"I shall do as I like, our Wilf, and you'll not stop me." Gertie opened the door and stamped her way upstairs.

"Well, that told you my lad. Our Gertie's growing up. Anyway, why can't she go up there. Alf will see to her."

There was nothing he could say. He couldn't very well tell them that he didn't want her mixing with Beatty. The chances are she would have to share a bed with her and who knows what might come to light? He just grunted and then suggested he walk Ada home.

She seemed to lose some of her gloom and starting planning her dress and Gertie's. "I shan't wear white or owt daft like that — beige or cream or pink, something like that."

If anybody had the right to wear white then it was Ada. She allowed herself a moment of daydream, seeing this tiny figure floating down the aisle in white and trailing a frothy white veil behind her. The man stood at the altar was dressed in a morning suit, like George had been. He was tall, dark — my God, she'd better stop. It was Wilf who would be at the altar — not Ralph, the man who had figured in her imagination. It wasn't as if she loved him, she didn't really fancy him all that much. It could be his position that held a little more appeal. Fancy, a solicitor's wife?

"You're miles away Ada. Are you planning your outfit?"

"Yes, and I'm not telling you about it. Groom shouldn't know until the day when he sees his bride. You see as you get yourself a new suit though — and one for Wilf. Get navy blue and don't wear a bloody cap."

That was a mark of the working class — a cap perched on the side of the head. She didn't want that, not with George and Isabella being guests. Wilf asked if she was planning a big do.

"Not all that big, but we'll have to have families, and with our lot, that's enough. Mam'll see to wedding breakfast."

As far as she was concerned, that was that. No good dreaming about white dresses and dark blokes — she was marrying Wilf — in a serviceable dress that could be useful afterwards.

Wilf put her funniness down to nerves. Women were funny creatures and none more so than Ada when she got a mood on. Still, they'd soon be wed and settled down and she would be fine then. He thought of her busy in the kitchen — the house all shining and bright — perhaps two bairns. Ada somehow didn't fit into that picture with bairns. She wasn't the motherly type at all. And if she kept on working, she'd not have much time for the house either. It wasn't a bit like he'd thought it would be. Still, they were better breached than most young couples and that was something to be thankful for.

The nagging feeling stayed with Ada throughout the night and instead of her usual sound sleep she tossed and turned, waking much earlier than usual and going downstairs as she heard her Dad raking out the fire.

"By hek lass, you're on it this morning. What's up then — getting nervous about wedding?" He smiled at her, teasing gently, but sensing that something was amiss.

"Might be Dad. I've to see Tinker again this dinner time and sign the lease. Could be a bit of nerves now that it's time to make things legal like."

Thom nodded, but thought it odd that Ada should be scared of signing a bit of paper. He'd have thought Wilf would have been like that, but not her. She was usually so self-assured. He made a pot of tea, took a cup up to Esther and then sat down facing Ada across the table.

She played around with the spoon on her saucer and then looked up at him. "Dad — ?" She paused for a long moment until he prompted her.

"Yes, hunny?"

"Is there going to be a war do you reckon?"

So that was it. Some silly bugger had been spreading all that rubbish again.

"Not if Uncle David has owt to do with it. We don't want war and I know he'll do all he can to stop it." He spoke of his idol, Lloyd George.

"They were on about it at our Isabella's. Said it looked a certainty. What would happen if there was a war, Dad?"

"Not a lot, lass. They'd ask for volunteers like they did for the last one and we'd send them off with army bands and that. But I can't see it making all that much difference to us."

"They said Wilf and the Territorials would have to go."

Thom grunted. "Well, I always did say it was a daft idea that, signing on in Territorials. I don't reckon they can make anybody go though if they've not a mind to."

But George had said they had to go. And that meant young Stanley as well. It would break her Dad's heart if he had to go.

Work passed the morning quickly. Visitors to the town meant that they were busy. Linen sheets, table cloths, pillow cases — there were thousands of them. Ada watched as they were being sorted and it reminded her of the hymn they sang at school, 'From Greenland's icy mountains.' The piles of linen with their folds jutting out here and there looked like peaked mountains — snow-capped and with the sun streaming through the thick panes of glass making patterns of shade and light.

"What the hell is up with you?" Lily Hartley asked the question bluntly.

"Nowt. I've got a lot on my mind, that's all. Come on, get on with it or we'll be here till Bank Holiday Monday."

It was only fourteen days away from the holiday weekend. For the laundry it meant extra work from the cafés and boarding houses, but they did manage to get the Monday off. If all went well, Ada planned to get Polly and Gertie to help her start scrubbing the house out. All being well, the signing would be done with, and as Wilf would be at the annual camp it would give her something to pass away the time.

She made up her mind to see that he resigned once this camp was over. They'd have enough to do with the wedding and things. The Territorials would manage. War or no war, she needed him more than they did.

The buzzer sounded and she took off her white coat and hung it on the peg at the side of her table in the little office. This was it — she was going down to sign on the dotted line. Wilf wasn't able to get time off and it was arranged for her to take the papers to him to sign that night, providing they got a witness of some standing. Maybe they'd go up and ask George to do it. His signature ought to be good enough for anybody.

Whenever she had gone down to Tinker's office before she had called home and got changed into what she called 'something decent.' Today, she decided not to bother. What the hell did it matter anyhow? What she looked like had nowt to do with the business in hand.

"Shan't be long Mam." She waved across the pavement to Esther who, as usual, was waiting for her family to turn the corner of the street and she could run in and get the dinner on the table. It was almost a ritual. They never came in from work to an empty table.

Esther shouted not to be too long. "I don't want that good food wasting."

Good old Mam — she wasn't a bit impressed about the prospect of her daughter going into business. In fact, she'd much rather have seen her wed and with a family. But Ada wasn't the family type.

"I'm sure she ought to have been a lad," she would often say to Thom, who would tell her to let Ada be — she knew what she was about.   But

149

the only thing a lass should be about, as far as Esther was concerned, was looking after a husband and a family — there was nothing in all the world better than that. But lasses were different now. All these new-fangled ideas — votes for women, women working — it was all my eye and pocket holes. Thank God, at least her lasses didn't bother about votes for women. Thom's interest in local politics had not rubbed off on any of the children — boys nor girls. Maybe with listening to him spouting on they'd had enough of it.

As she drew nearer Tinker's office, Ada's steps quickened. It was as if she wanted to get there and get the meeting over with. It wasn't nerves or anything to do with seeing Ralph again. She just wanted things settled and done with. It might put an end to her funny feeling.

The secretary — a man — showed her straight into Ralph's office. He stood behind the large leather-topped desk as she entered and held out his hand.

"How nice to see you again, Miss Skipton," he addressed her formally and she was a little taken aback. Perhaps it was because this was a business meeting.

The clerk brought in a folder and placed it on the desk in front of Ralph who waited until the door had closed behind him before unfastening the red ties that held the papers together.

"I have drawn up the lease with your interest — and Mr. Tanner's — in mind. Shall I read it over to you?" he asked.

She shook her head. "I'll take it as read, thank you. We can look through it tonight when Wilf signs. I don't think you'd do anything to cause me bother." She looked at him and smiled.

Ralph wondered at her last remark. Could she guess how he felt, how she disturbed him, this bit of a slip of a laundry girl? Even though he could see she had come straight from work, she looked neat and tidy. She wore a neat grey jacket over her skirt and blouse, and the black sided buttoned boots were clean and shining. Her hair, in once again its usual braids, was plaited around her ears, but no amount of pulling and tightening could stem the waves that curved onto her cheeks from the centre parting.

He walked around the desk and placed a legal document before her, offering a quill pen from the gilt inkstand as he did so.

"You sign here, Ada, where I have put the pencilled crosses."

She took the pen and wrote her name with a swift neatness, ending each one with a flourishing curve.

"I shall witness them," and he signed his name underneath hers.

He stood towering above her, trying to resist the temptation to place his hand upon her shoulder. He could see that something was disturbing her and hoped it was nothing that he had said or done.

"Are you alright Ada?"

150

She nodded and made to stand up and take her leave.

"Might I say something Ada, before you leave?"

Again she nodded. "Aye, spit it out lad. No good keeping things back."

He laughed quietly. "I just want you to know that if you ever need any help or advice, or someone to talk things over with, then I hope you will come to me. I hope you will consider me as your friend." How he wished it could have been more.

"That's most kind of you — er — Ralph. Yes I would like to think of you as my friend."

"I mean it Ada. I'm not just saying this because of our professional association or our meeting over the weekend."

"I know you do lad and I mean it and all." Her face lit up in a smile.

Somehow, the words comforted her greatly, though what she had to worry about God alone knew. But it was good to feel someone of Ralph's standing was there in the background should things go wrong. It made her feel safe and protected.

Her smile warmed him and without thinking he put out his hand and touched her face. "I would like to think we could have been more than friends, but I know that is impossible. But I am here Ada if you ever need me."

She didn't back away from him as she would have expected. His touch was not creepy or sinister. It was sincerity itself and a calming sensation swept over her.

"You must come and visit when we get things settled — if you'd like to that is."

"Yes," he said. "I would like that very much."

It might be upsetting to see her with another man, but the thought of not seeing her again rode over that feeling.

"I shall need the papers back tomorrow."

"But I've done now haven't I? Property's ours now isn't it?"

"Of course it is. As far as the legal side is concerned you have the lease for the next ninety-nine years."

There — it was done now — no going back or changing their minds.

"Well, I'll be off then. See you tomorrow. I must get on or I'll miss my dinner." She held out her hand and he took it between both of his and held it for a moment.

"Goodbye then, Ada."

"Not goodbye lad — cheerio — and thank you."

He held open the door and as she left he went to the window that overlooked the main street and watched as she walked by, listening to the clip clop of her tread which echoed lingeringly long after she was out of sight.

She started to run, thinking she would be too late to have her dinner before going back to work. The Town Hall struck a quarter-past the hour and she was surprised to see that the whole thing had taken only ten minutes. It had seemed much longer. But still she ran on — up the old street, past the school where she and Wilf had gone as children, over the railway crossing — running, running as if the devil were at her heels, until she stopped, breathless, outside Kidd's arcade of shops.

She went across and looked at the furniture. They'd have to start thinking about all that kind of thing now. She looked at the double bed and thought of sharing it with Wilf for the rest of her life. She giggled as she thought of them huddled up together in the great expanse of mattress. It would drown them both.

But first things first. They had to get on with arranging the wedding. Before they shared a bed or owt else, she'd have to become Mrs. Tanner. Mrs. Wilf Tanner — her knees trembled at the thought of sharing all her life with Wilf — all her life, day in and day out. Sobered, she walked home, wondering what lay before them. Would the business succeed? Would they be happy? Well, they'd have years to find out — about fifty if Mam and Dad were owt to go by.

She felt physically sick, her stomach dropped again. "Come on lass," she said silently to herself, "What's bothering you?" She wanted to wed Wilf — she wanted the house and the business — they would be comfortably off. What the hell was there to worry about?

CHAPTER 17

All that week Ada busied herself with getting the house organised and arranging the wedding. It was to be a quiet affair not only because they needed every penny, but also because both of them wanted it that way.

"Let's face it Wilf, I'm not exactly cut out for long white dresses and trains am I?"

They laughed together in perfect honesty at the thought. No, a long flowing dress would have drowned her. She decided to wear pink — pink corded silk with cream accessories. That would be fine. Gertie would be in blue to set off the theme and she too would wear cream accessories.

"Are you having flowers — a bouquet or anything, Ada?" Mrs. Price, the laundry manageress, asked.

Ada hadn't thought about that and she raised her eyebrows saying flowers were a waste of good brass.

"Let me buy them for you and Gertie. It would be a token of how much I appreciate you."

Ada smiled and nodded in agreement. They discussed the colour scheme and decided on pink carnations for Gertie and cream roses for Ada.

It was nice of her, Ada thought. They didn't always hit it off because Ada would stand up for lass's rights — that much she had learned from her Dad — but, all in all, they worked well together. Mrs. Price envied Ada's ability to get on with the girls, to make them work well and efficiently and yet remain friends. It was a difficult position which she had handled well. She knew of the business plans and was thankful that Ada would need to work for a year or two before becoming a full-time housewife. That was of course if a family didn't come along. Somehow she thought Ada would take control of that, as she did most aspects of her life. In fact she doubted very much if there would be any family — Ada didn't fit the image at all.

They had proudly taken the lease up to Sewerby for George to sign and had been a bit hurt by his off-handed attitude. At least Ada had — Wilf seemed not only to accept it, but to expect it.

George was a funny bloke and no mistake. One minute he could be as right as rain and then he would be as pig-mannered and off-handed the next. Although he didn't like to think so, Wilf was beginning to realise that Tutt Bradley was right about his future brother-in-law.

"Your being in business must not give you ideas, Wilf," George had said upon signing, after carefully reading every bit of the document. Tinker had done a good deal on the lease and it was very favourable.

"What do you mean, 'ideas'?" Ada asked the question sharply.

"I think Wilf understands what I mean," George sidetracked, not

153

wanting a confrontation with Ada. She was far too sharp to tackle.

"It's alright love, I know what he's on about. And he's right and all." Wilf knew that George did not want him to think above himself and that they were in any way equals. Wilf was still only a ranker in the Territorials and George wasn't having any embarrassment in that area.

"Ralph Tinker is joining us Wilf. He was enrolled this morning and is joining us on Thursday night. He has an automatic commission of course, with his standing." George emphasised the words and looked at Ada, who shrugged her shoulders and murmured, "And he'll be a good one and all."

Wilf saw the look on her face and began to realise what George had been up to. The sly devil was trying to get Ada away from him. Well, it was too bloody late now. As they walked home he suggested bringing the wedding date forward.

"Let's have a September wedding lass. It's not all that much sooner, we can manage it if we try."

Dear Wilf — he wasn't as daft as they thought. Happily she agreed and felt the weight lift from her shoulders now that things were getting settled.

"Right you are lad — last weekend in September, that's when we'll get wed." They sighed happily. Ada stopped herself adding that they would also be in business by then. Wilf was so happy it would be cruel to bring business into it.

He was to leave his work at the end of August and start on his own the Monday after. Ada was finding out Wilf was no fool and he had secured a good contract from Kidd's furnishers that would last him well over a year. He would be able to pay Alf's wages and keep Ada as well. She insisted they ploughed the money back.

"I earn enough to keep us. You think on the business and make a good · job of it."

He would, oh he would. He would work his fingers to the bone for Ada.

Polly had suggested that Alf move in with her when Wilf left, but seeing that he and Gertie were interested in one another, Ada had said it would be best to get him lodgings up the High Street.

"Lily Hartley's Mam will be glad of the extra brass and she keeps a good house and table," she said.

It wouldn't be good to put temptation in the way of the youngsters, not if they were serious about one another. Polly reminded her that she too could do with the extra brass, but Ada said not to worry, she and Wilf would see Polly was alright.

"You're a good lass Ada. I know I keep saying that, but I feel I've wronged you for that long I want to make it up to you."

Polly was close to tears. The lass had never mentioned Harry's birth since that day when she had confessed all to them. In fact it had seemed to draw them closer together. Wilf was a little more reserved and she wished

154

she could turn the clock back a few years and give him the love and attention she had showered on Harry.

These days he was more sly and secretive than ever. God only knew where he got his money from. He gave Polly very little and only when pressed, but he always had enough to go for a drink or out with his mates. Maybe it was best she didn't know where it came from, but it certainly wasn't from working.

She would miss Wilf, though he had never spent all that much time at home, and she couldn't blame him for that. Still, no good dwelling on things past. The future looked good for him and Ada now, and maybe young Gertie and that Alf Aylward and all.

Wilf had to attend the Territorials on two nights of the last week in July ready for the annual camp at the August Bank Holiday. Ada was glad for it meant that she could get the wedding breakfast and that planned with Mam. Peggy Shipley had said she would make hers and Gertie's dresses. That would mean another night for choosing the pattern and cutting out to fit. It was as well just now that he would be otherwise occupied.

When they mustered at the Drill Hall, Tutt signalled to Wilf to go to one side, obviously wanting to tell him something either of importance or great interest.

"Slip in here, lad." He led the way to his small office at the back of the building. "We've got something on Wilf — something big," he said.

Wilf asked what it was, thinking that some big brass hat was going to visit the camp.

"The Major is going to announce that the camp is to be for a full week. It's all over wind up they've got about Kaiser Bill starting a war. I reckon there's more to it than we realise."

"Oh hell, I could have done with that time at home, Tutt. There's not a chance of me getting off it is there?"

Tutt shook his head firmly. "Not a cat in hell's lad. This is something too important for any of us to be let off. That young solicitor, Tinker, signed on and he's here tonight already in the uniform of a first lieutenant. He's coming on camp and all. If they're rushing things like that it must be something big."

"If there's a war Tutt, do we have to go or do we volunteer?"

"You go lad, that's what you joined the Terriers for. If the Kaiser starts anything we'll be some of the first in."

"We'll leave home, you mean?"

God, what did he think he had been doing in the Territorials — playing games? "If war starts Wilf, you'll become a soldier and go wherever you're sent. I only hope to God they all remember what I've tried to teach them. I don't fancy a shindig with the Major in charge."

155

"Kaiser won't start owt with us mate. He's King's cousin. It's just a family quarrel. It'll all blow over."

The simplicity of Wilf's attitude irritated Tutt. If they were all like that, what chance would they have if war was declared? He hoped the coming week at camp would get them in a fighting frame of mind.

They mustered into ranks and Tutt noticed how quickly Tinker caught on. He must have been having a bit of private coaching. He handled himself well, was smartly turned out and looked promising. The uniform suited Ralph and he gave the impression of being quietly in charge of himself.

George marched smartly into their midst and ordered the men to stand easy. "I have an announcement to make. As you all know, we are due to go on our annual camp on Friday night until Tuesday — a long weekend. However, due to certain hostilities from our German cousins, the powers that be have decided we are to spend a full week at camp. We shall study modern warfare and act as if we are at war. You must make all necessary arrangements with your employers and if you need confirmation, I or one of the other officers will send a formal letter. There are no exemptions. That is all — carry on, Sergeant Major."

As he finished, the men began to gasp and grumble. Like Wilf, none of them entertained the thought of war. It was daft talk and they didn't take too kindly to having a week at camp. A few days were fine and got you away for a bit, but a week — that would take some explaining to the women folk, who were convinced that the Territorials were just an excuse for a binge.

They began to grumble amongst themselves and George tried to pull them to order with very little effect. He grew red in the face and was clearly embarrassed when no-one took any notice of him. "Sergeant Major, call the men to order. Do your job, man," he barked at Tutt and, turning quickly, left the hall.

"Aaaaaatention." Tutt's voice roared over their heads and immediately they drew themselves up and obeyed the command.

"It's no good you all bawling your heads off now. You joined the Terriers to meet an emergency if needed. That time looks like coming, so just pull yourselves together and get on with it — and I might as well tell you all now, I'm not having any slackers or moaners in my lot. You'll bloody well do what you joined to do and there'll be no buggering about."

His voice held the ring of authority and the men divided into their various companies to study and drill. Rifle drill was of paramount importance and after the momentary lapse, he was proud of the way the men reacted.

He watched Wilf's small figure crawling along the floor — watched as he aimed at the makeshift target and made a direct hit. Young Stanley

Skipton copied his every move and was just as accurate. Tutt marked Wilf for further promotion if trouble brewed up, and Stanley for a stripe.

Mr. Tinker joined them and it was obvious that he knew how to use a gun. He had been on shoots since a lad and though these military guns were somewhat different, he soon got the hang of it. With a bit of polishing up he would make a hell of an officer. Even the rough and readys pulled themselves together, shaped up better than Tutt would have imagined. Well, they did say it took a bit of trouble to bring out the best in a bloke. They'd be alright if needed.

Ada took the news of the week at camp grudgingly. It had become clear that there was no way of getting out of it, but as far as she was concerned, it was a waste of time.

"Ruddy war — who would be barmy enough to start a ruddy war?" she grumbled, as did all the women folk.

Wilf called on his way to muster at the Drill Hall before leaving for Beverley and found young Stanley waiting at his Granny's for him.

"Can we go down together, Wilf?" he asked shyly.

"Lance Corporal, when we're in uniform, lad."

Ada stared. Good God — he sounded like George. Whatever happened to blokes when they put on a uniform? Power went to their heads.

He kissed her fondly and told her not to worry, the week would soon pass. "And don't listen to the rumours, it'll not come to owt," he assured her.

She and Esther watched as the two men marched smartly down the street and felt a little tinge of pride.

"Kaiser won't tackle us with lads like that," Esther said.

It was a blazing hot weekend, and the work at the laundry piled up so much that Ada decided to work on the Saturday. She could scrub out on Monday and then have the rest of the week's nights to see to the other things.

The family gathered around the table for Sunday dinner and Esther had to rouse Thom from his favourite Sunday paper, "*The News of the World.*"

"Do you know, Esther, I reckon there will be a ruddy war if this bugger Kaiser doesn't pull his horns in," he stated after carefully reading all the editorials.

They laughed, and told him not to be daft.

"You just wait and see then," he warned, feeling troubled at what he had read, adding darkly, "It'll be a blood bath if it does start."

It was such a lovely day that Ada went up and called for Gertie and Polly and they went for a long walk along the sea front, taking note of the latest fashions and hair styles that the visitors wore. They had afternoon tea at Oberon's cafe and then sauntered leisurely home.

157

Early on Monday morning the three of them were up at Scarborough Road, buckets, mops, scrubbing brushes and Sunlight soap at the ready for a good clean out.

"By gum lass, this place will be a palace when it's all done." Polly looked proudly at their handiwork. It needed decorating, but the floors, paintwork and windows gleamed and shone in the bright sunshine of early evening.

Ada stood staring into the yard. It looked desolate.

"Owt up lass?" Polly asked.

Ada shrugged her shoulders. "I've got wedding nerves Polly. Me — after all these years. I'll be better when Wilf gets back from that ruddy camp."

They took off their pinnies, wiped themselves down and made to go down to Esther's for tea.

"Ada — will Alf be at that camp with Wilf?" Gertie asked.

Ada told her that she expected so.

"It sounded as if it were going to be a big do and I reckon most of them will be there."

Gertie smiled in the assurance that her lad would be with Wilf. He would look after Alf for her.

When the had arrived at Beverley, Alf had been waiting for Wilf's battalion to arrive. He had explained to his superior officers that very soon he would be living and working in Brid and they had arranged an immediate transfer. Wilf was delighted, and so was Tutt Bradley, who could see that Alf had the makings of a good soldier.

"Get in line then lad. Just because you know the Lance Corporal doesn't give you any privileges," he shouted, but they saw he was only joking.

Alf fell in line in the last rank and found himself beside young Stanley. Tutt noticed and could not resist saying it was more like a bloody family outing than a battalion. But it seemed right — they were a good set of lads and, being in one family so to speak, would pull well together. They pitched tents, drew rations and then bedded down for the night. Lights out echoed across the row after row of tents and the men listened in silence.

"Lights out always gives me the creeps," Alf laughed to cover his feelings.

"They do me and all lad, but not half as much as reveille." Wilf sighed, turned over and fell into a deep sleep

On Tuesday morning Ada had to rouse herself when she heard her Mam calling up the stairs. God, she had slept well. She felt ten times better this morning.

"I'm glad you seem in a better frame of mind my lass," Esther told her as she left for work.

"It were nerves, I told you that. Tar-ra Mam, see you at dinner." And laughing and waving she set off to catch up with the other streams of lasses who were making their way towards the laundry.

They worked steadily through the morning, singing, laughing and joking with each other.

Just after eleven o'clock, Mrs. Price called Ada into her office. "I am going to make an announcement Ada, but I thought it better to tell you first," she spoke softly.

"What's up Missus — has war been declared?" Ada asked.

Mrs. Price heaved a great sigh and said, "Yes, I'm afraid it has Ada. I've just been given the news that we have officially declared war on Germany."

Ada was stunned. She must be joking. But she could see from her serious face and tone that she wasn't.

"Tell the girls to stop the machines."

Automatically Ada did as she was bid, too stunned to say a word.

The girls gathered outside in the sunshine and were told simply, in plain words, what had happened.

There was not a sound, not a whisper nor a sigh. Silence hung all around and it was if the whole town had stopped breathing. They stood looking at Mrs. Price, unable to take in what she had said.

"God help us now and God save the King," her voice rang out, as clear as a bell.

Someone struck up the national anthem and soon they were all singing in strong voices. But not Ada, she was far too stunned and angry to sing praises to the King.

"Bugger him. He'll be alright. It's us lot that will suffer."

CHAPTER 18

At dinner time the talk was all about the war.

"I told you — I told you, didn't I — and you wouldn't listen to me," Thom thundered.

"What'll happen now?" Ada asked, wishing that Wilf was here to put her mind at ease.

"Aye, I don't know lass, but I'll tell you what, this afternoon I'll nip over to our Isabella's. She'll maybe know something, being an officer's wife."

Esther smiled across at Thom — he would sort it all out for them.

Ada was thankful that at least somebody was trying to do something to find out what was likely to happen next. It all seemed so muddled. Typical of the bloody government to let this happen now.

"I'll be a bit late home for tea, Mam. I'm going to pop up to the house and see that it's all dried out nicely."

Esther nodded, knowing the feeling of a young bride wanting to get set up in her own home.

"If I can do owt, hunny, let me know," she called after her disappearing back as Ada returned to work.

The laundry was alive with rumours — the Germans were going to land at Hunmanby Gap or Danes Dyke, and somebody had seen them sailing past Flamborough lighthouse.

"Don't talk so bloody daft," Ada told them, and for a while they were silent.

But it was all so exciting. A war meant something different was happening and it stirred patriotic feelings. Ada had to admit that she felt a bit of pride when they all began to talk about the Brid lads away at camp. "They'll soon see the Kaiser off," was the general feeling.

"Ted Chasey says they'll send them straight off to France without bringing them home." Bessie Tumm was quoting the postman.

"Nay, never — Charlie Clarkson told my Mam that they'll all get leave first."

Charlie was the cobbler and he heard all the news. What he didn't hear he also made up as most of them knew, but every bit of information added to the spice of the moment.

Ada hoped they would come home first if they really were going off to foreign parts. If they had time, they could get wed. They could even get a special licence if necessary. She cheered up a bit at the thought.

She decided to go straight home after all and see if Dad had got any news from Isabella. Her face lit up expectantly as she went into the house.

"It's alright lass, our Isabella has heard that they're going to bring them home first. After that, anything could happen. But they'll be home afore the weekend."

Relief swept through her. They could get something settled then. She knew Thom and Esther were glad too — glad for her and also glad they would see young Stanley.

After tea she went up to see Polly.

"I'm glad to see you, lass. I've been right bothered about all this lot."

Gertie had tried to tell her what had been going on, but like all mothers she hadn't taken all that much notice of her bairn.

"Well, they're coming home — that's official from our Isabella. You'll see Alf by the weekend, Gert — that's if he comes here instead of going back to Barnsley."

Gertie smiled thankfully. Sometimes being related to gentry had its points. Gave you a bit of an edge on others. Somehow she knew that Alf would make his way to Brid.

"I wish our Wilf had never . . ." Polly bit on the words, remembering that it was Ada who had encouraged him to join the Territorials.

"Aye, and so do I, love," Ada spoke ruefully. But how could she have known this would happen. It seemed a good idea at the time. Sort of keeping in step with Isabella.

The girls worked steadily through the next morning feeling, if anything, an anti-climax after all the rousing patriotism. It was if they had expected the war to start there and then, to hear the gunfire and to see soldiers charging about in the streets.

She was lost in daydreams of the house when Peggy Arter tapped her on the shoulder. "The lads are coming home tonight — it's right enough — Fred Jameson popped his head round to let us know."

Ada heaved a sigh of relief, looked across at the clock and saw the hands pointing to eleven.

"Are you coming down with us to the Drill Hall at dinner time to see if we can find out more?"

Ada realised Peg was thinking about her Charlie. It was funny, but you thought at times like this you were the only one with worries.

She nodded and went off to the sorting room to tell Gertie.

At twelve the buzzers screamed through the laundry and in an instant the machines stopped dead. The silence was eerie. Within seconds some fifty girls gathered at the gates to make their way down to the Drill Hall. Ada and Gertie walked behind them and as they passed Esther's door she called out to tell her what was happening.

"Don't be over long, lass, or it'll be wasted." She looked at her daughter and Gertie. They were nowt but bairns. It bothered her to see Ada so worried. Oh, the war would be over in no time. They all said so, but Esther had begun to absorb some of her daughter's concern. Ada was always one for thinking things out. She wasn't easily swayed by others and she'd not

161

joined in any of the shouting or cheering. It was if she knew different.

Outside the Drill Hall there were crowds gathered, mostly women, who were now desperately waiting for news of their menfolk. They chatted loudly and it sounded to Ada like a flock of angry seagulls hovering above a storm. She and Gertie stood silently on the edge of the crowd, leaning up the wall.

"They're here already. I just saw our Jack's face at the window."

They all turned and saw faces peering at them — they were back.

"Psst — psst."

Ada turned her head and saw Wilf looking through the double iron gates. Quickly she and Gertie went across to him.

"What's happening, love? They said you weren't coming back until tonight. Will you be home soon then?"

"Big-wigs are talking it over now, but I don't reckon it will be long before we hear something. Hang on if you like."

He smiled at Gertie. "Your Alf's here and all. He transferred when we were at camp. Look across yonder."

Gertie looked and her face broke into a beam as she saw Alf waving to her from the doorway.

Wilf had to go and once again the two were left standing with the other women. Now there was no sound — the talking and chattering had stopped and each stood waiting in silence.

Memories began to flood through Ada's mind — how many times had they walked past here on the way to school or some other adventure? She thought of his golden cropped hair, of his first suit. How they had shared their goodies, and racing each other to the beck to see who could spit furthest over the bridge. They had shared almost everything. The only thing she had not been able to share with Wilf was Ralph Tinker and really there was nothing there to share. A glimpse of feeling, hope from another man, was nowt to share with Wilf. That was a secret to be locked away and brought out in romantic moments.

"If they don't get a move on we'll be late back for work," Gertie said but no-one showed any inclination to move. Laundry could wait.

Ada saw an officer come out of the big iron studded doors and jumped as she recognised Ralph. It hadn't taken them long to make him an officer and get him in uniform. He was followed by George and Tutt Bradley.

The crowd broke into loud murmurings. "Ladies, ladies," he called out. "Please calm down and listen." His voice was strong and clear and the authority silenced the noise.

"The men have been given twelve hours leave from six o'clock tonight until six o'clock tomorrow morning. Twelve hours mind you. They will be in your trust and I know we can rely on you all to see that they report back here at six sharp tomorrow morning."

"Oh hell, that's not very long. My Dad makes me come in by nine. We shan't have long together at all," Pansy Wilkinson started to grumble.

"Well it's better than nowt. Come on Gertie, let's get off. I expect Alf will be coming to you. He won't have time to get home to Barnsley."

She started to walk away and Gertie followed. The crowd dispersed, each one going their own way to prepare for the short time they would have with their menfolk. For some, it would be the last meeting.

The afternoon dragged by, hour by slow hour. Every five minutes one of the girls would turn and look up at the clock and seeing the hands move so slowly would sigh deeply.

At last it was time to go home and never before had the place emptied so quickly. In less than five minutes there was not a sight nor sound of any of the girls.

Ada and Gertie literally ran home and fifteen minutes after she got home Gertie was knocking on the door.

"I didn't bother with any tea. I thought it best to get straight down there."

Ada was ready and waiting and Esther had to swallow hard to stop the tears as she saw how both lasses had got themselves smartly dressed in their best suits.

"You look a right pair of bobby dazzlers, I must say," she said and, bending forward, kissed Ada. "Take care now and don't be too late. Bring the lads back here if you've a mind to," she said.

She had to laugh when Thom called after them, "Keep yourselves decent." As if they wouldn't.

Well before six they were waiting with many of their friends and workmates outside the Drill Hall. Ada looked round and saw that most of them had made the effort and dressed up in their best. Not many of them bothered during the week, but this was a special occasion. The odd one or two, mainly married women with bairns, had come down in their pinnies with just a shawl thrown over the shoulders. Annie Boden and Sal Whittaker, both with big families, were still wearing their black scrubbing pinnies. Poor devils, she thought, what chance did they have to get dressed up for their blokes? Well, thank God she and Wilf were not going to turn out like that.

"If they are going off tomorrow I shall have a hell of a night with our Jack. More than like I shall be expecting again," Sal chuntered.

The remark made Ada tingle. If they got wed soon she would be thinking of the nights with Wilf. But she wouldn't be expecting, not if she had owt to do with it.

Finally the doors opened and the men surged forward in a great wave.

"Hold on there you randy buggers. Don't disgrace the King's uniform by rushing in a rabble. It's all waiting for you and make the most of it. You

163

might not get another chance for a long time," Tutt Bradley laughed.

They stopped dead in their tracks and, after pausing, hesitantly walked more smartly over to the waiting women.

Wilf and Alf were two of the last to come out and when he reached Ada he took her hand and tucked it beneath his elbow and gave it a squeeze. She held tightly on to his arm. Alf blushed and then smiled at Gertie, who, thinking on the sergeant's words, made no more to-do and took his arm.

"What shall we do then?" Wilf asked, hoping that Alf and Gertie would want to be on their own. He didn't want to share these last moments with anyone but Ada.

Again Gertie made the move and said in a firm voice that she'd thought of going up round the cemetery road and on to Flamborough.

"You do that then. Me and Ada'll go up round cliffs, eh love?"

She nodded her assent.

They walked in silence until they reached the sea front. The sun was setting and it sent a red glow above the white topped waves. There was so much to say, so many plans to make, but the words wouldn't come.

Finally Wilf broke the silence. "It's a right do is this, lass. We've only got these few hours and don't really know what to do with them for the best. I'll bet tomorrow night we'll be thinking of all we should or could have said and done, shan't we?"

"You'll have to spend some time with your Mam." What on earth made her say that? She wanted Wilf to stay every moment with her. She wanted to tell him of her idea about getting wed as soon as possible. She wanted to tell him she loved him, that she couldn't bear the thought of him not being there. The words would not come.

"Oh, I'll sleep at home tonight. I want to be with you."

They walked on talking about silly things — the weather — the view of the laundry — anything but what they wanted to say. On and on they walked until they came to the cliff top.

"Let's stop a bit — sit down and look over the bay. Mind you don't mark your suit," Wilf said.

"Oh, sod my suit." She sat down beside him.

Wilf shaded his eyes from the reflection of the sun. "I'm going to miss this," he spoke softly.

"And what about me?" She spoke sharply, beginning to feel disappointed and let down.

He placed both hands on her shoulders. "Little 'un, I'll miss you most of all, you know that. I can't tell you how I feel lass — how much I love you — I can't find the words. But the thought of leaving you is tearing my heart out."

And then the tears came. Totally out of character, Ada burst into tears and, laying her head on his shoulders, sobbed as if her heart would break.

164

"It's all gone so wrong, Alf — so wrong. And just when we were getting set up."

As best he could, he comforted her. "Tell you what — as soon as I come home again we'll get wed. It won't be more than a week or so. You get things arranged and we'll get wed and then you can take on the house and see that all's ready for when this lot is over and done with."

That was what she wanted to hear. She hugged him close and they kissed and embraced, not caring if anyone could see them.

"Do you reckon it will be over by Christmas?" she asked.

Wilf shook his head. "No I don't. The big-wigs can say what they like, but I reckon this lot will go on a hell of a lot longer than that." He told her of the rumours that had spread like wildfire through the camp — how the Jerries were supposed to have shot, bayoneted and burned old men, women and children in the Belgian town of Liege. They were even supposed to have raped nuns and young girls in the open streets.

"I reckon it's a lot of codswollop myself. No decent human being could do that. It's the top brass spreading things like that to get us riled up and ready for attack."

"If you ask me lad, I reckon the whole bloody thing is a set up. I reckon we are pawns being played by barmy glory-seeking fools."

He reckoned she had put it in a nutshell.

"Old George is feeling his feet a bit. He's got his mate, that Tinker solicitor, made an officer and he isn't half chucking his weight about." It was the first criticism he had openly made of her brother-in-law.

"Tinker's alright though, isn't he?" she asked.

Wilf nodded, repeating Tutt's words that he would be alright once he was knocked into shape.

"Tutt's a decent bloke, Ada. Do you know, just before we came out he shook my hand and sent his best regards to you. I reckon that was decent of him, don't you?"

Ada blushed, but said nothing, knowing the underlying message in the brief words.

"You'll keep your eye on Mam and Gert won't you?"

Again she nodded and turning away from him, leaned forward and wrapped her arms around her hunched knees.

"Wilf . . ," she paused for a long time, and then the words came out in a rush, "Shall we go up to the house?"

He stood up, stretched out his arms and pulled her to her feet. "Yes love, I'd like that — give us a bit of privacy."

They walked quickly round the top of the cliff, along Sewerby Road and then Scarborough Road. When they reached the house they stood and looked up at it. It was dusk and the light played games on the shining window panes.

165

"It's all ready, Wilf — ready and waiting for us." She delved into her pocket and pulled out the key, offering it to him.

"You open the door and see what we've been up to. Me and Gertie and your Mam scrubbed it from top to bottom."

He held her hand and with the other placed the key and slowly turned the lock.

"Race you upstairs," he cried and like two children they raced through the hall and up the staircase, reaching the front bedroom in a breathless haze.

Oh how they loved to be together — how they had loved to race and tumble when they were children. Nothing had changed, nothing would change, nothing could change what they had — not the Kaiser or his bloody war. She and Wilf were permanent fixtures.

For a time they stood, arms around each other, looking out of the window down onto the yard.

"I can feel it all happening. I can see you and Alf at work, busy as bees. I can see me working on the books, keeping house — with a daily woman too, I'll tell you — I can even smell the varnish." She spoke excitedly as if to assure herself that it would all happen.

Wilf held her closer. "I can smell you, little 'un. The only thing I can think of at this minute is leaving you. Oh Ada — I do love you."

They clung together and he began to run his hands over her body. She responded by pressing herself closer — so close that she could feel every part of him.

Blindly he kissed her — kissed her neck, her eyes and then her throat. She made no move to stop him, but answered his kisses with the same longing.

Oh, it would be easy to make love to her and he was very tempted, but with Ada it wouldn't be right. If the war had not been thrust upon them, she would never have allowed him to go this far. Roughly he pushed her away and she stared at him in disappointment.

"I thought you said you loved me?" Her voice trembled.

"I do lass — Oh God I do — but not this way. This is not for us, love. I love you too much to let owt like this happen." He sighed and taking her hands in his, he looked into her face. "Don't you see, lass, I want you like bloody hell, but not like this. We've got more than a quick shifty lark. You're going to be my wife."

He looked so intense in his sincerity, his face puckered and troubled as he spoke, hoping that he had found the right words to explain his feelings. Ada could be so funny at times and take things the wrong way, but she smiled and ruffled his hair.

"You're right, lad. Come on. Let's be getting off. It'll be a long day tomorrow."

166

Never had she spoken a truer word — tomorrow would be a long, long day.

Esther was waiting up for her and looked surprised to see that Wilf was not coming in.

"It's only right he should be with Polly. I'm going to see him off in morning," Ada explained.

The familiar warmth of the kitchen and her Mam's love almost made her cry. Oh God, why had they waited — why had she been so set on things being right before they wed?

Esther saw she was upset and putting her arms around her said, "Come on lass, get this supper down you and then get to bed. You'll need a good night's rest if you're to be up early in the morning. And don't fret. We'll see this through."

Ada hugged her Mam and took comfort in the warmth of her flesh. She'd often laughed at the smell of her Mam — carbolic soap and disinfected dusting powder, but it was a smell that always brought comfort and hope.

As she entered the bedroom she heard the regular breathing and snorting of her two sisters and thankfully they were asleep. She wouldn't have to talk and answer any questions. But it was many a long hour before sleep came to her. Her thoughts were tangled and she couldn't think why. Most of her friends had lads going away. It wasn't as if she were the only one. Maybe they were troubled too, at the thought of separation. Finally she fell into a fretful sleep and woke with a start to hear her Mam calling up the stairs.

"Come on our Ada, Wilf's here waiting for you."

Quickly she swilled her face and body down in cold water which Esther placed each night in the big jug, dressed in her working clothes and went downstairs. She'd thought of getting dressed up a bit, but what was the use of that? Best let things be as normal as possible and act as if they were just going off to camp.

Wilf was at the kitchen table with a cup of tea in one hand and a hot buttered bread cake in the other.

"By hell missus, I'm not half going to miss your cooking," he smiled at Esther.

"Was your Mam alright when you left?" What daft things you said at times like this. She honestly couldn't have cared less at that moment how Polly felt.

"She's a bit down like, and I said you would call in after work. Our Gertie is going down with Alf and we had tears from her this morning, but she'll be alright."

"Well, she'll have to be like the rest of us — lump it like cat's do dumplings."

167

Ada spoke sharper than she intended to and an uncomfortable silence hung in the room.

Esther started poking the fire and tidying the hearth. "I'll take some tea up to your Dad," she clumsily excused herself to give them a few moments of privacy.

"She's alright is your Mam," Wilf said.

"Yes." It was all Ada could say and they sat facing each other across the table, words dry in their throats with the unspoken emotion.

"I love you," he spoke softly and the words brought a smile to her face.

"Aye — I know you do lad — and I love you. I'll wait for you, Wilf Tanner, no matter what happens. I'll wait for you forever."

"I'll remember that, love, until the day I die." He smiled as he spoke, but the words struck an icy chill through her bones.

"Come on then lad, let's get you off to settle old Kaiser Bill. Soonest done soonest finished, and then we can get on with living our normal lives."

"Remember what I said Ada, I want to be wed on my next leave," he reminded her, but she needed no prompting. She was going to spend her time whilst he was away getting the wedding arranged and setting up the house. She flung her arms around him and they clung together, seeking desperately some assurance and consolation from their closeness.

"Look after yourself, little 'un," he whispered and kissed her tenderly.

Her Mam came back into the kitchen and they broke apart. Esther went to Wilf and taking his hand in hers, placed it gently against her cheek.

Ada tried not to cry but as she saw her Mam's tears falling she could not stem her own. She could feel her Mam's heart reaching out to them.

"God bless you son, look after yourself. I've got a little box of things packed for you to eat on the train. I've done enough for you and Alf and our little Stanley. Look out for him lad — he's nowt but a bairn." She picked up a brown paper parcel and gave it to him.

"You're a right good 'un, Mrs. Skipton, and don't you worry about your Stanley, I'll look out for him. Thanks missus." His voice disappeared into a whisper, but he smiled bravely.

Esther followed them to the door and watched until they were out of sight. They held hands tightly as they walked, not giving a damn about military law.

An almost deathly silence surrounded the Drill Hall in spite of the great crowd that thronged the street. The one sound was of whispered goodbyes, tender kisses and deep intakes of breath as tears were bravely stifled. The sound of horses' hooves made them turn and they saw the Sewerby open carriage turn down the street, parting the crowd and stopping outside the great doors. She saw Isabella and George — well at least she'd come down like the other wives to see her bloke off. Ada raised her hand to attract her sister's attention and thought better of it. It would embarrass her in front of all those officers.

She also saw Ralph walking through the door and as he did so he turned, looked into the crowd and saw Ada leaning against Wilf. Their gaze held for a long moment and then smartly he raised his hand in a salute and walked briskly into the hall.

"He's a bloody good officer is Tinker." Wilf had seen the look and the salute. He had half a mind to add, "A damn sight better than your Isabella's husband," but he thought better of it. This was not the time to start a family to-do.

The doors opened again and Tutt came out and called out, "Get yourselves in here my lads. Let's be having you."

There was no time for any lingering farewells. With a brief kiss on the cheek and, "I'll write as soon as I can," Wilf was gone.

She wondered whether to go on home, there was another hour or so before work, but the crowd didn't seem to be making any move to leave and so she waited. The chattering was stilled by the sound of marching feet and all the heads turned to see, coming out of the yard, the 5th Yorks — the cream of the Brid lads. Heads held high, they marched like seasoned troopers, full pack on their backs, down the street towards the station. You couldn't help feeling proud as they marched, strictly in step, led by George and the other officers including Ralph. In spite of her forebodings, her heart swelled with pride. The early morning sun peeped through and caught the dazzle of the shining cap badges — it was a grand sight.

"Come on my lads, let's leave with a song and a smile," Tutt yelled and as one man they whistled and sang 'My gel's a Yorkshire gel,' keeping in step to the tune.

Oh what a grand sight they looked. They'd soon settle the Kaiser. And then the singing and the footsteps faded and the women were once again stood, not knowing quite what to do.

"Well, this won't get owt done. I'm off to get on with my work."

Sensible woman, thought Ada, whoever she was. No good brooding. It was far better to keep yourself occupied and she had plenty to do that. She looked around for Gertie and finding her asked if she wanted to go home with her for a cup of tea.

"No, I'd best go back to Mam. She's a bit put out. I don't think she can really take it all in. But I want to see you Ada. I want to have a talk some time this week."

Ada raised her eyebrows and looked at Gertie. Last week she was a bairn — today she talked and acted like a woman. "You planning on getting wed then?"

Gertie blushed and said she would tell her all about it later. "I'll have to

169

be off. I reckon our Mam will kill our Harry if I'm not careful. She seems to blame him for Wilf going off. I reckon she thinks he started the war." They laughed and Gertie was off.

What an anti-climax, after all the comings and goings of the past week.

"Ada — Ada." It was Isabella's voice calling out from the carriage. "Come on back with me for a bit. You've plenty of time before work and I could do with a bit of company."

Of course she could. Money didn't make any difference when your man had gone away. Nothing could compensate for that. Thankfully Ada stepped up into the carriage and leaning back on the buttoned leather seat looked across at her sister. Tear stains streaked her cheeks — she'd been crying.

"Oh I know I look a sight our Ada, and I know it's not the correct thing to do, crying in public, but I just couldn't help it. Bugger social graces at a time like this."

Ada had to laugh — this was the old Isabella — Isabella Skipton.

"Well, we're all in the same boat, lass, brass or no brass. I'll miss Wilf just as much as you will George."

Isabella shrugged her shoulders and frowned. "George did everything for me Ada, you know. At least you still have your independence. Sometimes I used to think he even breathed for me. Somehow he was afraid I would put a foot wrong. Oh, I'll miss him alright. I love George, I always will, no matter what circumstances we wed in, but at least now I'll be in charge of myself for a change."

Well, that was a turn up. Who would have thought her sister — the future lady — would have felt like that.

"Aye, and you'll have that damn great house to run and all."

"Aye — and I'll damn well do it and all," she snapped back.

Their eyes met and they laughed. George had only been gone a few minutes and already she was coming into her own. He'd see when he came back just how well she had coped. It would put paid to his 'I'll see to it darling — after all you're not used to these kinds of things and there are certain ways of doing them.' She supposed he was being kind and loving, trying to save her any undue work and worry, but sometimes it would have been nice to have done something on her own for once.

He had left her strict instructions that she was to consult his father before she did anything. Well, she would if necessary, but first she would have a go on her own.

They drew up at the door and automatically it was opened by the maid.

"I always have a giggle when that happens — it don't seem all that long ago I was doing the same thing."

Arm in arm the sisters went into the house, where a pot of tea was already laid out in the morning room.

170

"Does all this ever bother you?" Ada asked.

Isabella shook her head. "No. George and his family are very, very good to me. They always made me feel one of them and never blamed me for what happened. But — but sometimes I get the feeling of being on the outside. Now I'll show them what's what."

The Kaiser had evidently given Isabella the opportunity she had been waiting for.

"You know I have always set you up as my ideal. I love this place and I always planned a big house. Oh, I knew I'd never wed like you did, but I've worked hard and so has Wilf and that bit from Uncle Joe looked like making all our dreams come true. I can't wait to get into our house and get started in business," Ada said, over her second cup of tea.

"Well, it's not all roses you know. There've been times when I would have loved to have a damn good row but couldn't in case the servants overheard. Oh, I've been happy enough, but by God I've felt I was going mad sometimes I've been that het up."

"Ladies don't get het up, lass."

"Well I weren't born a lady was I — I were born a Skipton."

They laughed again. This was just how it should be — warm, loving and free. They didn't care what they said for there was no-one hovering around to listen or stop them.

"I'm planning to get wed on Wilf's first leave. I'm going to busy myself with the house so that as soon as this lot's over and done with we can get on with our lives."

"There's never been anybody else for you but Wilf, has there, our Ada?" Isabella was thinking of Ralph and Ada knew it.

"Not in that way — no, never. I've liked one or two fellows, took a fancy to them in a way — but it's always been Wilf."

"Do you think you've given yourself a chance. You've never really gone out with or met anyone else have you?"

"I've never wanted to. I know damn well what you and George were up to with Ralph, and I can't deny I like the bloke, but Wilf and I fit."

"Like a pair of old shoes."

Ada reddened at her sister's remark. "No, not like that at all. I love Wilf — really love him like a woman should love a man."

Isabella raised her eyebrows. Oh she did look like Dad when she did that.

"We've not been up to owt so you needn't look at me like that. I'm not daft enough to saddle myself with a bairn. In fact I — we don't know as we want any at all. We've a lot to get on with, never mind a brood round my skirts."

"And how do you plan to stop it then? You got a remedy tucked away somewhere?"

171

"I've been reading things. There are ways and means — but don't you tell our Mam or I'll murder you."

"She'll murder you more like." They sobered at the thought. "What's put you off bairns?"

Ada thought for a bit before telling her about the way she felt. She'd seen her Mam with her big family — a happy family she couldn't deny that and all of them loved and wanted. She'd seen lasses wed and before you knew it they were bogged down with a family. As far as she was concerned, Isabella was the only one who had got it right — they had two bairns, young George and Anastatia — they could well afford them, and suffered no hardships.

"It would have been different if you'd wed a working lad. By now you'd have had five or six, be as poor as a church mouse and look twenty years older than you should. Anyway, what's your remedy?"

It was Isabella's turn to blush.

"We haven't one. Somehow it just hasn't happened after Anastatia." It was as far as she was prepared to go, but in truth, George had become far too occupied with the estate and the Territorial duties. He tired himself and didn't bother her much these days. Bother her — that was a laugh — for sometimes she had lain beside him crying out for him to reach out to her. Tentatively she had, once or twice, reached out to him, but he had just sighed exasperatedly and turned away. Embarrassment and hurt had stopped her trying again.

Ada stood up and went over to kiss Isabella. "I'd best be off now love. It's been grand talking like this. Made me feel a damn sight better about things."

"Come up again soon, Ada. Come and stop overnight if you want. The bairns and me would like that."

"And George?" She couldn't resist that.

Isabella playfully cuffed her ear. "He won't mind. He likes you — says you've got a good head on your shoulders."

"And Wilf?"

"He likes him alright, but you must realise it's a bit difficult with him being an officer and Wilf in the ranks. You can't hold that against him."

Ada didn't hold it against George. He was what he was — gentry — and she accepted that.

"Aye, and Wilf's only a working lad. But we'll alter that when he gets back. They'll be on a better footing then."

She refused the offer of a ride to work preferring instead to walk. It would give her time to be on her own and think things over.

With her usual briskness she set off down the lanes that led through the back part of the town to the laundry. She passed the house and looked up at the sun streaming across the windows. It seemed to her like a sign that

172

all would be well. She could almost see smoke coming out of the chimneys and hear the grinding of the saws and hammering of wood, as it would be when Wilf was busy at work in the yard.

An inspiration came in a flash.

"Tanner's Woodworking Company" — that's what they'd call it. She'd get the sign done and hang it for when Wilf came home on leave. What a surprise that would be.

She mulled the words over again. They had a ring to them — a ring of certainty that filled her heart with hope and gladness.

CHAPTER 19

The feeling of being treated like heroes, of being somebody, faded as Wilf looked around the crowded carriage of the troop train that was to take them God knew where.

They were crushed up and numbered about three times as many as the carriage was designed to hold. You could smell it too — the windows were tight shut. It would have been impossible for anyone to open them. There were no corridors and the air stank with the stale sweat of unwashed bodies. He eased himself behind the kitbag which rested on his knee, trying to hide his face in its folds and stop the stale air going in with each breath. Many of the men had been out on the town before they left and the after-effects filled the air to suffocation. They were packed like cattle on trucks with no thought for human needs or decency. Bet George and that lot aren't packed in like this, he thought to himself. What a shambles they looked. With the heat, some of them had opened the top buttons of their uniforms, showing angry red welts where the heavy serge had rubbed against their flesh. Others had pushed their caps to the back of their heads in the hope that it would stem the sweat pouring down their faces. The heat became overpowering.

"For God's sake, open a window," a voice cried out from the corner of the carriage.

"If you do, some of us will tumble out. Don't be so bloody barmy," another voice came from the bowels of crushed khaki.

It might not be a bad thing if some of them did fall out — again Wilf was thinking to himself. He wished it could be him, for the thought of fresh air was becoming vital. Why the hell did he get himself into this lot? He could have been at home with Ada. The thought of her devoured him in homesickness and he buried his head deeper into the kitbag, biting the cord to hold back a rush of tears. Good God, I'm worse than a bairn. And he wondered if any of the others were experiencing the same feelings.

His belly felt like an empty bucket, not from hunger, but from a void of nothingness that longed for the comfort and warmth of Ada. Fumbling, he managed to get his watch out of his top pocket and looking down saw that it was almost twelve noon. Ada would soon be leaving work, and so would Gertie. He could picture them walking down St. John Street, see his Mam sat with Gertie at the table over a slab of bread and dripping. If this lot hadn't happened, he would have been working out his notice ready to start up in business. He felt an anger at Ada for encouraging him to join the Territorials. It had only been because she wanted him to make something of himself — and now look where it had got him.

"If I don't soon piss I'll bust." The voice roused him from his thoughts and looking across the carriage he saw Alf, squirming uncomfortably, wedged between two others. He had not realised they were in the same carriage.

"Hang your tail out of the window and let go," he advised.

"I would if I were near it," Alf replied, his face contorted in the agony of trying to control his bladder.

"Try and ease yourselves round a bit and let him get to the window and open it." Wilf was surprised to hear the authority of his own voice above the rest.

Instinctively the men twisted and turned until Alf was near enough to the window to prise it open and relieve himself. It set off a chain reaction.

"Let me through next. I've been wanting to go ever since we left Hull station." One by one they made for the window where the wind caused by the rushing train took the night's beer and morning tea and slashed it into the air. After each man who needed to had been relieved, they settled down a bit. They passed through station after station and once or twice stopped to find ladies of various organisations waiting to hand them mugs of tea and wads of bread and jam. It was a welcome relief, but Wilf hoped the liquid would not mean more slashing out of the window.

Surprisingly, after a while, they settled down into some sort of orderly arrangement and even managed to get a few minutes' sleep or at least be left alone with their thoughts. He grinned at Alf, who sat looking wide-eyed and lost at all the goings on. Alf winked at him and sighed.

The hours dragged on into the night and it was pitch black dark before the train finally lurched to a standstill and with its force awakened the men.

"Are we here?" a voice heavy with sleep asked.

"Where's here?" another asked.

"I don't bloody know — France or wherever it is we're going."

"Don't be daft. We have to go over water first."

Wilf had to laugh as he listened to the conversation coming from the dark.

Someone hammered on the outside of the door and they heard Tutt's voice shouting out orders.

"Stay put all of you. I'm going further up to see what's happening." He opened the door, letting in a welcome breath of air.

The station under the gas lights seemed to be swarming with khaki. Everyone was in a tearing hurry, but he made his way to the front carriage and asked the Major for some instructions. The reply startled him, for George didn't seem to have any more idea that he had of what was going on. Tutt snorted to himself — he should have expected that.

Lieutenant Tinker saw his agitation and spoke up. "Let the men smoke and relax. We'll issue orders as soon as we can."

Well, at least that was something. He went down the carriages telling

175

the men to light up and relax but stay inside. Soon hundreds of cigarette stubs glowed in the darkness, but the night air was cold and carriage doors began to bang shut as they tried to keep the cold air out. By dawn the doors had been opened and closed time and time again as they alternated between freezing and sweating.

Alf had managed to swap places and sat huddled next to Wilf. They talked in whispers and Alf told him that he planned to marry Gertie. "It's alright with you mate, isn't it?"

Wilf smiled, nodded and tried to shake his hand.

"I want it to be right for me and Gertie — like you and Ada are. I don't want owt like out Beatty has done, Wilf."

Wilf had almost forgotten about Beatty and her predicament. He asked after her and when the baby was due.

"Not yet for a bit, but she seems alright. She only got what she asked for, you know."

Wilf said nothing. He still had a feeling of guilt about Beatty, still a lingering thought that the coming bairn might be his.

It was hard work keeping the men under control throughout the night. They had not eaten or drunk since about eight and mouths were parched, throats dry, eyes sore, and bellies rumbling. A stubble of growth showed up on unshaved chins. They felt and looked filthy.

"I itch like hell."

Wilf recognised young Stanley's voice. "I shall tell your Granny if you swear like that," he teased and Stanley raised a fist to him.

As daylight came from behind the clouds of dawn, an order rang down the platform to fall out. Thankfully, heaving sighs of relief, they obeyed, stumbling stiff and weary onto the platform.

Wilf tried desperately to get his men into some kind of order. They were tired, dirty and unkempt looking. Tutt came down to them and gave his customary 'tutt tutt,' but he too knew the men were not in the best frame of mind or condition to stand stiffly to attention.

A staccato of feet coming down the platform heralded a retinue of high ranking officers, sticks held smartly underneath their arms.

"What a sad looking rabble. Is this the best you can do? Better get 'em smartened up before our Allies see them or they'll lose faith in us," scoffed an officer who sported red tabs on his shoulders.

Wilf could hardly believe his ears, but Tutt was well versed with the attitude of some officers, particularly those who were not 'regulars.'

"But Sir. . ," Wilf started to protest.

Tutt interrupted sharply. "Don't speak to the officer unless requested, Corporal."

He stepped before the men and shouted, "Come on then my lads. Let's show 'em what a bit of Yorkshire is made of."

At the sound of their native county they automatically straightened up and stood to attention in orderly rank.

"That's more like it Sergeant. See this doesn't happen again or someone will pay for it," George snapped. And then he apologised to his senior officer for what he termed as his 'rabble looking lot.'

Tutt could not believe his ears and he saw that Tinker was also not happy. Anger showed in his face and he looked like speaking up for the men. Tutt caught his eye and, winking slightly, shook his head. Tinker was worth a bit of helping into shape. He would be a good bloke in a month or two. Thankfully he heeded the signal and kept his mouth shut.

How the hell they expected them to look any better under such conditions was beyond him, and any decent officer would have realised this.

"Permission to ask for water, Sir, so that the men can get cleaned up," he requested of the Major, who turned again to the senior man and tentatively murmured "Sir?"

"Good idea, Sergeant. Detail two men to fetch water from the horse trough just outside the station." With a brief acknowledgement of a salute he turned and, followed by his faithful band, marched on.

Wilf stood beside Alf, rigidly to attention, full pack on his back, rifle held slightly by his side. Sometimes he wondered about the gentry. Why hadn't they thought about getting water for the men? Surely that was one of the first things needed. He recalled one of Mam's bitter sayings when referring to such folk: "They're all wind and piss, lad, all say but no do unless it suits them." How right she was.

"Tanner — take two men and fetch water," Tutt ordered, and Wilf shouted to Alf and Stanley. They found two buckets and after waiting in line filled them with clear cold water from the trough. The line of waiting men appeared to be in good spirits — but what was the use of being anything else? They had to make the best of things and they jostled, joked and jeered good humouredly.

On returning, the Fifth Yorks took out their white enamelled mugs and filled each one half full from the buckets.

"How the hell are we supposed to shave and clean up in this drop?" Bill Harkness looked down his long thin nose at his ration of water.

"Well, it's a sight more than you've ever used in a morning," Wilf laughed, referring to Bill's usual early morning appearance as he went to work in the gas works. He only shaved about twice a week and that was for the Territorials meeting.

"What are we supposed to see through?" another one called.

"Use your bloody fingers and feel round yourself. You'll find what you're looking for," he snapped.

And so, by feel and touch, they shaved and washed as best they could. It

177

made Wilf feel like a lad again and he almost waited for his Mam's voice to shout out that he hadn't got enough water in the bowl to wash a cat's face in. He smiled, in spite of the discomfort, and then burst into laughter as he saw the contortions of the men's faces. Chins in air, noses held gingerly between finger and thumb, they scraped gently over the bristled features with the open razors.

"Bloody hell — I've slit my throat," someone called out, but it broke the tension and they returned to good humour once more.

When they had completed the task, Tutt returned and lining them up marched them to the urinals. When everyone had been relieved he told Wilf to take over while he had a 'riddle.'

"Where does Bradley keep his water then? He must be like a camel," Ted Pickering started off a line of laughter again.

"Quiet there in the ranks — keep order," Wilf's voice rang out.

"Bloody hell — who does he think he is? A stripe and he's God Almighty," Ted muttered.

Wilf ignored it. If he was an NCO then he'd better act like one. You couldn't run on both sides of the fence.

And then they waited around for what seemed like hours. Tutt had gone off again to see what orders were, and Wilf stood them men at ease. Surely to God they couldn't be expected to stand to attention for that length of time. The sun came blistering out of the sky heralding a beautiful, hot summer day. They wouldn't half sweat in this lot.

With relief they saw coming towards them a group of ladies in white aprons with bright red crosses on the front. They were carrying white buckets of steaming hot tea and food which they were handing out to the grateful men.

Wilf took the refreshment and smiled at the middle aged woman.

"Thanks missus — this is a right welcome and no mistake."

She answered by asking where he came from. It was more out of politeness than interest, but she felt sorry for these young men thrown together in such circumstances.

"Bridlington — East Yorkshire," he spoke with such pride.

"I know Bridlington. I've spent many a holiday there. What a lovely place. You must be very proud of it."

Wilf wished he was back there at that moment. He stuffed the bread plastered with butter and jam between his teeth to stem the lump in his throat.

He felt a hand on his shoulder and turning saw that Tutt was standing behind him. He looked tired and weary and Wilf realised that he had first seen that all his men were fed and alright before he himself took anything. Funny that — you never thought of men like Tutt being human beings. But they were, just like the rest of them. He marvelled at the self-discipline and strength of the man. Not by an eyelid or twitch did he show that he was almost all-in and just as hungry and thirsty as the rest of them.

"Where are we, Sarge?"

"To tell the truth, I'm buggered if I know. I reckon it's Dover from what I've heard, but they are keeping it a guarded secret. It's as if they don't want us to know where we are going."

He took a drink and the food offered, but paused before touching it, looking round to see that everyone else had been served first. Carefully he ate and drank, not shoving the food in his mouth as the men had done, but savouring it slowly and sipping the tea as if it were vintage wine. Tutt had been hungry and thirsty before. He knew it was better to take things slowly for you never knew when the next meal would come.

Wilf thought he could smell the sea and told Alf, who laughed saying, "You and your ruddy sea."

But Wilf was sure. He'd know that smell anywhere.

Noon came and went with no more food or drink, just a blazing hot sun shining down on them. The order to form rank and move came around two o'clock and as smartly as they could they marched down the platform, heads held high and shoulders back under the watchful eye of Tutt. There was no sign of the officers.

As they marched, the wooden platform narrowed and then ended abruptly leading to a jetty from where they could see the bulwark of a great ship.

"Oh hell, not water again? I thought we'd left that at home," young Stanley's voice whined over Wilf's head.

"Oh get yourself on. You'll be fine. Think of it as a trip on Boy's Own to Flamborough Head," he tried to encourage the lad.

"I never did like water and the only trip I've been on made me that sick I've never been since." Stanley was not to be appeased.

They walked in single file up the narrow gangplank, weighted down with packs and rifles.

"On top deck Yorks," came the order, and thankfully they realised they would at least be in the fresh air and not down in the hull of the ship.

Wilf had never seen one so big. Its funnels reached to the sky and there were rows and rows of portholes below the decks. They climbed around and around the iron stairs until they reached the top deck. What a view — they were looking at the white cliffs of Dover — very like the Flamborough cliffs. Alf and Stanley joined him at the rail and they stood looking in wonderment at the sheet of white rock that stretched before them. By hek, this would be something to write back home about. They saw figures on the cliffs waving flags and shouting, but their voices were carried away in the noise and rushing wind. But they waved back and shouted. Before darkness fell they found themselves a place on the wooden deck and settled down. Games of shove ha'penny, cards and dice soon got going.

Tutt brought Wilf a pack of green cards and told him to hand them round to the men. They were for writing brief messages home. It would take about six short lines to fill them, but as most of them had never written a letter before this did not bother them.

"I'm going to write to Gertie and ask her to let Mam know I'm fine," Alf said and busily started licking his indelible pencil, thinking what to put down.

Stanley decided Granny Esther would get his card. He could ask her to send him some grub.

Wilf thought deep and long before writing and then painstakingly he put, "Dear Ada, we are on a ship bound for somewhere — France, I think. The journey was not too bad but a bit crushed. Give my love to Mam and take care of yourself. I am thinking of you and hope to see you soon, Love Wilf." It didn't seem much, but it took all the space on the card. Still, Ada would know how he felt. He collected the cards, helped with the spelling and addresses and then delivered them to Tutt.

"Settle the lads down now Corporal and see that they don't make too much mess."

He wondered what Tutt meant, but soon found out, for though the crossing was calm and uneventful, many of them were sea-sick and only just managed to reach the sides to bring up what little food was left in their insides.

Rumours ran wild — they were off to France — they were destined for Belgium — they were off to kidnap the Kaiser — men battened down below were suffocating to death, choking on their vomit. It couldn't all be true, but when the men down below were let out the next morning the stench that floated up to the top deck showed that they had suffered a pretty rough time.

One told Wilf that there was only one closet between two hundred of them. "It were bloody awful, mate, and I'll tell you this, I'm not going down there again — not for a ruddy pension."

Wilf complained to Tutt, who tersely told him to mind his own business. "You look after your own, Corporal Tanner. It's every man for himself in this lot."

Mid-morning, they landed at Calais in a drab looking harbour which, apart from the khaki figures moving about, was desolate.

"Ooh-la-la, a bit of Frenchy tonight, eh lads," the joking started again.

"The only bit of French you'll get my lad is another train journey." Tutt had been given the destination and whispered it to Wilf — they were bound for Belgium.

Again they boarded a troop train, but this time there was enough room for all and the journey was quite pleasant. Wilf looked through the window at the passing scenery. It was just like England. He soon lost interest and fell asleep, waking only when the train stopped with a screeching lurch.

They were at a small Belgian village just outside the town of Monsand and this time the organisation had improved. Billets were allotted for the night and before they bedded down some found local estaminats and bought food and drink.

Wilf's company was in the village school. They were brought food and wine by the locals and after drinking heavily fell into a deep sleep. Reveille sounded at five o'clock the next morning, giving the sound sleeping men a rude awakening. Wilf gathered up his men, got them into the school cloakroom and saw that they shaved and washed properly and were correctly dressed and on parade for breakfast. It consisted of porridge, bread and jam and tea. His stomach retched as he looked down at it. Lumps of grey-looking concrete substance lay amongst the porridge, the tea was milkless and large tea leaves floated across the top of the tin mug. The only edible item as far as he could see was the bread and jam, and God he was sick of eating that. He'd had enough during the past few days to last him a lifetime. He could hear the men beginning to grumble. By hell, they'd appreciate home cooking after this. In exasperation he was just about to throw his away when Tutt walked over and stopped him.

"That's no example to set the men, Corporal. If they see you chucking your grub away, they'll follow suit and start grumbling. You could start a mutiny that way. Close your eyes, swallow hard and eat it up — all of it.'

Wilf knew he was right and felt like resigning his stripes if it meant sacrifices like this, but manfully he did as he was ordered.

Alf watched and gathered what was going on and bravely followed his friend's action. "Come on, lads — get eaten up — this is the stuff wars are won on," Wilf bawled out between each swallow. Opening his mouth and shouting made it easier for the grub to go down. At last it was all gone.

"I want a bloody medal for that, Sarge." He threw down the dregs of the leaves away as he spoke.

Tutt laughed and told him only heroes got medals — and they were usually dead.

They paraded in full pack and were then marched some five miles to the town centre of Mons where they were met by a small crowd of Belgians who had come to see the brave heroes who would rid them of the Bosh.

"Straighten up lads — show 'em we're here to knock hell out of Kaiser Bill."

They responded and were met with cheers of 'Brave Tommee.' It made them feel like heroes before they'd even fired a shot.

Once in the square it seemed to Wilf that the whole world was encompassed within its vicinity. Horses, carts, guns, carriages and khaki

181

men — it was all mingled together. But everybody was cheerful and going about their tasks with a purpose.

"What are we here for then, Sarge? I can't see a ruddy war." There was always one joker in every battalion.

"You'll find out soon enough, my lad. The Fifth Yorks are here to win the war."

"Then for God's sake, let's get on with it," said Corporal Wilf Tanner.

CHAPTER 20

When Ada received the field card she was thrilled to pieces and ran with it up to Polly's to find Gertie reading out the one she had got from Alf. It said almost the same as Wilf's had done — he was fine — they were on board a ship — and love to his Mam.

"I reckon I'll go over and see them one weekend, Ada. It wouldn't be forward or owt would it?" she asked.

Ada thought it would be fine and offered to go with her. Gertie gratefully accepted and even included Polly in the plans.

"By hek, I've never been to so many places in my life what with Hull and then that day in Scarborough and now Barnsley. I reckon I just might go with you lasses."

They smiled indulgently at her excitement.

Harry came downstairs, rubbing his eyes and ruffling his hair. It was easy to see they were not full brothers — Harry was as dark as Wilf was fair and he did not have the same open face.

"It's a rare time for a young bloke like you to be getting up." Ada had taken on the role of man of the house since Wilf had left.

"You mind your own bloody business, madam. I shall do as I like in my own house."

"But it's not your house, mate — it's your Mam's and don't you forget it. My Wilf makes an allowance and if anybody's got a say he has." She was not afraid of him and he knew it. Sullenly he sat down at the table, leaning his head on his hands.

"He had a bit too much last night Ada, that's what's up with him. I don't know why he doesn't get himself a decent job or join up like our Wilf has," Polly said.

"Our Wilf — our bloody Wilf — I hear nowt but him day in and day out. By hell, you've changed your tune our Mam. Once upon a time it were me that were the blue-eyed boy. What's gone off to change that — or maybe you daren't tell me — aye?" He smirked at Polly, who got flustered.

She had wondered many a time if he'd found out anything about his birth. Lately, since Wilf had left, he had dropped some dark hints. She'd best have a word with Ada when she got her on her own.

"How long do you reckon they'll be gone, Ada? Alf hasn't made any mention of leave." Gertie was thinking about her wedding.

"Give 'em a chance love. I reckon they'll be gone at least three months. I'm planning on getting wed around November or Christmas time. They say it will be over by then and a bloody good job too."

They words reassured Gertie as she spoke them and Ada too. They felt happy. Mam had had a card from Stanley and she was busy cooking and baking in answer to his request for grub. At the rate she was going there'd be enough to feed the whole army, but for once it was good to feel happiness in the air.

The two girls walked up to work chattering away telling each other of their plans and hopes.

"If all goes well Gertie, I still want you to stand for me," Ada told her.

"I've been thinking about that, Ada. Would you do the same for me and all? Alf was set on getting wed as soon as possible and if we could make it around the same time as you and Wilf, Wilf could give me away."

Ada took Gertie's arm and squeezed it in acceptance. She felt close to the lass and, in a way, protective towards her.

"Let's go up to the house tonight Gertie. I'll start measuring for curtains and lino. Our Isabella say's she'll give a hand with planning and there's one or two things in the hall barn I can have. We'll go up there from work and have a look."

Most of the girls with men at war had received cards or messages from their sweethearts. The air was full of plans and excitement. They knew the men were safe and well. This daft war would soon be over and then they could all settle down.

Thom wasn't as sure as the womenfolk and told them so.

"The jerries aren't fools you know. They won't give in that easily. I've been told by good authority that we could be in for a long slog."

Thom had been asked to take full charge of the council yard as the man responsible had gone with the Fifth Yorks. He didn't really want the job, but if it would help the war effort then he would do it. But by hek, the world was changing — women wanting to vote — half the town's lads sent to foreign parts — recruiting campaigns that pressurised young men to join up — it was a funny old do.

As soon as the machines had stopped, Gertie and Ada walked together to see Isabella. Tea was waiting and to Gertie it was like a party. Sandwiches and cakes, tea served in china cups — it was coming up in the world. Shyly she told Isabella of the plans she and Alf had made.

"Well if I can help, lass, just let me know. I consider it as much my duty to see to the women of the regiment as it is George's to look after the men. And we shall be related in a way shan't we?"

Everyone was so nice and helpful. The war seemed to have brought people together and it was not surprising as most of them were in the same boat.

They looked over the furniture, Ada and Gertie wondering how folk could ever afford to chuck such good stuff out, and Ada chose what she wanted. Isabella offered Gertie what was left. Gertie replied she would see what Alf said, and if it was alright, then thank-you.

Isabella decided to go with them down to the house offering to do some of the sewing whilst Ada was at work. She was thoroughly enjoying it all, having missed out on planning and preparing her own home, which had been ready and waiting as soon as the wedding was over. Gentry didn't do things for themselves, and if she were to be honest, it was something she had regretted.

As they passed through the Old Town Market Place they heard the sound of a band and marching feet.

"Let's stop and see what it is," she said to Ada, making the most of her freedom. She'd not walked through the town for years.

It was a small parade which stopped outside the corn exchange, set up a small platform upon which two glamorous ladies stood and began speaking. As soon as they opened their mouths it was clear they were not ladies — glamorous yes — but not ladies.

"Come on you Brid lads — where are you — you country needs you. Come and enlist and help beat those jerrie bastards."

Soon a crowd had gathered. They had chosen the spot well, for it was surrounded by several pubs and they knew that once a bloke was full of ale they could get him to do anything. And they were right. Men poured out of the pub doors and after a rousing song and dance from the women they surged to enlist. Most of them would regret it the next day, but having accepted the King's shilling — promptly spent on more ale — it was too late.

Gertie nudged Ada and pointed to a group of men where stood Harry — more than a little worse for wear. Devilment took Ada over and she sidled across to them and gave Harry a shove in the back.

In an instant his hand was grabbed, a shilling placed in it and he was wreathed in kisses from the women. He had no idea what had happened and when the recruiting sergeant came over to take his particulars, he tried to get out of enlisting.

"I was pushed. I'm not joining any bloody army, war or no war."

The sergeant held him firm by the scruff of the neck. He wasn't letting this one go. A recruit meant money — Harry was worth five bob to him.

"Now, don't be like that, my lad, your country needs you and just think of all that booze and women you can afford on regular army pay."

Harry was in the army.

"You bugger, Ada. I don't know what our Mam'll say." But Gertie laughed as she chided, knowing full well that Polly would be delighted.

They wondered if he would be sent out to the others and then thought of Wilf's anger if his brother joined his platoon. They decided to keep quiet about the circumstances of his patriotism and he had no idea who had pushed him, blaming one of his cronies who had been standing there with him.

Three more were recruited and the small parade, with the newcomers lined up in the middle, made their way down the town.

They giggled and laughed about the incident all the way up to the house, but Ada warned Gertie not to mention a word to Polly.

"Let Harry tell her and then no-one will be wiser," she advised.

Busily they measured, decided on colours and worked together for about two hours until Isabella stretched up from the window sill and said it was time to be off.

"I'm going to the Hall for dinner and I have to get dressed."

She looked alright to Gertie — her dress was grey silk with a shawl collar, fit for a wedding dress. But she had no idea that Isabella would have to wear something far more formal to dine with her parents-in-law.

"I know, we'll dine in style and all. Let's get some fish and chips from Rimmington's and take them down to your house," Ada told Gertie.

"You lucky devils. I wouldn't mind a good bite of Rimmingtons' fry up." Isabella's voice was wistful, and Ada realised, perhaps for the first time, that it wasn't all honey and skittles being married to gentry. They didn't have half the freedom people thought.

With a promise to take the curtain stuff up at the weekend, the sisters parted and, linking her arm in Gertie's, she and Ada made for Rimmingtons.

They were so happy as they entered Polly's cottage — a happiness that money could not buy.

"Come on Mam, get vinegar and salt out, we've bought supper." Gertie's voice stopped abruptly as she saw Harry sat in the chair in front of the fire.

"He's gone and joined up — he's bloody gone and joined up. I never thought he had it in him," Polly gasped out, and patted his shoulder.

Harry preened. "Well, I thought it was time I did something to help the country — go and give our Wilf a hand like."

The bugger — he was making out he had joined up of his own free will. A look passed between the lasses and they burst out laughing.

"Well done, Harry lad," Ada too patted his shoulder.

"When are you off then?" Gertie asked him and he told her the following Monday.

"'I'm to report to Drill Hall for six weeks' training and then it's off to join the Fifth Yorks.''

Polly frowned, but said nothing except, "As long as you behave yourself."

"I shall spend my last days of freedom enjoying myself. I'm off up to the Ship to see if I can get any more willing recruits." Smiling, he bade them farewell and left the house.

The trio ate in silence, each lost in their own thoughts.

186

"I don't reckon Wilf will be all that pleased," Ada said firmly.

"Nor do I, and I only hope he doesn't start any bother," Polly rejoined, praying to God he didn't know anything and start using it against his brother.

"Just look at that hole in the fire — it's a sign of death they say. I wonder who it will be this time." Polly leaned forward and poked the dying embers, filling in the hollow that had glowed in the red coals.

Ada laughed and went on eating. These daft suspicions — Polly was as bad as her Mam about them.

Suddenly Gertie shuddered heavily and pushed her unfinished packet of fish and chips away. "You turned chilly, love — shall I put a bit more on fire?" Polly asked.

Gertie shook her head. "No — it's alright — somebody just walked over my grave, that's all."

A deathly silence filled the room. No-one spoke and they sat as if transfixed, looking into the fire.

"Well, this won't do. I'd best be off or I'll never be up for work in morning." Ada broke the silence and, shouting goodnight, went out of the door. As she opened it a cold blast blew the fire into a blaze and leaning forward Polly went to warm her hands.

"Hurry yourself along then and don't dawdle. It feels a mite chilly out there."

Ada ran all the way as if someone or something was chasing her until at last she reached her own front door. God, these daft sayings didn't half put the wind up you. That's what had made Gertie shudder — poor lass would be scared out of her wits. She was thankful she had more sense than to believe any of that — a hole in the fire indeed.

The Fifth Yorks stood around smoking and talking and listening to the gunfire in the distance. They were waiting for orders and it was with a sense of relief that Wilf saw Tutt coming towards his battalion at the double.

"I want a detail of six men to repair a communication line." He explained to Wilf that along the line from Mons, communication to a vital position had been cut during the night. Hill 20 was a strategic stronghold and it was imperative that the line be repaired.

"They've picked us to do it. I want you to detail the men and then send them to me at headquarters for orders."

"Who shall I send, Sarge?" It was the first time Wilf had tasted the meaning of real authority.

"That's your bloody job. Send five of the best you have — five who know that they are about."

"Shall I go as well, Sarge?"

187

"No you bloody well won't. I said send five men — a Lance Corporal and four lads — and be quick about it."

Wilf shouted out the first names he could think of. "Lance Corporal Aylward, Skipton, Simpson, Wallace, Pickering and Johnson. Come with me and report to Sergeant Bradley for orders."

Quickly they ran and joined him and then marched in twos to the headquarters, which was situated in what appeared to be the Town Hall.

Tutt was waiting on the steps and they followed him inside. He held up his hand, barring the way when Wilf made to follow. "You wait here, Corporal."

The detail stood before a large desk, behind which sat Major Burlingham. "This is an important mission, men. It's our first baptism of battle and I look to you to keep the honour of the regiment. Hill 60 is up here on this ridge to the right of town. At point 29 the line is broken. That is your job, to repair the broken wires. I suggest you take this route." He pointed to the large map of the area which was pinned on the wall behind him.

"Sir?" Tutt ventured. "Is that route not a bit long, sir — it takes them very close to the enemy lines."

"A more direct line would take them straight through the enemy lines, Sergeant. Those are my orders — see that they are obeyed." They men were dismissed.

Tutt took them to the stores to draw supplies and watched as they made off in the direction of the lines.

"Where's your bloody rifles? It's not a practice match you know — this is the real thing. Jerry won't be waving at you — he will be shooting at you with real live ammo."

Red faced, they turned and picked up their rifles, slung them over their shoulders and once again made off.

"I hope he's right — I hope he knows what he's doing," Tutt muttered to himself.

"What's that, Sarge?" Wilf had walked over to him.

"Nothing Corporal — nothing for you to worry about. Return to your men and see that they get bedded down for the night. There's no telling what tomorrow will bring."

As night fell the gunfire became louder and the men uneasy.

"Don't fret yoursens about that lot, it's too far off to hurt anybody here. It's yon poor buggers up there that want to watch out," an old sweat, seasoned to the war, spoke up and pointed in the direction of the blazing guns.

Wilf could not settle down. He kept wondering where Alf and Stanley were — what they were doing — did they know enough about communication lines to repair them quickly — and under fire? Had he made the right choice of men? He hoped so, or Tutt would have his guts if any blunder was made. What the hell was expected of him now? No more orders had come through and he felt at a loss just sitting there. He had got the men to wash up, clean equipment and eat. It didn't seem like war — a bit rougher than camp, granted — but with the blazing guns it was more like bonfire night.

Now there were groups of men creeping into the square — they must have come back from the front line. He went over and tried to talk to them, but they were reluctant to converse — too tired and weary for chat. They lay down in front of the fires and slept or sat looking into the flames and listening to the wailing sound of mouth organs being played. It was an eerie sound made more so by the shadows that danced up and down the grey buildings surrounding them.

He fell into a state of half sleep with Tutt sitting beside him, arms folded on his breast, head hung down as if slumbering. But his eyes never closed — he was listening — looking for the return of his men.

"Sergeant Bradley — Sergeant Bradley — report to company headquarters at once," a voice rang through the darkness and Tutt sprang to his feet and made off into the night.

Wilf roused himself and wondered if orders had come through at last — anything would be better than just sitting around.

Tutt returned shortly, stumbling through the dark of the grey dawn. Wilf sensed something was wrong — now what the hell had happened?

"Corporal Tanner — come over here will you?"

Wilf went to the beckoning arm.

"We've lost them, Wilf — we've lost them." Tutt looked shattered.

"Lost what, Sarge?" Wilf asked stupidly.

"The lads, the detail we sent out, all of them — Aylward, Skipton, Simpson, Wallace, Pickering and Johnson — all gone."

"Gone where?" Wilf was dazed.

"They were blown to bits — all dead before they got a chance to set up the lines." His face sagged to ashen pulp.

Wilf could not speak. He was stunned beyond belief. Dead — Alf and young Stanley dead — there must be some mistake. Why they were all here a few hours ago, laughing, grumbling, writing letters home.

"I said they shouldn't have gone that route — I said they shouldn't," Tutt was muttering again.

"Sarge?"

Tutt looked at Wilf and pulled himself together. "Nothing for you to worry about Corporal. Return to your men and inform them of the situation. Let me have some names for promotion to Lance Corporal within the hour. Come on lad, get to it." He spoke harshly. He had to, or Wilf would have gone to pieces.

189

"But Alf, Sarge — he were my mate — he were going to work for me in business after this lot were over. And young Stanley — what am I going to say to Ada about young Stanley? Are you sure, Sarge? — there can't have been a mistake can there?"

"The British Army don't make mistakes, Corporal. Get to your duty now before I court martial you." It was an idle threat, but Wilf knew that if put to it, Tutt would carry it out.

"I can't, Sarge — I can't."

"Yes you can my lad, and you'd bloody well better, or I'll have you on orders this morning. This is war — no time for cowards or wasters." Still Wilf stood shaking his head and shivering until with angry desperation Tutt removed his revolver from its holster.

"I'll count to three, Corporal Tanner, and if you haven't got up your pluck by then, I'll put a bullet up your arse." He spoke quietly and calmly.

Wilf squared his shoulders and looking him straight in the eye replied just as quietly, "You bastard — you cold bloody bastard."

Tutt knew he had won — Wilf would obey his command.

Smartly he turned, brought up his right arm in a meticulous salute, said briefly, "Sergeant," and returned to his men.

Now he felt nothing — the shivering had gone and he just felt icy cold.

Briefly he told the men what had happened, adding, "Your name is going forward for promotion to Lance Corporal, Hardacre. Any questions?"

Numbly the men looked at him.

"Get your heads down now. Reveille is in about an hour. Come on there, get on with it." His voice rang out loud and clear.

"The bloody bastard — he's got no feelings at all," he heard a voice from within the ranks.

"Quiet that man there or I'll have you on orders in the morning."

"Well, I never thought I'd live to see the day when you'd act as heartless as this, Wilf Tanner," Hardacre spoke up.

"There's a war on — or hadn't you noticed?"

The jibes meant nothing to him. He was intent on getting the men to obey his orders, which they did on seeing his intense purpose.

He curled up apart from them, and buried his head in the folds of his kit. They must not know his fears, they must not see his tears or hear his tortured cry for Ada.

190

CHAPTER 21

When the news of the deaths reached the families, the town blew up in an uproar. Three of the men had left wives with young families — and two — including young Stanley — were single lads only in their teens.

Esther got the news of her grandson just after dinner on the 27th August — a date she remembered well. Resting beside the fire after they had all gone back to work, she was daydreaming — thinking of the days when her family were all at home. Oh, things hadn't been all sunshine, but there was none of this worrying about them being in foreign parts.

She was roused by the scurrying of feet down the passage and jerked out of her chair to see who was in such a rush. It was Sarah, Stanley's mother. One look at her face told Esther that something was sadly wrong.

"It's Stanley, Mam — he's been killed."

Esther stumbled and almost fell with the shock of the words. "He can't be, he's only a bairn — they've bloody murdered him," she cried out in pain that almost burst her heart.

Young Stanley — dead in some foreign parts. Heavily she sank back into her chair and slumped down. She thought of how he left, singing his heart out as he marched down the street.

"I've just ordered him a suit from Machin's for when he comes home." Her voice was bewildered.

"He'll never wear it now, Mam — he's never coming back — never," Sarah was sobbing.

Ada had no idea how to break the news to Gertie and decided to let common sense prevail and just come straight out with it.

First she spoke to Mrs. Price and asked permission to use the office. With the pretence of wanting to show Gertie some new work, she took her into the office and quietly and calmly broke the news. After gazing at her blankly, Gertie fell in a heap on the concrete floor — she had fainted.

Ada knew she should be crying with the lass — she should feel a sense of grief that one of her family had been killed, but all she felt was a tremendous relief that it wasn't Wilf. When she came round Gertie was hysterical. "I've got to see for myself, Ada. I shan't believe it until I see it in black and white. Come with me to the Drill Hall to see the list." She gathered up her apron and ran from the laundry with Ada on her heels.

"Take it steady, lass. Of course I'll come with you, but just wait on a minute."

But Gertie paid no heed and ran all the way down the street until she reached the glass case that held, in one short sentence, the whole of her life.

His name was the first one, Lance Corporal Alfred Aylward. She let out

191

a piercing scream and, with her fist, banged on the glass again and again until it broke into fragments and fell upon the pavement. Her hand was pouring with blood, which fell in stark contrast upon her white apron.

Ada did nothing — best let the lass get it out of her system. Passers-by looked at the scene, but on learning the reason shook their heads in sympathy and walked on.

And then, with a shuddering sob, for the moment her grief was spent. Leaning heavily on Ada they walked home to tell Polly. They talked in whispers, Ada trying to comfort and Gertie pledging her undying love for Alf.

"I'll not wed now Ada — never. I'll love and keep Alf's memory for always."

Polly was a bit non-plussed — she couldn't feel any real sorrow for she had not known Alf all that well. He was a nice enough lad and she had been glad that Gertie and he were planning to wed. But, well — he weren't her lad. All she could feel was a sadness for her lass. "Did his folks know you were to be wed?"

Gertie had no idea, for there had been so little time to talk of things like that. He had said he would like her to visit them, but what was the use of that now?

"We'll still go — just me and you, love — his Mam would like that and you might feel better and all," Ada said.

Gertie nodded — yes — to see his home and meet his family might make her feel closer to him. She wanted that so much. There were so few memories, only dreams.

Ada promised to write and they would go to Barnsley the next Saturday. "Don't come back to work, love. I'll make things right, and I'll call on my way home."

But she did not go straight back to work either. As she walked through the town she half expected to see a riot — a funeral procession or people moaning or groaning. There was nothing to indicate that any lives had been lost or indeed that there was a war at all. The sun was shining, folk were busy shopping, some cleaning windows or stood in groups gossiping.

"Aye, it's a bad job, right enough, but we must expect that sort of thing now there's war on," she heard the tail end of a conversation. Yes, that was war. All they could do was to carry on as best they could until it was over.

Without thinking of her direction she found herself near the house and automatically she went inside. Nothing had changed here either — no doom or gloom, sun streamed through the windows as if in welcome and as she strolled through each room she found a warmth and comfort, as if Wilf were here with her.

There was a heap of circulars in the wire cage behind the front door and she took them out. It was funny how folk knew when a house had been

192

taken. They soon started to let you know what miracles they had to offer.

A stiff blue envelope caught her eye and on looking she saw it was addressed to her personally: Miss Ada Skipton, The Red House, 55 Scarborough Road, Bridlington. Well, someone knew the full address. She paused before opening it, thinking that although the writing looked vaguely familiar, she couldn't place it. It certainly was not Wilf's and anyway he would write to St. John Street. She ripped open the envelope and out fell a beautiful silk embroidered card upon which were two union jacks entwined above a bunch of pansies. Underneath, embroidered in the same silk, was written 'Thinking of you.'

Who the hell could have sent her that? It was obviously from somewhere foreign — France or somewhere — but who could it be from? She looked again at the postmark — it was a British Forces Field one. She turned the card over — no signature — nothing. But that writing — she'd seen it somewhere before. Oh well, maybe it was Wilf getting one of his mates to write for a joke. Still it was beautiful. She would treasure it, but decided to keep it to herself.

At work a collection was made to give the widows of the men who had been killed. There was some talk of a memorial service, but that was put to one side. They decided to take the money up to Isabella. As the wife of the Commanding Officer she could share it out and see if there was anything else the women needed.

"I feel a great responsibility you know, and I shall make it my job to keep an eye on all the wives from now on — my bit for the war effort," she told Ada.

And Ada knew she would make a damn good job of it and all. It seemed that Isabella was coming into her own.

After tea she got out her writing paper to let Alf's Mam know of the intended visit. At least that would be something for Gertie to look forward to. She was surprised at the way the lass had pulled herself together and was even talking of volunteering for some more vital war work.

"I might even join up," she said to a startled Polly. "Become a nurse or something."

Ada toyed with the idea herself, but then decided not to. She had the house and everything to see to.

There was no reply from Mrs. Aylward and none was expected, for Ada doubted if any of them could write properly. They took the Saturday morning off work and set off on the first train at 7.30.

"I love this time of day — everything seems to clean and fresh, like a new start," Gertie said as they walked down to the station.

"And after this, that is the way you've got to think. You've all your life before you, lass."

Hushed tears came to Gertie's eyes and she just nodded her head forlornly in answer.

The Aylwards were pleased to see them and had prepared a nice meal which was ready and waiting on the table.

"I got a bit of money from the government for our Alf. I know he'd have wanted me to make a bit of a spread for you. He held you and Wilf in great store, you know." Mrs. Aylward's drawn face showed her grief and she burst into tears.

But it was Gertie and not Ada who comforted her. Gertie ran forward and put her arms around the old woman and murmured comforting words.

"Did you know Alf then — are you the lass he was sweet on?" she asked.

"We were going to be wed," Gertie whispered.

"Aye, I'm sorry lass — taking on like this and not thinking about you. Did they let you know he had gone?" She pointed to the telegram which held pride of place on the mantlepiece.

Ada told her how Gertie had heard the news. She felt a bit left out — these two women were sharing their grief for a son and a loved one. She had no place in it.

Footsteps echoed on the stairs and the door was pushed open with a creak. It was Beatty creeping down and holding a bundle in her arms. "I heard you all talking, Mam. Are you alright?"

Ada saw that the bundle was a bairn. Of course — she'd forgotten about Beatty's condition. Was it all that long ago since she and Wilf were here?

"Beatty's only been confined a week. It wasn't really due and they reckon the shock of Alf brought it on. Come on lass and sit down or you'll make yourself bad."

Her Mam brought forward a chair and Beatty collapsed upon it with a sigh of relief. She too looked drawn — so much older than when Ada had last seen here — old before her time. Well, if she would bugger about what more could she expect?

As she sat down the bairn almost slipped from her grasp. Automatically Ada stepped forward and took it from her. She opened the grubby bit of cloth that served as a shawl and looked into the tiny crumpled face. A shiver ran through her. The tiny face, topped by a mop of blonde hair, was so familiar. She tickled its face — the eyes opened and looked up at her — they were so blue. Quickly she folded the shawl over again and handed it back to Beatty. All babies' eyes were blue weren't they? But not all had blonde hair like that, a voice whispered inside her.

"What is it then?" she asked abruptly.

Beatty looked her straight in the eye. "A lad — like his father." Her voice was firm — cheeky — almost insolent.

The rest of the day for Ada was an uncomfortable one, but it seemed to

194

have done the trick as far as Gertie was concerned. She sat talking away to Alf's Mam as if they were old friends and promised to visit again.

Beatty went back up to bed, seeming far too weak to cope with all the fuss. As she went upstairs she turned and pointedly addressed Ada.

"That lad of yours — alright is he?" she asked.

Ada nodded, briefly.

"Give my regards when you write." It was a statement more than a request.

Ada had watched as she fed the bairn at her breast and changed him. Gertie held him and cooed over him, but Ada could not bring herself to touch him again. He was a right enough bairn — pretty, if she were to be honest — but this feeling that was sweeping over her, this buried sensation that was coming to the surface, made her seem awkward and a little hostile.

"You not used to bairns, Ada?"

She just smiled. It was best to let them think that if they liked. She just managed to bring herself to ask what they intended to call him.

Mrs. Aylward answered, "Well, we were going to call him Wilfred, after your lad. Alf was so fond of him. Wilfred James after him and his grandad. But now Alf's gone, it's to be Alfred James. That seems only right."

Ada thanked God for that. Wilfred indeed — how dare they? But that voice inside said they might well have every right to do so.

Gertie noticed that she was unusually quiet on the way back and asked if anything was wrong.

Ada shook her head and put it down to the trauma of the day. "I was thinking about Wilf and Alf, and all that might have been," she said.

"And still will be for you and Wilf."

Ada was sorry she had spoken like that. Poor old Gertie — old now aye — she'd thought of her as only a bairn until all this happened. Now — and particularly today — she had grown into a woman, ready to take on responsibilities of joining up or whatever. Why couldn't it have all stayed like it was?

When they reached Brid and got to Ada's house, she didn't ask Gertie in. She wanted a few minutes of her own, to think quietly and try to sort out all that was going on in her mind. That bairn of Beatty's — why had it disturbed her so? That card — who the hell had sent it?

"There's a letter for you, hunny. Dad says it's from Wilf," was her Mam's greeting.

"I'll take it upstairs to read. I'm a bit worn out, what with one thing and another today."

Esther nodded. The lass had taken a bit on herself with Gertie and Polly. She seemed to have taken charge there, and with all the extra work

195

at the laundry, and planning to get wed, there as no wonder she was dead beat.

"I'll bring you a cup of tea up in a minute," she promised. That would give the lass time to read her letter.

Excitedly she tore open the envelope, but as she read the lines, disappointment swept over her and she almost screamed out in anger. Wilf had written to say that as far as he could see they were far too busy for any leave yet.

"I mentioned it to Tutt yesterday and he reckons we'll be out here for a year or more. So it looks as though we'll have to wait a bit yet to get wed."

She couldn't believe it was happening. Was there something against them getting wed for things to go so wrong?

"Damn the Kaiser, damn, blast and bugger him," she sobbed into her pillow.

Esther brought up a cup of tea and sat down beside her until the tears were spent.

Ada told her what Wilf had said. "It's not fair Mam. We've got house and everything to go into and this bugger happens."

Esther tried to console her, but what could she honestly say?

"He might not have to wait all that time. A year does seem a bit much." It was weak, but it was all she could think of.

"Take the tea down, Mam. I'll just get changed and come down."

"Aye, love. Best not to brood on your own."

As she undressed to change, she began to wonder if she was going mad — first thinking that the bairn looked like Wilf — then imagining all sorts about the card — and now she was beginning to think there was never going to be a wedding. She began to wonder if Wilf really existed.

"I know, I'll look in my deed box. I'll look through the house lease — just to make sure — that'll put me right."

Hurriedly she got out the black box, turned the small brass key and rummaged in the papers. She read through the lease — it was real enough. And then she came to the signatures of her and Wilf and the witness, Ralph Tinker. That writing — she took the card from the bottom of the box, looked at the envelope and compared it — it was Ralph's writing. Now what the hell was he playing at sending her a card like that — and unsigned and all?

Angrily she pushed back the papers and slammed down the lid as if to shut away the doubts and bewilderment that engulfed her.

CHAPTER 22

Thankfully for Ada, Gertie, in spite of herself, seemed to take on the responsibility of the home and Polly. Having fallen in love for the first time, having known a little happiness only to have it ended in an untimely death, it appeared to have brought her sharply and cruelly to womanhood.

Poor little lass had never had much of a life and if Alf had come back and wed her it wouldn't have been all that much better. But with Wilf and Ada behind them, they would have stood a better chance than most. At least they would have had a decent standard of living. And that was something neither Gertie nor Alf, for that matter, had ever really known.

It was all so unfair — and so unnecessary. It was, as far as Ada was concerned. What did they want to get mixed up in a war for? She couldn't see that it was going to do anybody any good at all. It might get rid of a few lives and stop a bit of unemployment, but that was about all. As Thom said over and over again, "They're taking the cream of our country — young working lads that never stand a chance when big buggers get going." Ada had to agree with him. Just when she and Wilf were set to better themselves, this lot started.

Gertie kept going on about wanting to join up, do something to atone for Alf's death. Ada told her to hold on a bit, let her feelings settle down a bit before she rushed off and did owt daft. She was also thinking about herself. If Gertie went off it would mean that Ada would have the responsibility of Polly again, and besides, if the lass did something in the first grief of her bereavement, she might live to regret it.

One morning just before she set off for work, Gertie heard the plop of a letter landing on the doormat. She went and picked it up and saw it was an official letter addressed to her Mam. With her new found feeling of responsibility she had no hesitation in opening it.

It was from the Army Military Board asking Polly to state how much she depended on Harry. What was his state of health, and would she suffer any hardship if he were called up for active service? So, she thought, the bugger was trying to get out of it now, was he? Well, she'd show him. Without saying a word to Polly, she ripped it up and lit the fire with it. If Alf and Wilf could go, then so could Harry. It would have been a blessing if he had been killed instead of Alf. He'd never been owt but bother to them as far as she could remember. Aye, it was right enough — best were always first to go.

Harry kept on asking if a letter had come for Polly, but she, knowing nothing about it, said no and Gertie kept her mouth shut. When one did finally arrive it was addressed to him and told him to report to the Drill Hall the following week.

He started to create hell until Gertie surprised him by rearing up and telling him to bloody grow up and be a man. "Get off your arse for once and get yourself down like any decent lad would do," she shouted at him.

"Just because your chap went and got himself killed doesn't mean as how we've all got to, does it?" he bawled back, and then ducked as Gertie threw her cup of tea at him.

Maybe he'd best watch how he treated his little sister from now on — she'd changed a hell of a lot just lately.

He tried in vain to flunk his medical, but the officials were getting wise to his sort. He passed as a 'B' class due to his attitude and was posted to Beverley for basic training.

He had a moan to one of his cronies who told him to act daft — if they thought you were an idiot, chances were you'd be sent home. And he tried damned hard. All through foot drills and arms drills he behaved as if he was three sheets to the wind — pretending not to understand any of the orders, marching as if he had two left feet and fixing the gun so that it wouldn't fire correctly.

He had stomachache, backache, cramp — everything he could think of — but it was of no avail. The only unfortunate thing was he became a batman and was posted to the Fifth Yorks to serve two of the high ranking officers.

On embarkation leave he swaggered about like a turkey cock. He thought he might as well make the best of a bad job and being a batman would have its advantages — he would see to that.

To Ada and Gertie's great aggravation, he boasted openly about Wilf and Alf. "I'm going over there to avenge that lad's death and give our kid a hand to beat hell out of them ruddy jerries."

On the strength of that he got many a free pint and spent most of his leave in drunken oblivion. He certainly omitted to tell his admiring listeners what job he had been given — he led them to believe that he would be in the front firing line.

But when he finally left, Polly could not help shedding a few tears. After all, he was her lad when all was said and done.

On the other hand, Gertie, who seemed to have lost almost all her sympathetic feelings, couldn't wait to get rid of him, for in the short time he had been away at training camp, she had enjoyed the freedom of running the house pretty much as she pleased. Polly wasn't past it by any means, but Gertie blossomed in taking over and Polly enjoyed being looked after for a change. The house was so peaceful and the bit of money they had between them went a hell of a lot further — and you could leave it lying around and all. No Harry's sharp fingers to help themselves.

Maybe Ada was right, she thought to herself, maybe she should stay put for a bit and enjoy a freedom she had never known, even if it was at the expense of Alf's life. Polly talked to her more — more like a woman, and treated her like an equal. But, dear God, she would have given it all up in an instance if only Alf would come home at the end of it all.

She and Ada spent a lot of time together and each week they went together to help at a canteen that Isabella had set up in the Royal Pavilion for soldiers posted to the town.

They worked on the house together too. Although Ada had given up any plans for an early wedding, she still had the urge to get the house ready. After the shock of Stanley and Alf's deaths she felt that if she got it finished it would be like a milestone to herald Wilf's homecoming — something to work and look forward to.

Often she would think about the mysterious card and take it out and sit pondering over it. She'd not said a word to anyone about it, for truthfully she could not understand why Ralph would want to send it to her — her of all people. She wasn't of his class, not the class he would be expected to be interested in.

But one day, when she was dead beat after a hard day at the laundry followed by a stint in the canteen, she mentioned it to Isabella.

"Are you sure he sent it?" Isabella asked.

Ada nodded firmly and told her about the handwriting. "What do you reckon to it?" she asked.

Isabella pursed her lips and thought for a minute. "Well, I think he's just being friendly. After all, he did help you over Uncle Joe's money and the business and the house. Ralph is a gentleman and this is perhaps his way of saying that he is still taking an interest in your affairs."

"And that's all?"

"Well, could there be anything else, Ada? Only you could answer that."

Isabella looked inquiringly at her sister, but knew better than to press the matter further. Ada would only say as much as she wanted her to know. With a shrug of her shoulders, Ada put paid to any further discussion.

They were washing up the final load of pots after having served over a hundred young soldiers, most of them only lads who had obviously answered the country's call in hope of a better life.

The army meant regular pay and regular meals and that was a compensation. Little did they know the price that some of them would pay. They would talk to the women who served them. Tell them of their homes and families. Oh, they bragged on a bit, some making things a lot rosier than they really were and others finding a kind of inverted joy in playing up the bad and rough sides of their life before they joined the army.

199

"We slept six to a bed at home — three at the top and three at the bottom, top to toe, with nowt but an old overcoat to cover us." That was a familiar tale and no doubt true, but it helped to get the pent-up excitement out of their systems.

Ada was amazed at how they all looked forward to going to France and the front line — as if it was a great big party. Somebody had done a damn good job in schooling them in patriotism, and the silly young buggers had believed them. Like lambs to the slaughter it was. Ada felt little if no patriotism. Not like Isabella who felt that the position of George's wife gave her responsibility that she should show to the men and the wives of her husband's battalion.

Ada was more ruled by Thom's thinking and he was a great admirer of Lloyd George who abhorred all senseless killing. "It's allus working class that pays the price," he would chunter away to himself and his daughter was in full agreement.

Wilf would have been been set up by now if he'd not had to go off to war. He'd have been a damn sight better off doing that than shooting guns at blokes he knew nothing about just because some silly big wig couldn't reach an agreement. She strongly suspected that the German working class felt the same, but she kept her peace. God, what a row that would cause — Isabella would have a fit if she knew how rebellious her sister felt. All her life Ada had one thing in her mind — Ada and the fulfullment of her ambitions. Now her life centred on her and Wilf and their future. Bugger everything else.

She received regular letters from him and one or two of the pretty silk embroidered cards. She read them time and time again and made a point of writing a long letter every week. She would tell him about his Mam and Gertie, how the house was going, what was going on at work and in the town, being careful not to write down her true thoughts of the war.

'Last week Winnie Hardacre was emptying a uniform pocket to get it ready to be steamed and she found a note addressed to "any unattached young lady." It gave a name and address and asked her to write to him. She did and all, the little monkey, and we are all waiting for his reply.' She wrote all these little bits to let him know that all in all things at home were fine. She told how grown up Gertie had become and how well they were managing now that Harry had gone — adding that she hoped he wouldn't run into him. 'I know how you would feel about that,' she added.

But, by an ironic twist of fate, some daft bugger in administration had posted Harry to Wilf's company as batman to George, Ralph and Captain Richard Hendicutt. After the first bitter shock, he had to laugh at the way Tutt Bradley soon had him jumping about and carrying out orders. But, as usual, Wilf bore some of the brunt, for Harry was forever moaning and grizzling about the army.

"I should never be here — I'm not fit for this lark, our Wilf."

Wilf told him to shut his gob and get on with it like the rest of them had to. Harry offered him some of the tit-bits that he got from the officers' bunks — extras bits of food that he had lifted without permission. Oh how wh would have loved to have sunk his teeth into a bit of that tinned meat, but he resisted, not so much from honesty as a feeling that it would not be right to the other blokes.

His admiration for Ralph Tinker grew, for, as Tutt had predicted, he was a damn good officer. Old George wasn't too bad — a bit of a ditherer about orders and sometimes he sent them on a daft reccy and nearly always in the wrong direction, but he felt that the man honestly cared for his men. There was never any mention of a possible future relationship between them, but nevertheless Wilf felt that, underneath, there was a sort of comradeship existing between them.

Tutt took George in hand and would make tactful suggestions when any plans were being laid. "That seems fine, Sir — but if I might make a suggestion — a slight detour in this direction," would be his opening gambit, and George nearly always fell for it. In fact, good old Tutt seemed to have them all in hand and Wilf felt that were it not for his leadership they would sometimes be in a sorry spot.

"A battalion is only as good as its RSM, Corporal Tanner, and I take that responsibility very seriously — officers and men alike," he said. Wilf thanked God that he did.

Once Harry got the lay of the land, he started up his old tricks of gambling and petty pinching. If prisoners were brought in he would try and trade food for watches, swords or revolvers. If they came across dead bodies that were not too decomposed, he would somehow manage to loot them, too — it didn't matter whether they were British or German — it was all the same to Harry.

Tutt threatened that if he ever caught the bugger he would have him strung up and shot. Looting of any kind was strictly forbidden, but Harry lived by his own rules and saw no sense in leaving good stuff to rot and rust in the muddy mires and carried on. He had lived by his wits for a long time and used all his tricks to avoid being caught.

He also learned how to butter up his officers and listened and noted every bit of information as he went about his duties. You never knew when these little gems might come in useful. He had plenty of opportunity to take sneaky looks at personal items when tidying and cleaning up their kit. But they seemed a decent and upright bunch and so far he had nothing on them. But he kept a careful eye open, particularly on Major Burlingham.

The winter and spring of 1915 was long and wet — God it was wet. The battlefield was a muddy swamp and the trenches, at points, were knee deep in water. The British Army squelched, slithered, slipped and fell into

201

the stinking stuff. They became lousy and filthy and drenched through and the wet made the khaki serge uniforms heavy and stiff as cardboard.

In nine months, no word of home leave came through. Periodically they were sent back from the line to rest in one of the towns or villages nearby and then returned to the lines. The battles and engagements were brutal and heavy. Casualties mounted and Wilf began to think they would run out of men. It must all come to an end soon or there would be none of them left to go home, nor to fight for whatever they were fighting for, but he tried not to think about that. It didn't pay to think in this war. Far better to keep your mind on the job. That way you might manage to stay alive.

During one fierce battle, the batallion was ordered to go over the top to try and capture a section of German trenches. They said it was vital and if successful would score a great victory and save many lives being lost.

As they waited, tense and scared out of their wits, for the whistle to blow, Wilf spotted Harry underneath the wooden lats that covered the officers' dug-out. He was excused such duties as usual.

"That bugger knows what he's doing alright — cushy sod. I might try it on if I get back," he whispered bitterly into the turned-up collar of his greatcoat. But in his heart he knew he could never act like that. No matter how they felt about the war, he knew Ada would never want him to shirk his duty.

He wished that whistle would blow and let them get on with it. Finally the piercing screech wailed over his head and bending low they swarmed over the top following their officers.

"Come on, lads — let's get the buggers." Softly the words of encouragement floated over the noise of the battle. It was by now a familiar sound and they paid no heed, being hell-bent on getting the job done and returning safety to their own lines. Funny, really, but when you were out on a job, your trench seemed like home and you longed to get back to it.

As they neared the enemy trenches a sickly sweet strench floated towards them. Wilf laughed to himself — bloody foreign food. And then the stench hit him full in the face — hidden in a thick yellow smoke that tore at his lungs and felled men like matchsticks in a gale.

It was a gas attack — the first they had encountered — and many of them without gas masks, Wilf included. Nobody ever dreamt they would actually use gas — that was inhuman. As it hit Wilf he fell forward, gasping, choking and retching his heart out. He lay writhing in pain, praying loudly for God to help him.

"Ada — Ada — Oh God help me," he called out. He felt himself being pushed over roughly and looked up through streaming eyes into a masked face.

Something was pushed over his mouth and nostrils and the mask shouted in a blurred voice, "Breathe in — breathe in, blast you."

He obeyed the order and a little relief from the pain came through before he blacked out completely. Through the darkness he felt himself being lifted and carried bodily, with stumbling steps, over the rough, muddy terrain. But the pain was so bad he just wanted to be left alone, and struggled to free himself.

"For God's sake, keep still, man. We're almost back to our own lines."

Through the surges of pain he recognised the voice of Ralph Tinker before he was hurled through the air. He landed in a deep crevice with Ralph falling heavily on top of him. He struggled to tear the cover from his face, but it was pushed back on again and tied tightly around his head.

"Keep that bugger on until I get you to a Red Cross station," came the order.

Thankfully oblivion swept over him and he knew no more until he awoke in a hospital tent just behind the lines. For a minute he could not think where he was, and turning saw several of the other men lying in the rows of canvas camps beds. Raising himself on one elbow he looked around.

"Who . . ?" he tried to find his voice, but only a rasping whisper came through his gullet.

"Don't try to talk, Corporal. You'll soon get your voice back and be as good as new. You had a lucky escape. A lot more so than many of your comrades." A doctor came to his bedside and taking his pulse chatted softly to him.

They brought him a cup of tea and he gulped it thirstily, feeling the liquid course down his throat and into the depths of his chest. God, it hurt to breathe and that tasted good. The effort spent him and he fell back on the bed.

"You can have as much of that stuff as you like. Nothing like good old army brew to make you feel better." The familiar voice spoke above his head and looking up he saw it was Lieutenant Tinker standing there. His left arm was in a sling.

Wilf raised his eyebrows in question.

"Only a bit of shrapnel, Corporal — it's not a blighty one like you. You'll have leave coming as soon as you are out of here."

Joy soared through Wilf's heart — leave — home — Ada. It was almost worth all the pain.

"What happened, Sir?" he gasped and Ralph answered honestly, seeing no good being got from hiding anything from the man. The severity of the gas attack had made them withdraw and the mission was not successful.

"We've lost some good men, Corporal — or rather Sergeant. You've been given a field promotion."

"Who, Sir?" Wilf ignored the promotion.

Ralph reeled off the names of those dead and added that Tutt was missing.

"Any chance, Sir?" He was looking for hope for Tutt.

Ralph shook his head sadly. "There's a new bloke coming in from headquarters. You'll be second in command now. I would have wished for other circumstances, but congratulations. Miss Skipton will be proud of you. After your leave you'll be as good as new. What plans have you got for your leave?"

Wilf told him he intended to get wed without any further delay. "Ada and me have been courting long enough — it's time we were wed."

Ralph turned away — of course, he should have known that would be Tanner's priority.

Wilf lay silent for a while, resting after the exertion of talking, but happy to find his breathing easier and his voice returning with each word. He tried to recall what had happened, but only remembered Ralph and something being shoved across his face. He felt a great sadness about Tutt — what a waste of a good bloke. By hell he would be missed.

"Sir — thank you Sir — you saved my life. I wouldn't be here if it weren't for you. Have you said anything about what you did for me?"

Ralph shook his head.

"Well, I bloody well shall, Sir. Er — what was it you shoved over my mouth?"

Ralph began to chuckle. "Do you really want to know?"

Wilf nodded.

"Well, when the gas hit us I was terrified and then I managed to get my mask on. I couldn't see a bloody thing and then I literally bumped into you — without a mask. You should be hauled over the coals for that. I whipped my scarf off and pissed on it as best I could and wrapped it around your face. The acid neutralises the gas to some extent. Anyway it did the job for you."

Wilf gawped blankly and then they both started to laugh. He never thought he'd ever live to see the day when he would have been glad to be pissed on. But by God he was.

Ralph put out his hand. "I'll be off now, Tanner. Your leave pass will be ready as soon as you're fit enough to be discharged from here. I'm off back to headquarters to rest a bit and do some administration work until I'm well again."

Wilf gripped his hand and held it tightly. Tears rose to his eyes.

Ralph coughed and then turned to walk away. As he reached the open flaps of the tent he looked back. "Wilf. . . ?"

Wilf sat up and looked across.

"Give my regards to Miss . . . Ada, will you? I know you will be very happy with her. You've chosen well."

He disappeared quickly, leaving Wilf thinking what a grand bloke he was. By hek, he'd have hell of a lot to tell Ada. He'd send her a wire and let her know he was coming on leave, tell her to arrange the wedding. That would surprise and please her. Not half!

He fell into a pleasant slumber and was awakened again by a hand on his shoulder.

"Now then, our kid, you got yourself a right good 'un there. Going home on leave and all — you crafty bugger."

It was Harry leering above him, but he couldn't be bothered to speak the anger that came over him. How the hell did he manage to get a brother like that?

From under his gas mask Harry brought out a package of souvenirs. "See what you can get for these back home, lad. I'll give you a bit for your trouble. We might make a tidy bit on the side if you play your cards right."

"Bugger off — I'm not taking your thieving bits back home or anywhere else. You heartless sod. Don't you ever think about owt but yourself? You've got that lot from dead bodies and it gives me the ruddy creeps. Bugger off and leave me in peace."

Harry could see his brother was not going to be of any help and sulkily he took back the package.

"Major Burlingham sent you this." He held out a bar of chocolate and Wilf took it and put it under his pillow.

"He's not a bad bloke really when you get to know him and we — or you — are almost related aren't you? That makes us sort of family like." His voice had a hidden meaning, but Wilf chose to ignore it.

"Just bugger off," he snapped and turning his head on his brother pretended to sleep.

CHAPTER 23

Once the hue and cry had died down, folk began to accept that war meant loss of life. Ada, in an odd sort of way, felt a little at a loose end. Now that Gertie had her new-found confidence, it meant that there was no real need to involve herself so much with the affairs of Wilf's family. She still kept an eye on things and called every day as she picked Gertie up for work, but any inquiries were purely courtesy. It seemed daft, but it left an empty void. She'd always had somebody to see to — mainly Wilf, who had taken up most of her life. But he wasn't there any more — he was miles and miles away. Each day was now spent hoping and praying that he would come home safe and sound and in one piece.

Even the house lost a bit of its interest and she would mooch about like a lost sheep. If you had asked her the reason, she couldn't have told you because she couldn't honestly put her finger on the way or how she felt. A funny sensation would sweep over her at the oddest times — when she was in the middle of something at work, during mealtimes and more often in the middle of the night. She would wake with a start and then be unable to get back to sleep. It was a strong feeling of anticipation — as if she were expecting something to happen — waiting for it to happen more like. A feeling like the calm before the storm — and yet it did not frighten her, just puzzled her.

Esther was quick to notice her lass's restlessness and one morning as she cleared the breakfast things away she saw that Ada's plate of fried tatties had not been touched. She might be a little 'un, but she could always put her food away — and fried tatties were one of her favourite breakfasts.

"You haven't eaten a bite, hunny — what's up?" she asked, looking at her daughter's frowning, puzzled look. Lass must be bothering about Wilf — she hoped it wasn't a sign of owt happening.

Ada shrugged and sighed.

"Come on, hunny — tell Mam," Esther encouraged.

"It's nowt I can put my finger on, Mam — just a funny feeling I've got."

"Not about the lad is it? You've not got a premonition?"

"Nay. It doesn't seem bad like that, and anyway I got a letter from him yesterday. Not that that's owt to go by. It were over two weeks old. But I'd have heard if owt were wrong."

Esther decided to leave it at that. No good going on — it would only bother the lass more. She couldn't find any words of comfort or hope for that matter. She could only hope to God that things were alright. Ever since Stanley had been killed Esther had feared the worst. Eh, it were a funny do and no mistake. Everybody worried to death and yet going about as if this were a great party. She couldn't see any sense in it at all.

Ada buried herself in her work and was thankful that they were particularly busy. A huge batch of uniforms had come in and she set the girls on spraying them with disinfectant to ward off any infection. The lasses took it all in good part — even when they were sprayed and given doses of jollop to send any chance of infection straight through them.

Most of them had somebody in the war and they looked on this part of their work as their effort towards victory.

"Bloody hell Ada — I shit through the eye of a needle and stink like our Mam's privvy after she's scrubbed it out on Fridays," Winnie Pearson laughed and shouted as she swallowed the horrible black mixture and allowed herself to be attacked by the spray.

"Don't do much for your love life does it lass?" Lily shouted back and for a minute hysterical laughter rang through the great wash house.

They started to sing choruses that had become popular. They sang in unison and Ada had to admit they weren't bad. She listened for a while to *Roses of Picardy, Pack up your Troubles* and, finally, *My Gel's a Yorkshire Girl.* Oh, that brought back memories.

Lily Hartley saw that she wasn't joining in. That was unusual for Ada, like her Dad, had an lovely voice — strong and vibrant.

"What's up lass — missing your Wilf are you?" she asked.

"Aye, happen so. But I'm not only one, Lil. It's a hell of a war."

"And a long one for some lass — for some poor buggers it'll last for ever."

Ada remembered that Lily had already lost two brothers — they were a lot worse off than her.

She worked until eight that night and after supper went up to her bedroom and again took out Wilf's letters and cards. Tears rushed to her eyes as she looked at the scrawling writing and offered a prayer that all was well with him.

The next morning her heart seemed lighter, and she felt brighter and more cheerful, more like her old self. Esther was glad to see the change of mood. She was fed up with all the long faces, but she knew how they all felt.

The morning passed quickly and as she walked home at dinner time her steps were lighter than they had been for a day or two. She began to feel excited, almost lightheaded. There would be a letter — she knew it. It might say he was coming home after all. But there was no letter waiting beside her plate. Sighing loudly she sat down and listened to her Mam going on about no news being good news. That was a lot of tripe.

All through the afternoon she worked quickly as if there was some great need to get it all done. She thought about Wilf and a feeling of being close to him almost overpowered her — she could even smell him — the carbolic soap his Mam always used and the mothballs his best clothes were put away in. Oh, please God, please don't let this be a foreboding.   Just

207

before tea break, Mrs. Price walked across to her. She hurried, and this set Ada's heart pounding. Now what was up?

"Your Father's at the door, Ada. There's a wire for you — I do hope it's not bad news," she said.

Ada stopped work and ran to the door, but before she could reach it Thom was through it and running towards her.

"It's alright, hunny — I've opened it — he's coming home on sick leave and he wants to get wed." The words tumbled out, stopping Ada dead in her tracks.

"Thank God — oh thank God — I knew summat was going on." She took the telegram and read the words that floated before her eyes. 'Arriving Friday on sick leave. Have been gassed but I'm alright. Make arrangements for wedding by special licence. Love Wilf.'

"Friday — Friday. Why that's day after tomorrow. By hell, I'll have to get a move on. Hold hard Dad, I'm coming home with you."

She went back and told Mrs Price that she was taking time off and gave her reasons. Her face was flushed with excitement and she grabbed at her overall to get it off. She wanted to get home and start things moving.

"I can't spare you for too long Ada, you know how busy we are. Can you make do with two or three days?"

"You can bugger off, Missus — I'm having time off with Wilf and I'll come back when he's gone and not before. Take it or leave it."

She turned on her heel and went to join Thom. She knew her value to the laundry and it wasn't as if she ever took time off. They could like it or lump it. She tucked her arm in Thom's and they walked, almost ran, down the street.

"What's our Mam say then?" she asked.

"You know your Mam. She's been up to Neil Simon's and got stuff ordered for wedding breakfast. She's even been up to our Sarah's to see about you stopping up there for the honeymoon and Sarah and bairns coming to us — you'll be on your own then like."

A wide smile stretched across her face — trust Mam to see to things.

"Hold on a minute Dad. I'm off to call and tell Polly. I forgot to go and tell Gertie afore I left work."

Polly was delighted and said she was glad they were going to get round to it. "About time you two were wed. I began to think you'd changed your minds."

The next two days passed as if in a dream, but she had a lot to see to. First the licence which had to be applied for — cost twenty-five quid it did. Still it was worth every penny. Then she and Gertie went up to Machin's and got their outfits. Ada decided on a dusky pink dress and a cream hat, Gertie had grey silk with a pink hat.

When Ada reminded Gertie that she wanted her to be bridesmaid she

208

said she would understand if she refused. "I don't want to upset you about Alf and bring it all back, lass."

"Nay, I'll stand for you Ada and welcome. Nowt's going to bring Alf back."

They preened and pranced in front of Machin's mirror and Ada's excitement got through to Gertie. They were like a pair of bairns getting ready for a Sunday School outing.

The wedding was to be held at the High Street Primitive Chapel. Uncle Johnny Sawden offered her his carriage and after a moment's thought she accepted. Might as well be a lady for one day.

"Who's to be best man, then?" Thom asked.

Ada had not thought about that, but supposed now Alf was gone that Wilf would ask Tutt Bradley — she did not know that he was missing.

When Friday dawned she was up and dressed before daylight.

"You maybe won't be in such a hurry after a year or two of married life," Thom teased her.

They sat together having a cup of tea — it was too early for Esther or any of the others to be up and they were enjoying this little space of privacy.

"I don't know what time he's coming Dad and I reckon if I meet first train from London I might be lucky. Anyway, they'll tell me what time the others arrive — that's if he comes from London."

"He'll be here some time today, hunny. Get yourself off now and don't hang about."

Shyly she went up and hugged Thom. They didn't usually show a great deal of affection and least of all Ada, but today was a special day — today was the last day that she would really belong to him. Once Wilf arrived she would begin to think about being Mrs. Tanner.

Wilf was not on the first train and she went to make enquiries at the booking office.

"Where's he coming from lass?"

Ada paused. "France — I think." It sounded a bit daft not to know where he was coming from, but the clerk didn't seem to notice.

"Oh, he'll be coming from London then. The next one's twelve-fifteen, but it's usually packed. They put extra ones on though and he could just be a few minutes late."

She smiled her thanks and went into the street. Her first thought was to go back home, but that would mean several hours to kill just chatting and sitting around. No, she'd go for a walk first.

Her steps turned towards the sea front, but not to their favourite place on the cliffs. Instead she went and looked out over the harbour, imagining that she could see ships in the distance. Wilf would be coming across water like that. She peered into the mist and then, laughing at herself, decided to walk slowly back to the station and look in the shop windows on the way.

She stood outside the folding iron gates and looked down the line — in the distance she could see the smoke and steam and hear, on the rails, the rumbling of the train. Her heart started to beat loudly — Wilf would be on that train — in a minute he would be here by her side.

The train drew into the station and she searched the crowd of khaki figures that poured out of the doors. They all looked alike except that some wore dressings where they had been wounded. She wondered if Wilf would be wrapped up or anything — what exactly did being gassed mean? She stood on tip-toe trying to spot him.

"Hello, short arse," a husky voice whispered behind her and she jumped around to find Wilf standing there.

She opened her mouth, but no words would come — Wilf, was this Wilf? He looked so thin — his face was drawn, his eyes had black rims under them and his skin looked yellow — even his voice sounded different.

For a moment they stood looking into one another's eyes, and then he opened his arms and she tumbled into them.

"What have they done to you, love — are you alright . . . ?" the words were buried in a kiss and Wilf held her so tight she could not breathe.

"I've missed you, Ada — you don't know how much I've missed you."

It was her turn to hold him tightly — to whisper words of love and comfort. "You're home now, love — it'll be alright now." They released one another and looking round saw that the station was empty.

"Come on love, let's go on up home. Let's get some grub into you and get you rested."

But Wilf didn't want to share her with anyone else, not just yet. "I'd rather go for a walk up cliffs first — I'd like to take in a bit of Brid air."

He left his kit bag at the station office and arm in arm they walked as they had done so many times — through on to Quay Road, up the Promenade and then onto Flamborough cliffs. On the way people called out to them and wished Wilf well, but it all sailed over her head. The feel of him close to her again filled her with excitement. In two days they'd be wed — she'd be Mrs. Tanner.

The cliffs were lush green, making a striking contrast to the white chalk below them. Wilf sank down and pulled Ada beside him.

"I never thought I'd see this lot again," he whispered.

"What happened then, love?" she asked.

He paused and then the tears began to roll down his cheeks — his whole body became racked with sobs. He fell forward on his arms and she let him lie until his grief was spent. There were no words to help him — these were the tears of a man who had faced death and destruction. And he wasn't the same. She could see that war had made Wilf into a man. He told her what

210

had happened — about Tutt being missing — Tinker saving his life and some of the daft things George had done.

"He means right enough, but he's a silly bugger at times. God knows what'll happen now Tutt's gone. Still, I suppose that'll be up to me a bit."

For the first time she noticed the three white stripes on his arm. Leaning forward she stroked them.

Smiling he asked, "Well — aren't you going to say it then?"

"Say what?"

"Does it mean more brass?" He laughed teasingly, but the words brought tears to her eyes — now it was her turn to cry.

"Bugger the brass, lad — you mean more to me than all brass in world."

He held her close again and she felt the hardness of his body against hers. "Let's go and have a look at the house shall we?"

Again a thrill ran through her body. "I haven't done much to it since you left, only cleaned it up a bit."

They went past the station to pick up his kit bag, called in to say hello to Esther and let Polly know he was home. Lots of tears were shed — Esther cried as she hugged him, his Mam cried as soon as he entered the door.

"Come on now — all this blithering is making me wish I'd stayed back yonder," he laughed, but he understood how they felt.

Esther asked him back for a meal, but he refused saying that he wanted to spend a bit of time with his Mam.

"I'll be married soon Mrs. Skipton and then I'll be spending all me time with the missus." He glowed as he spoke — his missus — it gave him a warm feeling of security, a hold on life.

Slowly they walked up the hill towards Scarborough Road. Wilf took in all the familiar landmarks and asked questions about life in the town.

"Have you got everything arranged then?" he asked and she nodded shyly, telling him about the wedding and honeymoon arrangements.

"Who's best man then?" she asked.

Wilf shook his head and shrugged and she knew he was thinking about Alf and Tutt.

They had reached the house and she handed him the key. He opened the door that led into the passageway — the sun streamed through the landing window and everything gleamed. They toured the house and chatted about furnishings and what it would all look like 'after the war.'

"After the bloody war — everybody says that everything will happen then — I only hope I live to see if it does." His voice was cynical.

"You'd better, my lad — I don't want this lot on my own." She spoke like the old Ada he knew and it warmed his heart.

They stood in the bedroom and looked down at the yard as they had done just before he left.

"What do you see down there now, love?" he asked.

211

Nodding her head she whispered, "I can see you and me, men at work, washing on the line — it's blowing in the breeze. It's a busy place — a proper home and business."

"No bairns yet?" he laughed.

She blushed. In spite of their nearness she and Wilf had never really spoken of private things like that — not to mean anything.

He took off his greatcoat and laid it down on the wooden floor of the bedroom. "Come and sit down a minute." He knelt down and she went and sat beside him.

"Is it very bad over there, Wilf?"

"Yes — it's worse than I ever imagined or could put into words. But I don't want to talk about that, not just now. I want to look at you — to talk about us."

Roughly he pulled her towards him, half-expecting her to draw away. But she held him close, feeling his urgency and welcoming his embraces. Their kisses grew deeper, more passionate, and within her there was a feeling she had never known before. Love rippled and tingled through her veins. Wilf was here — he was here beside her holding her close. Oh God, how she had missed him. His hands began to explore her body — to delve inside her bodice and caress her breasts. Still she held him tightly.

He buried his head into her neck and cried, "I've longed for this, Ada. I've laid awake night after night thinking and dreaming about holding you like this."

She drew away from him and looked deep into his eyes — his blue, blue eyes. "Wilf, do you want to do it — now I mean, afore we get wed?"

He couldn't answer. He had felt her responding to him, but with Ada you never knew how she would react. Instead he gazed at her.

"Wilf?"

"Yes — yes I do — I want to make you mine, to feel that you really belong to me — here in our own home and not some strange bed."

To his surprise, she got up and going to the corner to hide herself from the windows, she slowly undressed, folding her clothes in a neat pile. He went and followed her and had to smile to himself, dear, naive Ada — she had left on her long bodice.

He kept on his long pants and on seeing them she burst into laughter. "You look daft in them, lad, and they're not a very good colour. Never mind, I'll get the copper going and soon have them white as snow." They laughed together and he pulled her down beside him.

They made love in a daze — he, savouring every precious moment, and she — she was thinking it was lovely to feel Wilf so close to her, but well, it wasn't all that much to get excited about. She had felt his thrill and had responded with all her heart.

"What if I'm expecting now?" she asked when the passion was spent and they lay in each other's arms.

"I don't give a damn and who'll know anyway? We'll be wed in a couple of days. I love you Ada — Ada Tanner."

Quickly she placed her fingers over his lips. "Don't say that Wilf, not afore we're wed. They say it's bad luck." She shivered and got up.

As they dressed she looked thoughtful and then asked in her blunt manner, "Have you ever done that before, Wilf?"

The question startled him — what on earth made her ask that ? He considered his answer carefully — he didn't want to lie to her, but he couldn't tell her about Beatty, that would ruin everything. The thrill of making love to her had not been the mad fleeting passion he had known with Beatty — this was real love — lasting and complete. He felt as if all the fear had left him in a gentle flood of passion.

"Now when have I had a chance to do that?" he answered with a question.

"Oh I don't know — in France or somewhere."

He breathed a silent sigh of relief. At least he could answer that truthfully. "No, Ada, I haven't."

She seemed satisfied with his answer. "Come on then, lad — let's be getting on with things. It's about time you made an honest woman of me."

Laughing they linked arms and left the house. It felt such a happy house now. She was glad they had made love there and felt no shame or remorse. They were to be married, so what did it matter and, anyway, it seemed right somehow.

They walked quickly, chatting and laughing about old times. "Do you remember?" Oh, they had so much to remember. As they rounded the corner that led into St. John Street, Wilf stopped in his tracks.

"Just look over there, Ada — at that officer."

She looked and saw that it was Ralph Tinker walking on the other side of the street. He had one arm in a sling and with the other carried a brown leather suitcase.

"Sir — Sir," Wilf called out, and ran across the street. "What are you doing here, Sir?"

"Now, that's not much of a welcome," Ralph laughed.

"You know what I mean, Sir. I only left you in France the other day. I thought you weren't due for leave."

Ralph explained that his arm was slow to heal and that the powers that be had decided he would benefit from some home leave.

"Well, I'm right glad to see you, Sir. Me and Ada are getting wed on Monday. Would you do me the honour of coming to the wedding, Sir? After all, if it hadn't been for you I wouldn't be here. I've just been telling Ada about it."

Ralph hesitated for a minute and then said he would be delighted to accept.

Ada had now reached them and she stood beside Wilf looking up at Ralph.

"My congratulations, Ada." Ralph spoke softly to her and had to clear his throat to get the words out. Ada nodded her thanks.

Wilf grabbed her arm and then said, "You wouldn't be my best man, would you, Sir? I wanted Alf, but well . . ." the words petered out.

"No, Wilf, you can't ask an officer to do that. Mr. Tinker might not want to — he might not think it right."

Ralph only wished he had other things to do than see Ada marry another man and he was just about to refuse when he saw Wilf's excited face. "Only on one condition."

Wilf raised his eyebrows in question.

"That you take good care of your bride. If I'm to be best man you'll have to answer to me." He spoke in jest and looked at Ada as he did so. Their eyes met and for a brief second locked. A shudder ran through her as she saw the deliberate blank look on his face.

Wilf finally broke the silence. "Tell you what, Sir, let's meet and have a drink tomorrow dinner time. I can give you all the arrangements. By hek, Sir, I'm right proud — I am and all."

"Right you are then. See you in the Ship Inn around twelve noon and Ada — I'll see you in church." He paused and stumbled over the last words, but smiled as he spoke.

Again her only answer was to nod briefly. She had been going to tell Wilf about the card, but how could she do that now? It would only create bad feeling. She couldn't spoil things now.

"That's a turn up then, lass." Wilf was bursting with pride.

Well, if that's what he wanted, she'd have to go along with it, but she wished it could have been somebody else — anybody else would have done, just as long as he was one of their own sort. Having Ralph Tinker there would make them all a little uncomfortable, and she would be on edge. Oh, damn the bloke. Why did he have to appear just now?

CHAPTER 24

The next few days passed by in a flurry of preparations for the wedding. Ada became so excited that Esther thought she might have a turn.

"Her brain's going nineteen to the dozen. I've never known her like this, Thom," she said and Thom had to admit that he would never have dreamt that Ada would ever get herself in a state about owt and never about getting wed after waiting all this time.

"Maybe it's the war and all the uncertainty, lass. Poor buggers never know if they'll come back or not."

Esther nodded in agreement.

Wilf kept his meeting with Ralph Tinker and the two men enjoyed a quiet drink in the lounge of the pub. Wilf had never been in the lounge before and had to admit he felt a bit uneasy, but once he had supped a couple of whiskies — yes whiskies — he began to feel better.

"I'm right glad you're to be best man, Sir — I feel proud." He spoke with obvious truth, but Ralph frowned.

"Are you sure Ada did not mind, Wilf? You didn't give her much chance to say anything."

Wilf brushed his doubts aside. Ada was as chuffed as he was — well she'd never said owt to the contrary and knowing her she would have done if she'd not liked the idea.

They chatted on a bit and then found that they were mainly talking about the comrades left at the front.

"Funny you know, Sir — when you're there you can't think of owt but home and getting away, and when you're out of it you can't talk or think about owt else but being there and your mates."

"You've got a brother with us, haven't you Wilf? — Harry — he's my batman. Not much like you, if you don't mind me saying so."

Wilf frowned heavily. "I hope not, Sir. Our Harry has always been a bit of a dark horse — a bit shady, although I says it as shouldn't being his brother. But he's always been a bit on the shifty side. We've never had much in common."

"No love lost, you might say."

Wilf shook his head. "He was never one for work — always swinging it. Now me — I've always worked, but I've got to say most of it's due to Ada."

"Yes — Ada — I can imagine that."

"She's not as sharp and biting as she seems at first, you know, Sir. She's got a heart of gold and a determination that would stick through thick and thin." He didn't altogether know why, but he found himself almost defending her.

Ralph smiled and playfully thumped his shoulder. "I can see that, man. Ada is made of stern stuff."

After arranging to meet on the morning of the wedding outside the church they parted with a warm handshake.

"Wilf, I'm honoured to stand for you — for you both — I don't know of any other couple that I'd be prouder to do so."

That Saturday night they decided to make a real family night of it and Esther invited Gertie and Polly down to the house to join in with the family in what would really be the wedding reception. Being married on a Monday meant that many of them could not get away from work — more so now that the war made much of their work so vital. Having a family night would be a celebration for the wedding and also for Esther and Thom. It would be grand to have most of them home together, sat round the big table as they used to do. Isabella thought it a lovely idea and offered to bring down some food to help out Esther, but Esther refused.

"I want to do this myself — make it like old times."

Isabella knew exactly what she meant but doubted if the old times could be recaptured.

When they were all gathered, Esther and Thom realised that the women far outnumbered the men. Sarah was there on her own with the bairns — young Thom was away somewhere down south with his battalion. Isabella was on her own — but two or three of the lads were there and with Wilf they made up a good enough party. But not like the old days — nowhere near it.

In spite of food shortages the table looked grand. Home made pork pie, home made bread, fruit cake, cut and come again cake and to finish off with that old family favourite prune pie and custard.

Thom beamed as he watched Esther setting out the places and giving a satisfied smile at the rich brown pastry, the crusty bread and the deep, almost black depth of the fruit cake. She'd not lost her touch and this little gathering had given her a new lease of life. He knew, like him, she worried about the lads being away, about the lasses being left on their own and about him having to work at a time when he should be giving up a bit.

"It's not right, Thom — it's not right at all. Men should be at home with the womenfolk, not off to some bloody foreign place getting maimed and killed."

That was right and all, but what the hell could they do about it?

Amid laughter and jokes they sat around the table as in days past with Thom and Esther in pride of place at each end. Cups and saucers rattled, knives and forks grated and cleaned the plates, as they tucked into their food.

"I'll say this Esther — and I've always said it even afore I knew you better — I don't know how you do it."

Esther beamed as Polly paid her the compliment, and she leaned forward and squeezed her hand. "Well, Polly lass, I had a good lad behind me. If you don't mind me saying so, you were left with a young family and I reckon you've done a damn good job with these two here."

Now it was Polly's turn to beam. "I wish the other one were more like Wilf," she sighed.

"Well, you never know lass, he might turn out alright in the end." They both doubted it, but the kindly words gave a little comfort.

As this was, so to speak, mainly for Ada and Wilf, Thom felt it was an occasion upon which a speech was called for. Oh, the bairns would have a wedding breakfast, but that would only be for the wedding party — about six in all. This was the time to say things he felt in his heart. As he rose to his feet the family gave a mock groan — Dad was off again and chances would be he would turn to politics.

"Na, then, you can all laugh, but it's a long time since this table has ha so many folk around it, and it's a grand sight. But what we're really here for is our Ada and Wilf who, as you know, are to wed on Monday morning — a good start to the week you might say. But it's also a start to a new life and for you both, life will never be the same again. You will take on new responsibilities — a responsibility for each other. You take on another life so to speak. And that is a very serious commitment — to be responsible for another life.

"We did wonder if you'd ever get round to it, but now you have, I want to say that we are all delighted. You've shown that you are a hard working couple, not afraid to graft for what you want. And prepared to wait for it too. You've shown that and all. God bless you both, and my only hope is that you'll be as happy and joyful in your life as me and Esther. And I'll tell you this lad — I couldn't have waited all this time for her. Keep safe and when you come back — God willing — you can start life as married life should be started — together."

As he spoke Esther and Polly wiped away a tear — and then Esther shushed him and blushed as he said about waiting for her.

Wilf took Ada's hand in his and gently stroked it with his thumb. He felt warm and safe — safe in a family love and in Ada's love. She'd proved just how strong that was in a way he had never thought she would. They'd be right enough.

Ada trembled as he touched her, but she wouldn't exactly have said it was with passion — more a feeling of dismay seemed to sink into her body, right down like a heavy stone. Please God they would start life together after this lot was over.

Esther would allow no-one to help clear away but Polly. "Let's give the bairns a rest. Us old 'uns can see to this lot. Get on that piano Isabella and get a sing song going."

217

Isabella did as she was told and Thom went and stood by her side leaning on the top of the piano, poised ready to sing. She struck up with *Just a Song at Twilight*, and Thom's voice, still clear and strong, rang through the room.

He was half-way through when Esther came rushing into the room, all of a bustle, wiping her hands on her pinny. "What the hell's that row?"

Thom stopped dead in his tracks and Isabella turned to look inquiringly. "I don't reckon I sound all that bad," he started to say.

"I don't mean that, you silly fool — that racket outside — just listen."

They cocked their ears and listened to a drone that got louder and louder until it seemed to be coming from right overhead. And then they heard excited voices and people running up and down the street.

Thom and Wilf rushed outside and then called, "Come on — come and look — it's a bloody Zeppelin — two of the buggers," Thom shouted through the door and then all hell let loose.

Most of them rushed outside and stood peering up at what was later described as a black cloud that appeared to cover most of the old town. Esther rushed to the sideboard drawer and took out the leather case that held her insurance policies — then went out to join the rest.

"I wish I'd got a bloody gun. I'd have a go and shoot the bugger down," Wilf called out.

By this time the police were out trying desperately to get people to go indoors.

"If they fire, we'll all be killed — get indoors before owt happens," they called out and just as desperately the folk resisted. This was a sight they'd never seen before and most likely would never see again.

Thom and Wilf went over to the poor bobby to try and help. "How the hell's it gotten here?" Wilf asked.

"We reckon it's on its way back from Hull and got off course. Just try and get your lot inside."

Wilf and Thom tried, and all but Esther obeyed.

"Play piano loud so as to drown out noise. Get 'em singing, Mr. Skipton," Wilf shouted.

But Esther would not be moved. She had brought out the old kitchen chair and there she sat — hat and coat on, and insurance policies firmly clasped upon her knee. "I'm not shifting — if owt happens we'll want these policies."

"If owt happens, you silly bitch, we shan't need policies or owt else — we'll all be gone." Thom was losing his patience, but she would not be budged. So he brought out another chair and sat beside her.

"Open the window, our Isabella, and play loud — I'll drown the bugger out."

Wilf could see they would not be moved and so he opened the sash window and told Isabella to get on with it. She played *Rule Britannia* and once again Thom's voice rang out. Ada popped her head through the window, and seeing the astonished look upon the poor bobby's face as he stood helpless watching Thom and Esther sitting there holding hands and the blessed policies, and Thom singing 'Britons, never never will be slaves,' cracked out laughing.

What a sight — by hell her Mam and Dad were a daft pair — but they were strong and always together. If Esther was going to go up through the Zeppelin, then Dad was going and all.

Her laughter caught on and soon the room and half the street, who had come out upon hearing Thom, were joining in the song. Wilf couldn't believe his eyes, but knew it was typical of this family. As the Zeppelin moved slowly across the sky and faded over the harbour, Thom got up, stood firmly to attention and sang the national anthem. Wilf couldn't have joined in if they'd paid him — he and Ada were doubled up, collapsed on the armchair in gales of laughter.

"I reckon we ought to have your Mam and Dad out there with us — they'd finish the war in no time," he laughed.

As the threat of a raid passed Thom and Esther picked up their chairs and amid cheers from the onlookers walked sedately and calmly indoors.

"What we need now is a strong cup of tea," she said, taking off her hat and, motioning to Polly, made for the kitchen.

"That's it our Mam — a cup of tea to cure all ails," Ada called after her and then turning saw that Isabella was transfixed, sat at the piano with tears rolling down her cheeks.

"What's up, love?" She went across and placed her arm around her shoulder.

"Nothing really. I were just thinking what a grand pair they are our Mam and Dad." She smiled and sighed and then went on to play a medley of popular choruses.

Then the party took off — charades, I-spy, hunt the thimble — oh how they enjoyed themselves.

"Trust our Ada to mark her wedding party with a Zeppelin — she can't do owt by halves," Thom laughed, and then asked her to sing a duet with him.

"Let's do that new one. I reckon I can remember it — *When the poppies bloom again.*" They stood together — Ada, tiny and raven-haired and so like his Esther — and Thom, tall, still straight and blonde, and their voices united beautifully as they sang, 'When the poppies bloom again, I'll remember you, down beside the river side, when we were two. Darling, till we meet again, I'll be forever true, and when the poppies bloom again, I'll remember you.'

Ada looked across at Wilf as she sang and felt his gaze bearing right

219

down into her soul. As she sang the words the thought of him leaving so soon after they were wed really hit home. She loved him so much — so much more than she had ever thought possible. She looked across at Gertie, trying to bravely smile through her tears as she thought of what might have been with Alf. Please God, send Wilf back to me. I don't care if he's wounded or maimed — just please, please send him back to me, she prayed silently.

As the song ended there was a silence that almost filled the room — each one lost in their own thoughts. As Isabella had played and listen to the part of the song that said, 'When you held me tenderly and told me not to cry, I knew it was our last goodbye, and you were gone from me,' she had had difficulty in playing the notes as she had heard Ada's voice tremble. But they were all in the same boat — Esther and Sarah were thinking of young Stanley, the other lasses were thinking about their husbands and she — she about George. Dear George, who always appeared to be so wise and manly, but who, she knew, could be so silly at times. She wished to God he were here now.

The silence was thankfully broken by the arrival of her carriage and the party broke up. As she left she hugged Wilf warmly, forgetting for once her position as his Commanding Officer's wife. Here and now he was to be her brother-in-law and she wanted to hold him and wish him well and a safe return.

"If you get a chance, tell George about this, won't you?" she asked, and Wilf nodded, returning her hug in the sentimentality of the moment.

He, Polly and Gertie hung on until the last and then Ada saw them to the door. "Stay with your Mam tomorrow night, Wilf. I've got things to do and after Monday we'll have all our lives together. Stay with her and have a chat."

He shook his head and smiled at her. Since coming on leave, although it had only been a day or two, he had brightened up and looked much better. His breathing was still a bit laboured, but easier now. Oh, if only he could have stayed longer — she'd soon have got him better.

"You're a good 'un, short arse. I only wish I'd had sense to wed you years ago, never mind what you said."

She silently wished so too, realising at only this late moment how futile had been her wishes to have 'things right' before they were wed. She went back into the front room and looked at the dying embers of the fire. Thom was stood on a stool turning out the gas chandelier, and she watched as each one plopped and died.

"You'll be alright with that one, lass. He's a good lad and when he comes back you'll have a good start in life."

She looked up at him. "Shouldn't you say 'if' Dad — if he comes back."

Her voice was quiet and low, but the words were spoken with such meaning that Thom and Esther stared at her.

"Now don't be like that lass. You mustn't think like that," Esther said.

"Well, it's no good burying your head, Mam. If's a little word with a big meaning." And she left the room and went upstairs to bed.

All through the night she tossed and turned — if — if — if. The word blazed before her mind.

"If only . . . " How many times had that been said when it was too late?

CHAPTER 25

She slept in fits and starts, but when she got up the next morning Ada felt surprisingly bright and cheerful. These moods puzzled her. One minute she was excited and looking forward to getting wed and the next she was right down in the dumps. She tried to fathom it out herself — were these black patches some sort of sign — or was she just worried about Wilf's going away so soon after the wedding? It was no use — she would just have to try and shake them off.

All through the day she chatted away to her Mam. They talked about when she and Thom got wed, about the troubles of their early life and, most of all, how it was the best day's work Esther had ever done.

"It hasn't been all roses, lass, but life never is. You'll have troubles same as rest of us, but you and Wilf have a hell of a lot more to start off with than we ever did — and a good many more and all. You'll be fine once he's back for good."

Again a shadow passed over Ada — whenever anybody said about Wilf coming back after the war, she felt a shiver run through her but she smiled at Esther — it was no use upsetting her Mam.

She had been surprised about a message sent down from Mrs. Price reminding Ada that she would be delighted to arrange for Ada's and Gertie's flowers. To be honest she'd not thought of a bouquet, but it was a nice thought and she asked for pink carnations for herself and blue asters for Gertie — it would all go nicely.

"You're a right one for being particular, Ada. I only hope you won't let it take you over when you get your own place," Esther tutted to herself and then got busy boiling the ham for the wedding breakfast.

Thom was a bit morose. He hated giving any of his lasses away and always made a pretence of trying to get out of it, but he wouldn't really have missed the wedding for anything.

"Makes me feel old, giving a bride away, as if my life is nearly over," he said.

Esther laughed and playfully thumped him. "You'll never be old, Thom Skipton."

He pinched her backside and she shouted at him, 'You'll never be too old whilst you still feel like that."

"You do know about things, don't you, Ada?" she asked when they were alone.

Ada blushed and nodded — my God what would her Mam say if she knew that she and Wilf had tasted 'things'? There'd be hell to pop. She'd not thought about what they did the first day Wilf was home — tasting forbidden fruits as she called it. To be truthful, it hadn't been all she thought it would be, and felt it had hardly been worth waiting all these years for. But it had passed and been pleasant enough and Wilf had seemed to enjoy it — maybe it would be better on the first night. They would be really alone with no fear of anybody finding them. She'd be relaxed and then it would be grand. Her body tingled as she thought of lying beside Wilf — being close to him — feeling his flesh against hers. Oh, if only she had had sense to get wed before.

As she lay in bed the thought crossed her mind that this would be the last time she would really be able to call it her home. From tomorrow she would be Mrs. Tanner and the bed and the room would only be on loan until she moved to her own place. It might be a good idea to start buying furniture and stuff and getting a move planned after Wilf left. If papers and that were right, the war would soon be over. Best get ready and not be caught on the hop. The thoughts and planning that ran through her mind gave her a sort of comforting confidence until she finally fell asleep.

Esther woke her with a cup of tea and a wide smile. "Come on, lass, we'll soon have Gertie and Polly here. Drink this and then I'll bring you up some hot water to wash yourself down. It's a grand day and your Dad is already up and dressed for you."

They laughed together and then she got up, laid out all her things and slowly and carefully washed and dressed.

Just before she put on her dress she unwound the rags her Mam had put in her hair before she went to bed. Her raven hair fell down her back in coiled ringlets. She stood before the mirror in her white chemise and looked at herself. She thought of the last time she had curled her hair and put it up — that night she dined at Isabella's. She recalled the ride home with Ralph. Oh aye — he'd be there and all today. But somehow the thought did not disturb her. In a funny way it gave her a kind of strength. He would be sure to see that Wilf didn't over exert himself and she knew he would give a good speech at the breakfast.

Her dress hung beautifully in two tiers — the latest fashion — and she had to admit it looked good. She pinned up her hair in large curls from the nape of her neck and then put on her hat and pulled the veil down under her chin.

"Aren't you ready yet, our Ada?" she heard her Dad call up the stairs and picking up her gloves from the bed she went downstairs.

"By hek, Ada, you look grand — a proper lady." She smiled as Polly spoke admiringly. "Our Wilf is a lucky chap and no mistake."

She looked at Gertie. The lass looked right pretty and she too had curled her hair and put it up to sit around her hat.

"You're a pretty pair — a pretty pigeon pair," Thom laughed and then heard Gertie sniff.

Ada looked at her sharply.

"Oh don't worry, Ada. I'm not going to get upset. Only I can't help thinking and wishing . . . "

"I know, love, and I've wished for you too, but when owt like that happens you've got to accept it and make the best of it." As the words came out they had a final ring about them — as if the final bell of a death knoll had been rung.

Polly and Esther started sniffing together and Ada and Gertie then started to laugh at them. It broke the tension and Ada took the bouquet of pink carnations from Gertie, held them in front of her dress and offered her arm to Thom.

"I wish you'd had Johnnie's carriage. It would have put the finishing touch to it all."

Well, he had to have his grumble, but after thinking about it was forced to agree with Ada that to ride in a carriage for just those few yards was a bit daft.

The procession set off — Thom and Ada — he was so straight and proud and she so tiny but upright and with the same proud hold of the head. Gertie came a step or two behind followed by Esther and Polly, who were marching in step, as proud as punch.

They entered the great doors of the chapel and heard the parson whisper loudly to Wilf and Ralph that the bride was here. She stood at her Dad's side for a moment and looked down the aisle. Wilf and Ralph had their backs to her, but she could see Wilf's hand fidgeting behind his back. Ralph spoke to him and he dropped his hand to his side and stood to attention. Esther and Polly walked forward and took their places — Polly behind Wilf and Esther at the other side to join Johnnie Sawden, who had been determined to be at the ceremony.

"Come on then, hunny, let's get going," her Dad whispered and he set off at such a pace that she had to tug on his arm to make him slow down. It might look as if he were in a hurry to get rid of her.

When she reached Wilf's side she passed her flowers to Gertie and then reached down and took his hand in hers. He held it so tightly that she thought he might break it and wriggled to free herself a little.

"Dearly beloved. . . ," she heard the words and also the sniffs behind. Carefully she took in every word and repeated her vows in a clear strong voice, "Until death do us part. . ."

"I now pronounce you Man and Wife." At last, at long last, she and Wilf were wed. They signed the register, hugged and kissed everybody and then each other.

"Well, I'm glad that's over. I never thought we'd get here, lad, she took that long getting ready," Thom said.

"But it was worth waiting for — aye Wilf?" Ralph smiled and then went on. "And don't I get a kiss from the bride then?"

Shyly she leaned forward and kissed him on the cheek, but as she turned his lips brushed hers and she felt him tremble.

"Be happy, Ada — be happy for me," he whispered and she looked sharply in case anyone else had heard, but no-one seemed to take any notice.

"Come on, Mrs. Tanner. I'm fair famished and I know your Mam — my mother-in-law will have a good spread ready."

Wilf took her arm and tucked it under his elbow and followed by Gertie and Ralph, Thom and Esther, Johnnie and Polly, they left the chapel and made their way home.

As always, the table groaned underneath all the food and soon Esther was busy mashing the tea and sharing out the ham. Wilf tucked it as if he'd never seen food before, but Ada picked at hers. It didn't seem right somehow for a bride to eat heartily.

The little speeches said all the usual things. Her Dad hoped they'd be as happy as him and Esther and Ralph spoke more about Wilf that anything, saying what a fine chap he was and how proud an occasion to be chosen as best man.

"I am only sorry that the wretched war has kept the rest of the family away from this happy day," he ended.

Polly, who was thoroughly enjoying a piece of fruit cake, spluttered and snapped, "I'm not. If our Harry'd been here, he'd have got pissed and shown us all up."

Wilf was clearly embarrassed by his Mam, but Ada caught Ralph's eye and they burst out laughing.

"What are you going to do with the rest of the day then, you two? Sal's coming down at six, but you've about four hours to spare. Why not go off to Sewerby or somewhere?" Esther suggested when everyone was ready for off.

Ada told her they'd think of something to do. They might go for a walk or maybe look at the shops.

"I'm going to change first. These things are far too good to walk around in." She went upstairs and put on a more serviceable suit, thinking that they might go up to the house — might start to plan things a bit.

Arm in arm they left the house and walked towards the shops. "We might get some ideas for our home and that, Wilf," she said and he smiled indulgently and hugged her arm to his side. Leisurely they looked in all the shop windows — picking out things they liked — getting ideas from the displays.

"Ada, look here — Harry Kidd's got one of them gramophones in. Let's go in and listen shall we?"

They went inside and asked for a demonstration. The assistant was pleased to oblige. Gramophones were at a premium and it was always a

pleasure to listen to a record or two. 'When the poppies bloom again...,"
the song droned out of the machine and instinctively they looked at one
another.

"Let's have it, Ada. It's like it was meant for us." Wilf was like a little
boy in his enthusiasm.

"How much?" she asked and then started to take out her purse.

With a wave of his hand Wilf stopped her and took out the money from
the top pocket of his uniform. "I'll pay for this. The first part of furniture
for our home. Deliver it will you?" he ended grandly, and gave the
Scarborough Road address.

They arranged for it to be sent later that afternoon. "Our errand boy
can deliver it on his way home," obliged the assistant.

Outside the shop they laughed and started to run up to the house. "If we
hurry we can get there before the lad. I bet he'll wonder what's going on
with no curtains or owt up," Wilf laughed as they breathlessly reached the
front door.

Eagerly they waited to take delivery and when it came tipped the
astonished lad two bob for his trouble.

They unwrapped it, wound it up and played the record.

"I've never bothered about music or owt before — have you?" Wilf
asked.

Ada had because her Dad was a bit musical, "We can get lots of records
and build up quite a repertoire," she said.

He laughed at the long word, but found himself enjoying the music and
began to hum in tune.

Dusk began to fall and Wilf looked at his watch. "Come on, Mrs.
Tanner, we'd best get down to your Mam's for a bite to eat before we start
married life proper."

"Oh, you and your belly," she laughed and they packed up the
gramophone carefully, placed it in the cupboard underneath the stairs
and went back home.

This time she did eat heartily. She had found the day a long one and a
bit tiring. She'd be glad to get to Sal's and get a good night's sleep.

In a small brown suitcase, Esther had packed her nightclothes and a
razor in case Wilf had forgotten his. He carried the case as they walked up
Applegarth Lane on to Sal's house. She had a good fire going and had left
some supper on a tray, but as soon as they got in the house Wilf locked the
door and took her in his arms.

"We're wed, lass — really wed," he sighed and kissed her lips gently.
She sighed and laid her head on his shoulder and he began to kiss her neck
and to gently undress her.

She always said it was a perfect honeymoon. Wilf was gentle but firm,
and she soon welcomed his caresses over the intimate parts of her body and

226

to even enjoy them. She'd been right after all — it was better in bed.   She still felt he had had some experience, but was far too wise at this point to mention it.

"You're glad we got wed — even in spite of war — aren't you love?" he asked her as she lay in his arms.

"Yes, of course I am. It was high time."

The three days passed happily and all too quickly. On the last morning she held him close as if his flesh would rub off on her and leave a bit behind. His train was due to leave in the early afternoon and with a heavy heart she went to see him off.

"Come on, short arse, let's have a smile. I'll be back afore you know it. You keep playing that record and think about all them plans." He tried to cheer her up.

As they whispered their goodbyes he held her close, leaping into the train only seconds before it moved off. She stood alone on the platform, waving her hankie until he was out of sight, and then turned and walked slowly home. She knew her Mam would be waiting with a cup of tea and had just reached the corner of Brett Street when she saw her Dad rushing towards her.

"Has he gone?" he cried out.

"Course he's gone. What do you think I'm doing here?"

"Well, there's a wire at Polly's telling him he's got another forty-eight hours. You go on home and I'll run to station and get train stopped at Carnaby."

Ada should have felt elated, but she didn't. Deep down somewhere a feeling of gloom was settling. But she smiled and told him to carry on and she'd wait at home.

"I don't like him being turned back. They say it's bad luck," her Mam warned, but what else could they do. They couldn't let him go back to camp before time — he'd never have forgiven them.

The next two days were something of an anticlimax. They stayed at Esther's and there was not the privacy that Sal's had given. Each day they went up to the house and played the record as if to give them both some assurance.

"I'm glad we've had these extra days, but it's been a bit unsettling hasn't it, lass?" Wilf said, and she had to agree.

"Never mind, love, we'll settle down when you come back."

Wilf did not answer but held her close and kissed her.

As she saw him off she could not help the tears falling. "Take care, love, won't you?" she shouted after the disappearing train and in answer he blew her a last kiss.

227

On the Monday morning she returned to work and met with the usual wealth of teasing. Ada took it all in good part.

"Come on lass, smile — you've just got wed," Lily teased, but Ada couldn't and worked as if in a dream. She couldn't even bring herself to go up to the house, but just worked all hours that God sent and then went home to sink into an exhausted sleep.

"I don't know what's the matter with our Ada, Thom, she seems that miserable. I hope they're alright together, her and Wilf," Esther confided in Thom.

"Leave her be. She'll tell us when she's ready."

Esther worried far too much at times, but he had to admit Ada was not her usual self.

On the Friday morning she was so upset she could not even bring herself to pretend to eat her breakfast.

"You're not expecting are you, lass — a honeymoon baby?" Esther looked inquiringly.

"I don't know Mam. I just don't feel right somehow. Maybe I'm love sick." And she tried to make light of her mood.

But it was much more than that. In Ada's heart and indeed the whole of her being there lay a feeling as heavy as lead. But she couldn't talk about it to anyone — not even her Mam and Dad.

CHAPTER 26

Wilf's return to the war was like the extra forty-eight hours leave — something of an anti-climax. He found himself back behind the lines with his battalion up at the front. Being officially still on the sick leave list he was first given a medical and then detailed to be in charge of the rations tent.

"You're O.K. really, Sergeant Tanner, but I don't want to take any chances with those lungs of yours — not yet a while, anyway," the Medical Officer told him.

And that day or two dragged out for almost two weeks. To Wilf it seemed more like years. The job was boring and the men were all basically conscientious objectors or those considered 'unsuitable for active duty.' They worked hard enough, but had no idea what it was like to be under fire and every time the smallest shot was heard they ran like scared rabbits to find shelter. It amazed them the way Wilf just stood with head raised to see what was coming over. If it looked like being a big one he would take cover or duck at the last minute. They might be way back behind the firing lines, but jerry had taught him never to take any chances.

One big problem was not knowing anyone — they were all strangers and he felt a strong loneliness for his mates. Being bogged down in the trenches was no picnic, but after a while it became a second home, like a family where everyone had a part to play. And when the shelling was bad and you had your head down, you got to really know the blokes — you talked as never before — talked about dying — about living — and sometimes cried together. Somehow it took away the great fear and cemented a comradeship that words could not describe.

After five days he was really brassed off and asked to see the Commanding Officer.

"Permission to return to my own regiment, Sir," he spoke clearly and stood smartly to attention.

"Is that so, Tanner? And what makes you think you will be more needed there than here?"

"Well Sir, I'm experienced in the field and besides I'm missing my own mates, Sir. Anybody could do this bit of a job," he answered with what he hoped was conviction. Ada always said if you wanted owt then speak up loud and clear.

For a few moments he became lost in thought as the C.O. considered his request. It was funny how his wife — he savoured the words — came to mind at odd times like this.

"I would be very surprised if many of your mates are left, Sergeant. Have you seen the latest casualty lists? They show awesome figures, particularly in the Fifth Yorks. But that is beside the point. You must stay here a bit longer. This section has never been run so efficiently. I don't get many good men of your calibre behind the lines. You must hold on — and besides . . ." he looked up and smiled, "Your battalion is being brought back in a day or two."

Wilf returned the smile and saluted. Now he knew the lads were coming back he would do a good job here and then re-join them. They couldn't stop him doing that, not once his own C.O. was here.

He worked silently and with firm authority that got the men in an orderly routine. His commands were given in a kind but firm voice, giving encouragement and a joke when needed. They in turn responded and rations were issued to the cookhouse at regular times and were never short — at least not if the food was in store.

The cooks, too, showed their respect by putting in orders for tit-bits they could never hope to get and Wilf took it all in good part. 'I apologise for the inconvenience, but my supplier has run out of this particular commodity. I have reprimanded him and if it is not here for next week I have threatened to take my custom elsewhere,' he would write on the order slips. It brightened things up somewhat and he felt that a bit of harmless fun helped things along.

He was bent over the ration list, examining the requests, when he heard the echo of marching feet and the sound of faint whistling. His ears pricked up and he caught the tune, *'My Gel's a Yorkshire Gel.'* And then the sound of laughter and shouting. He'd know that voice anywhere — it was young Bill Jenkinson, egging on his mates. Hurriedly he went out of the tent and saw coming through the mist of the morning the Fifth Yorks marching towards him.

Like a little lad let out of school he ran towards them. "You buggers — you buggers — about time and all — where the hell have you been — I've got fed up waiting for you."

He stopped short as he spoke and looked at the tired faces before him. They were covered in mud and grime and looked as if they hadn't slept for weeks. Poor buggers — they were all in — but with true Yorkshire spirit they were still laughing and joking and greeted him warmly.

"Trust you, Wilf lad, to sod off when things got rough. You knew what you were doing alright — you and young Tinker both cleared off together." It was Arty Watson shouting to him.

Quickly Wilf dropped into step and marched with them, asking about his mates. God almighty, half of them had been killed — Wilkinson, Johnson, Sawden, Kettlewell, Harrison, Beedale — all gone. His heart sank and once again Ada flashed across his mind. "What a waste — what a bloody waste," he could hear her saying the words in her sharp way.

Would it ever end? Would he and Ada ever get the business going? Was

230

he going to stay in this Godforsaken muck heap for ever? He could see no end to it. First they would advance and then retreat, gaining nothing and losing the cream of the men. But there was nothing he could do. When the country called you answered — that is if you were not to bear the label of coward for the rest of your day.

He drew in his breath and said the only thing he could think of, "Come on then, let's get some grub inside you. I'm in charge of rations and I've saved some spicy bits for you lot. Once you're rested up I'll be back with you then you'd best watch out." Laughing, he joined in the whistling and then spotted George coming to the front of the line.

"It's good to see you Wilf. Did you have a good leave — how is Ada and the family — did you see Isabella?" He grasped Wilf's hand and held on to it as the words tumbled out.

It took Wilf by surprise, but he answered civilly, telling him that he and Ada were wed. George congratulated him warmly. He seemed changed, more warm and human than he had been before. Maybe the suffering of war had brought out the best in him.

A fist banged him on the shoulder and before the voice spoke he instinctively knew who it was. "Now then, our kid. You're a cushy bugger getting off like that." It was Harry. Wilf shrugged away the proferred hand, but answered politely and asked how things were.

"Couldn't be better mate. I've not been right up at the front, but near enough to get the spoils. I'll have a right good business when I get home. Souvenirs of la France and Kaiser Bill."

Trust him, Wilf thought, knowing just what he meant. Loot from dead and wounded which he would try and sell for large sums of money.

"You've not changed much, our Harry. I wonder the Major doesn't put you on a charge, doing what you do."

Harry winked knowingly. "Oh, he won't do that mate, he won't do that, never you fear. Me and the Major have got a nice little thing going."

Wilf wondered what the hell he meant. He couldn't think George would condone looting, not Harry's sort, for he would have respect of a person whether he was British, French or German. It sounded a mite funny.

The men fed, washed and then went to their allotted tents to rest. Soon most of them were snoring their heads off as if in the sleep of the dead. He decided to take a walk, rest his mind a bit and try to take in the loss of so many of his friends. He lit a fag, drew heavily and stretched.

"Wilf — Wilf — can you spare time for a chat? I'd like to hear about home and the family." It was George, stood in his shirt sleeves and resting against a tent pole. "Hold on a minute, I'll join you for a stroll. I could do to get away from this atmosphere for a while." He didn't bother to dress and took his place by Wilf's side, walking head down and in silence.

It struck Wilf as being a bit queer. Fancy George coming out like that — improperly dressed. Fancy him wanting to walk with Wilf at all. That was something new. He looked so down and all. Maybe it was being away from his family for so long. Maybe George was missing them as Wilf missed Ada.

The silence lasted so long that Wilf felt bound to break it. It had got a bit uncanny. "Owt up then, Sir?" He was careful to use the title.

"Oh, cut that out, Wilf — let's be as we were before — family."

The silence continued until Wilf stopped dead in his tracks and faced George. "What's up, George? You've not come out with me like this just to say nowt."

"I've been a fool, Wilf — a damn fool . . ." the words petered out quietly.

"Why have you been a fool? Most of us are fools sometimes."

"Not like me. I'm being blackmailed Wilf, blackmailed."

Instinctively Wilf knew it was something to do with Harry. He waited for George to continue. No good saying owt just now. It might stop him getting it all off his chest.

"When we came back up to rest, just before you went on sick leave, I became friendly with a French family — out at that farm across the field. I met the man working in the field when I was strolling and we got talking and he asked me in for a glass of wine. I met the family — his wife, two sons and a daughter. Pacalle — Cally I called her. I started to go up there every day and soon Cally and I became friends. I would help her to stack the sheaves in the barn and before you could say 'Jack Robinson' we became lovers.

"I never told her I was married — even gave a false name. Stupid, I know, but I never meant any harm. I miss Isabella and the children so. I never really loved Cally, but she gave me a warmth I missed and needed. I'm no hero, Wilf. This lot has shown me that I need love, the feel of a woman to comfort me. I yearn for Isabella." He fell silent again.

"Well, that can happen to anybody. It . . .," Wilf stopped himself from saying anything further. He was tempted to mention the Beatty episode but decided better not to.

"That's not all, Wilf. Your Harry found out and followed me there one day and caught us red-handed. Cally called me by the name she knew — 'Berty' — and of course he quickly cottoned on to what was going on. I shall never forget the look on his face that day — all smug — filthy is the only way I can describe it."

"Aye, that's our Harry. And he's blackmailing you now, is he?"

George nodded. "I had threatened to court martial him if I ever found him looting again. I had actually put him on report, but I had to cancel that when he decided to 'tell me all' as he put it."

"What does 'all' mean?"

"I think you know, Wilf — about him being related to me and nobody but your Mother and the immediate family knowing about it. He said to ask you if it were true. It is, isn't it, Wilf?"

Wilf did not answer. He had no need, for they both knew it to be true.

"He's threatened to let it all out and I can't have that, Wilf. I can't let the family name be disgraced by it all. It would kill Father to know about me — and Harry — and I couldn't inherit the title under those circumstances. We'd be done for. And think what it would do to Isabella and her family if they ever found out I had let her down so. You know we had to get married — that was bad enough — it looks like this kind of thing runs in the family." He was close to tears and so very ashamed.

Wilf felt a surge of sympathy followed by one of anger against Harry. By hell — what he needed was a damn good hiding.

"What can I do to help, mate?" The familiarity came out unthinkingly.

"Nothing — nothing. But I feel better now that I have unburdened myself. God knows where it will all end. My fellow officers know he's a bad lot and already wonder why I don't have him on a charge. I wish to God I had got killed."

"That's enough of that. I'll see what I can do with our kid. Just you get off and get your head down."

They returned to the camp and before they parted George again gripped his hand and held it tightly for a long minute. "One thing Wilf — I don't regret marrying into Isabella's family. Oh, I showed off a bit at times, but I'm proud of them now — proud of them all — and that goes for you too."

Wilf turned on his heel and went in search of Harry. If there was nowt else, he could give him a piece of his mind. Mam would be wild if she knew.

"Get your arse out here." He went into the tent where Harry was sleeping and dug him in the back with his boot.

"What's up — what's up — is war over?" He roused himself and looked up at Wilf.

"No, more's the pity. That would put an end to your little games. Get yoursen out here." Roughly he pushed his brother outside.

"What's up?" Harry spoke sulkily.

"You know bloody well what's up. What the hell do you think you're playing at with the Major?"

"Oh, he's told you has he — silly sod. Still it's nowt you didn't know, except about him and that French piece that is."

"Do you realise what you're doing? If you open your gob — and I've no doubt you will if you're pushed — it will hurt not only him but our Mam, Gertie, Ada's family and me and all. Did you think about that?"

"So what. You've none of you ever thought about me, I've never been good enough."

"If you'd shown willing it would have been a help, but you just sat on your arse and lived off me and Mam. You've always been a wrong 'un. But I'll tell you this — if you so much as say a word about any of it I'll bray you myself."

Wilf was getting angry and Harry remembered the strength he could muster when roused.

"I shan't say owt as long as the Major plays the game."

"You'll not open your gob — ever — or I'll shut it for good."

With that Wilf marched away, leaving Harry leering after him. What the hell could Wilf do? There was no way he was going to let this little racket go without bleeding it dry. He laughed sardonically, his lips curling in anger. It was alright for him to talk, but what chance had he got to make money any other way? Them and their loyalty. Who'd ever shown him any loyalty? But they'd pay up alright, they'd never let this lot get out. It was a gem and he meant to keep and make the most of it.

During the following days rumours spread through the camp that the enemy was advancing and making a big push through the lines. Wilf felt that something was in the air and he became full of a tense expectation. Being behind the lines was falsely safe. He felt he should be up there at the front, helping to end the war. And how he wanted that — he wanted more than anything to end this bloody senseless slaughter and to return to Ada. His thoughts were constantly filled with the plans they had made during his leave. Once this lot was over they could get on with them all and start living again.

"Best not to make too many plans, love. They say it's bad luck and summ'at always goes wrong," Ada's voice came back to him. But nowt would go wrong — Ada would see to that.

The rumours were verified when the order came through to pull out and take up positions in the nearby village which had been evacuated during the night. Almost immediately the barrage began. Shells began to fall and the firing of rifle shots could be heard quite distinctly.

Hurriedly they began to pack and were caught right in the middle when the real bombardment started. It was a well-planned operation and accurately aimed shells fell everywhere. Chaos reigned as Wilf vainly tried to shout orders to get the men moving and under what cover the countryside offered. He ducked, ran, and veered from the path of falling shrapnel. Bodies lay all over the place and the cries of the wounded rent the air. Smoke, debris from the trees, and earth clumps covered the area and then just as suddenly as it had begun, the shelling ceased.

He looked up and saw the havoc — what a bloody mess. But, for the moment, there was a respite and he began to look for his mates. Everything was so muddled that it took him a while to find anyone. They were scattered in shell holes, ditches and some buried under great mounds of earth.

"Have you seen the Major?" he asked and was told that he had been seen to fall as a shell landed.

"I reckon he's had it, Wilf. He was over there in that field across yon ditch."

Wilf ran in the direction of the wearily pointed finger, leapt the ditch and stumbled into a small crater. Muck filled his eyes and mouth and his breathing was laboured. He began to clear his eyes and raising himself up looked over the top of the hole. All was silent and still. The sun was just peeping through the smoke and clouds. For a minute, its rays blinded him and then as the golden roundness emerged he began to feel better, almost lighthearted.

"Come on, lad — get a move on — you might win a gold watch." Clearly, and quite distinctly, he heard Ada's voice. It was so vivid that he turned, half-expecting her to be at his side. He smiled again. She was not there, but he felt as if, for a brief, precious moment, she had reached out and touched him. The feeling was warm and reassuring. He looked again into the sunlight — it was like that gold watch she was always on about.

Peering into the rays he searched the area for George and stared in anger at what he saw. There was his brother, Harry, bent over a figure — a figure he knew to be George — systematically going through each pocket, searching for his despised booty.

A blind red anger filled Wilf. "You bugger — you rotten bugger — I'll kill you for this," he yelled at the top of his voice, and, like a madman, leapt forward. With his heel he rolled George's body out of the way and made to jump upon his brother who was smiling and examining something in his hand.

"Look Wilf — I've found his gold watch. What. . ." The sentence was never finished, for with an animal shriek, Wilf jumped on his brother. As he did so the edge of his boot touched an unexploded shell. He knew no more.

In that split second, Wilf and Harry were blown to smithereens.

CHAPTER 27

Ada's moods continued to swing high and low. She ate very little and buried herself in work. She had to keep busy to occupy her mind enough to drive away the terrifying thoughts that had begun to creep into it.

On the morning that the fatal telegram was received she worked quickly and fiercely, wrapped in her own thoughts, trying desperately to work off the feeling of doom that engulfed her heart.

At half-past eleven she looked across at the clock. As she turned, she saw her Dad coming towards her with the dreaded buff yellow envelope in his hands. Showing no surprise or emotion she walked slowly and purposefully towards him.

"I know what it is, Dad — it's Wilf. He's gone, hasn't he?" She spoke quietly, stopping Thom in his tracks.

Tears welled up in his eyes as he looked down at his bairn. "Aye that's right, hunny — that's what this says."

"I've known all week it was coming. I knew I'd never see him again."

She was too calm for Thom and it unnerved him. Tears, a tantrum, he could have dealt with that. But this — this was not like Ada.

"Come on lass, you'll have to call and tell Polly."

In the same quiet voice Ada told Mrs. Price and then she and Thom left to walk home in silence, each of them deep in their own grieved thoughts.

When they reached Polly's cottage they found her standing at the door holding before her another buff envelope.

"Have they let you know and all then?" Without thinking Ada assumed the wire to be about Wilf.

Polly looked puzzled and then saw Ada's identical buff envelope.

"Our Harry's gone — he's been killed — I've just sent up to let Gertie know."

Ada had forgotten all about Gertie, and Polly's words didn't sink in.

"Harry? Harry? What do you mean — it's Wilf that's been killed. What the hell's going on?"

Thom realised what had happened and quickly ushered the two women through the cottage door.

"Here, gie us that, lass." He took the wire from Polly and read it. Sighing heavily he turned to Ada. "They've both gone — Wilf and Harry. Polly's lost them both."

Polly sank down in her chair and buried her head in her hands. Ada stood in stunned silence. She felt nothing about Harry, but losing them both would be a shock for Polly.

"Come on, love. Crying won't do any good. We've got to be brave. They wouldn't want this — at least not Wilf." Ada spoke calmly and put her arms around Polly's shoulders.

Polly raised her head and looked at Thom, her eyebrows raised in a question at Ada's apparent calm acceptance of the death of her husband. Thom shook his head and closed his eyes. "Leave it lass — leave it," he was mouthing the words silently.

"Try and keep calm, Polly. Remember Gertie has only just got settled down after Alf. Think about her and try and keep up," Ada said, and the words were as if she was talking about someone else's death — someone not related and nothing to do with her.

Thom shivered and said they'd best be getting along.

"I'll pop in later, love, and see how you are." Ada turned at the door and smiled. Thom wondered if the shock had turned her mind.

She felt like an empty bucket. Where her heart should have been, there was an empty void that no tears would fill or ease. Without Wilf she had nothing to look forward to — she was nothing. They might just as well have killed her too.

It was all too much for Thom, but he struggled on trying hard to bring back some interest in life. "What about house and yard, love?" he asked.

"I expect I'll have to give it up, Dad, and let somebody else have a chance."

She made an appointment with the solicitor and discussed the arrangements.

"In the circumstances, Mrs. Tanner, I am sure there will be no difficulties, in spite of it being a long lease. I am very sorry, very sorry indeed that things have turned out like this. I know our Mr. Tinker had great faith in the success of your venture, but I am afraid you are one amongst thousands," he tried to console her.

"Maybe so, but you only know the devil when he knocks on your own door. It doesn't hurt so much when it happens to somebody else." Ada spoke tersely.

It was arranged that she would give up the keys by the end of the month and although she could not bring herself to go near the place, or even pass by it, she kept the keys tied on a string on her bodice. It gave comfort and seemed to bring Wilf closer.

Night after night she would lie awake reproaching herself. Why had she pushed him into doing all those things? Why hadn't they got wed years ago like any other couple would have done? Suddenly she thought of Barnsley and Beatty — if that bairn were owt to do with Wilf, she would take it — bring it up and give the lass a chance in life. That would be part of Wilf. Why hadn't she got a part of Wilf too? Why had they waited so long?

But when day broke she dismissed all thoughts of Barnsley — best let sleeping dogs lie.

237

When the parcel containing Wilf's bits and pieces arrived, Esther hoped it would unlock the floodgates. Ada placed them on the table — a handkerchief, some of her letters tied up with a bootlace and a small photo of herself. She stood and looked down at them. Was this all she would have left to remind her of Wilf? Surely his life meant more than this? Carefully she sifted through the things and then re-wrapped them and put them back in the box.

"Is there owt in the house you should have, lass?" her Dad asked, and Ada remembered the gramophone. She had better fetch that out.

"I'll go up and give it a scrub out, leave it clean for whoever takes over."

And on the day planned she dressed up, in her wedding clothes, and set off as if on an outing. She could not have explained why she wanted to wear her wedding dress — the dress she had so carefully saved for Wilf's homecoming. She just had to wear it.

As she walked up to the house, her steps gathered speed until she was almost running as she turned the corner of Scarborough Road. She unlocked the big gate and winced as the key squeaked in the lock. The sound scratched into her heart. She walked across the yard and opened the front door, taking a moment to gaze around. This had been her planned world, this was where it was all going to happen.

Pushing open the door she stepped inside and found the atmosphere cold and unwelcoming. Shivering, she took off her hat and hung it on the banister knob and then going to the cupboard took out the gramophone. She filled the bucket with water and then struggled with it and the gramophone up the wide staircase to the top bedroom. She wound up the machine and put on the record before starting to scrub.

Each room was thoroughly scrubbed and her dress became wet and covered in grey spots where the soapy water had splashed. On and on she scrubbed, playing the tune as she went — 'When the poppies bloom again.' She scrubbed to the rhythm of the song, humming tunelessly to herself.

In the main bedroom where she and Wilf had made love for the first time, she paused and went over to the window to look down into the yard. It was empty and bleak — no working — no washing — no bairns — no swings. All gone now. All had never been, except in her dreams.

Finally she reached the bottom passage and she was scrubbing away when she heard the door open. She turned on her knees and saw through the sunlight streaming in the skylight window, a pair of brown boots and khaki legs.

"Wilf — Wilf," she cried out and before she could stop herself ran with arms open towards the figure and encompassed it in an embrace.

"Ada — oh Ada." The voice startled her into stark reality. It was not Wilf, it was Ralph Tinker.

She released him and fell upon her knees in a crumpled heap, leaning of the rim of the steel bucket to support herself.

"Ada — I had to come before I went back to the front. I had to say how sorry I am — and I had to see you again." He bent and stroked the crumpled heap. She looked as if all the life had drained from her body. This couldn't be the Ada he knew — the spirited, tough woman he had grown to love.

"Have you seen the Observer? Wilf has been awarded the Military Medal for bravery. From the evidence gathered, it appears he tried to save George and his brother Harry. I checked at the Drill Hall and they confirmed it."

She sat up and stared as if in a trance. Wilf — her little Wilf — saving George and Harry.

"Aren't you proud, Ada?" Ralph asked.

She looked straight into his eyes. "What the hell did he have to go and do that for? Why didn't he save himself first? I'd rather have a live coward that a dead hero." Her voice held some of its former sharpness.

In the background the record was almost at an end — 'When the poppies bloom again, I'll remember you.' The scrape-scrape of the needle against the record grated around the room and filled it until she felt the walls would cave in on her. Each scrape was a scratch on her heart and each scratch bled and left an open, gaping wound.

Her eyes travelled up Ralph's uniform and then the tightness inside her snapped. She realised that never — never again would she see her beloved Wilf. A loud sob ran through her body and she cried out in pain, "Why — oh why — why Wilf, when we had all this? Why did I push him into being what he wasn't? Why did I ever let him go? It's all such a waste — such a bloody waste."

Her body was racked with sobs and the tears at last fell like an unleashed storm falling into the murky water. Ralph stood back in the shadows to let Ada give vent to her grief.

"I loved him so, I did truly, and I didn't just want things and money. They are no use without him. We stood here — here on this spot and talked about our life together — our future. We've been together since we were bairns — Wilf was my whole life."

Ralph stepped forward. "Listen to me, Ada — listen — please. You gave Wilf Tanner a lot more than he would have ever had without you. You made him the man he was. Wilf told me that himself, just before you were married. Don't give up, Ada — think of the man he was, think of that."

"Man — but he's not a man now is he? — he's a corpse — he's dead — what's the good of that?"

"He didn't just die, Ada — he died a fine brave man — a hero — he won a medal — that's something, isn't it?"

"And I'll tell you what they can do with it and all — they can stick it up the Kaiser's bloody arse. What the hell can I do with a medal? I promised him a gold watch not a medal. A medal can't give me bairns — it can't bring me Wilf."

"You gave him love, Ada — real love — and no man can ask for more."

The words sank into her heart and the sobs grew softer. Ralph knew it was time to leave Ada in her moment of private grief.

"Perhaps I will see you on my next leave. If I can help in any way, please let me know."

Proudly she raised herself up and held out her hand. "I only want Wilf — you can't perform that miracle, can you?"

He shrugged his shoulders helplessly, but took her hand and shook it formally. "Well, if I can help in any other way. . . "

"That you, Sir — thank you for coming — it was right kind of you, but I'll manage."

The words were stilted, almost mocking.

Poor dear Ada — so brave — so strong and yet so weak and vulnerable without Wilf. He saw her face pucker and then her shoulders straighten and she held her bottom lip firm with gripped teeth.

Without another word he left, and as he walked through the yard he heard the record, but this time above its tones a strong clear voice sang out the words, 'Down beside the riverside when we were two.'

Her grief came through every phrase and he paused to listen. As the song went on her voice grew defiant and angry. That was good. If Ada got angry she would be alright.

Perhaps it was her way of telling him that she would see it through. It might take time for her feelings to subside, but she came from stern Yorkshire stuff.

Ada would be fine!